OIL

a novel

OIL

a novel

———

JEFF NESBIT

New York, New York

Oil

ISBN 13: 978-1-60936-114-3

Published by Guideposts
16 East 34th Street
New York, New York 10016
Guideposts.org

Distributed by Ideals Publications, a Guideposts company
2630 Elm Hill Pike, Suite 100
Nashville, TN 37214

Guideposts and *Ideals* are registered trademarks of Guideposts.

This novel is a work of fiction. Names, characters, places, and incidents either are the product of the author's imagination or are used fictitiously. Any resemblance to actual events, locales, organizations, or persons living or dead is entirely coincidental and beyond the intent of either the author or publisher.

Library of Congress Cataloging-in-Publication Data has been applied for.

Scripture taken from the New King James Version®. Copyright © 1982 by Thomas Nelson, Inc. Used by permission. All rights reserved.

Cover design by Studio Gearbox | www.studiogearbox.com
Interior Design by Müllerhaus Publishing Group | www.mullerhaus.net

Edited by Ramona Cramer Tucker

Printed and bound in the United States of America
10 9 8 7 6 5 4 3 2 1

A FEW QUICK THANKS TO . . .

The members of the "relentless, positive storm" family. You dream big, do the right thing, set your direction, take your compass, and never stray from the path.

You are the salt of the earth. You change the world and make it a better place.

PRAISE FOR *OIL* . . .

"Jeff Nesbit knows how to make some of the most urgent subjects of our time both entertaining and educational."

—BRIAN KELLY, EDITOR, *U.S. News & World Report*

"The action pings from Aqaba to Tehran, Bogota to Pyongyang, Moscow to Mecca, and smart phones to laptops. There's palace intrigue, insider sabotage, eleventh-hour twists, and rumors of a Twelfth Imam—and under it all is a powerful black current of crude oil, desperation, and greed."

—BETH NISSEN, FORMER SENIOR CORRESPONDENT, CNN

"Entertaining, terrifying and uplifting. Jeff Nesbit has turned one of the world's most dangerous challenges into a thriller with a high-tech twist."

—DARREN GERSH, WASHINGTON, DC, BUREAU
CHIEF FOR PBS TV's *Nightly Business Report*

"Nesbit's powerful storytelling abilities are on full display in this series. As usual, he's interpreting headlines before they happen."

—DAVID KESSLER, M.D., FORMER FDA COMMISSIONER
UNDER PRESIDENT BUSH AND PRESIDENT
CLINTON AND BEST-SELLING AUTHOR

"This book weaves intellect and imagination to forge a compelling and timely look into the future. It considers one of the most vexing questions of our time: will oil power us through this century or hold us hostage?"

— FRANK SESNO, DIRECTOR, SCHOOL OF MEDIA,
GEORGE WASHINGTON UNIVERSITY

"In *OIL*, Jeff Nesbit riffs on our murky understanding of Middle Eastern politics, beliefs, and ambitions to craft an absorbing tale of intrigue that enlightens as much as it entertains. Ingeniously plotted, and featuring characters and settings that add to its air of credibility, *OIL* relentlessly rises to its ultimate finale: it makes you think."

— DAN AGAN, PRESIDENT, PANTHERA GROUP

"A well-informed page-turner that stimulates fresh thinking about the Middle East."

— TOM DUESTERBERG, PH.D.,
EXECUTIVE DIRECTOR OF MANUFACTURING AND
SOCIETY IN THE 21ST CENTURY, THE ASPEN INSTITUTE

"With keen insight into escalating tensions in the Middle East and impeccable research, Jeff Nesbit gives us a mesmerizing read in his much-anticipated sequel to *PEACE*."

— MARLENE CIMONS, PH.D.,
FORMER WASHINGTON REPORTER, *Los Angeles Times*

"Jeff Nesbit has that rare talent of taking today's headlines and making them even more real in his fiction. A must read for anyone who wonders what in the world is going on in today's Middle East."

—Jim O'Hara, Washington, DC, Policy Strategist

"It's inspirational to see young characters like Nash Lee on the same stage with world leaders, changing the world and living the 'relentless, positive storm.' One person, no matter what age, can truly make a difference. Jeff Nesbit brings that point home vividly in these novels."

—Shepherd Smith, President,
    The Institute for Youth Development

For when they shall say, "Peace and safety!"
then sudden destruction comes upon them...

1 THESSALONIANS 5:3

MARYLAND

Baltimore

WEST
VIRGINIA

Washington, D.C.

VIRGINIA

PROLOGUE

Dulles International Airport
Washington, DC

"Why is it late?" the American president's secretary of state, Jennifer Moran, asked a young aide for the third time in the past ten minutes. "Do the Saudis think we all serve at their pleasure? I know this is important, but..."

"This *is* an important trip, Madame Secretary, for both sides," answered the aide, Katie Devlin, a gifted woman who'd managed new media for Moran through a long presidential campaign and had immediately joined her when she'd agreed to become secretary of state. "They wouldn't be late, not without a good reason."

When it did arrive, the "flying palace" would be hard to miss. Seven stories tall, with a wingspan the size of an American football field, the commercial Airbus 380 jumbo jet could hold nearly a thousand economy-class passengers quite comfortably.

But this particular Airbus 380 jet had been built for only one customer—a member of the Saudi royal family who had spent nearly half a billion dollars to buy and outfit the plane. It carried only fifteen crewmembers and private parties that often included other Saudi princes. Private bedrooms, a dining hall, an equipment gym, and a movie theater were engineered throughout the plane.

The Airbus 380 was so large that the members of the secretary of state's delegation, who had gathered at one end of Dulles International

Airport west of Washington, DC, would likely be able to spot it a mile away as it made its descent.

Today's flight had been shrouded in secrecy. Only a few in either Saudi Arabia or the United States had any inkling of its purpose or its passengers. There had been no stories in *The Washington Post*. Later, if the discussions proved fruitful, someone would mention the outcome publicly.

This trip was the culmination of months of careful planning with the United States, the Saudis' most valuable Western ally. The Saudi prince had agreed to meet with the American secretary of state, in person, to discuss the highly secretive plans approved by the Bay'ah Council. The Saudi grandsons were about to take power in Saudi Arabia. And a new king was emerging.

The small delegation on the ground, though, was growing restless. They'd been told to arrive at Dulles well ahead of time. But the plane was at least an hour late, and no one on the ground seemed to know why.

"So what's the reason?" Moran snapped. "That they're more important than us?"

"I doubt that," Devlin answered. "The royal family has been meticulous in their planning."

"Then what—?"

Katie's cell phone rang, cutting the response midsentence, and she glanced at the caller ID. It was a direct line from internal security at the State Department. As a close aide to the secretary of state, Katie had Top Secret clearance and was well known to the security team. She looked at her boss, asking with her eyes if it was all right to answer.

Moran sighed, closed her eyes briefly, and nodded.

Katie took the call.

"Ms. Devlin, we've just received something from NSA," the caller said quickly. "We're going to move the delegation off the tarmac, inside."

"Why?" Katie asked.

Five more cell phones suddenly went off. Katie glanced at other members of the delegation. Some were obviously receiving the same information simultaneously.

There was a loud thud behind them. Katie looked to her left. A half-dozen uniformed TSA guards burst through double doors and began to run toward them.

"Ms. Devlin," the caller said loudly on her cell, "*please* ask your boss to begin moving off the tarmac. This is credible information."

Katie reacted instantly. Stepping forward, she grabbed Moran's shirtsleeve. "Madame Secretary, we need to move inside."

Jennifer Moran was long accustomed to security. She'd already served a stint as the First Lady at the White House, and security for her was nearly as tight now that she was the American secretary of state. When folks assigned to protect her told her to move, she moved. She could ask questions later.

But even as they headed toward the double doors, there was a sudden commotion. Members of the delegation stopped and peered toward the west.

Two military jets appeared, seemingly out of nowhere, and raced east toward the enormous Airbus 380 jumbo jet that had begun to land at the airport.

The delegation watched, horrified, as both fighter jets fired several missiles toward a target on the ground. Fireballs exploded as the missiles hit their intended target, and the cacophony of multiple explosions reached them moments later.

Whatever the jets had fired at had vaporized instantly.

The security detail urged the delegation to move inside, even as the Saudi plane continued its long, slow descent onto the Dulles runway. The firefight they'd all witnessed was directly in the glide path of the jet, which now flew right above the billowing smoke.

Katie could only imagine what had happened. But one thing was clear: a threat to the Saudi jet and its occupants had just materialized. The American fighter jets had been dispatched at the last minute, based on intelligence picked up by NSA.

Still, even with her own high-clearance level, Katie wondered whether she'd ever learn the truth about what she'd seen.

01

He barely glanced at the pedestrians on either side of Jaffa Road, one of the longest and oldest streets in Jerusalem. He'd never been much of a tourist, and this day was no different. He paid no attention to Safra Square or other landmarks as the cab made its way from the old city to downtown. Instead, he spent the time studying his notes and answering e-mails to his boss.

The partnership they'd put together was a complicated one, and he didn't want to make a mistake with the registry. Far too much was at stake. He'd spent most of the trip to Israel examining the limited partnership papers to make sure he had all the players identified correctly.

"We're here, sir." The driver pulled the cab over to the side of the road.

The man looked up from his notes. "Two sixteen Jaffa? The Ministry of National Infrastructures?"

The cab driver pointed at a small sign near the building. Spotting both address and name, the man paid the cab fare, including a generous tip, and hurried toward the entrance.

The Ministry of National Infrastructures was a quaint, serene place. The folks who worked there never had to worry about titanic power struggles over control of Israel's natural resources—because the country had precious little in the way of natural resources. Oil was nowhere to be found, and Israel's leaders had struggled for a generation to meet the country's energy needs.

The man stepped up to the front desk. There was no line. "I'm here to speak to someone about the oil register," he murmured to the clerk.

The clerk folded up his copy of *Ha'aretz* and peered at his log. "Do you have an appointment? I don't see a notation."

"The deputy oil commissioner indicated that I would not require an appointment," the man said quickly. "When we spoke on the phone, he said I could meet with someone when I arrived."

The clerk grunted and muttered something under his breath. He picked up a handset and punched in a number. "Someone here to see Abe about the oil register." He nodded several times then hung up the phone. "He'll be here in a second to take you back."

"Abraham Zeffren will see me? The deputy oil commissioner?"

"Yeah, Abe himself." The clerk laughed. "He's got nothing better to do right now. He might as well give you a guided tour of the register." The clerk held out his hand.

The man looked at him, confused.

"Your identification papers?" the clerk said with irritation.

"Oh, yes." The man extracted his personal passport from his suit jacket and handed it to the clerk, who copied the name down on his ledger and handed it back to the man. The man had a government passport as well but chose not to use it here.

The clerk barely glanced at the passport. Apparently, it wasn't all that surprising to see someone from Russia in Israel, even at the Ministry of National Infrastructures. The clerk handed the passport back to the man and returned to his newspaper.

The man scanned the lobby. It was empty, save for the two of them.

Then a door to one side opened, and an elderly man strode across the lobby. He was in short sleeves with no jacket. His shoes were worn, and his tie angled off to one side. His gray hair was cropped close. He didn't look like a deputy oil commissioner, but the man hadn't really known what to expect.

"Abraham Zeffren?" The man extended a hand.

"Please—just Abe," he answered. "We don't go on ceremony much around here."

"I see. So, Abe...I called about the oil register?"

"Yes, I recall. I have it on my desk. We can look at it in my office."

The man followed Abe Zeffren to his office—a square, windowless office toward the back of the ground floor. Abe gestured to one of the two chairs in front of his cluttered desk, then moved to the other side. A battered leather binder perched on top of a pile of papers. It was held together by red electrical tape.

"That's it?" the man asked. "That's Israel's oil register?"

"It is." Abe smiled. "A sight to behold, isn't it?" The deputy oil minister opened the binder carefully. The crumpled pages inside seemed like they might disintegrate on touch.

"How old is that book?" the man asked.

"Don't know, exactly," Abe said. "But there are exploration permits in here going back at least thirty years or so."

"So that holds all the permits—leases, licenses, everything?"

Abe nodded. "Sure does. Only a handful of companies have had the courage or finances to go looking for oil, either onshore or off."

"But the big natural gas find last year off the coast of Tel Aviv?"

"Sure took us all by surprise," Abe said. "That was quite a shocker, hearing one of those areas held all that gas."

"Enough to meet Israel's energy needs for a decade, if I remember correctly?"

"Assuming they can get at it, yes."

"But it looks like they'll be able to, doesn't it?"

Abe squinted one eye. "That's what the newspapers say, I'll grant you that."

The man decided not to press the issue further. He knew more than he was letting on about the huge natural gas find in the Mediterranean. But he was here to register an oil license—not gossip about Israel's energy needs.

"So," the man said casually, "what do I need to do to secure a license in your register there?"

Abe turned the worn pages carefully. "If I remember from our conversation, you said you had partnership papers, some preliminary geological surveys—and a check? And you'd like to register a license at the northern end of the Dead Sea, in a new area?"

"Yes, that's correct." The man opened his briefcase, removed a folder, and handed a sheaf of papers to Abe. A check was stapled to the top of the file.

Abe glanced at the papers and then at the check. "It's all here," he said finally. "This is what I'll need to start the process."

"Good," the man said. "And I won't need anything else?"

"Not right now. But can I ask you something? How'd you manage to get INOC to put a privately held limited partnership inside its Dead Sea Partnership? That isn't easy."

Israel's National Oil Company was state-owned and had been around since the 1950s. Most of its financing came from public investors. But some of its financing came from private or foreign groups outside Israel. INOC had been aggressively exploring two lease areas under licenses at the southern end of the Dead Sea.

INOC's Dead Sea Partnership had recently begun to drill for oil at the southern end of the Dead Sea, with some reports indicating that the drill site might yield small amounts of oil, somewhere between one hundred to two hundred barrels of oil daily. It was a tiny amount, but it *was* oil, at least. No one had ever pursued anything at the northern end of the Dead Sea, though.

"INOC has its hands full at the southern end of the Dead Sea," the man said calmly. "This gives them a piece of any action in an area they've never explored and don't have the resources to go after."

"I see." Abe raised an eyebrow. "I guess that makes sense. But this paperwork says you have all the financing you need for a well-defined petroleum system and a viable geological conceptual model. You don't need any public financing?"

"We have what we need."

"Assuming you find anything." Abe smiled.

"Yes, assuming we should find something at the northern end of the Dead Sea."

Abe leaned back in his chair. It creaked and groaned. "You do know that Israel is a terrible place to drill for oil, don't you? This isn't Iran. No one's ever had even a whiff of anything like Ghawar in Saudi Arabia. You're likely throwing money down the proverbial rat hole."

The man didn't take the bait. "As I said, we have what we need. And we know what we're getting into. We're here for the long haul. We've pledged a firm partnership with INOC on this…and other matters."

"That's good, because no one's likely to get rich drilling for oil around here." Abe cocked his head toward the paperwork sitting on top of the oil register, loosely covering the electrical tape that kept the binder together. "So I have only one additional question. You mention in here that you might also be doing some work out in the Negev. Can you give me an idea of what you might be looking for exactly?"

The man stood to leave. "As I said, we've pledged to be a good partner to INOC. They've asked us for some exploratory help in the Negev. We won't be digging, if that's what you're asking."

"I'm not sure what I'm asking—though I *have* heard rumors that someone has stepped forward to help INOC make the pipe that runs from Ashkelon to Eilat two-way in order to allow oil to flow north to south and then out to China and the Far East," Abe said. "It was just a question."

"And when we have an answer," the man replied, ignoring the first part of the obvious question, "I'm fairly certain you'll be one of the first people to hear it."

Abe stared hard at him. After a minute, his gaze softened, as if he realized any further questions would be pointless. No answers would be forthcoming. "Fair enough. But if you *do* happen across anything interesting, you'll be sure to pay me a visit again and let me know?"

"Absolutely," the man said in earnest. "Should we find anything interesting, you can be assured that I will be back to see you."

"The Dead Sea is a curious place, isn't it?"

The man didn't answer this question either. "I'm sure we'll be in touch." He nodded politely.

"That would be nice." Abe closed the tattered oil register. "We don't get many visitors around here."

02

Somewhere off the southern coast of Yemen

"In range," Captain Samuel Bingham radioed to Vice Admiral Asher Truxton, who was listening in from a radio post at the US naval base in Manama, Bahrain, hundreds of miles away.

"What do you see?" Truxton asked.

There was a brief pause. "There are motorboats on one side," Bingham answered. "The *BPX* is dead in the water. Our guys said they can see some activity on the decks."

"Any sign of the *BPX* sailors?"

"Not that we can see, but we'll know more when we get closer," Bingham said.

Vice Admiral Asher Truxton—fresh off his successful defense of the Strait of Hormuz during the brief conflict with Iran—was troubled. It was hard to imagine that pirates could threaten big ships like the *BPX Limited* in open waters on the high seas. But that seemed to be the case.

"Can you take control?" Truxton asked.

Samuel Bingham, captain of the USS *John McCain*, had read the reports. He knew what the *BPX Limited* meant to the pirates that roamed the high seas off Somalia and Yemen. It was worth more than a ransom—its oil cargo was like black gold for the new breed of terrorism that was beginning to destabilize nation-states.

"I believe so," Bingham radioed back. "The men are preparing to board."

"So what do you make of the brief broadcast we got last night, right about when the pirates would have been coming aboard?"

"About the crew shutting down the engines and then locking themselves inside the engine room?"

"Yes," Truxton said. "Do you buy it?"

"Actually, ever since the Russians freed that crew from one of their own tankers, I do," Bingham answered. "We've been told that they're training sailors on board to do more of that. The owners are moving away from hiring private security forces and opting to get their sailors out of the way of the pirates."

"So you could board the ship?"

"Yes, Admiral, we could. I'd like permission to go in full force," Bingham said.

Truxton didn't hesitate. "You have it."

"Thank you, sir. I'll report back as soon as I have news."

The *BPX Limited* was an ugly ship. There were no visible markings and certainly nothing that might attract attention. So many heavy coats of paint had been applied over the years that it was nearly impossible to determine its original color. The *BPX Limited*'s engines always churned loudly and unimpressively when it sailed through the seas one hundred miles or so from the coastline of Yemen.

But to the sailors aboard a mother ship recently launched from the Somali town of Harardhere, Bingham knew the *BPX Limited* was a beautiful sight to behold. The ship might be ugly, but the light crude it carried was more wondrous than anything they could imagine. The oil was easily worth $50 million, even on the black market.

The Harardhere pirate group had their orders, and they were relatively straightforward. Take the ship by force, secure the unarmed sailors aboard in the cargo hold, and move the ship away from the waters off the coasts of Yemen and Somalia as quickly as possible.

This particular group of pirates had shifted its tactics in recent months, since pirating had become big business around the world.

Gone were the days of targeting small passenger ships and extracting ransoms. Now the Harardhere pirates and several others had their sights on oil tankers and commercial ships. There was a market for their contents.

Yes, both the EU and the United States Navy patrolled the Indian Ocean and the Arabian Sea, but they weren't fast enough to catch pirates using mother ships and motorboats. What's more, countries near Yemen and Somalia had grown weary of the chase and the efforts to lock pirates up. Some of the countries had already told the EU and the US that they would accept no more pirates.

The pirates of Somalia also benefited from their relationship to al Shabab, the terrorist organization that had long tried to overthrow the government of Somalia. While the deals were three and four times removed from the high-seas drama, the pirates discovered that someone, somewhere, was buying the oil from tankers such as this.

And that funding, in return, set al Shabab up to be a force to be reckoned with on the global stage. Big money tended to do that. It allowed al Shabab to export its own notions of jihad to other parts of the world.

It was hard to imagine, but three tankers nearly the same size as the *BPX Limited*—and their oil cargo—had simply vanished from the Arabian Sea in the past six months. Their crews were later found alive, wandering in either Yemen or Somalia. That's why Truxton had chosen to redeploy a dozen Reapers from Afghanistan and Iraq for duty in the seas south of Yemen and Somalia. The pirates knew nothing of these drones, which at least gave the US Navy some sort of an edge.

The Reapers were all-seeing, with infrared "eyes," and could fly for up to eighteen hours at a time. Their cameras could look down on suspected pirates from fifty thousand feet up, making them virtually invisible to the pirate mother ships that launched from Harardhere and Hobyo. The drones also could scan large areas for activity, so they were ideal in the vast waters where the pirates operated.

The trick, of course, was to spot a hijacking in progress and get there in time to find the pirates still aboard. Convincing his superiors at the joint chiefs to redeploy so many Reapers away from Afghanistan had been a tough sell for Truxton, but the change in pirate tactics to go after oil tankers had finally convinced the Pentagon leadership that more was going on than simple ransom hijackings. The pirates were beginning to fund terrorism, and that got the attention of the top brass at the Pentagon.

One of the Reapers had picked up a mother ship out of Harardhere two days ago. And just a day earlier, it had made the connection between the *BPX Limited* and the mother ship. So Truxton had quickly deployed the USS *McCain* to intercept both.

The firefight was intense, but brief. Captain Bingham could see it from the deck of the *McCain*. The pirates had opened fire immediately. They were well armed but no match for the American navy. Two of the pirates died in the gun battle. Another dozen, immediately arrested, were being detained aboard the *McCain*.

Once the *BPX* had been secured and swept, Captain Bingham came aboard the oil tanker. They'd guessed right. There were no *BPX* sailors to be found. They were either dead and tossed off the ship— or safely locked away.

Minutes later, one of his men shouted over the radio that the *BPX* sailors had been found, alive and well, inside the engine room. A minute later, other forces that had simultaneously boarded the Harardhere pirate mother ship also reported back.

"All clear here," said one of the sailors under Bingham's command. "But…"

"Yes?" Bingham asked.

"Well, we found things here in the hold of the ship that don't make any sense."

"Just report it, sailor," Bingham said patiently. "We'll make sense of it later."

"We found boxes and boxes of white flags."

"White flags?"

"Yes, hundreds of them. All new—piles and piles in boxes."

"That's certainly interesting," Bingham mused.

"And we found other things. Maps of an overland route from al Hudaydah to Mecca."

"Mecca, in Saudi Arabia?"

"Yes, sir. It appears to largely follow the coast. And there's one other thing."

Bingham smiled. "I can only imagine."

"There's a cache of weapons on one side of the hold," the sailor reported. "But they're useless."

"Because?"

"They're only a bunch of double-edged swords. Worthless in a fight. No one's fought with swords like these in a hundred years. I can't imagine what they're for, or why they're here."

"I can't either. But there's a logical reason for everything—and someone will make sense of this, I'll hazard."

"Flags, swords, and a route to Mecca? That makes sense?"

"It certainly makes sense to someone," Bingham answered.

03

Beersheba, Israel

It was hard to tell the friends from the enemies. That was what any casual observer noticed in Beersheba since the uneasy peace between Iran and Israel had remade the world. So many different nationalities visited on a daily basis now that it was nearly impossible to recognize the city known informally as the capital of the bleak, forbidding Negev desert.

But one thing was certain. The old wars were back in Beersheba, which had served twice on the front lines of war in the twentieth century. Many of the city's residents who'd migrated there since the Israeli Defense Forces had taken it from the Arabs in 1948 wondered if their city would soon become a symbol of war for a third time—or a harbinger for lasting peace in the troubled region.

It was odd to Dr. Elizabeth Thompson to see such a large US presence in Israel. She'd grown accustomed to seeing military in the refugee camps and places she frequented in East Jerusalem, the West Bank, and Jordan. But it had been a long time since she'd seen US military personnel operating so visibly in the region. It was a bit jarring.

Israel had been adamant about one thing as the peace talks between the leadership of the Palestine authorities, the US, and Israel had begun. There were no "blue helmet" peacekeeping forces in the Negev. They'd insisted that only the US military be allowed to move earth in and around Beersheba. Countries that wanted to send troops to the Negev to help the Americans had to equip their soldiers in the uniforms of the country's origin and operate under US military command.

"Dr. Thompson, you're back so soon?" asked an American soldier at a checkpoint ten miles or so south of Beersheba. He moved close to her jeep to inspect her papers.

Elizabeth smiled. "I expect you'll be seeing a lot of me for a while—at least until the hospital is finished." She handed her papers to the soldier, who glanced at them for only a second, then handed them back. He knew Dr. Thompson. He didn't need to examine her papers or the logo of her NGO, World Without Borders, on the side of the open-air jeep.

The American military had set up dozens of checkpoints in and around Beersheba, which made it virtually impossible for casual visitors to find their way around the city. It was frustrating. But Israel was allowing the operation—for now—while the peace talks were underway. They'd promised a show of good faith toward the creation of a free Arab state, so they allowed the operation to move forward.

A large transport truck—now empty—rumbled by from the opposite direction. Elizabeth winced as the truck kicked up a storm of dust. She and the soldier both shielded their eyes.

"I'll be glad when they've paved this road," the soldier said wistfully.

"I'll bet," she answered. "But the temporary authority central office said it will be at least six months before they get to things like that. They've got a lot of dirt to move first."

The soldier stepped back from her jeep to allow her to pass through the checkpoint. "You're probably right. But it sure would make this job more bearable—"

An air siren started up. Elizabeth instinctively looked up and south, toward the massive structures rising above the desert. The new "city" being built quickly by American-led forces was several miles to the east of Beersheba—between the old city and one of two Israeli air bases in the area.

The siren went off many times a day, and it always meant the same thing—another missile launch from somewhere in Gaza. Some of the Hamas forces had not yet fallen in line behind the call to peace from Iran's leaders.

Elizabeth caught the soldier's eye, and both watched in silence. Several moments later, a muffled explosion sounded as a missile landed and exploded harmlessly in the desert. Most of the missiles from Gaza either fell short of their targets in and around Beersheba or landed in the open desert.

"You sure you want to head into the compound today, Dr. Thompson?"

"I'm sure."

"The missiles have been more frequent of late," the soldier offered.

"I'll be fine." She laughed. "I'm a small target, and they never seem to land in the compound anyway."

"Except when they veer off target."

"True, but I'll take my chances."

"So what brings you back here today?"

She shifted gears in her jeep. "They're breaking ground for the new pediatric ward at the hospital. I promised I'd be there for it."

"Got it," the soldier said. "Be careful."

"Always. I'll keep an eye out for those missiles." She smiled easily.

As she drove toward the hospital under construction east of Beersheba, Elizabeth marveled at how swiftly events were transpiring since Iran, Israel, and the United States had moved the world back from the precipice and toward an uneasy peace.

The Korean peninsula was being transformed since North Korea had agreed to give up its nuclear weapons. The US military presence was rapidly shrinking and would be completely gone from the region in months. It was hard to imagine, but the situation in North Korea seemed to be stabilizing since American president Camara had traveled to Pyongyang and forged an agreement on the tarmac of the airport with its young leader.

Tehran had been true to its own promises. Press reports indicated that the leadership there was willing to negotiate with the Americans in good faith. Very public meetings in several cities had been fruitful and productive.

The hospital east of Beersheba was a good example of the fruits of those talks. Israel, reluctant at first, had finally agreed to a military presence, earth-moving infrastructure, and some permanent construction in and around a new Palestinian refugee camp already swelling with new arrivals.

The plan, Elizabeth knew, was to build a small suburb to the east of Beersheba as quickly as possible to accommodate an influx of Palestinian leaders and their families—people who would take over Beersheba as the capital of a new Palestinian state as soon as peace had become permanent and treaties were signed.

It would also give people currently living in Beersheba the time and space to move from the city to somewhere else in Israel—assuming they wanted to move.

Beersheba had been a centerpiece of the proposed Arab state in the original United Nations Partition Plan after World War II—until the Israel Defense Forces settled the issue by taking the city from the Arabs in 1948 and making it a part of Israel.

While it was still being debated, the thought was that Beersheba could become the capital of a new Palestinian state. It would be a real capital city and give the new state a fighting chance of success. The Americans had pledged to build up the infrastructure in and around the city to prepare for the day that such a free, Palestinian state was actually realized.

That concept, though, was proving much harder than anyone could have possibly imagined. Beersheba had once been firmly Arab—until the IDF had defeated Egyptian forces there in 1948 and driven them from the region. Since then, Jews from Arab countries, Ethiopia, and Russia had moved to the city and had no intention of moving until they were ordered to leave by Israel's government.

People thought the fights over Jewish settlements in East Jerusalem and the West Bank had been bad. The fights that erupted on an almost daily basis over the status of Beersheba in the proposed Palestinian state were much worse.

Elizabeth, though, focused on her own tasks. She'd promised to help create a hospital east of the city, within the compound that was starting to receive Palestinian families from refugee camps throughout the region. She knew many of the families personally through her work at all of the refugee camps. More families arrived at the compound on a daily basis.

What Elizabeth could not predict was what might happen when the compound reached critical mass—when the population of Palestinians had swelled to the point that they outnumbered the people who currently lived in Beersheba. She feared it might turn violent. Was anyone truly prepared for that day? It was something she often pondered.

As Elizabeth left the checkpoint, she looked off to her left. More American military convoys moved slowly in the distance. While no one said much about it, she knew from her many conversations with friends that one of the highest priorities for Israel was to secure facilities in and around Beersheba while the peace talks were underway in Washington and elsewhere.

At the top of the list was an oil pipeline that ran through the Negev desert and connected Ashkelon on the Mediterranean and Eilat. The pipeline, which had been built and co-owned by Iran once, was a crucial piece of the national infrastructure in Israel. Securing its safety was paramount to the Israeli authorities.

As Elizabeth drove toward the brand-new Palestinian compound, she wondered if all of this wasn't just a dream—one that would disappear when the dust settled.

Time would tell.

MARYLAND

WEST
VIRGINIA

Baltimore

Washington, D.C.

VIRGINIA

04

Dulles International Airport
Washington, DC

"Madame Secretary, I'm sorry, but I have my orders," the hapless aide said politely at the other end of the line. "The information is contained at the highest levels, on a need-to-know basis. As soon as I have clearance, I will certainly inform you."

"And you don't think I have a need to know?" Secretary Moran asked the aide, a colonel who now served the chairman of the Joint Chiefs of Staff. "I'm about to meet with a Saudi prince who was obviously the target of a terrorist attack—on our own soil—that we narrowly prevented. And you don't think I have a need to know why it happened?"

"It's not what I believe," the colonel explained. "But I have my orders."

"I understand," Moran said evenly. She had learned long ago to keep her anger in check, but it wasn't easy at times like this. "But I'll tell you what, Colonel. I'm going to ask you to put this call on hold. I want you to walk across the hall and ask your boss a simple question. Do I hear the information from the joint chiefs, or do I hear it from President Camara five minutes from now?"

"Madame Secretary, I don't think you need—"

"Go. Ask the question. I'll be here when you come back on the line."

Secretary Moran handed her cell phone to her aide, Katie Devlin, who'd been listening to one side of the conversation discreetly from a couple feet away. "Here—hold on to this for me until he comes back on the line. His name is Colonel something-or-other. I'm heading back out onto the tarmac to greet the Saudis."

"Madame Secretary, shouldn't we wait until they tell us it's clear?" Devlin asked, even as she pressed the phone up to her ear to listen in.

"I don't care at this point," Moran said. "Let them stop me. I intend to meet with the Saudis." She whirled and moved through the double doors to head back outside. Her internal security detail scrambled to keep up with her.

Katie Devlin smiled. This toughness, this resoluteness, was what she most admired about her boss. The detail would detain Secretary Moran briefly before she made her way out to the Airbus 380, but she would get her way sooner rather than later and manage to greet the Saudi prince on the tarmac.

There was an audible *click* on the cell phone Katie was holding as the aide to the joint chiefs chairman came back on the line. "Madame Secretary, if you can hold for a moment, I have General Alton on the other line. He would like to talk to you about the situation."

"Hold on," Katie said, but it was too late.

General John Alton came on the line. Alton was the first army general appointed vice chair of the joint chiefs stationed at the White House to serve the president directly. "Madame Secretary, they've relayed your concerns to me—"

"General Alton," Katie interrupted nervously, "the secretary of state is about to meet with the Saudis. She handed her cell to me. My name is Katie Devlin. I'm one of her aides."

"Of course, Ms. Devlin," the general said smoothly, without missing a beat. "I'll wait, if you'd like to see if your boss is available. Or I can call back."

"No, no. Let me see if she can talk right now."

Katie hustled through the double doors, but she was too late. Secretary Moran had managed to shake loose from her detail and was striding purposefully across the tarmac to greet the Saudi prince and his delegation planeside.

"General Alton," Katie said, "it appears that Secretary Moran is going to greet the Saudis planeside in a few seconds. She'll have to get back to you."

"That's fine," General Alton said. "But perhaps I can help clarify things somewhat. It would be helpful if the secretary had this information prior to her meeting with the Saudis." He paused. "As I understand it, Ms. Devlin, you have clearance? Top Secret, I believe?"

"Yes, I do," Katie said, hurrying across the tarmac to catch up with her boss.

"Well, then, if you could relay the following to Secretary Moran, I'd be grateful. But please be discreet. I'd prefer it if this information remains with the secretary."

"Certainly."

"You witnessed the two military aircraft that engaged shortly before the Saudi plane landed?"

"Yes," Katie said. "They seemed to come out of nowhere and then fired missiles at something on the ground."

"A target directly in the flight path of the Saudi plane, is that right?"

"Yes, it appeared to be right under the plane as it was landing."

"Ms. Devlin," the general said slowly, "we just stopped a terrorist attack aimed at the Saudi plane. We received credible information and confirmed it right before the plane was scheduled to touch down at Dulles. Those planes destroyed two MANPADS on the back of a truck that were about to fire at the Saudi plane."

"MANPADS?" Katie asked.

General Alton chuckled. "'A man-portable air defense system. They're surface-to-air missiles. They can be fired from the shoulder or mounted on the back of a pickup. In this case, it appears these were set up on the back of a truck. The gunner was about to use optical line of sight to guide both missiles at the Saudi plane."

Katie tried not to gasp. "The gunner? You mean a person?"

"Yes, Ms. Devlin, there was a gunner, a person, at the back of the truck. We don't know if he drove the truck there, parked, and then moved to the back of the truck to fire the weapons, or if there were more with him. We're analyzing the satellite photos, before and after. But our initial assessment is that there was only the one person who drove the truck there and then moved to the back to guide the surface-to-air missiles."

"This...MANPAD. Is it a defensive system?"

"They're designed as defensive systems," General Alton clarified, "but they can be used to target low-flying aircraft. You need line of sight, and the aircraft has to be well below twenty thousand feet. As you saw for yourself, that Saudi plane presents an awfully big target."

"And it was landing when your jets intercepted. So...this gunner? Do we know who it might be?"

"Not yet," General Alton said. "But we'll know soon enough. We know that al Qaeda in Yemen has been talking about something like this for weeks, which is what we'd locked on to. But we only confirmed the real threat right before the plane landed."

Katie took a deep breath. "General, is it possible this person, this gunner, was an American citizen? If so, that would change everything."

"I seriously doubt we're looking at an American. But as I said, we'll know soon enough."

"Who would do such a thing? And how could they get weapons like that into this country?"

"Ms. Devlin, it's conceivable to bring a shoulder-held surface-to-air missile across the border with Mexico on the back of a truck, to answer your second question. And who would do such a thing? Clearly, someone who has their sights set on the Saudis and the House of Saud."

Katie nodded to herself. She knew al Qaeda in Yemen had nearly assassinated the Saudi prince, who was the head of intelligence. They'd made no secret of their intent to pursue terrorism against the House of Saud. But taking the fight to American soil? That was new.

There could be only one answer. Someone within the House of

Saud knew of the emerging succession plan—and didn't like it. More specifically, they didn't like the Saudi prince, Muhammad al Faisal, who was about to meet with the Americans, and had chosen an opportune moment to target his Airbus 380 when it was in vulnerable airspace.

Prince Muhammad al Faisal, the governor overseeing Mecca, was about to move up in the House of Saud. Katie's boss had been in discussions with the Saudi royal family for months. A succession plan was emerging in the House of Saud, one that would shuffle the deck and bring both a new foreign minister and a defense minister into the picture, a new crown prince, and, ultimately, a new king of Saudi Arabia.

While she could only guess at this point, Secretary of State Jennifer Moran had told Katie she was certain she would learn today that Saudi King Faisal had decided to allow a change in the power structure.

Aging Saudi Crown Prince Saud bin Abdul Aziz would make way for his brother, Prince Natal, who would be named the new crown prince for a time. It was a risky but necessary move for the House of Saud. Natal was the long-serving minister of the interior who'd always taken a hard stance against Israel—which played well domestically but less so outside of Saudi Arabia.

But Moran had told Katie that the House of Saud was making moves that would lead to royal stability in the long term. Even as Natal was moving up, Crown Prince Saud would name his son, Ahmed bin Sultan, as the new defense minister. Meanwhile, the current foreign minister would shortly name his younger brother, Abdul al Faisal, as the new foreign minister. It had been a long road from the days of a previous king, Abdullah, who had long ruled the kingdom.

Muhammad al Faisal, who currently ran the foundations, philanthropies, science centers, financial investments, oil enterprises, and other assorted domestic operations for the House of Saud, would become the new Saudi minister of the interior—and the obvious crown prince in waiting. Muhammad al Faisal would almost certainly become the king of Saudi Arabia at some point soon.

The House of Saud was a byzantine network, Katie knew, and

you could never be certain your assumptions were correct about any of the sons and grandsons who ruled the kingdom. But her boss had an uncanny sense of timing and intuition about these things. And if Secretary Moran said Prince Muhammad al Faisal would become the king, then that was good enough for Katie.

"So how much of this should I relay to Secretary Moran? And what can she tell Prince Muhammad?"

General Alton hesitated only briefly. "The prince needs to know that we kept those missiles from being fired at his plane," he answered firmly. "Have the secretary tell him that we will debrief him and his government more fully once we have all the details in hand."

"Got it." Katie had almost reached her boss.

"And Ms. Devlin, I don't think I need to impress on you that we are not going out of our way to tell anyone about the true nature of this threat or what we averted?"

"I understand, General. A few of us saw what happened, but I doubt anyone could grasp what it all meant. It happened so quickly."

"We are preparing a standby statement. But we'll release it only when—or if—there's any press inquiry."

"And if no one in the media hears about it or asks about it?"

"Then it didn't happen, Ms. Devlin," the general said. "It won't be the first time an incident such as this simply did not happen."

05

Dammam, Saudi Arabia

It began with a rumor.

They've sent troops to the university, someone posted from his private account on the mVillage network.

They've put students from Dammam University in jail, another quickly followed on his own mVillage account.

An instant later, a third posted a video on mVillage that had been captured with a mobile device. Showing Saudi soldiers using force to halt a protest by dozens of "Young Turk" students in a public square in Qatif, the video was mischaracterized as a new effort to imprison religious Shi'a students from Dammam University.

But no such effort was underway at Dammam. Students there knew nothing of any such protests or arrests. It was merely a rumor.

Nevertheless, the video went viral immediately on mVillage. Mobiles lit up across Arabia with news that the Saudi's White Army internal security forces, under orders of the crown prince, had arrested and imprisoned young Shi'a students from Dammam.

More mVillage reports emerged, claiming that the Saudis intended to execute one or two of the students as part of their "iron fist" approach to halting even the beginning of any Arab Spring revolt that had rocked Egypt, Tunisia, Yemen, and nearby Bahrain.

This, in turn, fanned the flames of dissidence among the many disaffected Shi'a youth across Arabia who'd grumbled privately against the Sunni Wahabi rulers in the House of Saud for years.

These students had never bought in to the theory of the "notables"—the time-honored system of bestowing wealth and some measure of power to certain Shi'a families in cities with significant Shi'a populations, like Dammam and Qatif—that the House of Saud had so expertly deployed to keep the small Shi'a minority in Saudi Arabia in check.

These students—even those whose parents were part of the favored "notables" granted status by the Saudi ruling family—had no interest in being part of such a charade. They wanted recognition, the right to say their prayers in public, and some sort of representation in the Saudi system of government.

There were no Shi'a mayors or governors anywhere in Arabia. There were no senior Shi'a military officials. Even the Shi'a schools were devoid of Shi'a leadership. The principals of every Shi'a school for girls were Sunni and therefore connected to the Sunni monarchy that had ruled Saudi Arabia from its inception. *The Day of Anger is upon us*, someone finally posted on mVillage.

That phrase caught fire immediately. There was already a sense of urgency and excitement in the air since they were only a little more than a month away from the start of Hajj. Pilgrims all over the world were making their way toward Mecca.

Within minutes, the planning for a "Day of Anger" resonated with those who trafficked in such things across the mVillage network. Chaotic, wildly unorganized, organic efforts to spur such a day of protests in Qatif, Dammam, Medina, Mecca, and Riyadh spread like a virus across mVillage.

One student happened to notice that the ritual "day of cleaning" of Kaaba in Mecca was about to occur. It seemed convenient. So without consulting anyone, he simply proclaimed this day as the Day of Anger. It made some sense. Kaaba was the single largest symbol of religious authority in the kingdom. So why not tie a day of protests to the same day they cleansed Kaaba?

No one was in charge. No one understood what the final aims were. There was no manifesto, no call to arms, no demands of the House of Saud, no clear path to toppling the royal family and the monarchy of Arabia.

There was only a phrase, a mischaracterized video, and years of pent-up anger from a largely lower-class Shi'a minority that had been subjected to years of oppression from the monarchy. But that was the only fuel necessary for the Day of Anger notion to leap from mobile to another mobile in an mVillage network that had only begun to take root in the kingdom.

This will be our time to rise up against the oppressors, a Shi'a student at Dammam University wrote as he ate a sub sandwich in the cafeteria. He had a class in forty-five minutes and time to kill. Largely because he was bored, he surfed the network's deep library of images for a symbol that might be fun to post along with his messages.

First, he came across the unofficial flag of the Tea Party movement in America that cropped up in rallies—an image of a coiled serpent with the words DON'T TREAD ON ME beneath it. That was too weird and not relevant, the student quickly decided. Plus, the Tea Party in America was dominated by the old, not the young.

Then he found an image that struck him—the flag of the kingdom of Hejaz. It was simple, with a red triangle off to the left—or to the west on a compass—with black, green, and white bars crossing the flag horizontally. The point of the triangle—or the tip of the spear, perhaps—pointed at the heart of the green bar.

In a couple minutes of surfing the network, the student discovered that the Hejaz had once used the flag as their symbol for the Arab Revolt, early in the twentieth century. A nearly identical flag had later emerged as the modern Palestinian flag.

Throughout the twentieth century, rulers in other parts of the Middle East had used the colors of the Hejaz flag. Faisal, the king of Iraq, had tried them. The colors eventually came to be known as the unofficial pan-Arab colors—should a day ever arrive when there was a reemergence of a pan-Islamic caliphate that crossed country borders and resembled the old Ottoman Empire.

The kingdom of Hejaz disappeared in 1925, when an Emir drove the Hashemites out of Mecca, Medina, and Jeddah. The kingdom of Saudi Arabia was born in its wake. The current Saudi monarchy—the House of Saud—had planted their family name across Arabia and erased all traces of the old kingdom of Hejaz that had once been centered on the western coast of Arabia and the Hejaz mountains.

The ancient history of the Hejaz mountains was intriguing to this student. New archaeological research, combined with enhanced satellite imagery, had identified an ancient river that had once originated in the Hejaz mountains on the western coast of Arabia and made its way north and east through the Arabian desert, terminating at headwaters near what was now Kuwait.

A couple of obscure scholars proclaimed with absolute confidence that this "Kuwait River"—which had likely gone dry due to regional climate changes in about 3500 BC—was the very ancient "Pishon River" identified in the second chapter of the Old Testament's book of Genesis.

This, in turn, led the scholars to insist that the Garden of Eden could be found by following the ghostly, dry outlines of the Pishon River that had emerged from the mountains of Hejaz and snaked its way north and east through Arabia to a lush land where Iraq, Iran, and Kuwait converged at the northern end of the Persian Gulf.

The student thought that notion was hilarious—that the Garden of Eden could actually be found by following the dry riverbed—but he was also intrigued by the idea that the colors of the old flag of the Arab Revolt had traveled around the Arab world for the better part of a century.

Why not adopt the old Arab Revolt flag—the flag of the long-dead kingdom of Hejaz that had once called Mecca its capital—as the new symbol of the mythical Day of Anger uprising in the Saudi kingdom? the student asked himself. The flag hadn't been of use since a local ruler—the Sharif of Mecca—had used it to plot the creation of a pan-Islamic empire that had never come to fruition.

So the student copied the flag image, attached it to a new mVillage post, proclaimed it the flag of a pan-Islamic Arab Revolt, pinned it to the Day of Anger protests in different Arabian cities, and hit the SEND button.

Within minutes, another bored student in another Arabian university picked up on the post and added yet another rumor to it—namely, that the heir to the long-dead Ottoman Empire would make a special appearance at one of the cities during the Day of Anger protests and lead them in a demand to bring back the kingdom of Hejaz and overthrow the House of Saud.

It was a ludicrous post, half in jest. This particular student didn't care that there was, in fact, an *actual* heir to the ancient Ottoman Empire. The government of Turkey had carefully kept the heirs to the ruling dynasty of the now-defunct Ottoman Empire—the family of the Osmans—from holding any positions of influence in their country and society. They'd only recently allowed some of the family members to even enter the country.

Nevertheless, there was an actual heir to the Ottoman Empire—a retired librarian in London named Mehmet Osman, who was in his eighties, had never married, and had no children. There was uncertainty, in truth, about whether the Osman "dynasty" would end with Mehmet.

This post was followed by another outrageous effort by yet a third, equally bored student. He merged the Arab Revolt flag, the old kingdom of Hejaz, the defunct Ottoman Empire dynasty heir, the Arab Spring revolt leadership in Bahrain, Egypt, Tunisia, and Syria, and the peace talks between Israel and Iran into one vast Jewish conspiracy.

Israel is behind the new effort to bring back the kingdom of Hejaz, this student wrote on mVillage. *The Zionists are encouraging the revolt against the House of Saud. They are playing the Shiites of Iran against the Sunnis of the House of Saud in Arabia.* The student knew fully that he was tossing gasoline-soaked logs onto the fire. But he didn't care. It was amusing.

Then others took this post seriously. Within the hour, cables whirred and whizzed to various corners of the globe. The notion of a Day of Anger took firm root in the soil. People started to plan for such an effort. Several self-appointed leaders in Qatif, Dammam, and Mecca reached out to others who could organize organic protests.

People in distant capitals heard about the Day of Anger protests planned in Arabia, fed by a growing rise of missives about Israel somehow engineering the protests to pit the Saudis against Iran.

A few trafficked in end-times prophecy for good measure, to show the Mahdi returning as a pan-Islamic caliph of one sort or another. One thread merged the Mahdism of pop culture with the notion that the Sharif of Mecca would lead a new Arab Revolt that would spread beyond Arabia to parts unknown.

Still another thread began to spread rumors that terrorists were planning to destroy the Kaaba, Islam's holiest shrine. There had been threats to the Kaaba in the past, and several actual insurrections in its square. Should someone ever seek to destroy the Kaaba, it would set off violent responses across the globe and usher in the era of the hidden imam as prophecy foretold, they wrote.

None of it was remotely based in truth. It had all begun as a rumor. Yet somehow a new pan-Islamic flag circulated through mVillage. An actual day of protest in several Arabian cities was identified. An heir to a long-discredited dynasty had been conscripted without his knowledge. And a kingdom-in-waiting was forming in opposition to the House of Saud.

PANAMA

VENEZUELA

COLUMBIA

PACIFIC
OCEAN

Bogota ●

06

Bogotá, Colombia

"Please don't go, Nash. Saudi Arabia is too dangerous."

Nash Lee could sense the fear in his fiancée's voice. Kim Su Yeong was tough. She could hold her own in any meeting at the White House or at Foggy Bottom even though she was only in her midtwenties. She was fearless—but not when it came to Nash. Whenever he got on a plane to a part of the world where the government wasn't totally stable or reliable, Su worried. And she was worried now.

"It's fine, Su. *I'll* be fine. Don't worry," Nash said. "I'll be in the State Department bubble—like I am here in Bogotá."

"I know, but…"

Nash knew precisely why Su was worried. The two often talked at length before he set off on some new adventure around the world. His current trip to Colombia was a good example. When he'd met with the president of Colombia and proposed a novel technology solution to the problem the citizens and military had with indiscriminate landmines in the country, Su had been very worried.

Colombia was the only country in Latin America with a landmine problem. Anti-government rebels planted or dropped them everywhere to protect trade routes and coca crops. Those mines killed or maimed hundreds of Colombian citizens every year.

Nash's mVillage network had potentially found a solution. More than 40 million Colombians had cell phones, and all were more than willing to send SMS messages into the mVillage network to identify where the landmines were located whenever citizens spotted them.

Once sent, the messages were then plotted with Google's geocaching software and incorporated into Google Earth. In the past two years, the project had become a huge success. Millions of Colombians had sent in anonymous SMS messages identifying and tracking the landmines.

Overnight, Google Earth had transformed the picture of Colombia, allowing anyone with an Internet connection to keep track of where the landmines were located and most prevalent throughout the countryside. And the mere fact of knowing that the citizens themselves were keeping track of the landmines had already begun to change the equation.

But Nash's next trip worried Su. She was convinced he was getting in way over his head and making himself a needless target.

"The pirates off the coast of Somalia aren't rational," Su said. "And al Qaeda in Yemen is in their same league."

"I'm not getting involved with either of those," Nash countered. "Trust me. I'm only going to Riyadh to hear about their plans to help extend mVillage in the region. And then I'm just joining a State Department delegation for a day trip to Yemen for a quick round of talks on what we can do to access medical and health information. You'll never see me getting involved with any of the military or counter-insurgency stuff. Never. You know me. I'm all about—"

Su cut him off. "I know, I know. You're all about doing good, making a difference, not getting involved in the actual battles and fights. You're the relentless, positive storm out to remake the world at the edge of battle and military conflicts."

She knew Nash's "pitch" better than he did. He lived the "relentless, positive storm"—the defining way of life and meaning for millions of the Millennial generation who'd grown up living and breathing technology and its benefits. Use technology to change things, make the world a better place, increase knowledge, and help the underserved. That was their war cry.

Nash was one of their global leaders. His mVillage network had connected hundreds of millions of people all over the world, and opened doors through simple methods of communication using existing technology platforms that could be modified for social good.

"So I don't need to tell you," Nash continued, "that I won't be going anywhere close to the Somalia pirates or the al Qaeda camps that Yemen's government is trying to track."

"Good! Because I won't let you go if you're planning to get anywhere near that stuff. Promise me you'll just go there to get mVillage established in Saudi Arabia. That's all. Okay?"

"Deal," Nash said, smiling. His fiancée—known as Su Kim at the State Department—could make her threat good if she really wanted. Su had made plenty of connections at State in her brief tenure there. Word of the role she'd played as a back channel to North Korea during a conflict that had nearly escalated into a nuclear confrontation had traveled far. Su was a force to be reckoned with, folks said. She had connections—beginning with her globe-trotting boyfriend, Nash Lee.

Su worked at State during the day and went to law school at night. Nash, the CEO and founder of the Village Health Corps and mVillage, flew in and out of Washington almost on a weekly basis. The two of them saw each other whenever they could. But they were always connected, either by mobile, Skype, or SMS.

The trip that Nash was contemplating next, though, was one that could contain all sorts of mischief. The mVillage network hadn't quite taken hold in countries like Saudi Arabia, Somalia, or Yemen, for one reason or another.

Nash was especially curious about Saudi Arabia and the general lack of adoption there, so he'd decided to visit the tiny mVillage office in Riyadh and see the situation for himself. He was far less interested in places like Somalia and Yemen. There was very little he—or anyone else— could do in countries like Somalia, where the landscape was so chaotic. The mVillage would take hold in both of those countries on their own, like it had in North Korea and Iran, at the local level if people wanted it to work. The technology was available for those who wanted to use it.

"I'm serious, Nash," Su said forcefully. "If I hear that you're getting involved in Somalia, or Yemen, I'm going to march into Secretary Moran's office myself and order her to shut you down!"

"You'd never do that to me." Nash laughed.

"Watch me—especially if I hear you're going anywhere near Yemen."

A loud voice in the background interrupted their call. "Hey, Su, gotta go," he said. "They're boarding the flight. I'll call when I land in Riyadh."

"Okay, but you remember what I said. I meant every word."

"I know, Su, and I heard you. I won't go anywhere near Somalia or Yemen. I promise."

Baltimore

WEST
VIRGINIA

Washington, D.C.

VIRGINIA

07

Washington, DC

"I beg to differ, Mr. President. It isn't the same thing—not at all," the national security advisor said. "You're being naïve and making a mistake. You're overreacting. I'm afraid you simply don't understand how the House of Saud will react to this."

DJ held his breath and scanned the room. Dr. Susan Wright, the president's deputy national security advisor, was clearly shocked by the statement. But the faces of the military staff and advisors were implacable masks. They'd seen this type of scenario play out too many times to react.

The Situation Room was full. DJ, as usual, leaned up against a wall at the back of the room. The president's chief of staff, Dr. Anshel Gould, rested his back against a nearby wall as well. Sometimes, DJ knew, Dr. Gould sat beside the president in the Sit Room. But not today. The president was flanked on both sides by two four-stars—General Sean Thomas, his national security advisor, and Dan Johnson, the former Republican senator from Missouri who'd recently become the secretary of defense.

Daniel James, or DJ to everyone in the room, always counted himself lucky to be included in these meetings. As the principal deputy press secretary on foreign policy matters, he'd asked the president for permission to sit in on briefings like this. President Adom Camara had given DJ that chance, provided he never abused the privilege. DJ was careful and never said a word in these meetings.

Right now, though, DJ found it difficult to hold his tongue. Everyone in the room could see that General Thomas had just challenged the president's ability to understand a complicated foreign policy matter. And yet President Camara didn't respond—at least not the way DJ would like him to respond.

"Perhaps you're right, Sean," the president said. "Perhaps I'm not seeing the situation quite right, or clearly enough. But humor me. Assume, for a moment, that *is* the same thing, and that I am right about this. Play it out for me." The president pushed his chair back from the table a couple of feet so he could look directly at his national security advisor. He leaned back in his chair, folded his arms, and settled in for the lecture he was about to receive from his imperious national security advisor.

"Okay, I can do that." General Thomas nodded vigorously. Known to relish a challenge like this, he forged ahead, blind to the president's body language. "But it's hard, because you're wrong about this. The Saudis will not see this attack as all that significant—and certainly not similar to the attack on the towers in New York City. You're equating this attack on the Airbus 380 to 9/11, like it's a direct attack against the monarchy in Saudi Arabia. But it's not. It's merely a hapless dupe they planted here in the United States, who took advantage of a window of opportunity."

"You're sure about that, Sean?" the president asked quietly.

"Quite certain," the general said. "Al Qaeda in Yemen has attacked a Saudi prince before. They nearly killed their head of intelligence not long ago. They've gone after other members of the Royal family. This is old hat to the Saudis. One more in a long line of efforts to go after individual members of the House of Saud. Remember, it's Saudi intelligence that provides us with a steady flow of information about al Qaeda's activities. They've warned us about serious activities a half-dozen times in the past decade. They know al Qaeda better than we do."

"So this is just one more incident? Nothing more serious than that?" asked Camara.

"Yes, just one more incident," the general responded. "The Saudis know where most of the al Qaeda financing activities originate. They follow the money quite well, which gives them access to al Qaeda's plans. They know full well that al Qaeda is an organization in name only, that leaders in various groups don't really answer to anyone, and that they all look for opportunities to go after the House of Saud. This is an isolated incident. It isn't organized and certainly isn't the same thing as a direct attack against the leadership of their country."

"Dr. Wright, is that your assessment as well?" the president asked without taking his eyes off General Thomas. "Do you believe this is only an unfortunate, isolated incident?"

DJ glanced over at Dr. Wright. He couldn't help himself. He really admired the president's deputy national security advisor. She'd brought badly needed stability and sanity to the national security office. DJ knew that, someday, Dr. Wright would head back to academia to become president of some prestigious American university. But for now, he leaned heavily on her wise counsel and calm demeanor during times like this. He wondered how she'd handle this one.

She did not answer immediately, and DJ sensed she was uncomfortable that the president put her on the spot. When she did speak, she seemed to choose her words carefully. "I believe this is a serious attack, one that the Saudis will view differently than previous attacks. I'm not prepared to say it's precisely analogous to 9/11, but nevertheless, it is something the Saudis will take very seriously. They will ask for our utmost cooperation on intelligence sharing."

"Why?" the president asked.

"Because it's Muhammad al Faisal—who I believe will become king at some point—and because it happened on American soil at precisely the moment he'd arrived in this country to dialogue about the succession of power within the House of Saud. It's as if someone within the royal family—someone who doesn't agree with the succession plan—helped orchestrate the act to disrupt the plans. Imagine if the attack had succeeded. It would have permanently altered the plan for the House of Saud. For that reason alone, I believe we need to take this quite seriously."

"But Mr. President, we don't know any of this with absolute certainty!" General Thomas jumped back into the conversation. "We still don't know if Prince Muhammad arrived here to brief us on any succession planning for the House of Saud. At most, we'll be reading tea leaves after he's gone back to Riyadh. He's not the king yet and may never be. So we can't impute all sorts of things into this, like it's an assassination attempt against the Saudi king on US soil."

"Well, General Thomas, I beg to differ with your assessment," the president said calmly. "I do believe our intelligence is correct and that Prince Muhammad is here to give us a fairly clear road map. I also believe Secretary Moran will confirm that for us shortly."

"No secretary of state—not even Jennifer Moran—can decipher that in just one meeting with someone like Prince Muhammad from the Saudi royal family," General Thomas said flatly. "That's not possible. The House of Saud covers its face with one veil after another, and you can never truly know what face will emerge."

"So you're a diplomat now, Sean?" The president cocked his head.

"I don't need to be a diplomat to know how cautious the royal family is about their business. There's no way for us to know what they may—or may not—have in mind. I continue to maintain that this was just another incident—not directed at disrupting the succession plan for the next king of Saudi Arabia. And our response, both militarily and diplomatically, should be calibrated accordingly."

"But what if you're wrong?" Camara asked.

The general's eyes narrowed. "I'm not. We don't know the Saudis' plans. What we *do* know is that this was almost certainly an isolated incident. My prediction is that we'll learn in the next day or so that the gunner on that truck was a lone operative with loose connections, like nearly all of the others we've tracked down over the years. It's the press that creates this grand al Qaeda conspiracy that we all know is bunk."

"Even if, in this particular case, there may be more going on? That this was more coordinated and timed for a specific reason?" the president persisted.

"We don't know that any of that is likely," the general answered. "And we can't assume something like that, without any knowledge in hand. I feel I'm right about this."

DJ closed his eyes briefly. He knew, at that moment, that this particular meeting was the last time General Thomas would have any significant role to play in the president's decision-making process. He would be eased out of the White House within months—if not sooner. DJ could see it quite clearly, even if the national security advisor was obtuse to the signs.

While he had nothing other than his own personal convictions to go on, DJ trusted Susan Wright. He would follow her advice and counsel on almost any matter, and this was no different. And, DJ knew, the president almost certainly felt that way as well.

"All right, we'll wait on a report back from Secretary Moran from the Saudi visit," the president concluded. He pushed his chair back to the table and looked out across the room. "But we are going to treat this as a direct, coordinated attack against someone that our best intelligence believes to be a future Saudi king. In short—this was an assassination attempt, on our own soil."

ISRAEL

EGYPT

JORDAN

Aqaba

GULF OF AQABA

SAUDI ARABIA

08

Aqaba, Jordan

General Ahmet Fahd was perplexed.

Fahd was on vacation in the Jordanian coastal town made famous by T. E. Lawrence's participation in the 1917 Arab Revolt against the Turks.

In the past hour, the real-life Saudi general had received a most intriguing phone call. The minister of the interior in the kingdom wished to see him and would arrive shortly to discuss areas of mutual interest.

The retired general spent the better part of the afternoon wondering what, exactly, Prince Natal could possibly want. General Fahd was a distant relative of a Saudi king several generations back. For this reason, he'd always taken more than a passing interest in the comings and goings of the royal family.

As a young man, Fahd had made the career-limiting mistake of falling in love with an extraordinarily beautiful young woman while they both attended university outside the kingdom. The young woman was from one of the "notable" Shi'a families in Qatif—but she was still Shi'a. Fahd had spent the rest of his life, and career, hiding this fact from those in positions of power in the kingdom.

Both of these personal complications had always made Fahd leery of getting too close to the Saudi royal family. But once he'd assumed command of a White Army that regularly did what it could to keep the Shi'a minority in Saudi Arabia from gaining traction, he was also acutely aware of the deep resentments harbored by the Shi'a families. His wife regularly reminded him of those injustices, even as he ordered those in his command to carry them out.

Those who'd studied the House of Saud closely knew that Natal would someday be given the title of crown prince—either upon Saud's death or by acclamation when Saud decided he could no longer hold the title.

But, the retired general knew, it was also well known among the close-knit members of the royal family that Natal would never be given the crown. He would never be king. No, that position was, even now, being negotiated among the various factions of the House of Saud. Balances of power would, of necessity, be struck to make sure no dynastic line held too much sway.

Most likely, the family members were grooming the governor of Mecca, Prince Muhammad al Faisal, for the crown. There would be an interim step along the way, perhaps with Natal as crown prince, but the line of succession would be known to the insiders.

The general wondered how Natal felt about that. *Perhaps I am about to find out.* Sitting on the veranda of his retirement villa with a lovely view of the waters west of Aqaba, the general carefully sipped his afternoon coffee.

When Natal finally arrived, the general was even more surprised that no legion of White Army guard was with him. Natal had, apparently, made the trip to Jordan to see the general by himself.

"Greetings, my friend!" Natal said as both shared a warm embrace. "It has been far too long."

"Yes, most certainly," General Fahd answered. "But I am enjoying my time here."

"Here, in exile?" Natal joked.

"Self-imposed exile." The general laughed. "I return to Riyadh and Arabia when business calls me there."

"But you prefer the solitude of Aqaba?"

"I do," the general said truthfully. "Here, I am just an old man. No one knows my status as a retired general who once commanded the vaunted White Army of the kingdom."

"I can appreciate that, my friend. There are times I would certainly like to travel in anonymity."

The general gave Natal a curious look. "It would appear you have somehow managed to do so on this day?"

Natal smiled. "Yes, it is a very small privilege I enjoy—the ability to elude the White Army that follows my every move throughout the day."

"Yes, I remember those days well. I received hourly reports on your movements, as I recall." The general gestured toward the veranda. "Please, let us speak outside. I've made coffee. And once we're settled, perhaps you can tell me why you, of all people, would wish to journey so far without the protection of the White Army."

The general was retired, but he still had some bounce to his step. He made his way outside quickly, served coffee to the kingdom's interior minister, then took his usual seat on a soft chair that faced the water.

"The view is quite extraordinary, Ahmet," the interior minister said. "I can see why you try to return here whenever you have a chance."

"I would spend all of my days here, if I could. But we are not here to discuss my retirement. So, my good friend, what is on your mind?"

Natal looked off in the distance. "As you know, I always considered you to be my most loyal commander. I knew that, no matter what intrigue might be playing out, I could count on you to watch my back."

"Yes, I was loyal," the general agreed. "I still am, even in retirement."

"And I appreciated that—then and now. So I am here to call on that loyalty one more time. The time is urgent, and the need is great."

"I am listening."

"What I am about to tell you today is in the strictest confidence. Can I trust you?"

"You know that you can," the general said. "We have always been candid with each other. So I would urge you to speak freely. Your words will remain between us, here on this veranda."

"Good." Natal nodded. "I'd hoped you'd say as much. So I will get right to it. The kingdom is under siege and in grave danger. The royal family has made decisions that are not in Arabia's best interests. Saud and the king have decided that the grandsons are to take power, and they are giving that power to the two most liberal members of the family."

"Prince Muhammad will be in line to become king?" the general asked.

"Yes, and they will make Prince Abdul the foreign minister. Saud will step aside as crown prince, giving that title to me. However, it is merely a transition. The plan is that I will very quickly give up that title and office in order to make way for an orderly transition for the grandson, led by Muhammad. He is to be king, not me."

"And I can safely assume that you do not agree with this transition?" the general asked.

"I do not." Natal's dark, brooding eyes flashed with barely controlled anger. "You and I both know that the liberal grandsons who have pushed the royal family to modernize and make peace with Israel, among other reforms, are guiding the kingdom to its ultimate doom. Now is the time to rule with an iron fist, not make peace with our enemies."

"But peace demands compromise," the general said in a calming tone. "We both know that."

"But not with our enemies," Natal said forcefully.

The general was quiet for a time. He took a long drink from his cup of coffee. He wanted to weigh his next words carefully. "So what would you have me do, Prince Natal?" he asked at last. "I can only assume that you have some plan in effect to keep this from happening?"

"Yes, General Fahd, I most certainly do. But once I have told you of these plans, you will then be a centerpiece of the conspiracy. Is that a risk you are willing to take?"

The general looked out over the waters beyond Aqaba. He knew instinctively that this idyllic life was about to change forever. "I am willing to serve. We live but once, as far as I know, and my own life is nearing an end. There is nothing left to fear. So I will join you. Now, please, what is the plan, and what is my role in it?"

"I want you to be a leader in exile," Natal said. "You are perhaps uniquely qualified to become the voice of a disaffected populace in the kingdom and can articulate those sentiments against the House of Saud."

"I don't understand."

"Your wife," Natal said. "I know how you have assiduously kept your wife's religious beliefs hidden from those in Riyadh, but I have known for some time that she is Shi'a."

"So what does that have to do with this discussion?" Fahd said, his voice steady.

"I will be direct. There are others in the White Army who are loyal to me and do not wish to see Saud and the king hand over the reins to Prince Muhammad and the other voices of liberalism. But in order to make that succession impossible, we need chaos to return to the kingdom. Once it has returned, then I can lead the security forces in an effort to shut it down and usher in a new era where I am able to become the rightful king."

"Why not just have Muhammad removed?" the general asked.

Natal pursed his lips. "I have tried that, through others. It did not work. Iran is being blamed, in private circles."

"So you are moving to a much more dangerous game? Fomenting revolt and uprising in the kingdom?"

"Those are happening now, whether we like it or not," Natal said. "Look around at Egypt, Syria, and elsewhere. The Arab Spring revolts occur without bidding or prompting on our parts. I am merely attempting to channel the inevitable in the kingdom in a way that will, ultimately, keep us all from marching over the cliff."

"So you would have me voice the stirrings of revolution here, from Aqaba? I use my wife's religious heritage, appeal to the disaffected Shi'a minority populations, stir up discontent through harsh words directed at the House of Saud?"

"Something like that." Natal smiled.

The general paused. "You *do* realize that my vacation home here in Aqaba will then become an actual place of exile?"

"For a time—but only until I become king," Natal said. "Once I have taken control, I will move quickly to forge a coalition monarchy. You will become the minister of defense. It will be time to heal the wounds. You will speak for the oppressed Shiites in Arabia, their first real representative in Riyadh in a generation."

"Which, of course, will be a lie," the general murmured.

"Not entirely. You have heard the sentiments of your wife all of these years. She has told you things that you have undoubtedly taken to heart."

"Perhaps."

"So you will accurately give voice to some of these things," Natal said. "And within that lies the truth. You will be their voice—a voice they do not have now."

"And if I do this—is there a plan?"

"Yes, and it will almost certainly require bloodshed. This must be perceived as the beginning of an armed rebellion. There will be fights, explosions, armed insurrections in different parts of the kingdom—all necessary to bring the pot to a boil."

"And I am to remain here, stirring that pot until it boils?"

"Yes. And just as the world saw in Libya, weapons will arrive, members of the Saudi White Army will begin to defect. And you will command those from here."

"It's quite a gamble, Natal."

"Yes, but a necessary one, General Fahd," the minister said. "History demands that we do whatever it takes to protect Arabia, and I believe this is the only route to salvation."

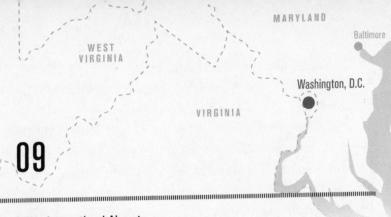

MARYLAND

Baltimore

WEST
VIRGINIA

Washington, D.C.

VIRGINIA

09

Dulles International Airport
Washington, DC

Katie Devlin did her best not to hyperventilate. She closed her eyes and told herself that everything would be fine. After all, she'd been through a presidential campaign and had managed to survive the eternal hazing from the national press corps that always waited like vultures for the smallest slip or mistake by her candidate, the boss.

So how hard could it be to insinuate herself between the secretary of state and someone who, by all appearances, was in line to become the next king of Saudi Arabia? She just needed to deliver a message to her boss, she kept telling herself. And then she would sit off to the side and watch.

The Airbus 380 was even bigger inside than it appeared from the outside. Climbing an entire flight of stairs—inside the airplane—she worked her way past several Saudi internal security forces toward the back of the plane.

Who builds such a monstrosity of extravagance? It seems so completely unnecessary and...excessive. Katie couldn't help but wonder what the people of the kingdom would think if they saw for themselves the ways in which the oil riches were spent. Would they care? Would they rise up against their leaders?

The world of billionaires was well beyond anything Katie knew or understood. Once, at the beginning of Jennifer Moran's presidential campaign, Katie had taken part in a private fundraising meeting with a reclusive billionaire who'd asked to meet with her boss. They'd met in public—but just barely.

This particular billionaire, who'd made his fortune buying and selling vast chunks of real estate in half the countries of the world, had cleared out the entire restaurant at the Four Seasons hotel in New York. When Katie had entered the Four Seasons, there was only one round table in the center of what, ordinarily, had been the entire restaurant at one of the most expensive hotels in the city.

Jennifer Moran and Katie had met with this particular billionaire for the better part of an hour. Throughout the meeting, a young woman who was not introduced had sat to one side of the elderly man, cradling one of his arms in her hands. She'd never spoken a word throughout the meeting. A dozen waiters had served them a four-course meal.

By the end, Katie had been nearly unable to process the meeting.

But her boss had secured a promise of support from the billionaire's network of friends, which, for an aspiring national politician, was all that mattered. Raising money to support a presidential campaign seemed like an endless parade of indignities, Katie had thought at the time.

Similar thoughts struggled to surface as she wandered through the opulence that confronted her at every turn in the interior of the Airbus 380. So much money stared her in the face that it seemed surreal—beyond a mere mortal's grasp. She'd had no idea, until that moment, how different the world of oil wealth really was in comparison to the rest of the ordinary world.

Katie entered through a massive set of double doors into what felt like a sanctuary. There was a stage at one end with a huge screen at the back of it. She struggled to understand why anyone would possibly need such a theater. The secretary of state was sitting at a small table off to the side, facing Prince Muhammad al Faisal. Aides hovered nearby.

Katie approached the table and waited for a natural pause in the conversation. "Madame Secretary," Katie said softly, "if you have a moment?"

Jennifer Moran glanced over her shoulder, annoyed. But the expression faded when she saw it was Katie who'd disturbed the meeting. She turned back to Prince Muhammad. "If you would excuse me?"

The Saudi prince nodded once at the secretary of state, then looked directly at Katie. "It must be important?"

"Yes, sir, it is," Katie said quickly. "I'm sorry to interrupt. It will only be a minute."

The Saudi prince smiled. "Take all the time you'd like. We have come here, to this country, for this meeting only. We will wait."

The secretary of state pushed her chair back from the table and walked over to meet Katie off to the side of the huge theater. "So I'm assuming you've heard from the White House about the attack?" Moran said without preamble.

"I have," Katie said. "And it's bad."

"How bad?"

"It was an assassination attempt on the Saudi envoy. General Alton told me that NSA had picked up the intel at the last possible minute, which allowed them to intercept the truck."

"Truck?"

"They were going to shoot the Airbus 380 out of the sky with a surface-to-air missile, from the back of the truck. Something called a MANPAD, which can launch a missile at a slow-moving target like this plane."

Secretary Moran was a tough woman. She didn't blink at the news. Katie knew she didn't want the Saudi prince to see her concern. "But we got it, right?"

"Yes, we got it."

"So the threat was removed?"

"It was, and it appears that it was only one truck, acting alone."

"It just takes one to alter the balance of world powers," Moran said. "We both know that."

"Yes, ma'am, we do. General Alton wanted you to have this information as you talked to the prince."

"I appreciate that. This helps. I can use that." Moran glanced over at the Saudi prince. "Okay, let's go put this information in play and see what it gives us. Come join us, Katie. I want a witness when we have this conversation."

Katie nodded and trailed in her boss's imperious wake. She loved working for Jennifer Moran. She would follow her to the ends of the earth, if need be.

"Prince Muhammad, I have news of great import," she said once she'd taken her seat at the small table that seemed so small at the foot of the grand stage inside the plane. "And I would like to share that information, in confidence, with you."

"I am at your disposal, Madame Secretary," the prince said.

Katie did her best not to stare at the prince, but it was difficult. The prince's robes had thin gold seams running throughout the folds. Katie wondered, fleetingly, if it was actual gold. *That couldn't be possible. Could it?*

"I will be direct, if that is all right with you?" Moran asked.

"Please, by all means. We are allies and friends. Information is the coin of our respective realms, and I have news for you as well."

Moran nodded. "Good. I am eager to hear of your news. But first, I must tell you that there was an incident, on the ground, as your plane was landing here at Dulles."

"An incident?"

"Yes, Prince Muhammad, we intercepted a terrorist attempt on your life. Two of our fighter jets took out a truck on the outskirts of the airport. This truck was about to launch a missile at your plane— a surface-to-air missile."

The Saudi prince stared hard at the secretary of state as he processed the news. "Did you receive help from our intelligence service? Is that how you were able to react in time?"

Moran didn't hesitate. She had no knowledge, either way, of the answer. But, Katie knew, that wouldn't stop her. "We share information in real time with the Saudi intelligence services. And I'm certain we would have shared information here. Without a doubt, it was the combined efforts of Saudi intelligence, combined with the quick reaction of the American military, that allowed us to neutralize this threat on your life."

The Saudi prince nodded. "Very well. I am glad for that."

"You're not surprised, then?" Moran asked.

"To be honest, no. We have been hearing rumblings for weeks that some within the House of Saud were not pleased with the news I was bringing here today. Clearly, someone was not happy at all and chose to move into action against me. I am quite grateful that you acted immediately on the information you received."

"It is our greatest pleasure to help you, one of our most trusted allies," Moran said firmly. "I'm glad we were able to deal with the threat swiftly and directly."

"I am, as well." The prince smiled. "The mere fact of this conversation—here, between the two of us—is proof that our enemies will not, must not, succeed."

"Yes, I agree."

The prince looked over his shoulder at one of his own aides. "Tell the pilots that we are returning to the kingdom," he called out. "We must fly back to Mecca, at once." He turned his attention back to the table. "I am sorry, but this news has changed things immensely. This will accelerate things greatly within our family."

"I understand," Moran said. "But before you leave, is there news that you'd hoped to bring us? About changes that will be underway soon in the kingdom?"

The prince did not hesitate. "Because you have saved my life here, today, I will answer that question. I was prepared to be more circumspect, but I see that events are moving more rapidly, so I will not waste words."

"Please. I will keep your words close," Moran said.

"I appreciate this." The prince leaned forward. "There are changes occurring within the family. The grandsons are going to be taking power in the kingdom. You can be assured of these changes. Pay no attention to anything else you might hear. King Faisal and Crown Prince Saud are going to step aside soon. They have agreed to make way for Natal, who will serve but a short time as the new crown prince until the transition can be completed."

"Natal?" Moran raised a brow.

The prince smiled. "I know, and I understand the concern you have not stated. Natal's views on Israel are well known. But he will be crown prince for just a short period of time—not long enough for his views of Israel to be widely known or acted on."

"Thank you for that."

"And once Natal has made the transition, the path will then be clear for the grandsons to take power. In fact, two of us will be named at the same time," the prince said quietly. "I will become the new minister of the interior and command our internal security forces. And Prince Abdul will become the new foreign minister. You know Abdul?"

"I know him well. He has our utmost respect."

"Good. Abdul is well regarded in the kingdom as well. It will be a good match, he and I, as we move to the new order. Between the two of us, I believe the ties between our two countries will be stronger than ever."

"I agree. And may I assume from this that you will be named the crown prince at some point, once you have taken over as the minister of the interior?"

The Saudi prince gazed off into the distance. "Yes, I suppose, though I'm not entirely certain this is something I would seek. But the times seem to demand service, and I have answered the call."

"You will make a good king someday." Moran's voice was steady. "The people of the kingdom will be well served."

"We shall see," the prince said. "There is much to do between now and then and many miles to travel. As we saw today, there are those who do not wish such a transition in the kingdom."

10

Riyadh, Saudi Arabia

Even though Nash had visited several dozen countries in the past few years, it was always a thrill to visit a new one. He'd never been to Saudi Arabia, and he was more than a little curious what it would be like. He'd heard and read so much about the land controlled tightly by the House of Saud. He wondered if it would live up to its reputation.

It was nighttime when they landed in Riyadh. As the Saudi Arabian Airlines plane made the long descent into the Saudi capital near the center of the country, Nash couldn't help himself. He pressed his face to the window and gazed out at the city. King Fahd Road stretched out before him. The colors dazzled him—blocks of green, orange, and purple mixed in with the usual lights of the city.

He kept his eyes glued to the sight as the plane made its way to King Khaled Airport north of the city. He tried to spot places he'd heard about, like Masmak Fortress, but it was hopeless. He did manage to spot two different golf courses, both lit by floodlights, during the descent. There didn't seem to be anyone on either course, though. *That's odd*, Nash thought.

One of his mVillage volunteers was scheduled to meet him at the airport and drive him to a hotel near the center of the city. He had a full set of meetings starting early in the morning the next day. He'd left no time for tourism, so this view from the plane's window would have to suffice.

He'd been told by his New York staff not to even bother going out at night in Riyadh. Alcohol was banned, along with movie theaters and nightclubs. His skeleton staff—volunteers for mVillage and Village Health Corps—gathered at a coffeehouse in central Riyadh, just off Tahlia Street. That would have to do for the evening's entertainment.

Nash turned his mobile on the instant the wheels touched down. With a couple of quick keystrokes, he'd switched his roaming to the local Saudi cell carrier. He had the mVillage network up and running before the plane had even begun to taxi.

The news jumped out at him almost immediately. Yemen's president—a man who'd been in power for more than three decades—had been forced to flee the country that night, while Nash's plane was in the air. Rebel forces now stormed different parts of the country at Saudi Arabia's southern border. There were no reports yet about an emerging leader.

So, Nash thought, *Yemen is falling—just like Egypt, Tunisia, and Libya. What's next?*

Large Middle Eastern countries like Syria and Jordan—and smaller countries like Bahrain—faced growing pressure from students and rebels. People seemed fed up with the status quo and leaders who'd been in power for years. It was the greatest uprising the Arab nations had seen since the Second World War, and no one could predict when and where it might stop.

Buried in the news reports, though, was an item that troubled Nash the instant he saw it. In order to protect itself from the unfolding events, the House of Saud had apparently invaded Yemen to contain one of the rebel movements aligned with the Shi'a leadership in Iran. Saudi Arabia had invaded once before to contain the Houthis, who had received funding and arms from Iran for years.

The world had ignored the Saudi move against the Houthis the first time, largely because the House of Saud had pulled the troops back into Saudi territory quickly after the initial invasion. But the world would notice this time, Nash knew. Iran, especially, would make sure the United Nations and others noted the Saudi action against the Zaidi Shi'a insurgent group.

The mVillage report was colorful:

Sporting replica "swords of Ali," or Zulfiqars, alongside their assortment of rifles, the young Houthi rebels are putting up quite a spirited fight against the Saudi forces. The Saudis have yet to make much headway against the rebels, and the fighting is scattered across the landscape.

One of the mobile videos was chilling. A group of young teenagers stormed Saudi troops with little more than swords and a few rifles. The Saudi troops, clearly uneasy at the prospect of killing teenagers, held back as long as they could, then fought hand-to-hand as the two forces clashed briefly. It was an unmistakable sign of the passion sweeping through Yemen and elsewhere.

The report concluded that thousands of Houthi tribe members had joined the fight during the night. If that was true, Nash knew the Saudis would have their hands full with this insurgency in northern Yemen for days.

Nash had planned to make his way through southern Saudi Arabia and into northern Yemen in two days—near the areas where the House of Saud had invaded and the fighting had broken out. He grimaced. Su would never forgive him if he went anywhere near the fighting. He'd have to play it by ear.

He scanned other mVillage news reports and checked the dozens of e-mails that had accumulated while he'd been in the air. There was nothing urgent or pressing that demanded his attention, so he sent a quick note to Su that he'd arrived safely. He finished the note as they arrived at the gate.

The young Village Health Corps volunteer would be waiting for Nash as he exited the gate area. Nash always marveled at the intensity and commitment of the young men and women who volunteered around the globe for both mVillage and the Village Health Corps that ran the network. They were constantly upbeat and relentless in their pursuit of social change. Nothing seemed to faze them. They truly were the "relentless, positive storm" generation.

"Mr. Lee?" True to his word, the young man approached Nash as he came through the exit.

"Please." Nash smiled crookedly. "Mr. Lee is my father."

"The US ambassador to Japan," the young staffer said. "Yes, I know, he's—"

Nash cut him off. "He's Mr. Lee, not me. I'm just Nash."

"Okay, well…" The young man seemed uneasy, as if not quite sure whether to take Nash seriously.

"So you're Badr? Badr Ahmad?" Nash asked. "You run the Riyadh operation?"

"I am," he said, lifting his head with pride. "And yes, I've been trying to build up an mVillage network."

"Good." Nash nodded. "I'm here to help with that effort. You've been working out of the Riyadh office for, what, six months?"

"Yes, sir."

"Straight out of school—out of KAUST, right?"

"I started helping out with VHC while I was still in school," Badr said.

"And you began working on some software applications for the local mobile carriers while you were still at KAUST?"

"Yes, sir, absolutely." Badr beamed. He seemed incredulous that the famous Nash Lee knew so much about him. "I believe I've come up with a way to add several new software applications directly to the mobile devices that people use here…"

"Which should make it easier for mobile devices of any shape or kind to communicate with each other?"

"Yes, regardless of the type of carrier, or the type of mobile device," Badr said. "I studied software design at KAUST, and this was my major side project."

"Good. That's going to be enormously helpful to us in the effort here. I wanted to thank you in person."

"My pleasure." Badr bowed slightly. "So please, my car is outside. I will take you into the city. There are others gathered at the coffeehouse."

Badr gave Nash a quick overview of the mVillage and VHC efforts on the drive into central Riyadh. It was rudimentary. They were just breaking into the tight control the House of Saud kept over the mobile networks. There had been some minor flare-ups. The Saudis were extraordinarily wary of anything that allowed even modest mass communications.

The Saudis viewed mVillage as a way around their control. For this reason, Badr said, they'd been exceedingly cautious about the groups and people they worked with—and the knowledge they shared. Unlike other parts of the world, where mVillage was freely and openly shared, the Riyadh staff members were much more circumspect in their actions.

Nash couldn't blame them. It was difficult to work in a country like Saudi Arabia, where there was a great deal of money dedicated to preserving the power of the House of Saud—and the status quo. Still, Nash was determined to make mVillage freely available here and in other closed societies in the Arab world. To Nash, it was only a matter of time.

Like the youth-led uprisings in Egypt, Tunisia, and now Yemen, there was no stopping a global mobile communications network like mVillage—especially when the open source code was beginning to make every single mobile device on the planet capable of talking to any other device across both platforms and carriers.

"Is downtown Riyadh always so quiet like this?" Nash asked as they made their way along Tahlia Street toward their coffeehouse destination.

"It is." Badr nodded. "At night. But it's very busy during the day."

"I see," Nash said. "So I will look forward to our day tomorrow?"

"Yes, sir. We have a lot planned."

11

West Bank

MEDITERRANEAN SEA

Jerusalem

ISRAEL   JORDAN

Gaza Strip

EGYPT

Jerusalem, Israel

Abe Zeffren wasn't easily fooled. He'd seen far too much during his years inside Israel's government bureaucracy to be easily taken in. He'd learned over the years that quiet persistence nearly always paid off and that questions asked in a benign fashion were more likely to produce results than bluster and confrontation.

But none of that had seemed to work with his Russian visitor. His questions had largely been parried. And his attempts to get to the bottom of what the Russian truly knew—and what his intentions were with Israel's National Oil Company and the Dead Sea—had gotten him nowhere.

Abe hadn't paid much attention to the nature of the visit when he'd gotten the initial e-mail. Exploring for oil in Israel was such a ridiculous, colossal waste of time that he hadn't been required to pay much attention to inquiries during his entire stint as deputy oil commissioner.

The visit had actually been set up by an assistant at INOC—not by someone from Russia. He hadn't even bothered to write the man's name down. He'd simply logged the meeting on his calendar and promptly forgotten about it until today.

But now Abe was intrigued. Something didn't add up. So shortly after his visitor had dropped off the check and the signed papers, Abe decided to do a little exploring of his own. He pulled the battered oil register held together by electrical tape down from the shelf and opened it to the section where the visitor had filed the paperwork.

Abe looked it over quickly. Every signature on it was from INOC, save the one signed by the visitor. Sadly, the signature was nearly illegible. He wondered vaguely if that was by design.

He pushed his chair back, ran his fingers through his gray hair, and sauntered back out to the lobby. The front desk clerk didn't bother to look up.

"I was wondering if you logged my visitor in when he arrived this morning," Abe asked.

The clerk glanced up at him then. "You checking up on me?"

"No, I'm looking for his name," Abe said with an easy smile.

The clerk appeared surprised. "He was your meeting. You didn't get his name?"

"He didn't offer it. And I didn't ask. He had proper papers and maps—and a certified check."

The clerk grunted and pushed the visitor log book forward so Abe could see it for himself.

"This is your handwriting?" Abe asked. The man's name still wasn't quite legible.

The clerk looked down at the log book. "It is."

"Perhaps you can help me out with the name. I can't make it out."

The clerk peered at it briefly. "Nicolai Petrov."

"And did he present a government passport?"

"No, a personal one."

Abe nodded. "Thanks," he said and began to saunter back to his office. He stopped, though, and turned back to the clerk. "By the way, I'll be going out in the field for the next two or three days, should any one ask or need me."

"I'll be sure to let anyone who asks know that," the clerk said.

Abe had to laugh. No one would ask. He doubted anyone would even realize he'd gone—not even the oil commissioner, who was almost never in the office himself.

He tried to place the name as he walked back to his cluttered office. But it was no good. The name was vaguely familiar but not so much that he could place it. And a Google search revealed a number of Nicolai Petrovs. It could be any one of them.

Abe clicked through several of the links, but none made much sense. The closest match seemed to be a patent attorney in Moscow, but he doubted that was the right Petrov.

"I wonder. Maybe you're with the government, too," Abe muttered aloud to himself. He found himself doing that more and more lately. Perhaps it was a sign of growing senility… Probably not. More likely he was spending far too much time by himself.

He started to search on different government Web sites, clicking through names that showed up. It seemed hopeless. Russia was an enormous place.

He was about to give up to pack for his field trip when he found it. He'd been staring at a picture from the *International Herald Tribune*— a picture from an event with Russia's well-known prime minister, Andrei Rowan—and the answer was staring back at him. The man was in the picture with Rowan, in the background.

"Which means you *are* government," Abe said to himself. He started a search on articles about Andrei Rowan. There were thousands of them, from his many publicized adventures. But after a couple of dozen, he discovered what he was looking for.

Nicolai Petrov was Andrei Rowan's chief of staff. He'd been with Rowan for years, always in the background. His name rarely showed up in the press.

Well, I'll be, Abe thought. *Why in the world would the prime minister of Russia send his chief of staff down here to sign a partnership agreement with our national oil company? What do they know that we don't—or, perhaps, want?*

Abe pulled the oil register out and studied the INOC oil license again. Nowhere did it say that their new funding partner was the government of Russia. He thumbed through the preliminary geological survey maps and findings.

It was impossible to know for certain, but it appeared as if they were going to commit some serious dollars to looking at the formations around the Dead Sea. Their scientists planned to conduct detailed studies in stratigraphy and structural geology—and the modeling of petroleum geochemistry—throughout the area. They also planned to work with an American university to generate 3D maps and algorithms of the area.

But the last two paragraphs of the preliminary report struck him as odd. They expressed an interest in experimenting with research on oil shale extraction technology in partnership with INOC. That was indeed strange. There had been a flurry of trade reports recently about interest in the previously worthless oil shale in the barren Shfela Basin south and west of Jerusalem.

Abe had heard promises of "new" technology to extract oil safely from shale for nearly as long as he'd been deputy oil commissioner. Almost none of it seemed to work, most of it was farfetched, and the technology that did actually work was both environmentally ruinous and much more expensive than drilling for crude oil in proven deposits.

But Abe also knew that hope always springs eternal. And should someone develop safe, inexpensive ways to extract oil from shale, well, then Israel was certainly sitting on one of the biggest deposits the world had ever seen in the Shfela Basin. That sort of scientific advance—combined with what the scientists were saying about the natural gas deposits in the Levant basin off the coast of Haifa—would make Israel an oil and gas superpower within a decade.

It was all very strange to Abe. Hunting for oil in Israel had always been a loser's preoccupation. To be honest, the Russian interest made no sense. Israel had no oil—at least not any that was worth the cost of recovering. There were more than four hundred dry wells in northern Israel alone. *So perhaps the Russians know something we don't*, Abe thought. *Either that, or there's some* serious misdirection going on. *Once the camel has its nose under the tent, it eventually makes its way inside.*

Either way, Abe figured, now was a good time to take a first-hand look at that area around the north end of the Dead Sea. It was a short drive. And while he was out, he figured he might pay a visit to the Shfela Basin, then take a drive south in the Negev to see the Ashkelon-Eilat pipeline work he'd been hearing about.

12

Somewhere on the border between Iran and Pakistan

It was an ordinary Boeing C-135 transport plane. But the American air force leadership was justifiably proud of it and its role. The RC-135 Rivet Joint plane had been extensively modified and outfitted with an amazing array of onboard sensors that could detect, track, and ultimately locate targets geographically throughout the electromagnetic spectrum.

The air force believed it could track anything—even people—if given enough information to feed into its onboard sensor network. It had been used extensively for all kinds of missions for the better part of twenty years, from Desert Storm to the effort to oust the dictator of Libya.

The two pilots of this particular RC-135 Rivet Joint were especially keen about their target right now. It was well after midnight, but Saudi human intelligence on the ground in Pakistan had provided some extraordinary information.

The claim was that the operational deputy of al Qaeda, Ali bin Rahman, had chosen to move from a safe house in the mountains of northeastern Pakistan, near the China border, and was traveling on a highway that ran south and west along the border between Afghanistan and Pakistan.

The hard intelligence placed bin Rahman—who had once been a Saudi citizen—in a small, nondescript vehicle moving past Quetta in

Pakistan. Incredibly, it seemed as if bin Rahman was headed toward the border of Iran and a town called Zahedan just inside eastern Iran.

Why bin Rahman would move into the open like this wasn't clear. But the two pilots aboard the Joint Rivet didn't care. Their job was to find and then track bin Rahman if he was, in fact, somewhere along the highway between Quetta in Pakistan and Zahedan in Iran.

The al Qaeda deputy was well known to Western intelligence officials, even if he wasn't to the public in America and elsewhere. He'd essentially run the fractured, disparate al Qaeda network for years. The House of Saud was especially focused on bin Rahman's intentions and his whereabouts.

The speculation at Langley was coalescing quickly around the belief that bin Rahman had set up the cell and the attack on the Airbus plane carrying the Saudi prince near Dulles airport. No one, as yet, had emerged to take credit for the attack. But the attack fit bin Rahman's style of operations, the CIA and NSA leadership believed. And if it walks like a duck, it's most likely a duck.

Ali bin Rahman was as anti-American as any leader in the loose al Qaeda network, but he was even more determined to remain a thorn in the side of the Saudi royal family. There were many guesses as to why, but the most logical reason seemed to be that he'd been denied a family inheritance in a family dispute and had then blamed politics inside the House of Saud for it.

One thing, though, was clear. Ali bin Rahman believed as passionately as anyone that the House of Saud stood firmly in the way of the true restoration of Sharia law across the Arab world and that it was centrally to blame for Western involvement in Middle Eastern affairs.

It was for this reason that Saudi intelligence had made special efforts to locate the al Qaeda deputy. They believed that removing bin Rahman would solve many problems for them.

"We have all the signature data we need?" the first pilot asked.

"Fed into the onboard computer by the tech crew right before we took off," said his copilot.

"Car and mobile device guesses?"

"Most likely."

"And if we get a hit?"

"I brought a bottle of single malt to celebrate." The copilot grinned.

There was a loud *plink* from the console. Both of them glanced instinctively at the place where the sound had come from.

"Well, I'll be," the first pilot murmured.

"We've got something, that's for sure."

They both quickly switched frequencies so they could listen to the chatter from the tech crew spread throughout the back of the plane. Genuine excitement rippled through the plane's crew. They'd gotten not one, but two, hits. The first was on the car, which had been confirmed almost instantly through an electromagnetic detection pattern. And they'd gotten a second hit on a mobile device almost at the same time. The car's occupant was talking to someone.

After several long minutes, the crew had confirmed that it was bin Rahman's car and his mobile device. He was talking to someone on the ground waiting to meet with them at Zahedan, inside Iran.

"Who is it?" the first pilot asked after listening to the crew discuss what they were eavesdropping on from their vantage point.

"Sounds like someone named Bader at the other end, they're saying."

"Bader? A German name? In Iran?"

They both listened for several seconds. "No, it's Bahadur."

The first pilot's jaw dropped reflexively. "Hussein Bahadur? The head of Iran's air force? That's who bin Rahman is meeting in Zahedan?"

"Sure sounds like it," said the second pilot.

The first pilot whistled softly. "That isn't going to sit well with the Saudis."

"Nope," said the copilot. "They'll call for action as soon as we send this out. So should we? Do we have confirmation?"

They did, in fact, have all the confirmation they needed for Global Hawk, the unmanned aerial vehicle made by Northrup Grumman, which was also airborne right now.

"Tell the crew to transmit," the first pilot said.

The orders went back, and the data was transmitted an instant later to the modern successor to the U-2 spy plane. The Global Hawk dutifully plotted the coordinates from the data. It had a rough calculation within seconds and then a very firm coordinate match shortly thereafter.

The Global Hawk sent the coordinates forward a moment later to analysts at a ground station. Once transmitted, the two pilots knew it was out of their hands. The information would soon be passed on to a command center for targeting.

From there, the command center would send the coordinates and likely route of the target to an E-3 Sentry AWACS command-and-control plane—essentially a flying battleship capable of directing warplanes in the area to the target.

From there, a fighter with advanced sensors could hunt the target without any further information needed, either from the air or the ground.

The decision to "acquire" the target was well above their pay grade. Neither pilot was quite sure whose call it was. Perhaps this one would go all the way to the president. But they'd done their job.

MARYLAND

Baltimore

WEST
VIRGINIA

Washington, D.C.

VIRGINIA

13

The White House
Washington, DC

The Saudi ambassador to the United States was literally knocking at the door of the White House complex a few minutes after the data and coordinates had been transmitted from the Rivet Joint, to the Global Hawk, to a command center, and then to an E-3 Sentry AWACS. The town car had pulled up to the gate, and the ambassador had asked to meet with President Camara. He had not called ahead.

Omar al Faisal was usually a polite man. But not at the moment. He'd already made sure that the Saudis and US intelligence agencies were sharing information in real time. The Saudi human intelligence asset on the ground had provided the lead, and the American planes had confirmed that bin Rahman was, in fact, in a car along a highway from Quetta to Zahedan.

He was here, at the end of the day in Washington, to make certain that the Americans would take the necessary action. And if they would not, for whatever reason, he intended to make sure that they shared the coordinates immediately so the Saudi Royal Air Force fighters could take the appropriate action.

"Mr. Ambassador," a tired voice said over the phone at the guards' box, "if you'd called ahead…"

"There is not time." Omar al Faisal closed his eyes to control his anger. "If you can just tell the president that I'm here, and that I need an audience with him immediately."

There was an uncomfortable pause. "Let me connect you with the chief of staff."

"No, I need—"

There was an audible *click*. Anshel Gould, the president's chief of staff, came on the line an instant later. "Mr. Ambassador, how are you this evening?" Dr. Gould said politely. "The president isn't available at the moment. Perhaps I can help?"

Dr. Gould was an inveterate gatekeeper. No one got to the president without passing by him first. Not even the vice president.

"If I may, Dr. Gould," said the ambassador, "there isn't time for a polite talk. I must see the president immediately."

"It can't wait until the morning?"

"It cannot," al Faisal said impatiently. "And I believe you know the reason for my visit."

"I may," Dr. Gould said noncommittally, "but still…"

"Can we meet, please?" the ambassador said curtly.

Dr. Gould didn't hesitate. He never did. "I will be out shortly."

Anshel Gould had just been reviewing the coordinate file from the reconnaissance planes in Pakistan—which included both a recommended course of action and the troubling news that the voice at the other end of the call in Zahedan was most likely none other than Hussein Bahadur, the head of Iran's air force.

He grabbed his coat from the back of a nearby chair, where it had been draped since 5 A.M. when he'd arrived at the White House. He made his way quickly through the West Wing complex, stopping only to let his executive assistant know he was headed out to the driveway to greet the Saudi ambassador.

"Do you need someone with you, Dr. Gould?" she'd asked as he'd practically flown by her desk.

"No, I have this," he said.

He took the spiral staircase that separated the West Wing from the Eisenhower office complex three steps at a time. He practically whirled down the narrow staircase. Just as he got to the bottom, he nearly ran over Daniel James—who had just been named a principal deputy White House press secretary for national security—as he was beginning to make his way up the staircase.

"Dr. Gould!" DJ said, stepping down and off the staircase quickly to avoid a collision. "Is there a fire?"

"No—at least not here." Dr. Gould started to hurry off but then stopped and turned around to face DJ. "You know what," he said quickly. "Come with me. I can use the moral support."

"With?"

"The Saudi ambassador."

"Omar al Faisal? Why is he here? He's not on the schedule today."

"He showed up unannounced. You'll find out why in a moment because you're joining me for the meeting. On the driveway."

"The driveway?"

"He's in a town car at the gate, demanding to see the president."

DJ nodded. While this was a little unusual, it occasionally happened with allies who felt they were justified in demanding immediate action from those in the White House they worked with closely—especially on sensitive national security or intelligence matters.

"You're going to meet at the gate?"

"You bet. It's as good a place as any. I needed the exercise."

DJ tried to keep up with Dr. Gould as he made his way down the corridor. He loved these moments. They almost made up for the fourteen-hour days, fast-food dinners, modest pay, and halfhearted office accommodations they afforded the press office staff. Almost.

Dr. Gould burst through the doorway that led to the driveway between the two White House office complexes. The guards had been forewarned and had already stepped aside from the doorway. This wasn't the first time Dr. Gould had raced from one building to the next. DJ could see that they were keeping a careful, respectful eye on the president's chief of staff as he marched briskly up to the gate and the guards' box.

"We'll just be a moment," Dr. Gould called out over one shoulder to the guards as he and DJ walked out of the complex to see the Saudi ambassador.

Omar al Faisal was already out of the town car and approaching the gate. He shook Gould's hand quickly, then said without preamble, "You know what I am seeking, Dr. Gould."

"I believe I do, and I can assure you we are prepared to take appropriate action," Gould said.

Only then did Omar al Faisal glance at DJ. "I can talk with him present?"

"By all means." Gould nodded. "The president regularly includes him in such discussions."

"Very well," the Saudi ambassador said. "What, exactly, do you mean by 'appropriate action'?"

Gould knew the Saudis would eventually see some version of the conversation picked up by the planes, so he chose not to conceal it. "There is a slight complication."

"Complication?"

"The person that bin Rahman is meeting in Zahedan is someone of note in Iran. Given the delicate situation we are in with our relationship to the leadership of Iran, we must be exceedingly careful."

The blood nearly drained from the Saudi ambassador's face. "We do not care if he is racing to meet the Supreme Leader himself…"

"Hardly. We both know that Reverend Shahidi rarely leaves Tehran. No, it is one of their top military officials."

"Fine!" the Saudi ambassador said brusquely. "Then let him—whoever it is—be collateral damage. We both know that bin Rahman is responsible for the terrorist attack on our prince at Dulles."

"We don't know that yet," Gould said mildly.

"We are arguing technicalities, while the opportunity slips through our grasp like the sands of an hourglass." Omar al Faisal's face darkened with anger. "If you will not act against bin Rahman immediately, then please do what you have always promised. Give us the coordinates so we may take action."

DJ held his breath. He was frantically trying to read between the lines of this conversation. It wasn't easy. But as far as he could divine, American reconnaissance planes had picked up the notorious al Qaeda deputy Ali bin Rahman on his way to a meeting in Iran. DJ was stunned that bin Rahman would risk exposure by leaving his safe house in the mountains of Pakistan. *There must be an awfully good reason*, he thought.

DJ could only guess the identity of the person bin Rahman was meeting in Zahedan. Most likely, he reasoned, it was either Iran's air force chief, Hussein Bahadur, or the head of the Revolutionary Guards, General Ali Zhubin. He couldn't imagine why either would be there, however.

What really complicated matters, DJ knew, was that the US government was in direct talks with Iran's leadership about a peaceful resolution of the Palestinian problem and a ceasefire with Israel. The near-nuclear confrontation between Iran and Israel was off the table while the talks were underway. But it wouldn't take much to derail the talks—and push Iran and Israel to the brink of war again.

If the US ordered a strike against bin Rahman, and there was any collateral damage against either of Iran's top military leaders, then the uneasy peace between Iran and Israel would be immediately shattered. It would be nearly impossible to predict what might happen in such a scenario. Iran's leadership was stable—but also highly capable of irrational overreactions.

DJ closely watched Dr. Gould. Instinctively, he knew that Gould would act to protect the United States' interests first, and then Israel's. The Saudi interest, while important, was a distant third. If pushed against the wall, Dr. Gould would let bin Rahman slip through the net rather than risk a move that set Iran against Israel again.

Anshel Gould took a deep breath and made his decision. The joint chiefs had recommended an immediate strike upon receipt of the coordinates at the Sit Room—or none at all.

They'd moved very quickly. The war fighters had set out for Zahedan instantly. But getting to the location wasn't easy. They'd been forced to navigate through not one, but two, air defense systems in both Iran and Pakistan.

By the time the fighters had reached the target, the car that had almost certainly carried bin Rahman had already arrived in Zahedan. They knew his location. They could take out both the car and the house where he was most likely meeting with Bahadur. That wasn't a problem—at all.

But taking out bin Rahman also meant that Iran's air force chief would be collateral damage. There would be no way to explain it away—not to Iran's theocracy. The fragile peace would be over.

So, Gould knew, the president and the joint chiefs had ordered the fighters to "sit" on their target. They would wait for bin Rahman to finish his meeting with Bahadur and cross back into Pakistan. They would wait until he was safely away from Iran before moving.

But he could not tell any of this to the Saudi ambassador—not right now. Because, Gould knew, the Saudis would not wait. They would act against bin Rahman immediately, no matter who else was in that house with him.

They wouldn't care if it ended the Iran-Israel peace talks. The Saudi royal family was generally still in favor of a confrontation between Iran and Israel. It was in their interests to see a vastly weakened Iran—and a war with Israel would do precisely that, provided it didn't spread beyond those two nations.

"Mr. Ambassador, I give you my word that we have taken appropriate action," Gould said.

"Which is, precisely, what?"

"We have sent fighter jets to the location. They have acquired the target."

"And have they fired on it?" the ambassador asked grimly.

"They intend to, at the first available opportunity."

"Again, when will that be?" the ambassador pressed.

"When and if the opportunity presents itself, they will fire on the target," Gould said. "You have my word."

14

Zahedan, Iran

Hussein Bahadur was an extremely impatient man. He demanded much of himself and his subordinates. He took orders badly—especially from politicians with no understanding of the needs of war—but always carried them out.

There were only two people on the planet he respected and followed blindly—Reverend Amir Shahidi, the Supreme Leader of Iran, and General Ali Zhubin, who commanded Iran's Revolutionary Guards Corps. Reverend Shahidi had risen through the ranks of the Revolutionary Guards, eventually taking command of the elite military that served as the lifeblood of the Shi'a regime. He'd then won the presidency and later become Iran's most powerful ruler as its religious leader. General Zhubin had proven himself so often in battle that Bahadur could only admire his record.

So when he'd been told by both Zhubin and Shahidi to meet with one of the world's most wanted men in a house near the University of Sistan at the southern end of Zahedan in eastern Iran, Bahadur had set off for the meeting without question. The mission, he'd been told, was simply to hear a proposal from Ali bin Rahman.

He'd arrived in time to stop at the university mosque for prayers. The mosque was full, but Bahadur wasn't surprised. Students in Iran liked to visit mosques, as much for social reasons as anything else. Bahadur liked to visit mosques when he traveled. It relaxed him and allowed him to think about something other than prosecuting military matters.

Still, he'd had a difficult time focusing on his prayers. He couldn't help but wonder why someone like bin Rahman would come out in the open like this. It had to be important.

The sun was beginning to set as he made his way to a nice but nondescript home at the edge of campus. It belonged to one of the professors who'd always been loyal to the IRGC, even in the worst of times when students and faculty were questioning nearly every action by Iran's leaders.

The professor had graciously left the front door open. There was a kettle of hot water on the stove, with a handwritten note about where to find tea, if he was so inclined. Bahadur made some tea while he waited for bin Rahman.

The past few months had been hard on Bahadur. He didn't trust the Americans, and he despised the Israelis. So it had been especially difficult to sit still while the peace talks proceeded about a Palestinian homeland and Iran's emerging role in those talks. Iran's grudging, but public, recognition of Israel's right to exist had shaken Bahadur to his very core. But he was a good soldier. He did as he was told. And right now, he was being told not to organize actions against his sworn enemies.

So it was with relief that he heard the front door to the home open. Bahadur knew instinctively that something was about to change the equation again. This man—so hated by the West—was not here for peace. He was here for something else.

"Brother Bahadur. May peace be upon you," Ali bin Rahman said quietly as he closed the door behind him. His driver remained on the front stoop.

"And with you," Bahadur answered. "I trust your trip was uneventful."

"It was." Bin Rahman took three quick steps across the floor, closing the distance between them.

Bahadur extended his right hand. Bin Rahman took it. They studied each other. Where Bahadur was stocky and muscular, bin Rahman was gaunt and emaciated from hiding in the rugged mountains of Pakistan. Yet both men instantly found mutual respect in each other's eyes, in their common story. This would be a fruitful meeting.

Bahadur, unlike the rest of the world, did not care what bin Rahman had done on the field of battle. All he wanted to know was whether bin Rahman could be trusted, whether he might prove an ally—and whether there was something he and his organization might bring to the table that would restore the balance of power in his country's favor.

For, as far as Bahadur was concerned, Iran was professing weakness by listening to the United States and Israel. A man like bin Rahman had it right—he would fight and die from the shadows and the caves if need be to remain faithful to his cause.

While Bahadur considered al Qaeda little more than a loosely held confederation of like-minded groups—and certainly not the fearsome threat painted by the Western press—he nevertheless admired their dedication to their cause. And bin Rahman was central to that obsession. It was hard not to like his passion. He also admired the enormous risk bin Rahman was taking by traveling down from the mountains to meet here, out in the open.

Even in the midst of peace talks, Bahadur was certain the Americans were keeping very close watch on nearly everything that happened in Iran.

In fact, it would not have surprised him to learn they were being monitored even now from one of the Americans' many reconnaissance and eavesdropping platforms. However, they would not attack this house—not as long as he was here. But Bahadur guessed that bin Rahman would not make it back to Pakistan alive—though that was not his concern.

"So you have come here, to Iran."

It was more a statement than a question, but bin Rahman understood its import. "In time. But first, what can you tell me of the most unusual terms of peace between your leadership and the West?"

Bahadur did his best not to flinch, though it pained him. "The Reverend Shahidi has pledged to work with the Americans."

"Why, if I might ask?"

It was a fair question—one Bahadur had asked Reverend Shahidi many times. "Because the United States has foolishly pledged to spend its capitalist dollars to build the Palestinian homeland and guarantee its security," he said. "Because the Americans have guaranteed the safe return of refugees, and given assurances about Jerusalem's status. Because they and the Russians have begun to provide for our energy needs."

"Provided you dismantle your nuclear weapons program," bin Rahman interrupted.

"Yes, that is what we have promised," Bahadur responded evenly.

"And you intend to honor that pledge?"

"We will see."

"So what else were you promised?"

"The United States, for its part, has agreed to lift all sanctions. The president has given us his full assurance that both our economic and national security will be assured and restored."

Ali bin Rahman exhaled. "And you believe that?"

"Not for a moment." Bahadur met bin Rahman's eyes. "But in return, we have only been required to tell the world that we recognize Israel's right to exist."

"And dismantle your nuclear weapons program."

"Such as it was. We shall see what will be."

"Interesting," bin Rahman answered. "Still, I must say I was surprised to hear of such things. I never expected the great and glorious leadership of Iran to be so easily taken in by the Americans and their promises."

Bahadur held his tongue. He was here, on orders, to listen to bin Rahman—not argue philosophy or diplomacy with him. "So," he said evenly, "will you tell me why you've risked your life for this meeting?"

The al Qaeda deputy took a seat near the window. He was calm enough—though Bahadur was certain the deputy also guessed that the Americans would find him once he returned to Pakistan. That meant the news was important enough for him to be willing to take the risk.

"I have news," bin Rahman said.

"Of?"

"Of the very thing your own president has predicted for some time, and your people have believed in for much longer."

Bahadur stared hard at his visitor. Unlike the Iranian people, Bahadur didn't think much of Iran's elected president, Nassir Ahmadian. But he was useful to the Reverend Shahidi, and he had a populist touch with at least some of the people. He often talked in apocalyptical terms that played well to the uneducated in Iran's society. But it was hard to take Ahmadian seriously.

"I can't even begin to imagine what this thing might be."

"Well, there is no need to imagine any longer," bin Rahman said, smiling for the first time since he'd arrived. "For we have found him. He has emerged, as predicted. We have found your Twelfth Imam and our Mahdi. And we are prepared to bring him to you, at your earliest convenience."

MARYLAND

WEST
VIRGINIA

Baltimore

Washington, D.C.

VIRGINIA

15

The Situation Room
The White House
Washington, DC

Between the Rivet Joint eavesdropping plane and satellite coverage, President Camara had hoped to glean something from the conversation between bin Rahman and Bahadur. But there had been only silence. Whatever the two men were discussing, they'd have to learn about it from secondhand accounts.

Not only was there no way to discern the nature of the talks, but they were forced to sit on their hands, unable to take any action against a man they'd sought for years as one of the most-hunted terrorists in the world.

The president stood up from his chair at the end of the large table in the Sit Room and began to pace. "We can't strike surgically? Really?" he asked no one in particular.

A half dozen of his most senior national security staff said nothing. They knew Camara was frustrated. But they also knew there was nothing they could do—not until bin Rahman left the house and made his way back through Pakistan.

Finally, the president's secretary of defense, Senator Dan Johnson, spoke up. "Mr. President, we've looked at every conceivable scenario," he said, glancing briefly at John Alton, the army general who served as the vice chair of the joint chiefs at the White House. "We don't have anything quite that precise."

"Seriously?" asked Camara. "What about the X37B we have up in the air?"

The X37B was easily the most closely held spacecraft the US had developed. Only the Gang of Eight in Congress—the Republican and Democratic leaders of the Senate and House of Representatives, and the chair and ranking members of both Intelligence committees for the two chambers—knew its real cost or what its true mission was. All the press knew was that a prototype of the thirty-foot craft had once been launched from Cape Canaveral using an Atlas V rocket, which looked something like a tiny space shuttle, and that it operated like an orbital test vehicle.

A couple of the military trade journals had speculated that one potential use was to launch small, directed satellites over a specific trouble spot during a conflict, giving the military highly specific "eyes and ears" over that location.

The X37B had begun as a NASA program in the 1990s. But it had been transferred to the Pentagon's Defense Advanced Research Projects Agency and then to the air force. A recent prototype had been able to test a new generation of laser systems.

"It's helping us," said Johnson. "It's one reason we were able to track bin Rahman so quickly. But we can't pick up conversations with it."

"And the laser system?"

"Not even remotely that specific," Johnson said.

The president sighed. "All right. Then what about that system we launched with the Minotaur from Vandenberg? What did you call it—the Prompt Global Strike?"

Senator Johnson shook his head. "It's just a prototype. It isn't operational."

"But your staff said it can hit any target, anywhere in the world, within a matter of minutes. That it could hit any site, from bin Rahman's safe house in Pakistan to a North Korean launch pad."

"Yes, it was designed with that in mind," Johnson said. "But it's a future weapons system, and it isn't nearly that specific. It would take out the house, along with everyone in it."

"Well," Camara said glumly, "then what good is it?"

The door to the Sit Room swung open. DJ followed Dr. Gould in and scanned the room to see who was with the president. As always, he couldn't believe they allowed him access to these sorts of meetings. But the president had made it very clear to the NSC staff that DJ could be trusted.

DJ had to smile as he saw the group of aides assembled around the table. Just as he'd thought, the president's national security advisor, General Thomas, wasn't here. In his place at the table was Susan Wright, the deputy national security advisor. Senator Johnson, the secretary of defense, was next to her.

"About time you bothered to show up, Anshel," the president said dourly.

"The Saudi ambassador is here," Dr. Gould answered.

"Here? At the White House?" Camara asked.

"Yes, at the driveway. He wants to see you. He knows we've acquired bin Rahman, based on their human intelligence asset in Pakistan. And he wants you to take action."

Camara frowned. "I'd like nothing better. But we can't—not while he's with Bahadur."

"I know," Dr. Gould said. "I said as much to the ambassador, without revealing too much. But you know, he'll see all of this in the shared transcript at some point."

"Undoubtedly, but he'll also see why our hands are tied," the president said.

"He won't care," Dr. Gould responded. "As he said, he doesn't care if bin Rahman is meeting with the Supreme Leader of Iran himself. We have a moral obligation to act, or something to that effect, because bin Rahman attacked their future king."

"Easy enough for him to say," Camara said. "He isn't managing peace talks with Iran and North Korea while several Arab nations are overthrowing their dictators on a weekly basis. We have to be exceedingly careful. Our shot at bin Rahman has to be clean, without complications that involve Iran's leadership."

"I understand," Dr. Gould said. "But the Saudi ambassador will not. And he is demanding that we give them the same intelligence, if we will not act, so that they can do something themselves."

The president turned his attention back to the table. He glanced at the array of monitors around the room that displayed real-time information and signatures. It was maddening to have bin Rahman in sight at last, yet not be able to act.

"What if we tell Iran's leadership that we thought bin Rahman was alone in the house?" the president asked plaintively.

Susan Wright leaned forward. "We all know that won't work," she said evenly. "Iran knows what we're capable of. It wouldn't be credible."

"Well, maybe I don't care," Camara said. "How can we simply sit here—and *not* act?"

There was an uneasy silence in the room. "Because we—as a preeminent superpower—are expected to at least try to do the right thing," Dr. Wright offered finally. "And the right thing here is to give peace with Iran a chance, for the greater good. We have no choice but to wait until bin Rahman has left the house in order to return to Pakistan."

"And if he doesn't return to Pakistan?" asked the president.

"Then we'll have to cross that next bridge," Dr. Wright answered.

16

IRAN

SAUDI ARABIA

Manama●
BAHRAIN

GULF OF OMAN

QATAR

GULF OF OM

UNITED ARAB
EMIRATES

OMAN

US Naval Base
Manama, Bahrain

Vice Admiral Truxton paced back and forth across the floor of the command and control center in the middle of the base at Bahrain. He was careful to dodge the debris that had been pushed to one side. The entire base was in the middle of a billion-dollar retrofit—ordered at the conclusion of the recent conflict with Iran's navy in the Strait of Hormuz—and there were parts loose in the center.

Truxton was on edge. The data from the unmanned X37B was being routed through their console at the base in Bahrain, and from there directly to the White House Situation Room and the joint chiefs at the Pentagon. But Truxton saw and heard it first. And what he was seeing and hearing was deeply troubling.

The X37B had been handling missions for the National Reconnaissance Office almost from the first prototype. Speculation had been rampant in the press that the unmanned mini-shuttle was some sort of space weapon. The truth was that it was infinitely more valuable as a deployable, movable spy sensor platform in space.

Combined with other electronic intelligence and news-gathering technology, or ELINT, that had progressed rapidly since the Second World War, the X37B could do very interesting things from a low orbit once it had a fixed target.

And right now, when the air force could not position planes

anywhere near the house in Zahedan, where Bahadur was meeting with bin Rahman, the X37B was doing an awfully good job of listening in from its position in low orbit directly over the house. A highly engineered narrow-beam antenna, among other things, had given the ability to instantly pick up a mobile device call.

Bahadur had placed a call to Tehran on a highly secure mobile phone. The encryption didn't matter. The call had been picked up and transmitted back from the X37B instantly.

It was clear from the electromagnetic data that bin Rahman was not heavily armed. In fact, he was traveling with virtually no protection whatsoever. But it was the very brief call from Bahadur to Tehran that had set Truxton on edge.

"General, I have news," Bahadur had said the instant the call had connected.

"I understand. So the meeting went well?" the person at the other end had said. Truxton, and the analysts at his side, had assumed it was General Zhubin.

"As well as could be expected," Bahadur had answered.

"And the news?"

"Not what we had expected." Bahadur had paused. "Actually, not what any of us could possibly have expected—except perhaps our president."

"Our president?"

"Yes, it is…something the president has spoken of on many occasions. It is what he has predicted. But I must confess, it makes no sense to me. I have never believed in the prophecies that speak of someone who can remain in hiding for hundreds of years. And I fail to see how this person can somehow emerge from the Jamkaran Mosque, as our president believes."

There was a deepening silence as the person at the end of the line began to realize what Bahadur must have been speaking about. "I see. So you will share the information—how such a thing might be possible—with us when you return?"

"I will. But I have called to ask permission to bring our guest with us."

"To Tehran?"

"Yes, to Tehran," Bahadur had said. "He wishes to deliver the momentous news to the president himself. He is quite certain that it is a development our president has anticipated for several years. "

"So he is unable to return to Pakistan, then?"

"Not if he wishes to live. I, at least, am quite certain he wouldn't make it much farther than the border. I'm sure our guest believes much the same thing."

"But surely, we do not wish to bring the same sort of wrath down on our heads?"

"That won't happen while the peace talks are underway."

"And of course, our president will want to hear this news firsthand, in person."

"Yes."

"Very well then. We will await your arrival."

The entire conversation had been cryptic and difficult to understand. But Truxton was convinced he understood the news that bin Rahman intended to deliver in Tehran.

Iran's president, Nassir Ahmadian, had shockingly delivered a speech at the United Nations, during which he predicted the imminent return of the Twelfth Imam. With leaders from around the world listening in rapt attention, Ahmadian had asked God to hasten the reappearance of the Promised One—a "perfect and pure human being"—who would fill the world with justice and peace.

He'd also said he believed that his mission on earth was to pave the way for the return of the messianic Twelfth Imam, who would only come back in the midst of an apocalypse.

Ahmadian had, in fact, spent $17 million to refurbish the Jamkaran Mosque, where the Twelfth Imam was said to emerge when he returned after remaining in hiding for hundreds of years. Much like the Jewish people placed notes of prayers to God at the Western Wall on the Temple Mount, faithful Shi'a Muslims had dropped notes of prayers down the well at Jamkaran for the Twelfth Imam for years.

Ahmadian seemed to genuinely believe in the return of a hidden imam who'd gone into "occultation" in the ninth century—and would return hundreds of years later with the Jesus of the *Quran*. What's more, he'd apparently convinced his Cabinet officials to sign a pledge—delivered to the well at Jamkaran—that they would work to assure the return of the Twelfth Imam. There were many prophecies that were popular to the masses. One well-known myth told of soldiers carrying black flags from the north and white flags from the south who would take control of Mecca, ushering in the era of the Twelfth Imam. Many, including Ahmadian, believed that worldwide violence and chaos were also necessary precursors to the return of the Twelfth Imam. Ahmadian had made no secret of his commitment to do everything he could to usher in the era of the Twelfth Imam.

Truxton had read much about Ahmadian. In part, he'd done so because he wanted to know what drove the man. But Truxton, a Christian in a quiet fashion, was genuinely perplexed by what appeared to be an insane doctrine that Ahmadian followed.

Right now, Truxton didn't like what he'd heard. If his guess was right, bin Rahman had just informed Iran's leadership that he had concrete news of the return of the Twelfth Imam, alternately referred to as the Mahdi.

That, Truxton knew, was impossible. There was simply no way a long-dead religious leader from the ninth century could suddenly spring to life. But evidently Ahmadian believed that such a thing was possible. And millions of pious believers in Iran and elsewhere—both Sunni and Shi'a—believed in the eventual appearance of a Mahdi.

Even more troubling to him than this, though, was the mere fact that al Qaeda's operational deputy was meeting with one of Iran's top military leaders. The Shi'a regime was fighting al Qaeda in several parts of the world. They were, in most respects, enemies.

Yemen's embattled president, for instance, had literally hired refugee al Qaeda mercenaries to fight the Shi'a Houthi tribe elements in north Yemen, near the Saudi Arabia border. On more than one occasion, the Saudis had successfully managed to keep al Qaeda elements at the throats of armed Shi'a rebels—and Iran proxies—in several countries.

But war made for strange alliances and bedfellows. It had always been more than a little curious to Truxton, and others in the Pentagon's leadership, that al Qaeda would have masterminded the September 11 attack against the World Trade towers in New York City in 2001. What seemed more likely was an attack inspired by Iran's leadership—not al Qaeda.

But here was proof that at least one of al Qaeda's leaders was perfectly comfortable reaching out to Iran's leadership in an effort to find common ground, whether religious, economic, or military.

Truxton picked up the secure phone. He wanted to make sure there was no misunderstanding about what might be taking place in Zahedan. He asked to be connected to the Situation Room at the White House. "I need General Alton. As quickly as you can."

Truxton knew they had no choice but to allow bin Rahman to leave, unharmed, with Bahadur. It was unfortunate. But they would do everything in their power to keep track of him.

But if bin Rahman promised news of a Twelfth Imam, then Ahmadian would listen. And there was no way to predict what Iran's president would do next, should he choose to believe what bin Rahman had traveled down from the mountains of Pakistan to tell him.

17

The Gulf of Oman
South of Chabahar, Iran

Captain Bingham stood on the deck of the USS *McCain* and watched the plane take off from the supercarrier group he was assigned to. It was a magnificent sight to behold—the navy's first-ever stealth fighter. *Some day*, he thought, *I'll have control of a ship with one of those to call on.*

The pilot of the F-35 C Lightning II was out over the water and supersonic so swiftly that Captain Bingham had trouble keeping his eyes on it as it made the climb up and over Iran's southern coastline. It was headed north, inland, toward Zahedan.

Captain Bingham knew the pilot's mission. Yet what no one in the supercarrier group knew just yet was whether he'd be given the ability to fire once he'd reached his target.

The navy's version of the F-35 stealth fighter had gone operational only in the past six months. As of yet, there were only a half dozen in service. This was the sole F-35 navy stealth fighter assigned to the Persian Gulf region.

A fifth-generation stealth fighter, the plane would have little trouble reaching Zahedan. Iran had no ability to track or fire on this plane, Captain Bingham knew. He just wished he could see it in action.

The F-35 pilot maintained radio silence for the flight of two hundred miles or so between the supercarrier group and Zahedan. There was no need to communicate anyway. This was an easy mission. The X37B was providing every conceivable piece of coordinate data he could possibly need.

While he knew there was virtually no way Iran's antiquated air-defense system could track him, he still kept an eye out for possible threats as he sped across Iran's countryside. None emerged. He was south of the city of Zahedan in a matter of minutes.

He took a hard right to buy some time and began a lazy arc to serve as a holding pattern. He wanted to make sure he didn't fly too close to the city.

He turned his mike on. "I've arrived at the destination. I'm ready for orders."

"Coming shortly," the answer came back an instant later. "Hold for now."

"I'll make a pass, and then circle back."

"Roger that. Keep the line open. We'll have your orders momentarily."

The F-35 stealth pilot—the first in the navy's history—continued a long, slow loop. He arrived back at the target area a minute later. He armed his missiles to be sure he was ready.

"Is the target painted yet?" he asked.

"Not yet. Hold."

"Roger. But weapons are going hot. I'm waiting on your command."

The pilot wasn't sure whether he'd be firing at a car or a house. But in either case, he'd be ready. He'd prepared for a mission like this his entire career. Very few of his fellow fleet pilots even knew where he was and who they were going after. If he succeeded—and there was no doubt whatsoever in his mind that he *would* succeed—they'd learn soon enough.

As he worked the plane north again, toward the city, he took several deep breaths and steadied himself. He was ready. The southern edge of the city was starting to come into view. He checked the console. The weapons were hot. Two targets, both the car and the house, had been painted. He only needed confirmation of his orders.

"Stand down," the voice came across. "The orders just came through. We won't be firing on the target today."

The pilot looked down, his face a grim mask. He could not believe what he was hearing. "I want to make sure I heard that right."

"Yes, you heard it right. Stand down. You are to return to the group. We will not be going after that target today."

"You're serious?" the pilot asked, frustrated. "We're going to let him go? Just like that?"

"You have your orders. Stand down, and turn back."

The pilot knew better than to ask why over essentially open airwaves. He could not see any possible explanation for it. But he had his orders. He took a hard left and headed back south toward the carrier group. He wondered if he'd ever be given an explanation.

18

Camp 16
North Korea

You Moon was beyond despair. His country had reached a peace with the United States. His boyhood friend, Pak Jong Un, was the new leader of North Korea. He'd heard scattered, unconfirmed reports as well that Pak's father had been murdered by the military.

You Moon knew, in his heart, that his desperate effort to reach out to his friend with a secret message from a hidden cell phone had somehow been instrumental in decisions that had led to the peace with the United States.

Yet he was still a prisoner at Camp 16 in the northern mountains of his country. Nothing had changed—not for him and not for his friend and fellow prisoner Kim Grace, who'd given him the critical information about the terrible nuclear doomsday weapon they were developing nearby.

Every day passed much like the previous one for both You Moon and Kim Grace. There was no news from the outside world. They'd confiscated his cell phone. And as punishment for bringing it into camp, the guards had cut food rations by a third for everyone in camp. Several of the prisoners were near starvation as a result.

So what good did I accomplish? You Moon often thought in despair as he worked his fingers to the bone, crushing rocks in a barren field inside the desolate Camp 16 compound. It seemed to him, in an ironic variation on a very well-known saying from the Bible, that he had gained the world some measure of salvation, yet somehow had nothing more than his soul to show for it.

Kim Grace often chided him when he would utter—or think—such things. "It is not God's punishment of us," she would say. "We grow and learn from our challenges. We become better people in adversity."

He loved Kim Grace dearly. She was like family to him, in many ways. But he could not, for the life of him, understand how she could possibly remain hopeful in the face of such absolute cruelty and unfairness. It made no sense to him.

Camp 16 was, even in the midst of the peace progress with the United States, a place of utter horror. The guards were worse than they had been before the change in power. If anything, the military had tightened its grip on the people, based on what he heard from new prisoners who arrived at the camp almost on a daily basis. You Moon wondered how long it might be until they removed his boyhood friend from power, as they had his father.

Just that morning, for instance, he'd managed to have a brief conversation with a man who had been the deputy mayor of a small town in eastern North Korea—until the military had stripped him from his post and shipped him off that evening to Camp 16.

"Why?" You Moon had asked him.

"I don't know," the man had muttered.

You Moon could tell the man was still in shock—much as he'd been when he'd first arrived at Camp 16 in the dead of night—so he probed gently. "But surely, there's a reason?"

The man shrugged. "I put up posters of Pak Jong Un around the town. I delivered several tons of food shipments from several NGOs to the grocery store so people would have food, now that they've allowed those shipments again. I was doing what I thought was being asked of me."

"But anything else?"

"I...I don't know, really," the man said, despondent. "I did tell the radio station to start broadcasting again, so people could hear news of the progress being made in Pyongyang."

You Moon shook his head. "Let me guess—you allowed news from the West in?"

The man looked surprised. "Well, yes, it was Radio Free Asia, from the US. I assumed that with the peace talks going on with the United States—and the new leader who was working with the Americans on a permanent truce—that it would be all right. It seemed like things had changed…"

"But they haven't really, have they?" You Moon said quietly.

"I guess not," the man said glumly.

"Which is probably why you're here. The military has no real intention of loosening its grip on the country."

"So allowing the station to broadcast Radio Free Asia was a mistake?"

"It would appear so."

"And nothing has changed? We're still at war with the Americans, and our military is still running the country?"

You Moon didn't have the heart to tell him his own circumstances, or how betrayed he felt by his friend, now North Korea's leader. "I would say that it seems so," he said instead. "I am so very sorry. Perhaps things will ease up in time, and you can return home."

What truly bothered You Moon, though, was that he'd heard nothing whatsoever from Pak Jong Un—even after he'd risked his own life to warn Pak about the threat to his life, and the nature of the threat confronting the country. You Moon was proud of what he'd done—but he simply could not believe that Pak Jong Un had not reached out to Camp 16 to free his friend.

As the days slipped by in monotony without any word from Pyongyang or any movement toward his release from Camp 16, You Moon slowly came to the realization that his friend would never acknowledge his mistake—and never order the military to release You Moon.

Barring some significant shift, You Moon now believed he would remain a prisoner in this awful place for the rest of his natural life.

SWEEDEN
ESTONIA
BALTIC SEA
LATVIA
LITHUANIA
BELARUS
RUSSIA
Moscow

19

Moscow, Russia

The news was much better than he could have believed. Andrei Rowan did not believe in luck, but he was glad to see so many world events moving in his direction—and so many situations bending to his will.

World leaders had badly misjudged the Russian prime minister for years. Dismissed by the global press as an overly ambitious, intellectual lightweight who'd been in the right place at the right time to jump to the very pinnacle of Russian politics, the truth was that Rowan was much closer to the likes of Stalin or Lenin than even his allies knew. His critics misjudged his aspirations to greatness at their own peril.

Prime Minister Rowan had carefully plotted Russia's return to superpower status for a very long time. Every move, from the grand to the mundane, had Russia's return to greatness firmly at the center. Rowan believed, quite passionately, that the fall of the former Soviet Union was the greatest tragedy of the twentieth century. He meant to right that wrong.

Rowan felt he truly represented the world's best hope of checkmating the rich, imperialistic overlords who controlled so much wealth in countries like the United States. The concepts and tenets of Marxism were personal for Rowan. He believed them utterly and completely.

If Russia did not serve as a hedge against the wealthy superpowers like America that operated across the globe with impunity, who would?

China might one day be able to counter the US in raw innovation and power—but not for at least another decade. The Chinese were still churning out a thousand engineers every year just to keep pace with the one or two engineers trained at US higher education institutions capable of creating, developing, and assembling engines of innovation. The Chinese were literally throwing massive numbers of bodies at social, economic, and scientific problems, knowing that 99 percent would fail. The Chinese society inched forward based on the small numbers who achieved in spite of the hurdles before them.

Rowan, though, had adopted a hybrid philosophy—mix in a little capitalism, a little Western-style education and democracy, and then overlay it with the historic Russian command and control system, a strong military, and a world-class intelligence network.

He was taking the best of the lessons the West had learned and mixing those in with the true ideals of the communist state. Build and inspire where you can, but take what you must.

Rowan was willing to make any deal, with any partner, that suited his grand purpose. Russia would return to its former glory. There was no question at all about his future success.

Russia's recent venture in Israel was a wonderful example. What could have been an unmitigated disaster for the Russian economy was rapidly turning into an intelligence and diplomatic success story. Even as the world's oil economy teetered and swayed toward chaos, Rowan believed Russia had at last found a viable path forward.

Russia depended heavily on oil but often relied on the good graces of unstable Middle Eastern partners in Iran, Saudi Arabia, and elsewhere. Rowan had made a series of moves over the years to seize control of the oil companies in Russia and bring them under his control. To set an iron example for the others, he'd presented the largest private oil company in Russia, Kosvo Oil, with a tax bill of $27 billion in 2003, declared it bankrupt, and then sold its assets to other firms.

Even though Russia's oil and gas industry was quite large, it was faced with enormous challenges. Though it had the largest reserves of natural gas in the world, the second largest coal reserves, and significant oil reserves, it was badly in need of massive investments to unlock those reserves. It produced a tenth of the world's oil, yet also consumed a vast amount as well.

Rowan had done his best to spread the wealth among the remaining state-owned oil, gas, and pipeline companies. But his latest move to position Russia at the cusp of the greatest explosion of oil extraction the world had ever seen was, he believed, the final chess move that would return his country to its former greatness.

Then his intelligence chiefs at the SVR had delivered precise information stolen from the world's largest private oil company on breakthrough technology to efficiently extract oil from shale.

The technology—designed to safely and cheaply super-heat the shale, forcing the oil to rise to the surface—was shockingly workable. It had no environmental side effects. No oil leaked into the surrounding environment. There was actually a net surplus of water, which had always been the major stumbling block in previous efforts to extract oil from shale.

And now, Rowan hoped, he was about to hear good news from his top aide on his return from Israel.

There was a knock on the door to his private study, away from the prying eyes and ears of the Duma. "Mr. Prime Minister?" his aide, Nicolai Petrov, called from the doorway.

"You've returned, signatures in hand?" Rowan answered.

Petrov stepped through the doorway. "I have. The papers have been filed with the Ministry of Infrastructures in Jerusalem."

"INOC's leaders are happy with our investment?"

"They are."

"And they are willing to work with us in the basin, on this new technology?"

"They are." Petrov paused. "But Mr. Prime Minister, there is potential conflict we'll need to work through."

"Which is?"

"We have competition."

"We've stolen what we need," Rowan said, laughing. "We don't need to worry about them. I've already given the research to our own companies. They've assured me that they can create a working oil shale manufacturing facility within two years. We already have the working schematics for it in the Negev. And we have what we need in our partnership with INOC...."

"No, it's not any of that," Petrov said uneasily.

"Then what?"

"It's Israel Energy Research."

Rowan glared at his top aide. "They're a glorified think tank. And they're not even Israeli to speak of, despite their name. So?"

"Their chief geologist just gave a talk in the United States at the yearly symposium of the Colorado School of Mines. He released their own assessment and presented data that the oil shale reserves at Shfela Basin near Jerusalem were the equivalent of 250 billion barrels of oil. That's roughly the same amount of proven reserves in Saudi Arabia."

"Again—so? It's an academic researcher, talking hypothetically about oil shale," Rowan said. "People have been talking about this for decades, and no one has taken them seriously."

"Maybe, but when you combine this with the US Geological Survey data showing that the Tamar and Leviathan natural gas fields off the coast of Haifa in the Levant Basin may hold as much as two hundred trillion cubic feet, people are starting to pay attention. There's speculation that, between the oil shale and the natural gas fields off its coast, Israel is about to become a world oil superpower."

Rowan thumped his hand on the table. "Idle speculation," he said, his voice rising. "They haven't extracted any natural gas yet. We have nearly that much in our own reserves here. And no one is taking the Levant Basin gas reserves and oil shale extraction technology story seriously—other than us."

Petrov waited a moment before continuing. He did not like to anger his boss. "That's not entirely the case..."

"Enlighten me."

"Well, Greece, for one, is actively talking to Israel about building out a transportation hub that would carry natural gas from the Tamar and Leviathan fields off the coast of Israel and distribute it throughout all of Europe. Greece is also talking about undersea pipelines that would carry the gas to Europe from the Eastern Mediterranean. That would seriously change the political situation in Europe."

"Fine. But it's still talk."

Petrov took a deep breath and forged ahead. "Yes, but Israel Energy Research says it will have hard numbers and research on the true dimension of Israel's undersea natural gas and oil shale deposits in the next few months. This won't be a secret much longer..."

"Which is why we are moving so quickly with INOC and the Israeli government partnership," Rowan said quickly. "We're there first."

"But we aren't," Petrov said anxiously. "Their chief scientist has also just said publicly that they have the same oil extraction technology that we do, perhaps even better. And I must remind you, Israel Energy Research is actually owned by the American telecom IBC group—"

"Which has nothing to do with oil and gas exploration."

"But their subsidiary, Aladdin Oil & Gas, does. It's a division of IBC. Israel Energy is run by Aladdin. And two very serious investors— two of the wealthiest men in the world—showed up in the past day. They took a ten percent stake in Aladdin—and seats on its board."

"Who?" Rowan asked, afraid of the answer.

"Joseph Rothman, the chairman of Vienna Financial, the world's largest network of banks and financial institutions, and K. Robert Moorhead, the chairman of Wolf Corp., the world's largest media empire. And for good measure, they also put Charles Raney, the former American vice president, on their board. Israel Energy and Aladdin are now very serious players. This is formidable competition."

"But still American, at the end of the day," Rowan said. "Which means our partnership with Israel's National Oil Company is even more central than we'd planned. We need to get to the Shfela Basin first, before the Americans. We *must* get there first. Our future depends on it."

SAUDI ARABIA

Dammam
Dahran

GULF OF OMAN

QATAR

Riyadh

IRAN

UNITED ARAB
EMIRATES

OMAN

20

Riyadh, Saudi Arabia

Nash was never a fan of indoor offices. It just wasn't in his nature. He much preferred to be outdoors, without suits and ties. It was one of the joys of serving as a young gun CEO of an NGO and global communications network. He could move around freely.

He liked nothing better than to be out on the back of a motorbike, headed toward a remote African village to see a patient with TB or malaria. To him, that was the real, central work of everything his Village Health Corps network did in several dozen underdeveloped countries. They saved lives, and Nash always liked being where that action was.

But he also fully realized the value of what mVillage had become in recent years. As totalitarian regimes and dictators had learned the rules of the Internet, they'd become much better at closing off gates and pathways for free information.

After all, Internet traffic everywhere on the planet was controlled and managed by only three hundred or so central "gigapop" centers, where virtually all information was routed. Big companies did a good job of building in redundancies. But at the end of the day, if a country wanted to literally turn off Internet access, it could. North Korea did it routinely—even now. So did other countries in times of high tension.

VHC's mVillage network, though, was a nearly unstoppable force. It was not dependent on the Internet, on satellites, or even on individual cell phone carriers. Its mobile apps could freely float across any and all networks. Black market SIM cards with mVillage apps had become ubiquitous across the world, allowing any user to access mVillage from virtually any mobile platform.

For this reason, Nash knew, mVillage had become the social network of choice for any revolution, any disaffected minority, any social group that wanted to effect change, or any community that simply wanted to stay engaged in a fractured media environment. Traditional media might have lost its ability to gather mass audiences, but mVillage was beginning to change those rules.

All of which meant that there were times—like now, in Riyadh—where he played by the rules and showed up at crucial meetings in a suit and tie. Su and several of his friends at the State Department had arranged for Nash and Badr Ahmad to meet in Riyadh that afternoon with Abdul al Faisal to discuss mVillage network—and the Saudi intelligence concerns about it. They'd just left VHC's modest offices and were making their way down the King Fahd Road in Badr's dilapidated Volvo.

Prince Abdul was an extraordinarily interesting figure. He was, to any astute observer, the member of the House of Saud who made everything work. He'd been the director general of Saudi intelligence, then the Saudi ambassador to the United States for a time. There had occasionally been a flurry of press attention to clandestine roles that Prince Abdul had played in keeping al Qaeda out of the kingdom, but nothing concrete had ever materialized.

He'd recently given up his post in Washington in order to return to Saudi Arabia for an academic and ceremonial post as the head of the King Fahd Center for Islamic Studies. The scientific and academic research center drew on some of the best minds in the kingdom to discuss emerging trends and held conferences on a regular basis.

But for those who understood what was happening in the very complicated line of succession within the House of Saud, observers believed that Abdul al Faisal had returned to this post to wait for an appointment as the next Saudi foreign minister—perhaps in the very near future.

Nash had been thoroughly briefed on Prince Abdul's situation by his friends at State. He knew that, in all likelihood, he was about to meet with the person whom the House of Saud had designated to manage the kingdom's foreign affairs going forward.

Today's meeting was absolutely critical to any forward movement for the mVillage network in Saudi Arabia. Their success—or failure—would depend on the outcome of the meeting.

Nash's mobile buzzed. He glanced down at the caller ID. It was Katie Devlin, who had been instrumental at State in arranging the meeting that Nash and Badr were now headed toward at the King Fahd Center in downtown Riyadh. She and Su were very good friends. Katie kept his fiancée occupied when he was running around the world.

"We're on our way to the meeting," Nash said as he picked up the call.

"So everything is set?" Katie asked.

"All set. We're meeting at the King Fahd Center."

"You *do* know how difficult this was to set up, right?" Katie asked. "So you'll be on your best behavior?"

"I'll be charming, as always," he said, chuckling.

"Yes, please. Be charming—as I know you can be when you choose to be."

"Hey! Not fair," Nash said.

"It *is* fair." Katie laughed. "Just remember that State set this up…"

"So I'm representing you. Yeah, I know. I'll behave."

There was a brief pause on the other end of the line. Clearly, Katie had called for a reason and struggled with how to convey the message. "You know," she said finally, "there are times when it's just a little more important than usual to be on your best behavior, Nash. This is one of those times."

Nash had known Katie for some time. He knew when she was speaking in a veiled way about something she really wanted to say. She'd done it, more than once, when she knew something from Su but couldn't tell Nash because Su had sworn her to secrecy. This was classic Katie.

"All right, Katie," Nash said, "I get it. There's more to this meeting, or to the guy I'm meeting with, or maybe both?"

"Not exactly," she said. "Let me just say this. Meetings with members of the House of Saud are especially important right now. And meetings with people like you are important. The Saudis are testing every single strand of their relationship with the US."

"But I'm not government," Nash protested. "Why would they care?"

"You might as well be, considering the power that mVillage has. And they all know your father is Ethan Lee."

"Who is the US ambassador to Japan and has nothing whatsoever to do with either the House of Saud or anything in the kingdom."

"True. But the Saudis are all about deep, tangled connections. Nothing is ever what it seems. They almost certainly view you as some sort of proxy for State. And they are currently critically examining every one of those proxies closely."

"Why? Has something happened I should know about?"

"Not a good question to ask," Katie said evasively. "I will say this. Be sensitive to what you're hearing from Prince Abdul. He's likely to test your resolve, ask your true intentions with mVillage, push you on what you might or might not know. I'm only urging you to be on your best behavior and to tell him the truth about your intentions."

"Which is that mVillage can connect people in ways he'd like and appreciate. Community health workers, for one, will benefit from the mVillage network. It's a positive force, not something to be feared or controlled by them. We can help them build bridges in communities."

"Yes, talk about that. And talk about how committed you are to working with them."

"Sure," Nash said. "But that's it?"

"Just keep your eyes open," she answered. "There's a lot going on at the moment. Some of it has to do with events that are likely to involve folks like Prince Abdul and others in the House of Saud."

"Like?"

"Like—just recognize that Prince Abdul and the others in the House of Saud are especially sensitive to events in other countries."

"You mean Yemen?"

"Yes, exactly like Yemen. Not to mention Egypt, Jordan, Iraq, and Bahrain on their other borders. The Arab Spring revolts are everywhere, all around the kingdom. The House of Saud is on edge in a way we've never seen."

Nash hated to talk about things like this. He was all about the "relentless, positive storm" and social change through action and technology, not conflict. But he also knew that he had to pay attention to conflict, because it was central to so much of their work.

"Got it. The Saudis are nervous. They're wondering if the Arab Spring revolts are about to show up on their doorstep."

"Exactly. Old enemies and old conflicts have a way of reappearing at times like these to cause trouble," Katie said.

"Like al Qaeda, I'd imagine," Nash answered. "They've never moved against the kingdom of Saudi Arabia. They've been awfully quiet of late in the middle of everything that's been happening in Egypt, Jordan, Syria, and now Yemen."

"Just be mindful of the times and the audience. And behave. Okay?"

"I promise," Nash said. "I'm wearing a tie."

"Shirt buttoned at the top?"

Nash reached to his throat reflexively and fastened the top button that he chronically left unbuttoned. "It is now," he said, laughing.

"Good. So now you're set."

21

Change Square
Sana'a University, Yemen

These were unusual times. Protesters from the Muslim Brotherhood, Islah, and several Houthi rebel tribes had managed to mingle and protest in the square on the outskirts of Yemen's leading university for the better part of four weeks without incident. They had a common goal—and a common enemy—that kept the peace.

Yes, there had been clashes. Early in the protests, half a dozen Houthis and Islah opposition party members had fought each other with their traditional Yemeni daggers, or *jambiyahs*, after one group had gotten too loud and boisterous in the square. But the Muslim Brotherhood and Houthi leadership had settled their differences.

Both, in fact, wanted the same thing—an end to the rule of Yemen's long-serving president, Ali Kahar. They were all united behind one common cause. They wanted him to step down and call for democratic elections.

Today, there were more protests in the square—led by Houthis, Islah, Muslim Brotherhood, and several other groups that spanned the continuum from one end of Shi'a to Sunni—designed to keep up the pressure on the government to call for democratic elections.

So when a battered, ugly, yellow VW bus pulled out of the square full of youthful protesters, no one cast a second glance. Had anyone bothered to look inside, they might have been startled to see that the bus was carrying members from both a Houthi tribe and a camp in north Yemen known far and wide as a place that refugee al Qaeda fighters frequented.

It was common knowledge that President Kahar, with Saudi Arabia's quiet urging, had once hired al Qaeda mercenaries to keep the Houthi rebels in north Yemen from causing too much trouble. Sporadic firefights had broken out between al Qaeda Yemen fighters and the Houthis, and there was plenty of bad blood to go around.

But something quiet and dramatic had changed in the past six months. Someone had reached out and provided desperately needed money, supplies, guns, and aid to both the Houthi rebels and al Qaeda in north Yemen. For weeks on end, it had been quietly been raining cash for projects the Houthi tribes had contemplated for years.

Specifically, the Houthi rebels had been given substantial assistance from these unknown benefactors in a five-year-old project to build a secret crossing from north Yemen into the southern reaches of Saudi Arabia.

The effort was similar to what rebels in Egypt somehow managed to accomplish by continually building secret tunnels into Gaza. Funded by Iran through intermediaries, Hamas in Gaza always managed to keep at least a few tunnels open, no matter how many the Israeli military destroyed.

But the Houthis were among the poorest people in the world and had virtually nothing beyond their own hard work to create a secret passageway into southern Saudi Arabia. Iran provided a small amount of food, money, and guns—but nothing beyond that which might give them the ability to finish their project and passage into Saudi Arabia.

Saudi forces easily controlled the border where the one and only highway—Route 5—connected Al Hudaydah in Yemen along the coast to Mecca in Saudi Arabia. There was no other way to get into Saudi Arabia from Yemen except Route 5, and Saudi Arabia kept tight control over that highway.

The Houthi tribes had been quietly building a narrow road through the wilds of north Yemen to cross into Saudi Arabia and intersect with Route 15, which also ran south and east from Mecca. But there was another reason the Houthis had been earnestly building and planning this narrow, secret roadway, with occasional encouragement from Iran.

One day, they believed, they would succeed in punching through. And when they did, they would be within a stone's throw of Dahran, the absolute nerve center of Saudi Aramco and the epicenter of the House of Saud's oil operations.

The effort had dragged on for so long, though, that some of the early leaders in the project had moved on to other pursuits—until an al Qaeda group with money had simply shown up one day and offered to lay down arms and join in the effort to finish the secret road project. The Houthi tribe leaders, after considering the offer, had accepted. The road was finished within three months.

Now the yellow VW bus made its way north from Sana'a University and Change Square. Today was an exciting day. They'd crossed the Saudi Arabia border almost six weeks ago. They'd cleared brush, trees, and other significant items in their way for days, careful not to make it appear from the air as if there was a road. And this very afternoon, they were in sight of Route 15.

What they were hoping to see was whether they'd managed to intersect with Route 15 far enough east to get past the three checkpoints manned by armed guards that kept everyone out of Saudi Aramco's massive headquarters compound in Dahran.

Once the group had reached the end of the existing highway in north Yemen—which was just ten miles or so from Dahran as the crow flies—they parked the VW bus and moved into three brand-new off-road vehicles that had been purchased with the al Qaeda cash in the past six months.

From there, they followed markers until they arrived at the border between Yemen and Saudi Arabia. The group had sequestered another brand-new vehicle purchased with the newfound al Qaeda cash off to one side. They inspected it to make sure no one had stumbled on it.

The truck was outfitted to look exactly like a Saudi Aramco truck, with the state-owned petroleum company's distinctive blue-green background and star logo carefully re-created in the right locations. Uniforms nearly identical to those worn by Saudi Aramco engineers were folded neatly in the back of the truck's cab.

Most important, though, were the rods and plates that had been carefully stacked and covered on the truck's bed. Most in this particular group did not know exactly what they were, beyond the general description told to them that they'd been carefully stolen from "swimming pool" nuclear reactors found at academic research universities around the world.

The material that sat on the truck bed had been taken, piece by piece, from academic research centers across the world. Surprisingly, it hadn't been especially difficult. Academic research facilities were not known for tight security.

And despite the fact that these reactors ran on enriched uranium mixed with aluminum or zirconium, they weren't closely guarded the way a military or commercial nuclear power plant was. In fact, it was even possible to use highly enriched uranium in these small academic reactors designed for research purposes.

True, highly enriched uranium had largely been phased out over the years at these nonmilitary reactors as a safeguard against proliferation. However, most of them continued to use alloys that were merely a fraction less than the 20 percent threshold for enriched U-235 that would make them "highly enriched."

The reason was simple. An alloy that contained a fraction less than 20 percent of U-235 had a much greater lifetime. So for this reason, most of these small, nonmilitary reactors continued to use alloys that were almost, but not quite, considered to be highly enriched. As a result, the fuel elements tended to be rods or plates with a considerable amount of uranium.

Only two nuclear engineers who'd recently come from Pakistan to join the effort—one affiliated with the al Qaeda group and the second loosely connected to the Houthis—knew anything at all about the "swimming pool" and miniature neutron source reactors that the Chinese had been outsourcing for years.

But neither engineer considered trying to explain the nature of the plates and rods in the back of the truck. For one thing, the Houthi and al Qaeda crew members did not trust each other. If either knew they were transporting what amounted to highly enriched uranium in the back of a truck, it was anyone's guess what might happen if a knife fight broke out.

But more importantly, the groups funding both parties had given very clear instructions to the two nuclear engineers that they were to keep the two groups from harming each other. Ignorance served that mission quite capably.

Once they'd made certain that the truck, clothes, and cargo in the truck were secure, the group drove their off-road vehicles across the border. They made their way slowly around boulders, up and over ridges, and then, finally, down a carefully mapped route along a line of trees until they were in sight of Route 15 in Saudi Arabia.

They parked their three off-road vehicles and did nothing for two hours except watch a number of trucks move in either direction. But none of them stopped for any length of time, which meant that, most likely, there was no checkpoint between here and their final destination.

What's more, they were able to see that, at several points on the road, the trucks moving along it were able to leave the road to head out into the oil fields that dotted either side of the highway. There were more than one hundred fields, and eleven thousand miles of pipelines, connecting seven refineries throughout this area, which were responsible for moving nearly ten million barrels of crude oil every day.

In the end, both groups were satisfied that they would have direct access to the Aramco fields and pipelines from here. Now it was simply a question of waiting for their orders.

22

Tehran, Iran

Amir Shahidi was furious. He'd just received a report through IRGC channels that one of the Americans' new F-35 stealth fighters had flown a solitary sortie north from the Gulf of Oman into Iran's interior, and there had been no resistance. None. He couldn't decide who to blame— or who to fire.

Without question, the F-35 had been on a mission to target bin Rahman. But, as Bahadur had guessed, the Americans had pulled back because he was not alone. Still, someone needed to be held accountable.

He called in Admiral Hashem Sanjar, his naval chief, while he was still fuming. Sanjar spent the better part of the meeting in Shahidi's private study explaining why it wasn't *his* responsibility for air defenses along the southern coastline, that his navy was still recovering from the recent conflict in the Strait, and that he'd never had the budget to counter a stealth fighter like the F-35 at sea.

"Then whose responsibility is it?" the Supreme Leader asked, exasperated at Sanjar's constant whining and backpedaling.

"It is…I would believe…that you should consult with General Zhubin," Sanjar said. "Overall, he has a much better perspective on what we have that can deal with that sort of threat."

"Yes, I suppose," Reverend Shahidi said. Everyone hid behind Zhubin. Was he the only military man left in Iran with any sort of courage?

"Reverend Shahidi, he is your top commander in the Revolutionary Guards," Sanjar said, "and would likely be in a better position to answer this sort of question…."

"Even though the F-35 came directly out of their fleet in the gulf?"

"And past our air-defense system inland, I believe, which your air force is responsible for…"

There was a knock at the door to the study. An aide peered in timidly. "Reverend Shahidi, Hussein Bahadur is here to see you, with a guest. And General Zhubin has asked to join the meeting."

"May I leave you to your next meeting?" Admiral Sanjar asked politely, relief visible on his face. Sanjar was clearly in such a hurry to leave that it didn't occur to him to linger and see who Bahadur's guest might be.

"Yes, you may leave," Reverend Shahidi told his navy chief, barely able to mask his disgust. Sanjar left the study quickly, leaving Shahidi to pace angrily while he waited for Bahadur and Zhubin.

It had been years since Shahidi had last seen Ali bin Rahman. In fact, it had been more than a decade, before the events of September 11, 2001, in New York and Washington. Because Shahidi never left Iran, for any reason, bin Rahman had come to him when he was still with the IRGC with a proposal to share intelligence occasionally about their common enemies—especially the Saudis and the United States—when possible.

The man who would later rise to become al Qaeda's global, operational second-in-command had made a persuasive case at the time. The differences between Shi'a and Sunni were not as great as some in al Qaeda believed. They certainly had more in common than their enemies in the west. Both Iran and al Qaeda were working toward the same pan-Islamic policies and a return of Sharia law, he'd argued. Surely, they could find common ground against mutual enemies.

Shahidi had turned bin Rahman down flat—largely because al Qaeda was nothing more than a flea on the elephant's back at the time. Had he known the successes al Qaeda would enjoy, he might have reacted differently.

Since then, the rift between al Qaeda and Iran's leadership had grown to the point that al Qaeda openly attacked Shi'a citizens in Iraq and elsewhere as legitimate targets. Western governments around the world operated on the principle that they could always keep al Qaeda and Iran proxies at each other's throats. It was a common, if slightly misguided, foreign policy.

The truth was much more complex and virtually impossible for Western intelligence sources to comprehend. After the events of September 11 in the United States, the al Qaeda leadership had split, with some fleeing to the mountains of Pakistan and others seeking safe haven in Iran. Ali bin Rahman, for one, had not set foot in Iran since his last meeting with Shahidi.

The IRGC had accommodated the al Qaeda elements after September 11, though. And why not? They were a steady source of knowledge and funding. But the IRGC kept them on a tight leash. The al Qaeda remnants in Iran simply did not make a move without the IRGC knowing precisely what they were doing. It made the Western intelligence officials exceedingly nervous, because it was then nearly impossible to understand what Iran's ultimate objectives were toward al Qaeda.

As he waited for bin Rahman to arrive, Shahidi wondered, as he had years ago, if he wasn't missing something—if perhaps there *was* common ground between the two that he and others had overlooked. The Saudis and the United States were most certainly mutual enemies.

But common ground between Shi'a and Sunni? *What could that possibly be*? he pondered. *And why had bin Rahman returned to Tehran to meet with me again*?

When bin Rahman entered his study, Shahidi was startled to see a gaunt, emaciated shell of a man. The years of hiding had not been kind to bin Rahman. His face was drawn, his skin loosely covering a skeletal frame. Yet the man's eyes still glowed with the intensity and fierceness Shahidi remembered.

"Reverend Shahidi, may you receive many blessings of peace," bin Rahman said without preamble.

"It has been many years since we last spoke," Shahidi answered. He glanced at General Zhubin and Hussein Bahadur as they followed bin Rahman into the study.

"I must thank you for your kindness, and your willingness to grant me an audience," bin Rahman continued.

Shahidi glanced over at his two military leaders and then back to bin Rahman. "I hear that you bring us interesting news."

He did not, for a moment, believe that the Mahdi—whether one thousand years old or thirty—had made his appearance. But that was not the sort of thing he would ever discuss with anyone. It was one thing for Nassir Ahmadian, and the masses, to believe in the reappearance of the Mahdi. It was quite another thing for the Supreme Leader to believe in it.

"Reverend, I *do* have news that I believe you will find of interest," bin Rahman said, "but I would like to discuss it privately with you, if that might be possible. But first, I have other urgent news I have not discussed previously. And for this, I would ask that both of your military leaders hear it."

Shahidi glanced at Zhubin and Bahadur again. Both nodded and took seats at the table in the study where they often discussed matters of war, intelligence, and diplomacy. Shahidi and bin Rahman took seats as well.

"So what is this urgent news," Shahidi asked, "that requires a personal audience?"

"It involves the Saudis," bin Rahman said. "I am here to offer you information of a very confidential nature and to extend a hand of friendship."

"I am most anxious to hear of it," Shahidi said.

"The Shura Council has met," bin Rahman continued, "and we have made two decisions. The first is that we must no longer be divided in our work with your country. We wish to form a strategic alliance. As you know, there are some in al Qaeda who have met with frequency in the eastern part of your country. The Shura Council has decided to take this to its most logical conclusion, and to seek an alliance of mutual satisfaction. We believe it is time."

"I will consider your offer carefully," Shahidi said. "And your second decision?"

"We have decided that we will no longer remove our hand from the kingdom of Saudi Arabia and the House of Saud," bin Rahman said. "We know the king has promised reforms to the Shi'a people and others, to keep the revolution sweeping other countries from appearing at its door. But we do not believe it will be sustained. We have decided to take certain steps that will bring the revolution to Saudi Arabia. I am here to ask if you will join us."

Shahidi said nothing to this offer at first. He'd known for years of the many, complicated financial arrangements that had been made to keep al Qaeda from attacking anyone in the kingdom of Saudi Arabia. But those financial arrangements had begun to go public, in various ways, and the House of Saud had been forced to gradually pull back its clandestine efforts to neutralize al Qaeda.

As a result, Shahidi presumed, the al Qaeda leadership had determined there was no longer any benefit—financial or otherwise—in not targeting the Saudi government as they did others.

"So you will act against the House of Saud?" Shahidi asked.

"In fact, we have acted already," bin Rahman said quietly. "We initiated an attack against one of the Saudi princes landing at Dulles airport in the United States. Unfortunately, US intelligence picked it up, and the attack never took place. But the Saudis know we were responsible, and they have begun to act accordingly."

"I see," Shahidi said. "So what would you have us do?"

"There is a second, much larger attack planned," bin Rahman said. "And it is imminent. In fact, you may know of it already, for it involves the Houthis, to whom you have supplied arms and supplies in northern Yemen. Whether you know it, al Qaeda and Shi'a are working together against a common enemy, and the strike will be heard around the world."

IRAN

SAUDI ARABIA   Dammam   GULF OF OMAN
                    Dahran

                              QATAR

● Riyadh

UNITED ARAB
EMIRATES   OMAN

23

Riyadh, Saudi Arabia

The King Fahd Center wasn't much to look at on the outside. But Nash knew it was the leadership who so casually made appearances there that made the center a place of great importance in the affairs of the kingdom.

Badr had parked the Volvo three blocks away on a quiet side street. They'd walked from there. It was wonderfully quiet in this part of the city. Nash noticed that trees and vegetation had been planted recently along the streets.

The green, bursting vegetation created a serene sense of life in full bloom, reminiscent of what it must be like to come across an oasis in the desert. So, Nash thought, *the Saudis must care about appearances. For this place, they wish the appearance to be much different from opulence.*

"It's nice here, isn't it?" Badr said as they walked along the tree-lined street.

"You like all the trees and vegetation?" Nash asked his colleague.

"I do. They've worked hard to bring some life to this part of the city. It reminds me a little of something…"

"An oasis, perhaps?" Nash asked.

"Yes…like an oasis."

Nash smiled. The Saudis certainly knew how to welcome guests, in many ways. He admired the thoughtfulness. But he also knew he had to pay careful attention to what he was being shown in the kingdom. "I agree. And yes, it's nice. Peaceful."

There were several new Mercedes-Benz sedans lined up in the private drive to one side of the center. So Prince Abdul was there already. Nash remembered Katie's admonition and checked his tie again. He glanced over at Badr, who grinned broadly as they walked up the steps to the center. He realized, with a start, that this was probably a very big deal to the volunteer who ran his office in Riyadh.

"You ready?" Nash asked Badr.

"All of my life," Badr answered.

The door to the center opened, and a man with elegant, traditional robes greeted them. "Welcome, my young friends," the man said, extending his right hand. Nash shook it gladly, as did Badr. Clearly, they were accustomed to Western visitors at the center.

"Should I remove my shoes?" Nash asked before he'd taken a step inside.

"No, please, it is all right. You are fine as you are," the greeter said. "You will be meeting with the prince in the library."

He turned to lead them into the center. Nash and Badr followed, glancing right and left as they walked along the hall. Original Islamic manuscripts and paintings adorned both walls. The effect was extraordinary.

When they'd reached the library, the greeter ushered them in and closed the double doors behind them without another word. They were on their own, awaiting Prince Abdul.

The library was unlike anything Nash had seen. Rows upon rows of books and bound manuscripts were arranged along every wall. At least a half-dozen reading stands were spread across various parts of the library. It was a place of scholarly learning. *Or, at least, it is what I am expected to feel while I am here,* Nash thought.

"There's an old Quran here." Badr peered closely at a bound manuscript under glass on one side of the library.

Nash walked over to look as well. "Really? How can you tell?"

Badr pointed to the lettering on the front. "Here, you can tell from this script. It's ancient."

They both leaned forward to study it more closely. "I wonder how old it really is," Nash said finally.

"It is from the seventh century," a mellifluous voice said from the front of the room, where they'd entered the library.

Nash and Badr both turned quickly, like two young boys caught with their hands in the proverbial cookie jar. "I was just admiring the manuscript," Nash said. "It is magnificent."

"It is. And it is but one of many such wondrous documents and books in this library." The man walked across the room, his robes flowing slightly. His countenance was striking. His face was dark, broken only by a welcoming smile. He also extended a right hand in greeting. "Welcome. I am Prince Abdul al Faisal, and I am most honored to meet you, Nashua Lee."

Nash nodded briefly and shook the offered hand. "I am the one who is honored. Thank you so much for seeing us."

Prince Abdul turned and extended his right hand to Badr. "Welcome to you as well, Badr Ahmad. I have heard much about your successes with mVillage here in Riyadh."

"Thank you," Badr said nervously.

The prince pivoted to face the rows of books and manuscripts. "I think you will be impressed. We have assembled the largest collection of Islamic manuscripts anywhere in the world, in this library here at the center. We have more than 250,000 volumes in Arabic."

Nash turned to look as well. "Here, in this library?"

"Not all here, at present," the prince said, smiling easily. "They're in different parts of the center. But many are right here. It represents the entire breadth of Islamic Studies and Islamic Civilization. We also have more than ten thousand films and videos that document everything we do here at the center."

"That's quite a resource," Nash admired.

"The center was built to preserve and celebrate Islamic culture," the prince said proudly. "We have dedicated ourselves at the center to acquiring, authenticating, or copying every known Islamic manuscript in the world."

"Every single one?" asked Badr.

"Yes, my young friend, every single one," the prince answered. "At this time, we've acquired tens of thousands of handwritten texts. Some in this very room are more than a thousand years old. And that particular manuscript you were looking at, as I said, dates from the seventh century. It is one of the oldest known manuscripts, we believe."

"I'm impressed," Nash said. "I haven't heard of any place quite like this."

"You have your Library of Congress and other places in Washington that go well beyond our modest library here," the prince said. "We have much to do, and many places to visit, to match that."

Nash looked around. "I would say you have a good start."

"Yes, I believe you are right," the prince said. "So please, should we sit and talk?"

They took their seats at the polished table at the center of the room. Nash watched the prince carefully. He'd learned, in his many travels, that you could learn a great deal about someone by watching how he or she handled himself during a conversation. Body language, especially in a place like Saudi Arabia, was nearly as important as the words themselves.

The prince appeared quite at ease in his surroundings and this room. That hardly surprised Nash. They were sitting in a room that quite possibly represented the epicenter of Islamic culture in the world. The prince, and his extended family, had gone to great lengths to create this place. They were justifiably proud of what they'd accomplished— and what it represented.

"So Nashua," the prince said, "can I assume that you have come here, to the kingdom, to offer us something of value? Or, perhaps, you are here for some other reason?"

Nash sat perfectly still at the table. He had to give the prince credit. He didn't waste time. "Thank you for the question, Prince Abdul. And please, you can just call me Nash."

"Nash, then," the prince said with a quick nod. "So the nature of your visit?"

"You're familiar with mVillage?"

"I am. It is a remarkable global network—elegant, simple, quite utilitarian."

"Thank you," Nash said. "It is that. But it is also more than that. It is a tool that can help engage disparate communities in ways that you might not expect. Used properly in a place such as Saudi Arabia, mVillage can help you and the other leaders in the country reach out to disaffected communities or places that otherwise might not feel empowered to speak up."

"So I've been told," the prince said calmly. "It allows rebels to communicate with mass audiences and allows those who might not be sympathetic with the direction of Saudi leadership to widely complain about its policies."

"That *is* one way to look at it," Nash said. "But I'd like to present another way to look at it."

"Of course."

Nash glanced over at Badr. They'd discussed this very conversation the night before. Badr nodded silently, and Nash plunged in. "Prince Abdul, what if you thought of mVillage as a way to allow dissenting voices to connect with the House of Saud and to propose ideas? What if you used mVillage to reach out to small businesses with offers of assistance? And what if you used mVillage to set up information networks that granted communities access to useful information? Mothers-to-be, for instance, might learn commonsense tips for having healthy babies."

"Perhaps you can elaborate?"

"Gladly," Nash said. "Take the first idea. Rather than allow disaffected groups of people to fester and complain in isolation, you could use mVillage to reach out to them and offer to listen to their ideas. It would be like an electronic idea box, only with mobile devices. Many American corporations have suggestion boxes for their employees, which gives them a chance to have their voices heard."

"And if we don't take any of their suggestions?"

"But you will—at least some of them," Nash said. "There will likely be some interesting ideas that you can act on and then talk about. It's a positive, constructive use of mVillage, which we've been experimenting with in other parts of the world. I call it mobile democracy."

"Fine. I will consider your offer. It has merit," the prince said. "And your other ideas?"

"The second is relatively simple. You're familiar with banking credits over mobile devices?"

"I am."

"Well, we've included that functionality, but we've also incorporated ways in which small entrepreneurs can offer their business ideas to the mVillage network. You could establish that, provide an Entrepreneurs Fund, and then establish a network of very small businesses that can succeed through such a network. The word will spread far and wide among communities that you've created such an opportunity."

"That would be interesting," the prince mused.

"And the third idea is at the core of what Village Health Corps has always been about. Using mVillage to connect groups of people with common health questions—like what to eat or do during pregnancy—is a logical thing for you to sponsor. Again, it's a positive, focused way to allow mVillage to be a force for good in your society."

Nash sat back. He doubted he could refine the pitch any further. If the House of Saud rejected it, there were still ways to bring mVillage to the kingdom. But it would certainly make things easier if they didn't have to work around the royal family.

"You know," the prince said, "I've seen you speak on three occasions. I was in the audience. I have always marveled at your ability to sell a big idea. You have the gift—one that is rare indeed for someone so young. You have the ability to see beyond borders, and to recognize the things that large groups of people aspire to see, hear, and understand. It is the mark of a leader."

"Thank you," Nash said softly.

"So I would ask you to consider something," the prince said. "I can see a way in which we can work together, you and I. But we will need shared terms of reference, a common foundation on which we might build something together."

"Such as?"

"Such as a recognition that the world before us is changing very rapidly. Even as we sit here today, having a polite discussion, forces are plotting for the overthrow of the House of Saud by violent or other means. Old alliances are ending, and new ones are being forged. There are news reports just this morning, for instance, that the ruler in Yemen has agreed to elections in a month's time. And that is only one country on our border. Others on our border are experiencing similar disruptions."

Nash nodded. "I recognize that. It is a very uncertain time, in many countries."

"And in every one of those places, there is the mVillage network," the prince said, "aiding, abetting, helping those who would advocate overthrow."

"But also educating, inspiring, teaching, broadening the base of knowledge," Nash countered.

"It depends on your perspective. So here is what I would propose. I would like to test your theories of mVillage in Saudi Arabia. I would like to see if it can, in fact, be used in the ways you've described."

"Wonderful," Nash said quickly.

"But the foundation that I am seeking—the common ground— is that mVillage be seen as a street with traffic going in both directions. Even as we are hearing from groups and communities, I would like the ability to communicate with them as well. That seems like a fair trade, does it not?"

"It most certainly does," Nash said. "I can foresee many ways in which the House of Saud can reach out to its people through mVillage— in unique ways."

"And not only in Saudi Arabia but to other countries as well. That is what I am proposing here—a chance for Saudi Arabia to tell its story to the world."

"Yes, absolutely," Nash said. "The network is global."

"And Islam is global as well," the prince said. "We are very quickly approaching a time where national borders are not nearly as important as they once were. Information and communication has changed that in ways none of us could have anticipated."

"I couldn't agree more," Nash said. "I believe we have found that common ground. I will help you with your efforts, in return for support behind the mVillage goals I explained."

The prince nodded firmly. He seemed genuinely satisfied with their informal agreement. "It would be a welcome opportunity for us— a chance to display to the rest of the world what our universities, our companies, and our people have to offer. It is a chance to reach out to the world."

"I would welcome that," Nash said. "And mVillage would be more than up to that task."

MEDITERRANEAN SEA

ISRAEL

Gaza Strip

West Bank

Jerusalem

JORDAN

● Bersheeba

EGYPT

24

<hr>

East of Beersheba, the Negev Desert

Abe Zeffren had been Israel's deputy oil commissioner for as long as anyone could remember. He'd seen crazy plans, lunatic con men, and scams designed to dupe gullible Americans into giving money for oil exploration in Israel. But he'd never seen anyone take oil or gas exploration seriously in Israel. Until now.

As he drove along a solitary desert highway into the Negev east of Beersheba, Abe wondered deeply about what he'd seen that day. In the morning, he'd made the short drive to the northern end of the Dead Sea. He'd expected to see nothing. Instead, he'd been greeted by cranes and trucks and all manner of drilling equipment.

The Russians were indeed serious about exploring the Dead Sea for oil. Abe was shocked as he got out of his car to visit the construction site. It didn't make sense—not when the Russians had vast oil reserves of their own to explore. Why bother with drops of oil in the Dead Sea when they had barrels upon barrels in their own country?

Every worker at the site spoke Russian, and Abe had grown frustrated at their unwillingness to convey—even in broken English—any sort of progress they were making at the site. After nearly an hour of fruitless conversation, he'd gotten back into his car and driven west and south toward the Shfela Basin.

One thing had been clear at the Dead Sea, though. The Russians were serious in their intent. Whether they'd find any significant amount of oil was another matter entirely. But they'd made a definite commitment to INOC to spend money at the Dead Sea, and they were following through.

Abe was in for another shock when he came to the Shfela Basin. He hadn't been to the region in years, and he'd expected to see nothing but barren rocks and shrubs stretching across one hundred miles or so. Yet here, too, Abe saw immediate signs of development and construction.

Almost from the minute he drove into the vast basin area, he was able to spot construction trucks lumbering from one place to another. He stopped at one of the half-dozen sites he'd spotted from the road and approached it. Here he found more Russians. And this crew was nearly as uncommunicative as the Dead Sea group.

Twenty miles farther south, Abe came across an entirely different construction site. The sign at the entrance said it was managed by Israel Energy Research. Abe was one of the few people in the country who knew what it was—and that it was not, in fact, an Israeli entity. It was an American oil and gas research outfit, working here in Israel.

The construction foreman hadn't been all that forthcoming, but he'd at least provided more information than the Russians. They were, in fact, testing oil extraction from the shale. Abe hid his surprise. The permits were in order. But he couldn't believe that, after all these years, anyone was actually trying to extract oil from the shale.

No one had held much hope of doing so at a price point that could compete with regular old crude oil. Unless there was a huge surge in the price of crude oil—something that could only occur if proven reserves in countries like Saudi Arabia, Iraq, and Iran suddenly disappeared like a thief in the night, driving crude oil prices sky-high—it made no economic sense. Yet in the space of just an hour, he'd come across not one but two tests of oil extraction in the barren Shfela Basin. Someone, somewhere, was confident enough that they could safely and cheaply extract oil from the shale that they were willing to spend money on it.

As he drove into the Negev, in the general direction of the overland oil pipeline that carried oil one way from Eilat north and then west toward the port of Ashkelon at the Mediterranean, Abe had spotted another convoy of trucks. He'd watched from a distance for the better part of an hour as the workers methodically lifted sections of the oil pipeline and replaced each section with new pipe. Abe knew enough about oil pipeline construction to see what they were doing. They were turning the Eilat-Ashkelon pipeline into a two-way system—capable of transporting oil in both directions.

The import of that stunned Abe. It had been a day of surprises, yet this was by far the biggest. It meant the INOC—or someone—was confident enough in the monetary value of shipping oil through Israel from Ashkelon and locations inside Israel south to the Eilat port in southern Israel that they were willing to retrofit the entire pipeline.

It was an enormous undertaking—and hugely expensive. The original Eilat-Ashkelon pipeline had been built largely with Iranian oil dollars prior to the fall of the Shah of Iran in the late 1970s. Israel had never seen the need to improve the one-way nature of the pipeline. Yet they were improving it now and preparing for something.

Abe's curiosity finally got the best of him. Driving up to the construction crew, he parked his car a safe distance away and ambled over to the closest truck.

"Can I help you?" the driver called down from the cab of the truck.

Abe fumbled in his pocket and eventually produced an ID badge that he generally kept in his shirt pocket. He was barely recognizable from the picture, but the words explaining that he worked for the government were clearly visible.

"I work for the Ministry of Infrastructures," he explained. "I was just wondering what you all were up to here. I'm assuming you have a permit for this work?"

The driver shrugged. He pulled a piece of paper down from the dashboard and handed it down to Abe. "It's all legal, as far as I know. We're here under INOC."

Abe looked over the permit. Sure enough, the work had been

authorized by INOC, and it was all legal. "How much of the pipeline are you working on?"

"All of it," the driver said.

"The entire pipeline?" Abe asked.

"As far as I know," the driver said. "They have at least three dozen crews working on it at different points. The plan is to have the entire pipeline redone by the end of this week."

"In a matter of days?"

"Yes. We've been at it for a month. We're almost done."

Abe couldn't believe what he was hearing. Granted, his office only handled exploration permits—not construction permits or work on pipelines—but he was still surprised that something of this magnitude could happen so quickly without his knowledge.

"And what about the oil that's supposed to flow through it?"

"We connect everything by the end of the day, and the oil flows at night," the driver said.

"You're all working together?"

"We are. They're paying us a lot to make sure we start and finish on time."

Abe shook his head. "And you'll be finished in just days? And oil will be able to flow south?"

"That's the plan."

"Thanks," Abe said and started to walk away. He turned back, though, and asked one final question. "So who's paying for all of this?"

The driver looked back at the permit. "Aladdin Oil and Gas," he called out. "I think they're American. But I don't care—as long as the checks clear."

MARYLAND

Baltimore

WEST
VIRGINIA

Washington, D.C.

VIRGINIA

25

Foggy Bottom, State Department
Washington, DC

Jennifer Moran did not like being kept in the dark. What was especially galling was that she'd witnessed the terrorist attack, and now it appeared the White House was deliberately keeping her at arm's length. It was more than frustrating.

She walked across the office quickly, her heels making a sharp *click, click, click* as she left the carpet around her ornate desk and headed across the wood floor that made up most of her rather large office. She leaned out of the doorway and spotted her executive assistant. "I need the president," she snapped.

"The president of the United States?" her assistant asked meekly.

"Yes, *that* president," said Moran.

"I should just call the White House and ask for the president?" her assistant asked.

"Yes," she said simply, then walked back into her office. She knew she shouldn't be so hard on her staff, but she was flat-out irritated. And when she got this way, her staff knew enough to stand clear. They had no choice but to get their assigned jobs done, without asking too many questions.

A minute later, the executive assistant buzzed her boss on the intercom. "Madame Secretary, I have President Camara's assistant on the line for you," she said.

Moran picked up the phone. "But does she have the president?" she asked her assistant.

"I—I don't know for sure," said the anxious assistant. "She said she would let you know when the president could speak to you."

"How about now?" Moran asked curtly. "Can you please tell the president's assistant that I'll be here in my office, waiting for his call?"

"Yes, Madame Secretary."

Moran hung up the phone and swiveled her chair away from the doorway. She closed her eyes and waited. Less than a minute later, the intercom buzzed again.

"The president is on your private line," her assistant said quietly.

"Thank you," she said, only slightly concerned that she'd just put her assistant through the worst five minutes of her young career. She switched lines. "Mr. President?"

"Secretary Moran, I'm delighted you called," said President Camara. "I was about to call with a briefing on the Dulles incident."

"I'm certain you were," she said with only a slight trace of sarcasm. "I've heard nothing from your national security team. Have they confirmed the nature of the attack at the airport?"

The president paused only briefly. "In fact, they have. Just in this past hour. As we suspected, it was someone loosely affiliated with al Qaeda. What made the person so much harder to track is that he'd been here, working in a nondescript job quietly from before September 11."

"Which nationality? Pakistan or Yemen?"

"Neither," the president said. "That would have been too obvious. No, he'd lived for years in Bahrain, then the United Arab Emirates, and London before that. He'd gone to school in England then transferred to the United States. He was in the final year of his PhD program at a school here in Washington."

Moran caught her breath. "That can't be. Really? It doesn't fit any known profile."

"No, it doesn't. But what that tells me is that this is all becoming much more difficult. And that our enemies are getting that much smarter about avoiding obvious traps and filters."

"What's NSC say about a rationale?"

"They're still working on that. I'm being briefed by Susan Wright within the hour. But the preliminary facts on the ground indicate that al Qaeda has determined they will no longer stay out of the kingdom."

"So Saudi Arabia is now a target?"

"It would appear so," the president said. "The complicated deals that the House of Saud has managed to make all these years are no longer working. Money bought peace for a time. But that doesn't appear to be the case anymore."

"It's not unexpected, if you think about it," Moran said. "The Arab Spring revolts—combined with the death of their leader— have changed everything for al Qaeda. They've lost the ability to convince the world that change occurs in these regimes only through violence and terror. The peaceful student uprisings have changed everything, and al Qaeda knows it. They will need to radically change their own plans, their allies—and their way of operating in many of these countries."

"It's hard to believe that the world could have changed this much, so quickly, through the rapid-fire dissemination of information and peaceful protest."

"No one could have predicted these movements in all of these countries. I know we didn't. And our enemies certainly didn't."

"But it means that the game has changed," the president said. "In fact…"

"What is it, Mr. President?" Moran said quickly. "Has something happened that I should know about?"

The president hesitated. Moran knew she'd once been the president's rival, and he probably wondered whether he could entirely trust her. Nevertheless, she was now his secretary of state, and she deserved to hear of developments that would change everything in the Arab world, regardless of whether there was any truth to what they'd heard.

"Can you make it here to the White House in an hour, for Dr. Wright's briefing?" he asked.

"I'm on my way," Moran answered, even as she grabbed her bag and jacket from the chair nearby. "In fact, I wanted to brief you on my meeting with Prince Muhammad."

"Was your guess correct?" the president asked.

"It was. Once I told him that we'd neutralized the threat on his life at the airport, he reciprocated with information."

"So he is in line to be the new king?"

"He is. He will become the interior minister first. Natal will become king for a time, and Prince Muhammad becomes the crown prince, while still serving as the governor of Mecca."

"Israel won't like the Natal play," the president said.

"It won't be for very long, I don't believe. The changes will occur quickly in the kingdom. Natal is quite old. They need to transition to the grandson as quickly as possible, and I think they know that."

"I think you're right."

Moran hurried toward the door of her office. "I'm headed your way. Can you tell me what I'll be hearing about?"

The president paused. "The Twelfth Imam, if you can believe it. And a meeting between Ali bin Rahman and the Reverend Amir Shahidi in Tehran not long ago."

26

**Camp 16
North Korea**

It was ironic. The very same person at the highly secret nuclear research compound who'd once turned Kim Grace in to the authorities for privately expressing doubts about the direction of North Korea's nuclear program was now entering the gates of Camp 16.

Times change, Kim thought. *There may be a new leader in Pyongyang, but the military still purges all dissenters.*

Yet Kim harbored no thoughts of revenge toward her former colleague as she watched him trudge down the steps of the dilapidated bus that had creaked slowly through the main gates of the prison camp. Kim felt only sadness for him. She knew that he, too, would die in this terrible place.

The guards generally allowed the prisoners to watch as every new group of prisoners entered the camp compound. It was a reminder of just how hopeless their situation truly was. They could see the desolate mountain range through the gates and the downtrodden prisoners enter with bewilderment, fear, and panic on their faces.

Kim had watched every bus enter the gates. Against all rational hope, she scanned every face, hoping to see one of her children or her husband. She knew it made no sense. Yet she refused to give up the only thing that kept her alive—the possibility of seeing her family again someday.

There had been a flicker of anticipation when the peace talks between the North Koreans and the United States had been announced. Some of the prisoners even talked of release and going home to their families.

Yet those days were long behind them. No one had been released. If anything, the days had become longer, the labor much harder, and the hope of an end to their misery a distant memory.

Kim approached her former colleague as he left the bus and made his way toward the throng of prisoners who'd gathered near the bus. "My friend," Kim said to her colleague.

Her former colleague looked up. Consternation, then recognition, and finally sadness swept across his face as he spotted Kim. "Oh my. It is you. I had forgotten that you were here."

"It is where I was sent after…" She didn't have the heart to remind him that he had been the one responsible for her imprisonment. When Kim had expressed doubts to him about her work with a nuclear doomsday device, in confidence, the colleague had reported her. She, her husband, and her children had all been sent to camps within days.

"Yes, I remember," her dispirited colleague said. "I am so very sorry. I had no idea they would arrest you and send you…to a place like this."

"It is just what they do," she said simply. "So can you tell me? Is there news of my husband? Of my family?"

The man's face fell even further. "Oh, I am so very, very sorry. I thought you'd have heard."

"What?" Kim held her breath.

"Your husband. He has…he died two years ago, in another camp. We heard the news. I thought they would tell you something like that."

Kim fought the tears. Long, hard years at Camp 16 had made it much easier to suppress her emotions. "No, they tell us nothing here. I've heard nothing of my family. Have you heard anything about my children?"

Her colleague shook his head. "I have heard nothing of your children. Prisoners were released at some camps. I know that…"

"Though not here."

"No, I suppose not. This is a camp for political prisoners, and I suppose it would be too much to expect that anyone would see freedom here."

"But you said some of the camps released prisoners?"

"Yes, as a show of good faith to the Americans. Some camps allowed prisoners to go home."

"But you have heard nothing about any of my children returning home?"

The man looked genuinely heartbroken. "No, I have not. I am sorry."

"At least there is still hope," Kim said wistfully. "Perhaps they have left their camps and are in other countries. Perhaps they did not feel it was safe to return home and left the country."

"Yes, we can hope."

"So my friend, why have they sent you here?"

The man shook his head. Like other prisoners before him, he was still mostly in shock. The fall from grace had been swift and severe. "There was nothing I could do about it. We were told to secure nuclear materials and weapons. We had to prepare some for inspection and others for shipment."

"Shipment?"

"Yes, not all of the nuclear weapons are to be destroyed. Many, many of them—along with a considerable amount of highly enriched material—were to be sent out of the country. The Americans knew nothing about any of it."

"Where was it going?" Kim asked.

"I don't know for certain, but it appears that it was going to Iran. Unfortunately, those of us who knew about the secret arrangements to ship the nuclear material to another country were felt to be a liability. We—all of us—were rounded up, forced onto a train, and sent here. It happened very quickly. I had no time... No time even to pack."

Kim could see that her colleague still wore the very same clothes he'd likely come to work in. He seemed dazed. "And your own family?"

"I—I do not know. I was sent straight here." The man glanced around nervously and then lowered his voice. "It happened so quickly, you know—and the police were so disorganized—that they did not search us." He patted his suit coat pocket. "I still have my mobile with me."

Kim moved closer. "Quiet. Say no more. The guards will take it from you if they think you might have something of value."

"But it is really of no use here—not any longer. Who can I call? And who would help?"

"You never know what tomorrow will bring. The guards have told me for weeks that my days are numbered because of my role in the Pak Jong Un matter, but I am still here," Kim said. "For now, let us hold to hope."

27

Northern Yemen

Neither the Houthi fighters nor the al Qaeda warriors who'd long taken refuge in the wilds of Yemen had heard of him. They had no use for a leader who'd made the long, secret journey from southern Lebanon to take command of the operation today.

But those who'd provided the cash had told them—both Houthi and al Qaeda alike—that this man would lead them into the heart of the Saudi Aramco complex. They were to obey his every command and heed his words, whether they liked it or not.

In truth, they should have known something about Sa'id Nouradeen. He was a legend to the Shi'a rebels in southern Lebanon and widely known as the only military leader to defeat Israeli forces on the ground in the past generation.

Granted, it had been little more than a war of attrition, with Nouradeen grimly holding enough land and ground to eventually force the Israeli army back into its own territory. But that was enough for Nouradeen, and his taskmasters in Tehran, to trumpet the fact that the Shi'a rebels he led had defeated the Israelis in battle. The legend had grown from there.

What made today's operation difficult was that Nouradeen was supposed to be engaged in peace talks with the Israelis. As Iran's proxy in southern Lebanon, he was loosely part of the ongoing peace negotiations between Iran, the US, and Israel.

Under the terms of the ceasefire, Iran had agreed to remove its support from southern Lebanon, Gaza, and Syria. Guns and supplies had stopped flowing to those regions while the peace talks were underway. But not money.

Nouradeen was privy to Tehran's plans. Reverend Shahidi liked Nouradeen immensely and trusted him with important missions. For this reason, Nouradeen was well aware of the recent talks in Tehran. In fact, he was here today, leading this operation, as a direct result of the news Ali bin Rahman had delivered to the Supreme Leader in Iran about the plot against Saudi Aramco.

As for the news that the Twelfth Imam had reappeared, Nouradeen was dismissive. He considered the notion of a reappearance of the Twelfth Imam the wishful thinking of the believing masses. His son believed in the fantasy but not Nouradeen. He believed only in the cold, hard steel of a gun in the hand of a fighter—and not much else.

Yet he was aware that the fantasy and legend of the Mahdi was useful to guide and control the masses. He also knew that, at some point, it held an almost mystical power to unite both Shi'a and Sunni, if someone should ever wish to do so. There was an allure and mystique about the Twelfth Imam that, if properly harnessed, could be quite useful.

Today, though, Nouradeen was focused. He needed to keep the Houthi and al Qaeda fighters from turning on each other. They had a mission and a common enemy, and it was Nouradeen's job to make sure they delivered their package to the heart of the Saudi oil complex.

Tehran had known there was some risk in sending Nouradeen to lead this mission. But once they'd heard of the plans from bin Rahman, General Zhubin had quickly convinced the others they needed someone of Nouradeen's stature to guarantee success. He'd been dispatched within the hour and had arrived in Yemen during the night.

"Move," he said to a Houthi fighter who was trying to finish a cigarette.

The Houthi fighter took one last drag on his cigarette and tossed the butt to one side. Nouradeen glanced over at the butt, which was still glowing, and motioned to the soldier to stamp it out. The last thing they needed was a brushfire. The Houthi fighter shrugged but stamped the cigarette out and then climbed onto the back of the pickup that carried the rods.

They drove across the southern Arabian border in silence. Nouradeen was pleased to see that both factions were generally getting along. They'd need to work together for today's plan to work.

What only Nouradeen knew was that they had to infiltrate the Aramco complex and place the rods in several precise places. He had long-forgotten plans tucked inside his jacket that none of the fighters traveling with him knew about. They were the keys to the success of today's mission.

Once upon a time, in a fit of paranoia and fear that they might be overrun by military forces led by Saddam Hussein in nearby Iraq, the House of Saud had decided to lay traps at key points in their Aramco complex. Secret triggers could be released in the event that military forces one day invaded and won control of Saudi territory.

With the fall of Iraq and the end of Saddam Hussein, the House of Saud had gradually removed most of the various triggers that could cause the Aramco complex to self-destruct. But some were still in place, known only to a few members of the royal family.

Nouradeen now kept a copy of those plans safely tucked inside his jacket. They contained locations where a few of the nuclear rods and highly enriched uranium could do the most damage. If they were lucky, they could either destroy or contaminate a significant part of the Aramco complex. In one strike, Nouradeen hoped to cripple the Saudi oil operation.

Once in Saudi territory, they proceeded quickly and efficiently. They changed into their Aramco uniforms and were ready to go by the time they'd reached the concealed truck that had been outfitted to look like just another Aramco service truck.

Nouradeen had been told of the road hacked into southern Arabia, south of Route 15, but it still amazed him to see it with his own eyes. Sure enough, the road did lead them to Route 15, behind every checkpoint that the Saudi forces maintained to keep unwanted visitors away from the vast oil complex.

They moved the nuclear rods from the back of one truck to the mock Aramco truck quickly and set off. No one challenged them.

There were more than one hundred oil fields, dozens of gas and oil separators, thousands of miles of pipelines, and a half-dozen refineries to choose from. But thanks to the plans Nouradeen carried with him, they had just three targets. If they were lucky, they would be able to drop the rods and plant the detonators in under an hour. From there, the world would change.

As they took the sharp turn onto Route 15, one of the Houthi fighters in the front seat leaned too closely in to an al Qaeda member. There was a brief scuffle, followed by a flashing knife. A fight was about to break out.

Nouradeen didn't hesitate. Sitting in the second row of seats in the truck, he pulled a gun and held it to the Houthi fighter's head.

"Put the knife away," he ordered.

"But he…"

Nouradeen released the safety on the gun. "I won't say it again. We don't have time for this. Not today."

The Houthi warrior reluctantly put the knife away. Why he would be carrying a knife on such a mission was beyond Nouradeen. But that wasn't his business. He was here to get a job done.

"Good," Nouradeen said. "Now we must move quickly. We have work to do."

Nouradeen knew they had just enough rods and explosives—combined with the remnants of the self-destruct network the House of Saud had once put into place—to cripple several refineries. It would take the Saudis months to repair the damage and clear away the potential radiation from the rods once they'd been placed strategically.

They weren't going to touch any of the pipelines, which could be repaired quickly. No, their target was several of the refineries and chemical plants. They could do the greatest damage that way.

They passed only two other trucks on Route 15. The drivers of both trucks had merely waved and kept moving.

They saw no one in any of the oil fields on the way to the refineries. They'd planted every single rod and their corresponding explosives with cell-phone triggers, in every location, without anyone challenging them. The Aramco complex was so large that it wasn't surprising they'd come across only a few people.

But Nouradeen was still amazed at how easy the entire operation had been. Clearly, this was something the Saudis had never imagined in their plans. After all, there was only the one road that led into and out of the Aramco complex. Who knew that a hacked road from the wilds of Yemen could bypass the elaborate security checkpoints and give them such easy access to the open complex?

Two hours later, they were back at their original spot south of Route 15. Every rod and explosive had been set. Nouradeen called Hussein Bahadur in Tehran.

"They're in place," Nouradeen said simply.

"Any problems?"

"None. I don't think the Saudis anticipated that something like this was even possible. We saw almost no one."

"Good," Bahadur said. "And you have the numbers to the mobile devices?"

"On speed dial," Nouradeen said.

"I'm assuming there's enough of a signature left behind that al Qaeda will be blamed for the attacks."

Nouradeen smiled. "We both know they'll take credit for this immediately. And yes, there's more than enough here to tie them firmly to the attack."

"Then proceed. And make sure you leave Saudi territory after you've set this in motion."

"I will," Nouradeen said.

"You know your next assignment?"

"I have the camp coordinates." Nouradeen grimaced. "But I'm having trouble believing you really want me to lead such a group…"

"Don't worry," Bahadur said. "We have our reasons. The Reverend Shahidi has agreed to it, within the hour."

"But Mecca? Why?"

"We have good reason. Trust me."

"The Mahdi," Nouradeen said. "Seriously? That's what you're planning for? They're all just ridiculous legends and old fishwife stories. You can't possibly believe in them."

"I don't have to believe in them, and neither do you," Bahadur said. "But if they serve a useful purpose and rally people to our cause, then why should either of us care?"

"I suppose. But still…"

"I know," Bahadur said. "Just get this done and move to the camp. We have this one opportunity, and Reverend Shahidi would like to take advantage of it."

"Understood. I'll act now."

Nouradeen ended the call. An instant later, he began calling the mobile numbers he'd programmed into his own cell phone. And several seconds later, the small group of unlikely allies began to hear muffled explosions off in the distance throughout the Aramco complex.

28

Dahran, Saudi Arabia

Very few people had seen the nerve center of Saudi Aramco. To get to it, a visitor had to pass through three checkpoints and by dozens of armed guards, complete with electronic screens to check for concealed weapons. For this reason, only people with a need to visit the center had seen it.

The actual Operations Coordination Center was at the center of the huge compound in Dahran. There were no windows in the high-security room, but a massive, curved wall extended more than two hundred feet with a digital screen displaying maps and visual shots of various points in the compound.

About twenty or so engineers kept a careful eye on the numbers and maps on the big screen. When something happened, the numbers on the screen reflected it.

And something had just happened. The engineers started scrambling long before the first phone call came in. Numbers started dropping on the big screen—first in one location and then another. After a few minutes, it was apparent that many different locations of the Aramco complex were involved.

"Find me a camera shot!" one of the engineers called across the room.

An instant later, a live video feed showed up on one corner of the massive screen. What they saw stunned them. An oil fire had erupted in a field near one of their seven refineries.

"Send a truck there!" the engineer ordered. But even as a truck was dispatched, they received news of four more oil fires that had erupted almost at the same time.

The engineers watched in growing horror as fires and explosions occurred in and around four of their refineries. More than half of their capacity would likely be affected, the engineers calculated. Numbers careened wildly on the big screen.

"Can we contain the fires?" asked one engineer.

"Do we even know what started them? And are they connected?"

Some scrambled for answers at their computer consoles. Phones started to ring. Chaos descended. No one could guess what might have happened at Aramco. It all seemed surreal.

But it was even worse than that, the engineers learned moments later. Monitors at one of the sites had detected traces of radiation. Where it might have come from was hard to imagine, but it was definitely contamination and radiation.

The chief engineer placed a call to Riyadh and asked to speak with one of the members of the royal family. He knew he'd likely be blamed for the events at the Aramco complex. But he had to let them know.

The political consequences were hard to imagine or calculate, the chief engineer knew. It depended on what, precisely, was behind the events. But clearly, they would alter the balance of power. Someone was orchestrating the chaos erupting at the Saudi Aramco complex, for whatever reason.

MARYLAND

Baltimore

WEST
VIRGINIA

VIRGINIA

Washington, D.C.

29

The White House
Washington, DC

"This is a joke, right?" DJ was incredulous when he'd heard from Anshel Gould about the nature of the briefing that afternoon in a small room in the East Wing of the White House. He'd hustled down the hall from his windowless cubicle in the press office to hover next to Dr. Gould's cluttered desk.

"No joke," Dr. Gould said. "There are millions of people, Sunni and Shi'a alike, who take Mahdism seriously. We have folks at the NSC who track it, actually. A couple of analysts at the joint chiefs are mindful of the literature as well."

"Really?"

"Yes, really," Dr. Gould said. "And if you think about it, Iran has been operating on the principle that it's preparing for the return of their Twelfth Imam since the fall of the Shah in 1979."

"So they honestly believe this stuff?"

"Yes, they believe this stuff—at least some of the Shi'a clerics in Iran do. But there are plenty of others, like the Grand Ayatollah in Iraq, who think all of this talk about the Coming of the Twelfth Imam that's been circulating inside Iran for years is hugely destructive for Islam in general. He's said as much recently."

DJ slid one knee onto a chair near Dr. Gould's desk. "But you said this briefing we're going to is about the actual emergence of the Mahdi?"

Dr. Gould rolled his eyes. "According to at least two conversations NSA picked up, bin Rahman delivered the news directly to Amir Shahidi that it was so."

"But I thought the Twelfth Imam was a Shi'a thing?"

"It is," Dr. Gould said. "But some of the propaganda that's been circulating is starting to confuse the two. To the Sunnis, they can witness the coming of the Mahdi to rule a pan-Islamic world. And to the Shi'a followers, that Mahdi is the reappearance of the Twelfth Imam, who's remained hidden for centuries. It's hard to see how it could be the same guy, but who knows?"

"Isn't there other stuff thrown in there—you know, like Jesus coming back with the Twelfth Imam? And that they'll defeat this evil Dajjal character who's leading the dark forces in Israel and maybe the United States?"

Dr. Gould laughed. "Something like that. The Dajjal from the mass literature is this fat, olive-skinned Jew with a dark beard, an ugly, misshapen nose, and a blind right eye. The caricatures that you see on the front of these books in Iran and elsewhere make him look like evil incarnate. To the Mahdists, the Jewish Dajjal is the Antichrist who will rise somewhere in either Iraq or Syria and rule for a time. Then the Mahdi returns, or appears, along with Jesus, takes out the Dajjal, and ushers in the age of Islam throughout the world."

"And what about Israel in this Mahdist worldview?"

"It depends." Dr. Gould shrugged. "Israel is either destroyed just before the Mahdi appears or immediately afterward as the age of Islam is ushered in. You can take your pick."

"And you know so much about this because…"

Dr. Gould sighed. "Because I've gotten a crash course on the sheer lunacy of it all quite recently." He pushed his chair back. "So let's go find out where this Twelfth Imam is supposed to be reappearing."

DJ followed the White House chief of staff from his office and down the hall. They wound their way through several corridors, toward the East Wing of the complex. DJ figured they were heading over to this side of the White House to make sure the briefing was "off the books" and away from prying eyes. The last thing any of them needed was a reporter picking up that senior White House staff was being briefed on the reappearance of the Twelfth Imam in Iran.

When they'd finally arrived at the smallish conference room that folks occasionally used for meetings like this in the East Wing, DJ was surprised to see that it was standing room only. Aides stood shoulder to shoulder around the conference table to listen in on the briefing.

DJ looked at the head of the table and nearly dropped the notebook he was carrying. Secretary of State Jennifer Moran had come here, just for this briefing. She was sitting by herself, studying the briefing materials. And he spotted at least two four-star generals in the crowd as well. *So this is serious stuff*, DJ thought.

He was happy to see that Susan Wright was to lead the briefing. For DJ, that meant he would understand the briefing, its context, and its relevance. Like DJ, Dr. Wright had quiet, deeply held Christian beliefs. Neither mentioned their beliefs publicly and did not wear them on their sleeves during the workday at the White House.

But those beliefs informed their worldview and shaped the way in which they understood policies great and small. DJ, especially, liked the way Dr. Wright seemed open and willing to follow the "still, small voice" as she lived her life. It wasn't easy to hear that voice in the chaos of Washington, but DJ knew Dr. Wright did her level best to do so. And he appreciated that.

DJ also knew the way Dr. Wright lived her faith was one of the reasons she and Anshel Gould got along so famously. While Dr. Gould often struggled to find the time to go to his synagogue, he likewise did his best to heed the "still, small voice" in his life.

There was an unspoken bond of common ground between the two that informed every decision they made on a daily basis.

Susan Wright was incredibly nervous. Never in her wildest imagination did she think she would one day be leading a discussion—at the White House—about the alleged appearance of the Twelfth Imam, or Mahdi, somewhere in the Middle East. It certainly wasn't in her job description, and it had never been featured in a single instance of foreign policy study.

And yet, here she was, about to brief White House, NSC, and Pentagon staff on what they'd heard from conversations in Iran—and its implications for both the peace process and the military.

Thankfully, she'd been able to call on several leading, local scholars at universities nearby who'd been studying the rise of Mahdism in recent decades. They'd gotten her up to speed quickly. She'd taken careful notes and was now prepared to talk about what NSA had overheard and what it might mean.

"Before I begin," she said, clearing her throat, "I'd like to set some ground rules about this briefing. This is strictly informational. I think it goes without saying that we don't want any wild speculation leaving this room about the reappearance of the Twelfth Imam. That won't do us any good and is likely to make us look foolish to our allies around the world.

"Nevertheless, the NSC staff and joint chiefs believe the information is credible enough that we need to pay attention. I'm certainly not going to make any judgments about the truth of what we've heard.

"But what I will say is that at least some of those in leadership positions in Iran are likely to believe the news—whether it's true or not and whether a person appearing as a Mahdi in Iran or elsewhere is an imposter."

One of the generals near the head of the table leaned forward. "Dr. Wright, may I assume that we're going to be using this concept of a Mahdi, or a Twelfth Imam, interchangeably during this briefing?"

Wright nodded. "That's a good question. And yes, largely because there's been quite a bit of propaganda circulating around the world—especially a recent twenty-eight–minute video sanctioned at the highest levels of Iran called *The Coming,* which makes no distinction between the two—we're going to use them interchangeably. If credible leaders in Iran, Yemen, or elsewhere throw their weight behind a human being that they claim is the Mahdi, it really won't matter much whether it's a plain old Mahdi or the reappearance of an imam who's been in hiding for more than a thousand years and is now resurrected."

Wright ignored the snickers in the room and did her best to keep her own beliefs and thoughts in check. She just needed to forge ahead with this briefing. "So what have we heard? First, that Ali bin Rahman delivered news to Iran's air force chief, Hussein Bahadur, that they were prepared to make the appearance of the Mahdi known to the world. And second, that he delivered this news, in person, to Iran's Supreme Leader, the Reverend Amir Shahidi, in Tehran.

"But what is infinitely more dangerous to the current situation is that bin Rahman is apparently willing to make common cause with the Shi'a clerics and leadership in Iran. We've known for years that parts of the al Qaeda leadership have been granted safe haven in Iran. Now it appears bin Rahman is rolling the dice on some sort of Mahdi that he believes he can convince Iran is the Twelfth Imam as well."

"Do you think bin Rahman believes it?" Anshel Gould asked from one side of the conference table.

"Who knows?" Wright answered. "And to be honest, I'm not sure it matters whether he believes it or not. If al Qaeda's leadership joins with Iran's to declare a live human being as the Mahdi, there isn't a whole lot we can do about it. We'll be forced into a posture where we'll have to deal with that person as a de facto leader of at least Iran and its orbit."

"And we're sure that's the news bin Rahman delivered to Shahidi?" Dr. Gould asked.

"We are," Wright said. "NSA is certain of the context of the conversation and its import. The problem, of course, is that the propagandists inside Iran have been laying the groundwork for this for some time. Whether we like it or not, films and books for years have been referring to Sunni and Shi'a hadiths alike."

"Hadiths?" someone asked.

"I'm sorry," Wright said quickly. "They're stories—collections, really—about the words and deeds of the Islamic prophet Muhammad. You can think of them like commentaries. And there are some inside Iran who've been handpicking certain hadiths to justify that real, live people like the Supreme Leader, Amir Shahidi, and Iran's president, Nassir Ahmadian, are fulfilling prophecy. What's more, they've even identified other political leaders, like Sa'id Nouradeen—"

"The Shi'a military leader in southern Lebanon?" someone else asked.

"Precisely," Wright said. "There is literature that identifies Nouradeen with a prophetic figure known as Yamani, who will precede the emergence of the Twelfth Imam. What makes this important is that, should Nouradeen be seen leading military forces into battle—possibly aimed directly at a holy site like Mecca in Saudi Arabia or Jerusalem—then others might very quickly rally behind him as the Yamani who is to precede the Mahdi's emergence."

"So it might not make any difference whether there's some messianic Mahdi waiting in the wings?" Gould asked. "If Nouradeen is hailed as a predecessor of this Mahdi, and people believe it, then it could start a chain of events…"

"Yes," Wright said, "which is why we're taking all of this quite seriously. We already know Nouradeen's reputation to the masses—as the one and only general to defeat the Israelis on the field of battle in southern Lebanon. If, for some reason, Nouradeen were to show up in Yemen, then, I would say, it's time to start worrying."

"And have we been tracking Nouradeen?" Gould asked.

The room grew quiet.

Wright hesitated for just an instant. "In fact, yes, we have been. And as of last evening, Sa'id Nouradeen is in Yemen. What we don't know is why—and what he might be up to. We lost him for a time, but at least one intelligence asset has reacquired him in the past three hours…"

Gould's cell phone buzzed. So did Dr. Wright's, and then several others in the room. A few received text messages. Dr. Wright stopped talking, glanced at the message, and tried to keep her composure. She glanced at Gould, who confirmed with an almost imperceptible nod that he'd received the same message.

"We need to wrap this up," Wright said quickly. "The president wants us in the Situation Room. We'll pick this up at a later date." She rose, and the others in the room rose as well.

DJ moved quickly to keep up with Dr. Gould as they exited the briefing room. "What happened?" he asked in a hushed whisper.

Dr. Gould sighed. "There's been a terrorist nuclear incident at Aramco's oil refineries in southern Arabia, just north of Yemen—which might explain what Nouradeen's been up to."

30

Riyadh, Saudi Arabia

Nash really wanted to take a quick jog through a park. He was starting to go a little stir-crazy in his hotel room.

But of course, that was nearly impossible to do in Saudi Arabia. First, he didn't particularly want to call attention to himself. Not many tall, young white men from America went jogging in the Saudi desert during the heat of the day. And second, he had dozens of e-mails and SMS messages from his mVillage network "friends" to deal with. Most had come in from other time zones while he was asleep.

So he did what he always did while he was traveling. He grabbed his iPhone, headphones, and iPad and headed down to the small gym in the hotel. To make himself a little less conspicuous, he wore sweatpants and a pullover jersey as he made his way through the hotel complex.

Thankfully, the gym was empty, though it was extraordinarily chilly. He wandered around the room, found a thermostat tucked away in one corner, and adjusted the air-conditioning to a more reasonable setting. He had his pick of stationary bikes and treadmills.

Nash set up shop on a stationary bike at the far corner of the room. The TV at the top of the room was set to CNN International. Nash turned the volume off but kept the pictures on. He couldn't help himself. He liked constant input and thought nothing of simultaneously watching video from CNN while he read his SMS messages and listened to his collection of songs on his iPhone.

He set his stationary bike to a comfortable aerobic course, placed his iPad in front on the bike, adjusted the volume on his iPhone, and set off on his imaginary bike trip through a virtual world of hills and valleys. It felt good to stretch his limbs.

Nash was still thinking through his meeting with Prince Abdul—and the offer the prince had placed squarely on the table. It was a gamble on the prince's part, one that no doubt had the backing of the royal family and the extended House of Saud.

Oppressive or totalitarian regimes rarely gave up power willingly. The House of Saud was far from an oppressive regime, but it certainly wielded extraordinary power over its people and commanded vast sums of private wealth for the elite of its society.

At some point, Nash knew, the House of Saud was vulnerable to an uprising from people who were disaffected with the Saudi rulers. It was this sort of disaffection from the youth and ordinary citizens that had led to the uprisings and the Arab Spring revolts that had toppled so many despots and regimes across the Middle East.

Saudi Arabia, though, was the crown jewel in the equation. It was the center of oil wealth and the core of pan-Islamic art and culture. Nash had just witnessed the House of Saud's impressive and grand design to create a science, arts, technology, and cultural mecca in Riyadh. It was impressive.

But the House of Saud was vulnerable. A well-financed and organized military excursion into Saudi territory would likely succeed, in part, until the Saudis could call on US military allies. A collapse in the price of crude oil on the world market—one that OPEC could not control—would also do serious damage to their wealth.

And of course, there was always the slim possibility that the Shi'a minority population could organize itself and mount a serious political challenge to the ruling House of Saud. Tehran had long plotted this sort of movement but had never made many inroads.

As usual, Nash's inbox was filled with dozens of e-mails. He scrolled through them quickly and efficiently. He responded to the business ones that seemed most urgent. He'd become quite adept at brief, one-sentence answers. He'd learned long ago that a short answer was often better than a lengthy reply days after an initial inquiry.

But his personal e-mails were another matter. He often felt guilty about not responding to inquiries from friends and acquaintances. It bothered him that there weren't enough hours in the day to sit and respond to the well-wishing and friendly back-and-forth that most people enjoyed during the course of their daily correspondence.

Su knew this about Nash, so she rarely sent him e-mails or SMS messages. If she wanted something from him, she just called him. But others hadn't quite figured that out about Nash and often sent him long, winding e-mails about everything under the sun, from the din-ner parties they'd been to the night before to new recipes for sun-dried vegetable soup.

"Oh my," Nash muttered to himself after he'd quickly perused one especially long e-mail from one of Su's close friends in Washington. They'd gone to DC Coast on K Street the night before and had appar-ently stayed quite late into the evening. Su's friend had recited the types of drinks, their appetizers, and then their main courses for the evening. None of which Nash wanted to read about.

But it was a friend of Su's. Therefore, by extension, he knew that he was required to care. So he typed in a few sentences, commenting on the wide variety of things they'd ingested for the evening, and hit the SEND button. The fact that he'd forgotten everything he'd read and written the instant he sent it off into cyberspace actually bothered Nash on a certain level.

But then he came to a series of SMS messages on his mVillage account that nearly stopped him cold. He slowed his fast-paced clip on the stationary bicycle in order to read through them carefully. They were drafted in a series of bursts, one after the other as the limit was reached on each message. Nash stared at the words.

The message was from You Moon. Nash had assumed—wrongly, as it turned out—that You Moon and Kim Grace had been safely moved from Camp 16 in North Korea after the president of the United States and the new, young Dear Leader had reached a tentative peace on the Korean peninsula.

Nash knew from his father, the US ambassador to Japan, that President Camara had made a special diplomatic request for the release of both You Moon and Kim Grace. Given that sort of interest, and the commitment to peace on the part of both parties, Nash and Su had both believed that the two people who'd risked their lives for peace would be allowed to leave Camp 16.

But nothing of the sort had happened. In fact, You Moon's SMS message was precisely the opposite of this hope:

My friend Nash,

This will be the last message I will be able to write to you. It will also be the last words I will write in my life.

I am to be executed in the morning. Kim Grace and I have both been sentenced to death for our part in the events that led to the peace talks.

There is no appeal. We cannot speak to anyone. I have tried, many times, with the guards, but they will not speak to my friend in Pyongyang.

I have not heard from him. And with our execution scheduled for the morning, I have lost all hope that I will ever hear from him.

There has been some change in North Korea since the peace talks began. But political prisoners still show up here at Camp 16 every day.

That is how I am able to send you this message. My mobile device was taken before, but a new friend was able to bring in his own phone before the guards took over daily life again.

I do not know anyone else. By the time you read this, I will most likely be dead. But I wanted to thank you for what you tried to do for Kim Grace and me.

I wanted to tell you one other thing, in the hope that it will mean something to you. It is something that we have learned from the new political prisoners at the camp.

The nuclear weapons that North Korea agreed to give up to achieve peace have been moved. Some of them were given to the Americans.

But there were many other weapons that the world did not know about. Those have been moved. The prisoners say they have been given to Iran.

I do not know if this is true. But I wanted to give you this information. I am sure you will know what to do with it. There is nothing more that I can do.

I am at peace. Kim Grace has given me the gift of the knowledge of Jesus and what He died for so very long ago. I am indebted to her for that gift.

I will die in the morning, knowing that she and I will see our God soon. I believe this. It gives me hope that I will soon be in a better place.

Kim Grace also sends her love to you. She hopes that you will be able to continue to make the world a better place.

Your friend,

You Moon

Nash simply could not help himself. He stopped moving on the stationary bicycle. The images on the television screen above him blurred. The music in his ears lost meaning.

He began to cry, uncontrollably. The tears streamed down his face and landed quietly on the plush carpet at his feet. It was so patently unfair. He felt helpless to do anything about what he was feeling at that moment.

You Moon and Kim Grace had risked their lives to bring peace to the world. Now they would pay with their lives for that act. And here he was, in an expensive hotel gym, with his toys and cultural pleasures surrounding him, a network of information at his disposal, and he could do nothing whatsoever to help two friends he'd never met avoid an execution they did not deserve.

The words of his unspoken prayer called out to a God that he believed was there—and listening. The words were unformed. Yet Nash knew in his heart that, if God existed, then He did not need words. Nash bowed his head in silence and continued to cry for a while longer.

Then he picked up his mobile phone. He did not care what time it was in Tokyo, or anywhere else in the world for that matter.

"Get me my father," Nash said when he'd connected with an aide. "I need to talk to him immediately."

31

Tehran, Iran

Nassir Ahmadian, the president of Iran, was not a stupid man. The world thought so, however. And for that, Ahmadian was grateful. It allowed him to make his way through the world without ever needing to reveal his true nature or his real thoughts.

Ahmadian bought the finest suits and dressed well. He kept his dark beard trimmed. He employed both a masseuse and a hair stylist. That allowed people to think of him as a cultured, fancy man obsessed by appearances.

But Ahmadian was anything but those things. His dark countenance masked a fierce belief in his own shining place in the world. He did not care about the material things of this world. He knew, in his heart, that he had been chosen to clear a path.

When he went to speak to the General Assembly of the United Nations in the great, sinful, sordid city of New York in the United States, he spent much of his speech scowling at the handful of representatives who'd remained behind to hear his words.

Ahmadian had not cared that much if the hall remained empty. There had been a presence in the hall as he'd spoken about the imminent return of the Mahdi on earth, and the others had felt it. He was certain.

Ahmadian truly believed he was chosen by his God and fate to serve as the president of the great country that would pave the way for the Twelfth Imam. It was not an act for his countrymen. It was, he was convinced, his calling, and the reason he was put on the earth.

Ahmadian had strongly objected to the path toward peace that Reverend Shahidi had pledged to forge. Ahmadian felt sure it was the exact wrong thing for his country. Iran was to be a beacon in a rapidly darkening world on the edge of apocalypse.

In order for the Twelfth Imam to return, the world must first be at war. There must be chaos on the planet. The principalities and powers, both seen and unseen, must surely know that the world was on the brink and that it was time for the Mahdi to return. Iran was the light on the path toward the return of the Twelfth Imam, and Ahmadian was the leader of that effort.

Perhaps the most direct route to worldwide chaos would be a terrorist attack on the Kaaba, Islam's holiest shrine, as part of an apparent uprising and effort to throw off the monarchy in the Saudi kingdom, Ahmadian knew. It was for this very reason that he'd authorized his own network to plot with others seeking to destabilize the Saudi regime.

Because of his firm belief in this doctrine—and his willingness to commit what was needed to usher in those days—Ahmadian knew his days were numbered. The Reverend Shahidi had been slowly drawing a noose around his neck. Some of the more conservative clerics who did the Supreme Leader's bidding had been calling for his impeachment of late.

For this reason, Ahmadian now traveled with an IRGC armed guard. He was certain that at least some members of the military guard surrounding him at all times were disloyal and answered in whispers and traitorous dialogue to those who served Shahidi.

Ahmadian didn't care. He would fulfill his destiny and lead Iran as long as his body and mind was willing and able.

He'd been thoroughly briefed that Ali bin Rahman had brought to the Supreme Leader news of the imminent return of Muhammad al Mahdi. But what none of them knew was that Ahmadian was several steps ahead of all of them.

Ahmadian had his own spies inside the IRGC's intelligence bureau who kept him apprised of developments. He knew the name of the Mahdi that was circulating among the al Qaeda leadership and was slowly making its way through the ranks of Iran's intelligentsia.

There were some who were calling him the new Caliph of God, from a direct lineage that belonged to the House of Muhammad and, perhaps, the line of Imam Hasan and the family name of Abul Qasim. Some said his father had been Abdullah, a Saudi king, and that he was even now in Mecca. His name, it was said, was known to a close circle as Muhammad Abul Qasim al Mahdi.

Ahmadian wondered, to himself, whether the name alone would be enough to bridge the great gulf that separated the beliefs and hadiths of both Sunni and Shi'a about the Mahdi. *Perhaps, if it can be proved that his lineage and family is directly from the House of Muhammad, it may be so.*

If it could be proved that he was descended from Fatimah, the Prophet Muhammad's daughter, and Ali ibn Abi Talib, the cousin and son-in-law of the Prophet Muhammad considered by the Shi'a faithful to be the first Imam and the rightful successor to Muhammad, then that would satisfy the Shi'a faithful. He could thus be perceived as an elect from God and descended from the Prophet's family.

And if it could be proved that he was also connected directly to Abu Bakr, the father-in-law of the Prophet Muhammad who is known as the first, true caliph to the Sunni faithful, then there might be a bridge. Election from the Shura—from the community—could be addressed in this fashion.

While the Prophet Muhammad had no sons who lived to adulthood—assuring he would be the Last of the Prophets, according to hadiths—both Shi'a and Sunni agreed that Fatimah had children. The Shi'a believed succession was through Muhammad's family. The Sunni believed that the Shura, or community of the faithful, selected successors. If this new Mahdi could draw connections through direct lineage while also indicating a connection to the Sunni line of caliphs selected through the process commonly known as Shura that had originated with Abu Bakr, then it would make things interesting.

It would not be an easy task. The disagreement that had split into the Sunni and Shi'a branches of Islam after the Prophet Muhammad's death had lasted for centuries. This Mahdi's direct lineage to the Ahl al-Bayt, the family of the Prophet Muhammad, and his service or direct lineage to the family and descendants of Abu Bakr would be critical to his legitimacy.

Recently, Ahmadian and his chief of staff had taken a highly secretive—and dangerous—trip to Iraq to meet with Shi'a warriors in service to Iran's leadership. These warriors were careful not to make their presence known to the US military forces that continued to occupy Iraq. But they were loyal to Ahmadian and the cause.

Iran had carefully planted the belief that the US had taken control of Iraq for one simple reason. They'd plundered Iraq's oil wealth. For this reason, there was a growing conviction among the Shi'a faithful in Iraq that it was only a matter of time before Iran would move and take control of Iraq as they had Lebanon, Syria, and other proxies.

Ahmadian knew the Americans would never truly leave Iraq—not since they'd allowed three of their largest oil companies to secure the vast reserves in the country for development. The world might have wondered why the US invaded Iraq, but Ahmadian suffered no such delusions. America had seized Iraq's oil reserves and turned them over to the Western oil companies.

Today was a great day. It was Tuesday, the day of great vision. Ahmadian had set in motion a great event at the mosque on the outskirts of Qom. They were, at long last, going to dedicate the cornerstone of the newly renovated blue-tiled mosque in Jamkaran.

Tens of thousands of pilgrims would be there to offer their prayers to the hidden imam and drop their thoughts down the well there.

"Let us go," Ahmadian said to his driver, who'd been waiting patiently for Iran's president to leave the city.

"We must hurry," the driver said.

"Yes, we must," Ahmadian said. "I wish to get there in time to speak this evening to the people who will be gathered at the mosque. How long will the drive to Qom take us?"

"Less than an hour," the driver said. "It is an easy drive south of the city."

"Good," Ahmadian said. "Then I will have plenty of time to prepare my remarks."

32

The Oval Office
The White House
Washington, DC

DJ made sure he didn't leave Anshel Gould's side. He'd been around the White House long enough to know that he could worm his way into almost any meeting—provided he stayed close to the blunt chief of staff.

Dr. Gould was an interesting guy. He kept two offices—one in the West Wing in the traditional chief of staff's office. But he also kept a much smaller office, away from the Oval Office, near the president's unofficial, private office.

President Camara spent much of his time in this smaller office, away from the ceremonial Oval Office. For this reason, Dr. Gould saw the president much more than the rest of the White House staff. Proximity to power was a curious thing.

DJ admired this about Dr. Gould. He'd watched and learned. So when Dr. Gould was on the move, DJ knew enough to stay by his side.

And Anshel Gould was on the move. DJ was hard-pressed just to keep pace with the chief of staff as he made his way from the East Wing briefing room to the Oval Office.

"There's no such thing, is there?" DJ asked Dr. Gould as they hustled through the corridors.

"As?"

"As a Twelfth Imam," DJ said. "It's a joke, right? What we just heard from Dr. Wright?"

Dr. Gould sighed but kept walking at a clipped pace. "I wish. That would make it so much easier."

"But some person who's been in...what was that word?"

"Occultation," Dr. Gould said.

"Which means what exactly?"

Gould glanced over at DJ with a smile. Of all the White House aides, he felt most comfortable with DJ. The two of them could speak in code, or directly, or in jest. It didn't much matter. Gould knew he could let his guard down with DJ—almost. The kid could be trusted.

"You've heard of those stories about Ted Williams?"

"The baseball player who had his head cryogenically frozen?"

"Yeah, that Ted Williams."

DJ got it right off. There were times Gould and he didn't even need to finish complete thoughts. "So occultation would be like that—bringing a body back to life from some sort of a deep freeze?"

"Something like that."

DJ snorted. "And they had cryogenic chambers a thousand years ago?"

"No, but they did have glaciers," Gould said dryly.

The two laughed as they continued to walk along quickly. "But seriously, how could anyone talk about some Twelfth Imam coming back from whatever you called that...occultation? And how could anyone in their right mind take it seriously?"

"So you remember Ahmadian's speech at the United Nations, right?"

"Where he talked about how he was paving the way for the Twelfth Imam?"

"Yep," Gould said. "That speech. He's the president of Iran. He's the elected head of one of the world's emerging regional superpowers.

So you tell me. The president of a country that's about to go hot with nuclear weapons says that he's ushering in the era of the Twelfth Imam. Then some human being shows up at a mosque south of Tehran who looks, walks, talks, and acts like he's the occluded Twelfth Imam. And the president of Iran recognizes that person as the Twelfth Imam, what do you call that? Is it real?"

"Hmm, yeah, good point," DJ mused. "That's about as real as anything else you see these days. If Iran's leadership says this is the guy..."

"Then it's the guy," Gould said. "And if others from the radical, militaristic Sunni factions like al Qaeda hail him as the Mahdi, come to usher in a pan-Islamic era of dominance over the West..."

"Then we have a Mahdi ruler as well," DJ said thoughtfully. "So how does that sit with the other Arab countries? There's no way that Saudi Arabia recognizes that Twelfth Imam."

"Not as *the* Twelfth Imam, no," Gould said. "But if it's the Mahdi, and there's pressure on the Saudis, or the Egyptians, or the Jordanians, to recognize this new religious figure, well, then I wouldn't bet against anything right now."

"But that's seriously crazy," DJ said.

"Crazier than some guy building ovens during the Second World War so he could exterminate millions of Jews, while the world hardly paid attention? Crazier than that?"

DJ knew enough not to take the bait on that one. If he'd learned anything about Dr. Gould, it was that he lived his anger at a past injustice against the Jewish people on a daily basis. He was loyal to the United States, but his dedication to Israel's survival as a constant reminder of the Holocaust was never far from his mind.

"Okay, not crazier than that," DJ said. "But I just don't see how any sane person could possibly think that some religious figure like a Twelfth Imam could stay hidden for a thousand years, and then come back to rule on earth."

"If the principalities and powers say that it's so, DJ, then I can assure you that it's so," the chief of staff said firmly. "Sometimes, that's all it takes. You know better than almost anyone else on this planet that perception is often much greater than reality."

Which was true. Propaganda didn't require truth to work. It merely needed the force of persuasion. A lie well told over and over worked as well as truth—and sometimes even better.

"True," DJ said. "But it would be a hard sell to the populations in many of these Arab countries."

"Really?" Dr. Gould asked. He didn't slow down as they took a corner. "Think about our own nation, about the level of willful ignorance that has swept across our country in the past twenty years. We have large parts of our own population who still believe, at a molecular level, in things that were long ago dismissed by science as nothing more than myths."

"I know, but…"

"Look around the world," Dr. Gould said forcefully. "There are millions of people who see video clips from isolated events in America, and they believe those clips to be indicative of American life. They have no basis in reality, yet they stoke populist beliefs in America, the Great Satan. There has been pulp literature for years about the emergence of either the Mahdi or the Twelfth Imam."

"So when he shows up, then they believe," DJ said. "Is that what you're saying?"

"Something like that," Dr. Gould answered.

They turned a final corner and nearly ran into Jennifer Moran and her aide, Katie Devlin, coming into the outer offices from another direction. DJ knew Katie by reputation only. They'd been opposite each other in the press operations during the presidential primaries and had since been involved in inter-agency communications meetings. Katie was a pro, DJ knew.

Dr. Gould moved quickly to greet the secretary of state. DJ sauntered over to Katie's side. "You're here for the briefing with the president?"

"I guess," Katie said. "I was with Secretary Moran at Dulles, and she grabbed me on the way out the door at Foggy Bottom. So do you know what it's about?"

DJ never knew how much he could let on in situations like this. "I think it has something to do with the briefing we just heard from Dr. Wright."

"Most likely," Katie said.

There was movement at the door. President Camara peeked out, caught Dr. Gould's eye, and motioned for him to join him in the Oval Office.

"DJ, come along," Dr. Gould said without missing a beat.

Jennifer Moran didn't wait for an invitation. She simply walked into the office. "Katie?" she called out as she walked in.

DJ and Katie glanced at each other, smiled quickly, and then joined their bosses in the president's office. Susan Wright was already there, sitting at one end of the room.

"So," President Camara said when they'd taken their seats. "We have quite a few items to go over, I believe." The president eyed DJ, then Katie. He said nothing directly to them but continued. "First up, you've all heard Dr. Wright's briefing on this notion of the Twelfth Imam?"

"Yes, sir," Dr. Gould said. "We're up to speed."

"Good. And while we know it doesn't make a great deal of sense, there are reports coming out of Saudi intelligence and elsewhere that there's been a flurry of talk about the reemergence of some powerful religious figure who can consolidate authority across nations."

"Mr. President, if I may?" Dr. Wright looked uncomfortable at the end of the couch. "We all know how ridiculous such a notion is, but I must say in all honesty that it isn't too farfetched to believe that any religious figure granted some measure of authority from Iran's leadership will be given some level of recognition by at least the masses. Beyond that, it will depend on the reaction from a country like Saudi Arabia."

"This Mahdi character, or Twelfth Imam—wouldn't it require

some sort of recognition by the Saudi royal family?" Jennifer Moran interjected. "Doesn't he rule from Mecca?"

Dr. Wright nodded. "He does, at least according to the popular legends."

"Which would mean that the Saudis would need to recognize his authority there," Moran continued. "Which hardly seems likely."

"Unless there's chaos in the kingdom, or a military threat that threatens their power," Dr. Gould said.

The president stood. "Which is why I've asked you here. Frankly, I have no interest whatsoever in this kind of craziness. We have a much greater threat at our doorstep. There's been a successful terrorist attack against the Saudi Aramco complex. And from our own intelligence reports, it has crippled a great deal of that complex."

"The world's oil markets will go over the cliff within a day or so," Dr. Wright added.

"The Saudis are almost certain to retaliate," the president said. "And if they go after Iran…well, then, we will almost certainly see war erupt overnight in the kingdom."

Dr. Gould nodded. "Which means we'll be forced to choose sides. We either intervene to help Saudi Arabia in a confrontation with Iran, or we keep the peace process intact with Iran and let events play out in the kingdom on their own."

The president looked at his advisors. "And you know where I'm likely to end up in that scenario. We *must* preserve the peace process. There's too much at stake."

"But we can't choose sides between the Saudis and Iran. Not now," insisted Dr. Wright.

"We may not have a choice. If the Arab Spring comes to the kingdom, and the Saudis are forced to deal with a threat inside their borders that threatens their leadership, we will almost certainly have to stand by and watch it happen," the president said.

"But there's more at stake here," Dr. Wright continued. "If the world oil markets begin to collapse because the Saudis can't control

OPEC, then we will quickly need to find other ways, other methods, of meeting our energy needs."

"Precisely," the president agreed. "That's the other reason I asked you here. There's been considerable movement in the past year on two fronts, and both of them are closing in on completion. And, I might add, not a moment too soon."

"On the energy front?" Dr. Gould asked.

"Yes, there," Camara said. "I'm not sure how much you know of this, but we've been working closely with Turkey and a privately held American firm for the past several years on two very ambitious projects near Israel. The first involves a pipeline at the bottom of the Mediterranean Sea connecting Ceyhan and Haifa, which—"

"Mr. President, I thought that was an aborted project," Dr. Wright interjected. "With Turkey sideways with Israel, I thought they'd put that on hold?"

"We—I should say the United States—interceded through private parties." Camara paused, taking the temperature of the room. "I think all of us would agree it is in the United States' interest to assure that there is at least one major oil pipeline connecting Europe and the West that isn't subject to the turmoil we're seeing in Saudi Arabia, Iraq, and Iran. Should those countries lose the ability to deliver oil to the West, we'd all be in considerable trouble."

"True, but how does Turkey figure?"

"They've completed the pipeline," Camara said flatly. "They're ready to go live, at both ends. Oil could flow from the Baku pipeline out of Azerbaijan right now, if we asked."

"Through Israel?" Dr. Wright asked, incredulous.

"Yes, through Israel."

"But the pipeline through the Negev…"

"Is also about to go operational and two-way," the president explained. "INOC received a massive influx of aid from a private company, Aladdin Oil and Gas…"

"Aladdin?" Dr. Gould asked.

"It's a subsidiary...of an American transnational. Charles Raney is on the board." Camara waited for that news to sink in.

"The former vice president?" Dr. Gould asked.

"Yes, that Charles Raney," Camara clarified. "They've overhauled the pipeline that runs north and south in Israel, and oil could conceivably run from Haifa to the south of Israel, and back again in the other direction toward Europe."

"But whose oil?"

"Israel's," Camara said. "At least that's what the energy secretary tells me. He's been over to see the Baku pipeline and its connection to the terminus in Ceyhan. He says it's ready to go online."

"That means there's a new pipeline that isn't part of any of the Arab states?" Jennifer Moran said, eyes wide.

"Right," Camara confirmed. "And there's one other piece. You're all aware of the earth-moving the US has been leading in the desert near Beersheba, as part of the peace settlement with Iran?" Heads nodded. The entire world knew of those efforts to create a new capital for a Palestinian homeland. "Well, Aladdin and its parent company have a new refining plant that's ready to go live on the outskirts."

"What sort of refining plant?" Dr. Gould asked.

"One capable of processing oil they pull up from the Shfela Basin," Camara said.

"The massive oil shale reserves southwest of Jerusalem?" Moran frowned. "That's impossible. There's no way that works. They don't have proven technology."

"They *do* have proven technology," the president said quietly. "At least, so I've been told. It's in the hands of a privately held company. And they're ready to begin pulling oil from those reserves right now. All it takes is a green light from Israel's government."

"Judah Navon would never go for it," Moran said.

Camara paused. "Are you absolutely certain of that? A chance for Israel to be energy independent for the first time in its history? No, more than that—a world oil and gas superpower, with the ability to control energy resources that flow to the West? Are you so certain Prime Minister Navon wouldn't sign off on that?"

"But if the plant and the pipeline are controlled by a private American company?" Gould asked.

"Is that so hard to imagine?" the president said. "Our biggest oil companies now dwarf most countries in terms of the resources and manpower they have at their disposal. But we were helpless during the Gulf oil spill. We had to rely on their money, and their own people, to deal with it."

"I guess." Dr. Gould hardly bothered to mask his feelings. "But I know the first call I'm making once I leave this meeting. I'm more than a bit agitated that my friend at the Mossad didn't bother to brief me on these developments."

"Be gentle with him, Dr. Gould," the president urged. "If things get out of hand in some of these oil nations, we're going to need friends."

"Good friends," Dr. Gould said.

"We're also going to need some security," the president added. "I've asked Egypt for permission to send a couple of ships up the Suez, so they can be there in the Mediterranean when the Ceyhan pipeline goes live. The joint chiefs have also recommended that we put a few boats at the other end, near the southern terminus of the pipeline through Israel."

Dr. Gould shook his head. "Go figure," he said ruefully. "Israel at the center of the world's oil economy, after all this time?"

"Strange times, Anshel," the president said. "Strange times indeed."

33

Su was devastated by Nash's SMS message and then his call. Like Nash, she'd believed both You Moon and Kim Grace would be safe and freed from North Korea's brutal Camp 16 complex. The news that they were to be executed just hours from now was more than Su could bear.

Nash and Su had quickly formulated a plan. Nash would talk to his father, relay the news about nuclear materials, and put his father on a path to deal directly with Pyongyang on the release of You Moon and Kim Grace. But that would take time—which their friends did not have. It was Su's job to intervene from Washington.

It was very late in the day at State. Most of the vast bureaucracy had gone for the day. But Su knew that at least one person would still be there. Alex Cooper, the secretary's brilliant, peripatetic director of science and innovation, was nearly always in his office long after the sun had gone down.

Today, thankfully, Alex was still there. "Can I talk?" Su asked as she fairly burst into his office minutes after getting off the phone with Nash.

Alex looked up from behind his terribly cluttered, messy desk. Stacks of paper were strewn across it and piled high on either side. "Always," Alex said with a wan smile.

Su was one of his favorite people in the building. They shared a common belief in the power of Nash's "relentless, positive storm" to remake the world for good.

"I need your help," she said breathlessly.

"Tell me what you need."

"Can you call the US ambassador in Seoul?"

Alex glanced at the map of world time zones he kept hanging to one side of his desk. He always struggled to keep track of the times in other parts of the world, and the map helped. "It's the middle of the night there. I doubt if the ambassador is—"

"Can you call him?" Su demanded, much too loudly for the small office.

Alex studied his friend. She was clearly troubled. He would find out why at some point. But now he would do as she asked, without question. "Of course, Su. You can tell me what this is about while I find the number at the residence."

"Thank you," Su said more quietly.

Alex typed in a couple of commands on the MacBook Pro that he used as his office computer. An instant later, the telephone number for the US ambassador in South Korea's capital appeared on his screen. He dialed the number from his Skype account and switched the video on. He wanted the ambassador to see him, via video, while he talked. He knew he'd likely get in trouble for this, but he didn't care. If this was important to Su, it was important to him.

"So quickly, why am I calling him?" Alex asked while the number rang.

"To ask him to intervene in something immediately," Su said. "They are going to execute two people in the morning—in just a few hours. We need to ask him to call the peace negotiators who are working through the agreements in Pyongyang…"

"Su, you *do* know that we can't really make demands of the North Koreans right now, not on something like prisoners," Alex said. "Internal security matters are their own concern. We can't intervene in those things. We're only concerned with matters of state—nuclear materials, troops on the peninsula, things like that."

"I don't *care*," Su said. "This is a matter of state. The lives of these two people are critical to the national security interests of the United States. They have information vital to us, and we must keep them alive."

Alex chose not to question Su further. There wasn't time. "Their names? And where are they?"

"You Moon. He's a personal boyhood friend of Pak Jong Un. He's at Camp 16, along with another prisoner, Kim Grace. She's the nuclear engineer who tipped us off to the nuclear activities near the camp."

Someone answered on the other end. A video circle swirled on the Skype screen. "And they're to be executed this morning?" Alex whispered. "How do you know that?"

"Nash got an mVillage message from You Moon."

Alex nodded. The Skype connection finished. "Hello?" Alex asked. "This is Alex Cooper at the State Department in Washington, DC. I am calling from Secretary Moran's office. Who am I speaking to?"

"My name is Emma Broddle," the voice said sleepily, as if the call had awakened her. "I'm the cultural attaché here at the embassy."

"May I speak to the ambassador?" Alex asked.

"I'm sorry, but he's on travel," Emma reported.

"Do you have a number for him? May I call him?"

"He's in Pyongyang," Emma said. "I think I can probably get a number for him, but I'll have to get it from his executive assistant here at the residence. Can I tell her what it's about?"

Alex glanced over at Su. She nodded. "Yes, tell her I need to speak to the ambassador about two North Korean prisoners who are about to be executed at Camp 16 in a few hours. These two prisoners are vital to the national security of the United States. I would like the ambassador to lodge a formal protest at the talks, which should halt the executions for now."

Alex could see that the news had startled the young woman, who was clearly new to this sort of thing. But Emma didn't blink or pause. "Yes, sir, I understand," she said quickly. "Can I have the names of the two prisoners, so I can relay that information to the ambassador?"

"You Moon and Kim Grace," Alex said. "You Moon is a boyhood

friend of the new North Korean leader. He is at their principal camp for ex-government leaders. Camp 16."

"And can you safely give me enough information about the national security implications I can relay to the ambassador?"

"You Moon has information that he wishes to provide—information that bears directly on the talks that are underway there in Pyongyang," Alex said firmly. "But the ambassador is not to share that information with anyone. It is for him—and no one else—to know."

"I understand," Emma said. "I will deliver the message to him and then report back once I have news for you."

West Bank

Jerusalem

MEDITERRANEAN SEA

ISRAEL

JORDAN

Gaza Strip

34

Jerusalem, Israel

Prime Minister Judah Navon dreaded the meeting he was about to attend. He was always perfectly comfortable addressing the Knesset or his own Cabinet members. He didn't even mind speeches to unruly crowds who disagreed with his policies. He liked a good argument.

What he'd never gotten comfortable with was the necessary evil of meeting with finance or corporate interests—especially those of oil or gas companies who'd long held his country hostage. He hated such meetings with a passion.

Today's meeting, though, was necessary. Long before Navon had become Israel's prime minister, the Knesset and a previous Israeli administration had made the decision to sell at least some of Israel's National Oil Company to private interests.

The logic, at the time, was that there was no oil or gas to be found anywhere in the country, so the only way to make money was to sell off part of INOC to private financiers. Some in the Knesset had tried to block it at the time—to no avail. The company was still referred to as INOC by the public, but it had long ago changed its name to Israel Oil.

Israel Oil's board of directors now included non-Israelis— including, unbelievably, members of foreign governments. It made no sense to Navon that Israel's largest petroleum company would form alliances and financial arrangements with foreign governments.

But it was what it was—and Navon was a realist. He always played the hand dealt him, and today's hand was a closed meeting with the board of Israel Oil. They'd demanded a meeting, based on the news that two of the wealthiest men in the world had just bought a 10 percent stake in a rival that controlled vast natural gas reserves in the Levant region in the Mediterranean and was circling around the oil shale question.

Worse news, this board had written him, was that this other company—Israel Energy Research, part of Aladdin Oil and Gas in America—intended to move swiftly on the Shfela Basin's oil shale. This must not happen, the board had insisted.

Navon knew the meeting would be difficult. There was little he could do about Israel Energy Research. Not only was former American Vice President Charles Raney on their board, but the two financiers who'd taken a stake in the company were so wealthy that they could swallow half of Israel's financial markets, if they so desired.

Navon also knew that the work Israel Energy Research—and Aladdin—was doing with the natural gas reserves in the Mediterranean would mean that Israel would not be required to import oil for at least two decades. The Knesset fully supported that work and would do nothing to block those efforts.

What's more, Israel Energy Research had also made arrangements to turn the Ashkelon-Eilat pipeline into a two-way pipeline, so that oil could flow south and beyond the port of Eilat to the oil-dependent countries of Asia. It had also begun to build an enormous oil shale refinery in the Negev desert—thanks to a recent massive infusion of capital from those same two wealthy men.

But Navon could not tell that to the board of Israel Oil, a company with a proud history, once owned and operated by the state. Instead he would do his best to hear their complaints and try to convince them to move quickly in the Shfela Basin, if that was their desire.

Navon was prepared to promise that he would order the bureaucracy at the Ministry of Infrastructures to clear a path for exploration and excavation deep into Shfela. But that was as far as he could go.

When Navon arrived at the board meeting, though, he was taken aback to be greeted at the door by the top aide to Russia's prime minister. Navon had been to Moscow several times to meet privately with Andrei Rowan, and his aide, Nicolai Petrov, had been present at all of their meetings.

"Nicolai, my friend, you are connected to Israel Oil?" Navon said as he entered the boardroom. "I had not heard that Russia was interested in our pittances of oil in Israel."

"Israel Oil is a new investment, Mr. Prime Minister." Petrov grasped Navon's hand. "And we have a joint agreement to explore the Dead Sea."

Navon studied Petrov. The Dead Sea had produced oil—but a terribly small amount compared to the vast reserves of oil that Russia commanded. It made no sense for Russia to express an interest in exploring the Dead Sea region for oil. But he said nothing about that.

"Well, the Dead Sea is a consistent producer," Navon said instead. "It has always turned a small but handsome profit for Israel Oil. One of the few, I might add, when it comes to oil."

"Yes, which is why we have come forward to help," Petrov said.

"I see. And that is all you are interested in here in Israel?"

Petrov raised an eyebrow. "Now that you mention it, I do believe we share a mutual concern. The Americans have expressed a great deal of interest in your pipelines, your Shfela Basin, the Levant, and relationships with Greece and Turkey."

"Is that all?" Navon smiled.

"Russia has decided that we could not allow the Americans to take over your country's oil and gas production, so we have come forward with the finances to allow Israel Oil to become the central provider of your energy needs again."

"And that is the subject of our discussion today?"

"That—and a request for you to intercede directly to block the American investments and actions, both at Shfela and in the Negev. We have heard they are already building an oil shale manufacturing plant alongside the new city that is rising west of Beersheba in the Negev," Petrov said.

"If they are, then I am not privy to their plans." Navon shrugged. "If they have the permits, and the land, then it is no real business of the Israeli government."

"It is against Israel's sovereign national interest to allow the Americans to control so much of your well-being," Petrov countered. "That is what I am here to represent and what Israel Oil's board wishes to discuss."

"Very well." Navon stepped into the boardroom. "Let us begin. I cannot promise that I will block the Americans' actions in the Negev. But if you are pledging to bring a significant investment into Israel through INOC, then I am quite willing to listen."

"Not only are we willing, Prime Minister, but I have brought my checkbook," Petrov said. "I am prepared to write a check to Israel this very day in order to cement our relationship and bring Russia fully into business within your country."

"And how large would that check be, do you think?" Navon asked.

"Larger than you can possibly imagine." Petrov's voice was deadly earnest. "We want to be your partner, and we are willing to pay handsomely for it."

35

Sa'id Nouradeen did not hesitate. He had his orders, and he was not about to let knife fights slow him down. He had an important job to do, and he would do it.

Yet another mindless, meaningless fight had broken out on the way back from southern Arabia. The same Shi'a Houthi fighter who'd pulled a knife on one of the al Qaeda Sunni fighters had come back for a second bite of the apple. This time, the Houthi warrior had gotten a piece of flesh before Nouradeen could intercede.

Nouradeen broke up the fight in the truck, separated the two, and then told both that there would be a very quick punishment back at the camp that they were heading toward north of al Hudaydah. The two combatants settled into an uneasy silence for the duration of the ride.

Back at camp, Houthi and al Qaeda warriors alike were preparing for a most unusual trip—one that generated both excitement and mystery for them. Boxes had arrived from several ships during the dead of night. Half of them contained dozens of white flags. The other half contained small, double-bladed swords—replicas of the one Zulfiqar, or God's Sword.

What's more, farmers from all corners of Yemen had begun to bring horses to the camp. A makeshift pen contained them at one corner of the camp. To those who knew the legends, this could mean only one thing. They were going to ride to Mecca to meet the Mahdi.

It seemed impossible, yet the warriors could come to no other conclusion. The legends were clear. Some would ride to Mecca with white flags and swords to greet the Mahdi. It appeared that this time had at last arrived.

But first, Nouradeen knew, he had to end the argument between the Shi'a and Sunni warriors. They had to act as one. If he did not do something—swiftly and decisively—then their journey to Mecca would be compromised.

They arrived at camp. Nouradeen ordered the two warriors to the center of the camp. He called on the dozens of fighters preparing for their journey to surround him.

"You all know who I am?" Nouradeen called out when they'd gathered around him.

"We do," said one of the fighters. "You are Sa'id Nouradeen, the great Shi'a general who defeated the Israelis on the battlefield in Lebanon."

"And they tell us you are Yamani, who will precede the Mahdi," said someone else.

"I am that general," Nouradeen said. "History will soon tell us the rest of this story, and whether the time of Muhammad al Mahdi has arrived. But first, we are here today, Houthi of Shi'a and Sunni of al Qaeda. We are acting as one. We are about to ride to Mecca as one, to fulfill our destiny.

"It is important that there be no dissent among us. For me to lead, I must be very clear that I am not here to prejudice Shi'a over Sunni. I cannot—and will not—do that. I wish to lead you both to Mecca, if that is my destiny.

"For this reason, I am going to render a judgment today, one that I believe you will understand. I tell you now that the Houthi will not like my judgment. But I ask you, my Shi'a brothers, to understand why I am passing this judgment. It is for this reason—you can no longer fight with the warriors who are here by your side.

"We have just returned from an important mission—one that has forever changed the balance of power in the world. It struck a devastating blow to the Saudi kingdom and crippled their oil complex. Yet, even as we succeeded, a Houthi struck an al Qaeda unprovoked on the return home.

"That can no longer happen. We must be one, Shi'a and Sunni, in this fight. We cannot quarrel or fight among ourselves. It is for this reason that I render this swift, immediate punishment. Let it be a lesson for any of you who continue to disobey me and fight each other unprovoked."

Without warning, Nouradeen grabbed one of the double-edged swords on top of a nearby box, turned toward the Houthi who'd fought in the truck, and pulled his arm toward him. With one swift, savage motion, Nouradeen cut the man's right hand off. The hand fell to the ground cleanly. Blood poured from the open wound as the man collapsed in shock.

Nouradeen picked up the severed hand from the ground and held it aloft. "We must no longer turn our hands against our brothers unprovoked," he said loudly. "Let this be a lesson to all of you. We ride to Mecca together, as one."

Nouradeen turned to the al Qaeda fighter who'd been struck by the Houthi fighter in the truck. "This is your brother," he ordered. "Tend to his wounds. Make sure he does not die of blood loss. I want this man to ride to Mecca with us, and I place the burden of saving his life on your head."

The Houthi and al Qaeda fighters were stunned. But the message had been received by all of them. If anything, their admiration of Nouradeen had grown immeasurably. Yes, it had been a brutal, savage act. Still, they knew instinctively, it was necessary. They would now act as one.

Nouradeen watched with satisfaction as the al Qaeda fighter tended to the Houthi warrior's mangled arm. The man would live to tell the tale of what had happened to him.

In time, the man would relate how Yamani had done what was needed to usher in the Mahdi. And he, the man with the severed hand, had played his part. He would become legend.

Nouradeen knew specific acts were required during war and on the battlefield. This was one, and he did not regret it.

He could now turn to other matters. He placed a call from his mobile to one of his trusted deputies who'd gathered forces at a highly secretive camp on the outskirts of the Bahr al Mihl Lake north and west of Karbala in southern Iraq.

The forces commanded by his deputy had been training for months. They'd recently met secretly with Iran's president, who'd managed to make his way undetected into the American-occupied country in the middle of the night to ensure that the carefully orchestrated plans were proceeding. They were.

Nouradeen often wondered if Iran's president and Supreme Leader were of one mind on the matters at hand. But he couldn't spend too much time on the question. There was too much to prepare for and too much work ahead. They had a plan for the oil fields of southern Iraq—the treasure that, Nouradeen believed, had always been at the heart of America's interest in the region—that would create serious problems for the occupying forces of the United States and others.

"You are ready for the ride?" he asked his deputy.

"Yes, the men are ready," his deputy replied. "It will take us several days, once we have left camp. We will make much of the first part of the journey in trucks, pulling the horses behind us in trailers. But we will abandon those once we are a day's ride out, as we have discussed."

"Good. We will wait a day, then set out," Nouradeen said. "Your journey is longer and more difficult through northern Saudi Arabia."

"Fine. We are prepared to create our diversion."

"That will keep everyone occupied. They'll be forced to focus everything on the oil fields. You may get two or three days in before anyone realizes you have entered the kingdom."

"And when we are challenged by the Saudi troops?" his deputy asked.

"Do what you must," Nouradeen said. "Just make certain that some of your men arrive in Mecca."

36

Prince Abdul was beside himself. He paced in the outer offices that surrounded the king's quarters. He desperately wanted to order troops somewhere. He was sure they were under attack. The enemy was at the door. A time the House of Saud had long tried to delay had arrived.

But he'd seen too much in the world to think that force alone would defeat the wolf at their door. No, they would need to convince allies like the United States and others to challenge Iran, forcing them out of the war against the kingdom they'd just launched. Diplomacy was needed more urgently than ever. Abdul wished he'd already been named as foreign minister.

He'd come to the king's office in an effort to convince them to go to the United Nations, to challenge Iran there and involve their country in the peace talks between the US and Iran. Abdul had heard talk among members of the royal family that a military strike against Iran was being contemplated. He hoped to convince the king of another path.

Abdul knew they needed to strike back—not at the terrorist camps in north Yemen but directly at Iran. If they did not respond with some show of force, then their weakness would eventually lead to chaos and revolution as their enemy gained momentum.

First, there had been the terrorist attack on a member of the royal family. But it had not been just any attack. It had been against Muhammad al Faisal, the governor of Mecca, who would one day become king of Saudi Arabia.

And now, like a bolt from the blue, terrorists had moved in behind security at Saudi Aramco, planted enriched nuclear rods in places very few knew about, detonated explosives, and destroyed or contaminated a vast portion of the huge oil complex.

Military retaliation against Iran would only incite more violence, solving nothing. But, Abdul believed, they needed to contain this now on the world stage—before it got much, much worse. And that required diplomacy, not force. They needed to surround Iran with others more capable of forcing the regime in Tehran to back down.

The world did not yet know the extent of the damage to the Saudi Aramco complex, but they would soon. Once that news was public, the price of crude oil would go through the roof on worldwide markets as the one, constant supply from Saudi Arabia dried up.

Saudi Arabia had always been the constant in OPEC. When other countries were in turmoil, the world could count on Saudi Arabia to boost production to keep oil prices from skyrocketing. No longer. The terrorist actions at the Aramco complex had changed that equation forever.

Abdul did not believe in coincidences. The attack against a Saudi prince who would become king was more than the work of a loose alliance of global terrorists. It was likely part of a plan by a nation-state bent on regional power. And there was only one country in the region with the resources and will to create such an opportunity.

He had pulled many levers—and forged many unholy and hidden alliances—to keep the dark forces of al Qaeda from working in the kingdom. But with the death of their leader at the hands of the Americans and the changing of the worldwide guard, al Qaeda had chosen to move against the House of Saud.

What seemed hard for Abdul to imagine was Iran's theocracy working by al Qaeda's side. Yet that appeared to be the case.

The problem, for Abdul, was that he was not yet Saudi Arabia's foreign minister—and Muhammad al Faisal was not yet the Saudi king. They were grandsons and had not assumed absolute power in the kingdom. He and Prince Muhammad were on the sidelines, pursuing designs without any real authority.

Prince Muhammad was on his way back from America to Mecca. Abdul had spoken to him briefly and had learned that the Americans had identified the terrorist who'd tried to bring his Airbus down. Neither of the princes had been surprised to learn of the terrorist's ties to the theocracy that ruled Iran.

"The king will see you," the receptionist said finally.

Abdul nodded. It was about time. He gathered his robes and swept into the king's office. He was surprised to see four other members of the royal family—including Crown Prince Saud and his brother, Prince Natal—in the offices with the king.

Abdul took quick stock of his surroundings, knowing his work was cut out for him with this gathering. Natal, especially, was adamantly anti-Israel and would not take kindly to any suggestion to pursue a military strategy against Iran.

"Prince Abdul, thank you for meeting with us on such short notice," said King Faisal.

Abdul studied the aging king, who appeared more tired and haggard than usual. The events of the past seventy-two hours had taken their toll. "It is my duty and honor to serve in such times."

"These are difficult ones," Faisal said.

Abdul eyed Natal, secretary of the interior and nominally in charge of the Saudi Aramco operations. "Do we know the extent of the damage yet at the Aramco complex?"

"The reports from the engineers in the field are coming in," Natal said somberly. "It is quite bad."

"How bad?" Abdul asked.

"Worse than if it had merely been explosives," Natal said.

Abdul cocked his head. "How is that possible?"

Natal glanced at the king, then back at Abdul. "You remember the plan we'd set in motion two decades ago, which allowed us to destroy the oil complex in the event our country was overrun?"

"Yes, I do." Abdul could feel his anger rise. "It was a foolish, short-sighted plan, by leaders who had no faith in our ability to manage our own affairs and defend our country. We removed all of those operations years ago."

"Not all of them," Natal murmured.

Abdul held his tongue. Nothing surprised him any longer. There were secrets within secrets within more secrets in the kingdom. He was guilty of generating such secret boxes himself on occasion.

"What's done is done," said the king. "We must decide what we are to tell the world."

"Do we know who is responsible?" Abdul asked.

Natal narrowed his eyes. "It is always Israel. No matter who pulls the trigger, it is the Israelis who are standing behind the man who wields the gun."

"Can you be certain of that?" Abdul asked. "Why would Israel care to attack our complex at Aramco? What possible good would it do them to cripple our complex or the supply of the oil that the world relies on?"

"Because Israel remains our enemy forever and will always seize any advantage where they see us as weak or indecisive," Natal stated. "They revel in chaos in our country and the other countries of the world."

"That is not necessarily true," Abdul said softly. "Israel has enjoyed peace with both Jordan and Egypt for years. They have come to rely on that."

"But not with the Saudis." Natal's tone was bitter. "They would like nothing better than to see us destroyed and our country in ruins."

"It is not the Israelis," a voice with a slight tremor from age said from another corner of the room. Everyone peered in the direction of Saud—the crown prince who'd never sought the throne and who held universal respect within the royal family for that lifelong decision.

"But how can we…" Natal started to say.

"It is *not* the Israelis," Saud said, more forcefully this time. "We know precisely who is responsible for this attack. It is the one scenario that we have pondered for some time. It is why we have crossed over into Yemen not once but twice in recent years to stop the rebel attacks by the Houthis and others in service to the forces that control Tehran."

"I agree," Abdul said. "But do we have hard evidence to support that?"

Saud nodded. "We have satellite surveillance footage already, from the Americans. It has arrived within the hour."

"And what does it show?"

Saud shook his head. "It shows something we should have predicted and prepared for. They hacked a road from northern Yemen to the Aramco complex."

"Behind our security checkpoints?" Abdul asked.

"Yes, behind all of them," Saud said. "And they slipped in with a truck in order to plant explosives."

"But explosives could not possibly have done the damage we're getting in the reports from our engineers," Natal said.

"What sort of damage?" Abdul asked.

Natal sighed. "They knew to plant the explosives near a few of the leftover trigger points in the complex…"

"Which we should have removed years ago," Abdul said. "It was only a matter of time before someone leaked those plans to our enemies."

"…and it caused a chain reaction," Natal said, ignoring the barb. "But as bad as this might be, it is much worse than that."

"How bad?" Abdul asked.

"There appears to be radiation—nuclear radiation—and fallout in every single instance. There's contamination. The explosives evidently were mixed with highly enriched uranium."

Abdul was aghast at the implications. "That means Aramco—big parts of it—is likely to be crippled for some time?"

"Until we can contain the fallout, yes," Natal agreed. "We will see our production cut, perhaps by as much as two-thirds, for the foreseeable future."

Abdul closed his eyes. The ramifications were unthinkable. "Do we have any hard proof that this nuclear material arrived in the hands of these homegrown terrorists in Yemen courtesy of our friends in Tehran?"

"Not yet," Saud said. "But we will, because we have also received word from the Americans that this incursion was likely led by none other than Sa'id Nouradeen. He has been seen in Yemen, they told us."

"Nouradeen is in Yemen?" Abdul asked.

"Yes, and likely in one of the camps near the border," Saud replied.

"Which means Iran is behind it." Abdul nodded. "He is Iran's agent of choice in Lebanon. You are certain he is in Yemen?"

"The Americans are," Natal confirmed.

"That's good enough for me," Abdul said. "So given Nouradeen's likely involvement and what we know of Iran's funding of the Houthis, are we prepared to confront Iran at the United Nations? To call the Americans and demand that we be included in the peace talks with Iran? If so, I am prepared to lead that delegation to New York."

The king and Natal exchanged glances. "I'm not sure that will be necessary. Natal and I have talked," the king said quietly. "We believe we may have another solution—one that takes the fight directly to Iran's own doorstep. It is time to get this fight off our soil."

Abdul did his best not to show his surprise. But he feared for the scheme that the aging monarch and the interior secretary had concocted. "Does it involve diplomacy?"

"Not immediately," the king said. "We, Natal and I, believe that it is time to bring the full force of the Arab Spring revolution to Iran."

"How?" Abdul asked.

"The oil workers in southern Iran have been unhappy with the leadership in Tehran for some time. A group, Jundallah, has taken action against Iran on their behalf in the past," the king said. "We have decided that it is time to give them some ammunition for the task at hand. Revolution can run both ways. And a nuclear option can be employed there—just as it was here at the Aramco complex."

Abdul looked first at the king and then at Natal. He could not believe what he was hearing. "You *can't*," he said finally. "No one in the world knows of that capability. We have kept it hidden for the entire generation we have conspired to create or acquire it."

"If ever there was a time, it is now," the king said firmly. "We created the capability for just such a moment."

Abdul rose from his chair. "If you allow that capability to be used in southern Iran, it will be impossible not to trace it back to us."

"We are not so certain," Natal said. "The Israelis have long threatened to use force against Iran. Who is to say that they did not act?"

"The Israelis, for one!" Abdul exploded. "They are in peace talks with Iran, even as we sit here debating this."

"But we must do something," Natal said plaintively. "We cannot simply allow our enemy to create a revolution from within. It is time to act against them."

"But there must be another way," Abdul argued. "Give me an opportunity to make the case at the United Nations."

"No." The king's tone was decisive. "We have decided on a course. And I would ask you to honor and respect it."

37

West of Basra, Iraq

It was a great irony that the United States had liberated Iraq—for the benefit of the largest oil companies in the world. Six years after the Iraq war began, large development contracts had been negotiated with the Iraq National Oil Company.

The largest oil companies in the United States, Norway, and Russia all had contracts to develop the oil field reserves dotted across southern Iraq. The amount of recoverable oil in the West Qurna oil fields west of Basra alone was staggering—43 billion barrels by most estimates.

Both the huge private oil company from the US and Russia's largest state-owned petroleum company were racing each other to develop West Qurna. Both had contracts with the provisional Iraqi government to develop export capacity out of West Qurna. Turkey had pledged to spend $2 billion to build a pipeline from the oil fields in southern Iraq.

In fact, West Qurna was the second largest field in the world after Saudi Arabia's gigantic Ghawar oil field. The field, long closed to both Western and Russian firms for years due first to sanctions and then the war, had been opened in 2009.

The massive American oil company signed a $50 billion contract to develop West Qurna, which included an even split between investment and operating fees. More than 100,000 new jobs would be created by the investment—an enormous boost to the struggling Iraqi economy.

Russia wasn't far behind, with its own commitment to develop

West Qurna alongside the Americans. They too had pledged both invest-ment and operating fees, though on a smaller scale than the private American firms.

Still, even with the race to develop, there was little security around West Qurna. The American military focused its attention elsewhere in Iraq, much farther north. Someday, once the fields were further devel-oped, security could be tightened in southern Iraq. But there was no real need at the current time.

That was the very opening the small forces at Sa'id Nouradeen's dis-posal needed. All Nouradeen wanted was a diversion. If it set the Americans back in their race to develop the massive West Qurna oil fields they'd won as a spoil of their successful war in Iraq, then so much the better.

With help from the IRGC military and intelligence planners in Tehran, Nouradeen and his deputies had plotted for months on their route to the fields west of Basra.

The plan was as simple as they could make it. They'd targeted every well that had been drilled since the fall of 2009. Individual trucks would drive to each and set off explosives. If they were lucky, they could set off oil field fires throughout West Qurna that might burn for a month or more. Nouradeen's men had learned how to set oil field fires quickly and efficiently by watching Libya's psychotic dictator torch his own oil fields as American forces closed in. Then they'd modeled their own efforts after what they'd seen.

The trucks secured by Nouradeen set off for their destinations that evening. All of them delivered their sets of explosives to the wells. Fires from the burning oil fields of West Qurna lit up the dark night within the hour.

Shortly thereafter, these same soldiers loaded horses onto trailers at the back of trucks and set off for northern Arabia. They would make the cross-ing from Karbala, Iraq, across the plains of southern Iraq, toward Mecca in Saudi Arabia. They carried black flags and double-edged swords.

Black flags from the north and white flags from the south—both were needed to fulfill prophecy in the surge toward Mecca.

MEDITERRANEAN SEA

ISRAEL

West Bank

Jerusalem

Bethlehem

JORDAN

Gaza Strip

EGYPT

38

Aida Palestinian Refugee Camp
Bethlehem, Israel

"Dr. Thompson, are you sure that you won't spend the night? It's late, and we have a spare bed in the back." Shira Dagher had practically planted her slight frame in front of the door, daring Elizabeth to push her way past her.

"Shira, if I didn't know you better, I'd say you were planning to hold me hostage here in Aida." Elizabeth smiled. "I can see the headlines— WORLD WITHOUT BORDERS PRESIDENT HELD AGAINST HER WILL IN PALESTINIAN REFUGEE CAMP."

They both laughed.

"Yes, for sure," Shira said. "An elderly grandmother holds an American physician much younger than her against her will."

"I don't know. You're pretty wiry."

"And tough. Don't forget that."

Elizabeth loved her visits to Aida, one of the larger Palestinian refugee camps in East Jerusalem that had long been at the heart of the conflict between Israel and the Palestinian people for control of the area. Aida had a large key over one of its entrances as a constant reminder to the refugees of a time when they would win their freedom in their own country.

Aida was easily one of the most beautiful Palestinian refugee camps—largely due to the efforts of residents like Shira, who built things of beauty throughout the camp with virtually no resources or money. It was part of Aida's "beautiful resistance" to Israel's settlements in East Jerusalem.

Shira had founded the Al Rowwad Children's Theater near the center of the Aida camp. Elizabeth periodically made a personal swing through the camp for a pediatric clinic day at the theater. Mothers from the entire camp would bring their children for the day.

Elizabeth could easily have delegated her prenatal and pediatric care duties to one of the physicians on her NGO staff, but she was obsessed with Shira Dagher and the people of Aida. She visited the camp as often as she could—and stayed as long as she could.

An elderly Arabic woman with six grandchildren living in Aida now, Shira had spent nearly her entire life in the refugee camp. She was a permanent fixture in the community. Shira knew everyone, and the entire town knew and loved her.

Elizabeth considered Shira a friend, and the feeling was mutual. They'd grown up in vastly different cultures, with wildly disparate educations and social upbringings. Their religious beliefs were quite different. Yet Elizabeth felt closer to Shira than anyone. She admired and emulated Shira's gentle yet fiercely positive spirit.

Shira Dagher could so easily have been distraught, distracted, and angry over her lot in life as a permanent refugee in the shadow of Jerusalem. But she didn't live her life that way. She spent her days teaching children and her evenings easing the fears and worries of the night. It was all she'd ever known.

"One more coffee?" Shira asked Elizabeth. "You can get an early start in the morning."

Elizabeth nodded reluctantly. "All right. I can see it's hopeless." It had been a very long day, with dozens of shots and vaccinations. She was dead tired. But she was interested in catching up with gossip from Shira, who seemed to hear news from all of the other Palestinian camps on a regular basis.

"Good!" Shira clapped her hands together. She hurried past Elizabeth toward the kitchen.

Elizabeth trailed behind. "So, what's the mood of the camps?"

"About the peace talks with Israel?"

"Yes. Do people believe the talks are real?"

"Oh, we believe they are real," Shira said, her back to Dr. Thompson. "What I don't think very many believe is that it will lead to a homeland for us. We have heard these promises so many times, only to see them vanish like an early morning mist."

"You know, they're building a new city to the east of Beersheba, between the old city and the air bases," Elizabeth said quietly. "They seem to be awfully serious about it. I've been there to work with the staff on the hospital."

"Oh, I'm sure they're serious about the buildings." Shira set water on to boil. "But I don't believe the city is for us."

"For Palestinians?"

"Yes, for Palestinians. That is what the people are starting to say— that the city is not for us. I've heard it many times, from those in some of the other camps who've been trying to find out information on what is happening there."

Elizabeth was confused. "But it's precisely what was talked about in the peace plans—that there would be a contiguous land, with a capital city. That's why they're building there."

"Jerusalem is my capital," Shira said. "No one ever asked me if I wanted to relocate south to Beersheba. And many, many others feel as I do."

"Even if you are guaranteed a homeland you can call your own? One that is finally, permanently free and is not separated from other parts of your country?"

"Geography does not make a country. Heritage does. And we have always lived in Palestine, in Jerusalem. We should not be asked to move."

"Not even in the name of peace?"

"Not even for that." Shira stopped rummaging for cups in the cupboard and glanced back over her shoulder. "You know, not all of your own country is connected, yet no one says anything of that. Certainly, the people of America consider everyone part of their country, whether they're connected or not by land masses."

"I suppose you're right." Elizabeth chuckled. "Alaska and Hawaii are part of the United States."

"The *United* States," Shira said. "It means that your people recognize who belongs in the country and who does not. It is that way with the Palestinians."

"But surely, you can recognize that there must be an end to this conflict at some point. After all, Israel recognizes Jerusalem as its capital. So do you. Both countries cannot claim Jerusalem as their capital. It can't possibly work."

"And why not?" asked Shira.

"Because it's nearly untenable, that's why," Elizabeth said. "Look at Berlin after the Second World War. East Berlin was separated from West Berlin by more than just a wall. The residents themselves yearned for one city, in one united country. However, it's very difficult for two sovereign countries in the modern era to share a common capital."

"But it is possible," Shira insisted. "All I know is this: Jerusalem is my home. It is rightly the capital of my country, even if the world does not yet recognize it."

Elizabeth felt like giving up. She'd been around and around on this subject with Shira and others in the Palestinian camps for as long as she could remember. It was the one impossible demand at the center of the interminable peace talks between the Palestinians and Israel that had dragged on for nearly a generation.

Neither side seemed willing to budge. Several Israeli prime ministers—including Judah Navon, at one time—had come close to partitioning Jerusalem and ceding land for a Palestinian state. Maps were drawn up, with parts of East Jerusalem settled by Arabs to go to a new Palestinian state, and the parts settled by Jews to go to Israel.

But inevitably, those maps and plans had been discarded. The plan to start fresh in Beersheba, in another part of Israel, was closer than anyone had come in quite a long time. It seemed strange to

Elizabeth that someone like Shira would simply dismiss the possibility out of hand.

"So what did you mean, that people are saying the building going on in Beersheba is not for you? For the Palestinians?"

"The word in many camps is that it is not." Shira had located the cups and was searching for the instant coffee.

"How would you know that?"

"Because we have seen many Jewish settlements start over the years. Some were begun for political purposes. Money shows up, buildings are constructed, and then the Israelis say that the land belongs to them and always has."

"I know the history of some of the Jewish settlements," Elizabeth said. "But that's not what's going on here."

"No? So why are they building a modern city next to Beersheba? Why are the Americans spending so much money there, at the edge of a desert?"

Elizabeth was puzzled. The answers to the questions seemed obvious. "My country committed to the peace process. We have our own construction crews involved, and we've committed to building there. It is the right thing to do, and the American people have supported the effort."

Shira turned and faced her friend. "But do your own people know who is paying for this new construction? And these people—these Americans—will see no direct benefit in anything they are doing in the Negev? They are building and constructing simply out of the goodness of their heart, with no other motive at all? Does that make sense to you?"

Elizabeth paused. She actually did believe that. Still, it was a fair question. After the United States invaded Iraq, toppled its dictator, and then installed a new, provisional government in the region, it had committed to large-scale construction in southern Iraq much like it had committed to building in the Negev.

In Iraq, the purpose of that vast American-led construction effort was to rebuild a country destroyed by back-to-back wars. Yet America now also had permanent, plentiful access to several of the largest supplies of oil anywhere in the world. Its construction efforts and partnership with both Iraq's new government and its national oil and gas infrastructure assured a permanent source of oil in a troubled region.

The American government had always maintained that access to Iraq's vast oil reserves was never part of the war equation. But the United States certainly was willing to take advantage of the situation in Iraq now that it had changed it through military force.

"I believe my country has honorable intentions," Elizabeth affirmed. "The Israeli government would not allow the building to go on there if it was not a serious effort."

"Oh, it is a serious effort," Shira said. "And perhaps, someday, it will be for the Palestinians. But in the event that it is not, and the peace process collapses again, then people say that the building in Beersheba will serve another very useful purpose."

"Another purpose?"

"I cannot say what it might be. But the Israelis—and the Americans—are not stupid. They build and plan, but they also prepare. Every settlement they've ever built has been that way. They build and plan with a purpose."

"But you have no guess as to what that might be?"

"I do not." Shira set the cups down on the table and took a seat. "But I can assure you that, if there is no peace, the Beersheba developments will be useful for something else. I am certain of it."

The water started to boil. Elizabeth took the instant coffee from Shira and scooped some of it into her cup. Shira grabbed a towel, wrapped it around the handle of the water pot, and poured the steaming water into their cups. The aroma of hot coffee was tantalizing—the perfect end to a very long, satisfying day in Aida.

"You seem awfully sure of your suspicions," Elizabeth said with a wan smile. "You have no hope for peace?"

"I always have hope for peace. But I also listen to what the people say, what they hear, what they believe as truth. Sometimes it is helpful just to watch what occurs and what is described, then wait to see what sort of reality and truth actually emerges."

Elizabeth had to grin. Shira, though she could not possibly have known it, had just neatly summarized a leading philosophical argument that social science scholars had studied for generations. Reality could be shaped by perceptions, and truth was often a difficult construct in a world where people relied on competing stories that defined what they saw.

Jerusalem was as good an example as any on the planet. Three competing world religions all saw the city that was a stone's throw from where they now sat as the epicenter of their faith, critical to their beliefs. Yet the city meant vastly different things to each, often in absolute, direct conflict to the simple truth on the ground.

Elizabeth nodded. "Wisely said, my friend. So you will wait on the peace process, to see what emerges, where it goes, and what might happen?"

"I will," Shira said. "It is what I know. I have waited for a generation for a proper homeland for my people, with Jerusalem as its capital. I can wait a little while longer."

SAUDI ARABIA

Riyadh

IRAN

Dammam
Dahran

QATAR

GULF OF OMAN

UNITED ARAB
EMIRATES

OMAN

39

Riyadh, Saudi Arabia

Nash was conflicted. Because he was the CEO of the mVillage network, he was able to see message trends streaming through the network that no one else could see. He was often in a position to see actions and events unfold in ways that no one else could. And when he saw something troubling, as he did now, he was often torn about what to do with that information.

The mVillage network was in near chaos. Hundreds, perhaps thousands, of reports were flooding in about the nuclear terrorist incident at the Saudi Aramco facility. The world oil markets were predicting that Saudi Arabia could lose up to two-thirds of its oil production for many months. The spot crude oil market was surging to stratospheric heights.

A series of oil field explosions had swept across southern Iraq overnight, setting back the efforts of several of the world's largest oil companies to bring a number of new oil reserves into the market. Analysts were saying that it might take years and new security to bring the oil fields back in the future. All of the mVillage reports were capturing the oil field fires at West Qurna.

No one had taken credit yet. But the world's largest oil companies were reeling from the attacks. They'd committed nearly $100 billion to develop the West Qurna oil fields following the American war in Iraq. And the attacks had set back those development efforts, perhaps by years, and caused untold damage to the world oil economy as a result.

Reports were spreading across the mVillage network of skirmishes and fights in Yemen, Saudi Arabia, and Iraq. It was as if unseen hands had deliberately reached out to stir pots in different parts of the world, setting one group against another.

It was hard to tell exactly who was angrier. Clearly, the Saudi royal family was reeling from the attacks at the heavily guarded Aramco facility. But the princes had largely been silent. And there had been no visible response yet.

The al Qaeda in Yemen faction had, predictably, taken credit for the Saudi attacks. The Saudi royal family had managed to keep video and pictures from emerging, but citizen reports streamed across the network about the radiation fallout and devastation at the facility.

Pakistan's military had begun to mobilize on two different borders. Because such a significant portion of what remained of the al Qaeda leadership was still in hiding in the rugged mountains of northern Pakistan, no one was quite certain what might happen next.

Iran's leadership, though, had remained strangely silent. Nash found that more than a little strange. They were usually quick to jump out with provocative statements. But the Revolutionary Guards Corps was nowhere to be found on the mVillage network reports, and Tehran was quiet.

American military forces had descended on southern Iraq to contain the oil field fires almost immediately, but they'd been unable to find anyone to pursue for the attacks there. It was almost as if ghosts had attacked, then vanished.

But none of these reports were troubling Nash. Messages about wars and rumors of wars streamed through the mVillage network on any given day. It was merely the nature of things in the modern era. Conflict was ever present in many parts of the world.

No, what was bothering Nash was a highly unusual report—actually, a series of reports that all pointed to roughly the same thing—that had him baffled. He couldn't imagine what it might mean. He wanted to check the report with someone. So, as he often did, Nash called his father.

But he was also desperate for new information on You Moon and

Kim Grace. He was still reeling from You Moon's text. Su had given him hope that they might be able to forestall the execution, which would occur within hours without some interference.

Nash hit the speed-dial number on his mobile without even thinking about what time it might be in Tokyo.

"Ambassador's residence," a voice answered an instant later.

"Hi, this is Nash Lee. I'm calling for my father, if he's in."

There was a pause at the other end. "You do realize that it's after midnight."

"I'm so sorry," Nash said. "I didn't realize. But I need to talk to my father."

"Well, I do believe he's still up, reading."

"If you can just check, please?"

After nearly a minute, there was a second *click*. His father's deep, rumbling voice came through clearly, startling Nash. "Is everything all right?"

"Yeah, Dad, no worries. I'm fine."

"But it's late."

"I know," Nash said quickly. "It's just that…"

As he often did, Ambassador Lee knew precisely what was on his son's mind and heart. "You're concerned about your two friends at Camp 16 in North Korea?" he said gently. "That's why you're calling."

"It is, Dad. Any news? Have you been able to reach the ambassador and the negotiating team there?"

His father grunted. "Well, yes. And I have some news. It took some doing. Our team on the ground there says the military wanted nothing to do with the calls, at first. But I kept insisting. I finally had to get our ambassador there involved directly. That shook things loose."

"And You Moon and Kim Grace? What will happen now?"

His father sighed. "They're now in the mix of the talks. The North Koreans will hold on to them and use them as they see fit."

"Which means?"

"That they've done this sort of thing before." Nash could hear the tiredness in his father's voice. "We pursue peace, and they use prisoners as pawns. In the past, they've used prisoner exchanges for food shipments or troop movements away from the demilitarized zone."

"And in this case?"

"Hard to tell. Usually, we're negotiating for the release of unfortunate hikers who happened to wander too close to the North Korean border and were caught. I know this is hard to imagine, but we've actually had to send in ex-presidents to meet with North Korean leaders in order to secure the release of ordinary prisoners."

"I remember some of those."

"But in this case, both You Moon and Kim Grace are North Koreans with very specific information about their military and security secrets. And in You Moon's case, he is also a personal, boyhood friend of the new leader. The military is going through gyrations to see how they can maximize this information for their own benefit."

"But they're okay? They won't be executed in the morning?"

"They're fine," his father said reassuringly. "The military leadership now sees that they have leverage in the talks with these two prisoners. They wouldn't dare execute them at the moment. They're valuable."

"Well, that's a relief."

His father was quiet on the other end of the line. His tone was somber when he spoke again. "Nash, there is something about all of this that I wanted you to realize."

"What, Dad?"

"You know me. I always tell you things in a direct fashion."

"Shoot, Dad. Give it to me straight."

"Okay. It's just this. The North Korean military leaders were looking for some leverage in our peace negotiations. They have a new leader, Pak Jong Un, who colored outside the lines when he met with President Camara directly, after the assassination of his father. The military can't control him. They needed some way in, something that gave them some measure of control over Pak Jong Un. And You Moon gives them that. Most likely, they used you to achieve that."

"I don't understand."

"They played you, Nash. The North Korean military may be ruthless, but they aren't stupid. They probably traced the first reports back to mVillage—the ones that allowed us to learn of their wicked nuclear ambitions that brought President Camara to Pyongyang in the first place. They knew You Moon had communicated with you. And that he would again, given an opportunity—and a reason."

"Okay, so?"

"So they probably allowed a new prisoner to bring another mobile into Camp 16, figuring he would connect. They then told You Moon that he would be executed—knowing he would reach out to you and trigger exactly what happened. Pak Jong Un's boyhood friend is now squarely in the middle of the peace talks, and the military feels they have some leverage over their young leader. The military needed a new chess piece. You Moon is that piece."

Nash took a deep breath. "Dad, I never imagined. I'm sorry. I just don't think like that. I got You Moon's text and simply reacted to save him."

"I know. It's perfectly normal. You're not a diplomat. You act swiftly and decisively. It's why you are so very good at what you do."

"But you're measured and deliberate," Nash said quietly. "And it's why you are so very good at what *you* do."

His father ignored the compliment. "Look, it's fine. We'll use this to our advantage. Truthfully, the news you gave us about their nuclear shipment plans is more than worth the trouble that this gave us in the talks. The North Korean military leaders didn't bargain on *that* piece of information winding up in our hands."

"Well, good. That's something, at least."

"It's more than something. We'll be able to track those shipments to Iran. And we'll be able to use that information in the talks, at the appropriate time. It's all good."

"You Moon and Kim Grace—what happens now?"

"They'll be safe at Camp 16 while the talks progress. They're not completely out of danger, though. If Pak Jong Un, for instance, is able to convince the military that he truly does not care about his boyhood friend, then I suppose that could change things. The military loses their leverage, and You Moon is vulnerable again."

"So can you move quickly?"

"We will, Nash. Don't worry. We're moving this along as fast as we can."

"All right. I'm sorry I caused trouble. But if it means You Moon and Kim Grace are released at some point, I'm going to call it a victory."

"You do that." His father laughed. "So was that it? Is that why you called?"

"That and something else I've been seeing on the mVillage network. It doesn't make sense. I thought you might be able to sort through it."

"Tell me."

"Just a few hours ago, we started to receive reports across the network that said roughly the same thing—farmers all across northern Yemen were gathering up horses and delivering them to a camp near the Saudi Arabian border. And on top of that, fighters—from different factions—were streaming in to that camp from across the country. The reports said that someone called *Yamani* had appeared in Yemen and was about to precede the reemergence of the Mahdi, the Twelfth Imam. What do you make of that? Does it mean something to you?"

"Not right now," his father answered. "But I can bet it will mean something to someone, once I've had a chance to relay the information. Are you comfortable with that? I know you always hesitate when you have information from the network."

"It's okay, Dad. This is information others can readily find. I'm not breaking any rules by telling you this. It's just that I'm seeing the reports from different places, and it will be a bit before others start to fit the pieces of the puzzle together."

"I understand. I'll let a few folks know, and we'll see what it means. In fact, I'll do that before I go to sleep. Right now, in fact."

"Great. And Dad—thanks. I mean it."

"I know you do, Nash. And you're welcome."

40

The White House
Washington, DC

DJ couldn't stand it any longer. He could actually *feel* himself being kept out of the loop. So he planted himself outside Susan Wright's office and waited. If need be, DJ vowed, he'd camp out there all day until Dr. Wright came by and gave him a couple minutes.

The administration professionals in the front office at the National Security Advisor's office liked DJ. They didn't mind that he was just hanging out. Actually, nearly everyone liked DJ. He was a living, breathing, walking example of the "relentless, positive storm" generation that was determined to remake the world. DJ, and those like him, didn't wait for opportunities. They made them.

"So how long, DJ?" asked one of the admin staff, a young woman who'd recently graduated from Georgetown's foreign service school and greatly admired DJ.

"How long?" DJ answered.

"How long will you wait here for Dr. Wright?"

"As long as it takes."

"And if she's tied up through the end of the day?"

DJ gave her a crooked smile. "Then I guess one of these chairs will have to do. You all will find me here first thing in the morning. I'm not moving until I get in to see Dr. Wright."

The admin staff laughed as one. They didn't doubt DJ. He actually *would* camp out until he'd gotten in to see Dr. Wright. So after a half hour, one of them took pity on him, checked Dr. Wright's schedule, moved another meeting back by fifteen minutes, and created an excuse for DJ to run into their boss in between meetings.

Susan Wright just shook her head as she walked into the front office, saw DJ leaning up against the wall off to the side of the room, then caught the eye of one of the admin staff beckoning her over to her desk.

"Dr. Wright, you had some time before your next meeting, and we…"

Wright held up a hand. "I understand. You created a few minutes on my schedule so DJ could see me?"

"Yes, Dr. Wright, I hope that's all right with you?"

Wright turned and gave DJ a big smile. She liked the deputy White House press secretary for national security nearly as much as her front office professionals. "For DJ, anything." She walked toward her office briskly, her high heels clicking loudly on the wood floor. "But make it quick, DJ. I have only a few minutes."

"That's all I need, Dr. Wright." DJ followed along in the deputy national security advisor's wake. He closed the door behind him as they moved into her office.

"So?" Wright asked him. She scanned the phone messages on the top of her desk before turning her attention back to DJ. "What's on your mind?"

DJ jumped right in. "I hear they're about to name you national security advisor."

"From whom?"

"Does it matter? Is it right? A reporter from the *New York Times* has been stalking me all day."

"You know I can't confirm that, even if it's true. That comes from Anshel or from the president. Certainly not from me."

"So it *is* true." DJ grunted. "I thought so. Some of us could see it coming from across the room. Your boss just kept getting sideways with the president and—"

"DJ!" Wright said sharply. "I don't want to go there. I like you, but I don't traffic in gossip about others. You know that. So we're not going there. The relationship my boss may or may not have with the president is none of my business. And it's none of yours."

DJ nodded. To be honest, he liked that about Dr. Wright. He respected the fact that she lived, breathed, walked, and talked her beliefs on both a personal and professional level. That wasn't easy to do in Washington. "Got it," he said. "And I respect that. But I will say this. Some of us saw this coming, whether you want to talk about it or not."

"Understood. And no, I will not talk about it."

"So are you going to be named the national security advisor?" DJ pressed.

Dr. Wright smiled. "I would advise that you go ask Anshel that question. And good luck with that. Is there anything else?"

"Yeah, of course. But I'd been meaning to ask you about the job, so I thought I'd get that out of the way first."

"Okay, it's out of the way. What's next?"

"White flags," DJ said. "I keep hearing about white flags, some guy called Yamani, and this guy you referred to as the Twelfth Imam in your briefing, or the Mahdi, or something like that. And that maybe they're connected to the attacks on the Saudi oil complex, the West Qurna oil fields in southern Iraq, and maybe even the uprisings in Yemen. And that there was a secret meeting between al Qaeda's leadership and the Supreme Leader in Iran. Maybe a deal between the Shi'a and Sunni factions. So what gives?"

"Wow." Dr. Wright smiled. "That's a lot of questions."

"Well, I feel totally out of the loop," DJ said wistfully. "And you know me. When I'm out of the loop this badly, the press thinks I'm flat-out lying to them when I say I don't know anything."

"But isn't it better not to know some things?"

"No," DJ said firmly. "It's not. You and I have talked about this. I need to know these sorts of things. That gives me the chance to deal with it correctly with the press. I've got a good relationship with the main reporters who cover national security in this administration. They know that, when there's a subject I can't talk about, I just tell them I won't talk about it."

"Okay, fine," Dr. Wright said. "So which question first?"

"The white flags. What gives with that?"

"I don't know, exactly. We do have some intelligence reports about a shipment of white flags and double-edged swords that were discovered on board a ship that one of our carriers intercepted from pirates off the coast of Somalia."

"Double-edged swords, like Zulfiqars?"

"Yes, they're known as God's Swords," Dr. Wright said. "There are legends in the masses about a legion of fighters, carrying Zulfiqars and white and black flags, who race on horseback to take Mecca. Soldiers carrying black flags come from the north, while soldiers with white flags come from the south. They're led by Yamani, who paves the way for the reemergence of the Twelfth Imam."

DJ frowned. "I heard you talk about some of this in your briefing. But seriously, that's insane. Flags and double-edged swords in a world where nuclear weapons make their way into the hands of unstable regimes?"

"I know. It makes no sense. But it is what it is. And I will say this—though it's not the sort of thing you should repeat to your reporter friends..."

"They're not friends," DJ shot back. "It's my job to talk to them and keep them informed enough so they don't go out of their way to harm us."

"Fine. I'm glad it's your job, not mine. But we do have reports of horses being brought to a camp in northern Yemen by farmers. There are reports on the ground of someone they're calling *Yamani* in one of the camps. Combine that with the reports of the white flags and the Zulfiqars on that ship, and you see why we're at least curious."

"Is it true that Sa'id Nouradeen is in Yemen?" DJ asked.

"True, and we have at least two reports that people are calling him this Yamani character."

"Yikes," DJ said swiftly. "That can't be good. So what's the chance that they're going to ride to Mecca?"

"Who knows?" Dr. Wright shrugged. "With everything that's going on in that region, I wouldn't want to predict. The Saudis are beside themselves."

"Which reminds me—one of Secretary Moran's folks told me about an aborted attack at Dulles—on a Saudi prince or envoy who was flying here to meet with us about some new line of succession to the grandsons in the House of Saud."

Dr. Wright pursed her lips. "You shouldn't know about that."

"Dr. Wright," DJ said, visibly trying to control his anger, "remember what I said about how it's more harmful when I *don't* know about something?"

"I know, but DJ, we really don't want folks to hear about that. You know our policy about stopping terrorist attacks on American soil."

"I know. It didn't happen, until and unless someone hears about it and makes it public. But did it happen? Did we stop a terrorist attack against one of the Saudi princes?"

Dr. Wright took a deep breath and stared at DJ as if trying to decide whether to trust him. Finally she spoke. "Not just any Saudi prince. The target was Muhammad al Faisal."

"The governor of Mecca?"

"And the person that Secretary Moran believes is now in line to become the next king of Saudi Arabia. He's about to be named as the new minister of the interior and eventually the crown prince."

"And that's who they tried to take out?"

"Yes. But no one knows any of this. We'd like to keep it that way."

"I'll bet," DJ said. "But that means someone in the House of Saud wasn't happy about the succession plan and they probably triggered the attack here."

"Precisely. And with the attack against the Aramco complex, it's gotten an awful lot more complicated."

"Where is Prince Muhammad now?"

"He met briefly with Secretary Moran, and he's headed back to Mecca as we speak."

"And if there's this crazy ride to Mecca?"

"Then he'll be there when they arrive."

DJ started pacing. "And the reports about the meeting between al Qaeda and the IRGC in Tehran, with the Supreme Leader—are they true?"

"You're pushing the envelope here. You know that would be well beyond something I could confirm with you."

"So it's true as well," DJ mused. "Wow. I've always thought it was only a matter of time before al Qaeda threw their lot in with Iran's leaders. They have a common enemy in Saudi Arabia. They were only going to stand clear of the kingdom for so long."

Dr. Wright nodded. "They're not standing clear of the kingdom now, that's for sure."

"The Twelfth Imam stuff or the Mahdi—any truth to that?"

"Who knows? And that's the truth. I don't know. I'm not sure anyone does at this point. We'll have to see how this plays out."

"So the Saudis…what do they have to push back against Iran? We've never heard a whiff of any effort to create a nuclear weapons capability—not ever. They've always relied on the United States to take military action when it gets hot. Like the Kuwait invasion, right across the water. They leaned on us to take care of that threat. Have they asked for our help?" DJ asked.

"They have, but only partially. They take the attack on Prince Muhammad and the Aramco complex as a declaration of war on the kingdom from Iran. I couldn't begin to predict what their response might be. But if I had to guess, it won't be a diplomatic one."

"But their options—it's not like they have many."

"We'll see," Dr. Wright said quietly. "I'm always surprised at the layers that get peeled back at times like this."

41

Azadegan Oil Field
Southern Iran

"It's a no-brainer. We get three for the price of one," the Saudi operative told his colleague privately as they drove by truck to the southeastern corner of Iraq.

The two Saudi operatives had chucked their UN "blue helmets" into the Iraqi desert once they'd passed the US-sponsored checkpoints in southern Iraq. Security was tightening as a result of the bombings at the West Qurna fields, but the two Saudi operatives had been in the field for years. They were able to travel toward the Iraq-Iran border with little trouble. The UN peacekeeping outfits had helped but were no longer necessary.

They were now dressed in a casual, nondescript manner. They didn't particularly want to attract attention to themselves. Not yet, at least.

The inside of the truck was littered with gear, maps, and papers that would clearly tie it to Jundallah, the notorious Sunni opposition group that the United States had only recently placed on its terrorist list after years of allegations that the US had financially supported Jundallah's efforts to violently oppose Iran's regime.

The two operatives had been gathering artifacts for the better part of a year for just such an event and need. Jundallah would be blamed.

Neither had known whether they'd ever need the artifacts. But as they drove toward a point at the Iraqi border where they could safely cross into southern Iran and head for Azadegan—the largest oil field in Iran, recently discovered—both were glad they'd put in the time to gather the artifacts.

One of the operatives peered over his shoulder toward the back of the truck and the precious cargo. Even the cargo had been carefully concealed to appear as if it had originated elsewhere—in this case from the bowels of a facility somewhere in North Korea with some old Russian parts thrown in for good measure.

Postmortems would likely tie the truck's contents to the IRGC efforts in Iran to secure nuclear weapons capabilities from North Korea's scientists. The speculation would be that the Jundallah terrorists, with US backing, had secured the cargo on the black market inside Iran.

The operatives had received their orders directly from the Saudi crown prince himself, without an intermediary. The handoff of the cargo had come to them from the personal plane of the crown prince. Just one pilot and one technician had been aboard that flight.

"So how do you figure?" the other operative asked.

"Obviously, we take out Iran's greatest hope, the Azadegan oil fields," the first operative said. "If this works, they won't be able to go anywhere near these fields for years."

"Okay, fine," said the second operative. "But that's our primary mission. What are the other two?"

"The US will be blamed for the attack. Everyone, Iran included, knows that the United States has been supporting Jundallah financially since 2003..."

"The United States denies that," the second operative countered.

"Yeah, right." The first snorted. "Like we haven't been supporting al Qaeda all these years to keep them away from the kingdom."

"True."

"The American CIA might as well have planted the bombs themselves when Jundallah targeted Iran's Revolutionary Guards Corps at the mosque and killed all those people. Every high-profile bombing inside Iran that Jundallah is responsible for has the Americans' hand-prints all over it. This will be no different."

"Perhaps," the second operative said. "We shall see. So what's the third?"

"China's national oil company has put a considerable amount of financing into Azadegan already. The Chinese will go crazy after this. They'll go right after the United States."

"How do you figure?"

"They'll assume Jundallah secured the nuclear components—and the portable device that can set something off—with US help. No one in their right minds will imagine Saudi Arabia had a hand in it."

"But we *do* have a hand in it. The world may think we haven't been quietly working on a portable nuclear device that can be deployed." The second operative gestured toward the back of the truck. "Yet, here we are, with precisely such a device."

"Yes, but the markings are North Korean and old, forgotten Russian parts. There's no way, not in a million years, that anyone will be able to trace this back to the kingdom. At best, it will come back to Iran's sloppy acquisition of nuclear technology. At worst, China will accuse the US of aiding and abetting Jundallah in their violent opposition to the IRGC. In neither case will any of this come back at us."

"Nothing is impossible," the second operative said evenly.

"Which is why we're being careful now—and why we've always been extraordinarily careful to mask any efforts to explore nuclear capabilities all these years. We don't have facilities, and we don't have nuclear scientists."

"But we *do* have people who can deploy something that's already been built," the second said.

"Precisely. We don't need to build or invent. We only need to acquire. And as we've seen, money can buy almost anything."

The two operatives drove in silence toward the Iraqi border. Once they were inside Iran, it wouldn't be difficult to get to the Azadegan oil fields and deliver their cargo.

From there, they'd travel to the southern tip of Iran in a second vehicle coming from a different, undisclosed direction. From there, they'd board a speedboat that could safely carry them away from the scene.

The covert operation was bold but fairly easy. Covering their tracks was the most difficult part. They just needed to ensure that everything left behind after the blast pointed directly at the North Korean nuclear weapons technology and then to the US support for the Jundallah organization that had previously bombed IRGC soldiers.

If they did their jobs right, no one would suspect—or blame—the Saudis.

The two operatives had no interest in the geopolitics of the moment. They didn't care that the decision had been made by the Saudi king and crown prince to retaliate against Iran's complicity in the attack at the Saudi Aramco complex. All they knew was that they had a job to do and that they needed to do it well and carefully.

They slowed the truck as their GPS coordinates told them they were crossing over into Iran. But there was no real need for undue caution. The land looked the same, on either side of the border. They maintained a safe, easy speed to Azadegan.

Once there, they drove to the point on their handheld GPS devices that, they were told, the blast from their cargo would have maximum impact. The first operative parked the truck, while the second climbed into the back to make sure that nothing had become dislodged on the trip there.

They checked and double-checked the two cell phones that would serve as a primary and backup trigger. Everything was ready. Even better, they'd only seen a couple of other trucks in the region as they'd made their way to the pre-chosen location.

The two operatives walked away from the vast Azadegan oil field complexes. Nearly an hour later, they were met by the second vehicle, with a single driver. Once safely on board, they headed toward the southern Iranian coast.

"So, is it time?" the second operative asked as they raced away from the massive Azadegan oil field.

"It is," said the first.

He dialed the number on the primary cell phone. The number rang. An instant later, there was a muffled blast in the distance and a small mushroom cloud spread heavenward.

"It is done," said the first operative. "We are avenged."

MARYLAND

Baltimore

WEST
VIRGINIA

Washington, D.C.

VIRGINIA

42

The Capitol Building
Washington, DC

Jennifer Moran dreaded these meetings with the Gang of Eight at the Capitol building.

First, there was the necessity of meeting in the sound-proofed, bomb-resistant, windowless room in the basement of the Capitol building. Then there was the smallness of the room itself.

While the eight congressional leaders were not allowed to bring aides to these briefings, the room barely accommodated nine or ten people. It was very close quarters.

But today's briefing to the Gang of Eight at the Capitol would be especially difficult. There were so many conflicts breaking out at various parts of the globe that she didn't even know where to begin.

The event that had triggered the requirement to meet at the Capitol was the most recent attack in southern Iran. The highly classified intelligence briefs, which she would share with the leaders at the Capitol today, placed the blame for the attacks on the radical Sunni Jundallah terrorist group that opposed Iran's leadership.

But Moran wasn't convinced. And there were doubts expressed in both the CIA and NSA briefs as well. It was too easy. She and others felt that Jundallah was an easy patsy.

The problem was compounded by the fact that a few rogue members of Jundallah had swiftly, almost gleefully, taken credit for the nuclear terrorist attack through posts on the mVillage network. This always happened with attacks of this sort. Everyone was always quick to take credit—whether they were responsible or not.

But that was only the beginning of her problems. She also felt compelled to bring the congressional leaders up to speed on the fast-moving developments elsewhere. At least two of the congressional leaders had already asked her about the follow-up actions to the Saudi Aramco attack.

They'd also demanded to know the American response to the attack against West Qurna in southern Iraq. Between the near-simultaneous attacks on oil fields or complexes in Aramco, Iraq, and Iran, the congressional leaders had told her in confidence that they felt like the desperate threat to oil on a global basis had triggered the most severe threat to US interests in the Middle East in a generation.

"What will the president do?" one of them had asked her in a confidential communiqué as a precursor to today's briefing. "Is he prepared to send troops back into Iraq to protect our oil interests there?"

But the big question that half of the congressional leaders had posed to her and the White House was the obvious, growing challenge to the peace process. Saudi Arabia had laid the blame for Aramco at Iran's doorstep. It was hard to tell who would ultimately take credit, or blame, for the attack in Iraq, but both Iran and Saudi Arabia were engaged in furious, back-channel finger-pointing.

And now, with the Jundallah incident, Iran was blaming Saudi Arabia—even if the Saudis could plausibly deny they were behind it.

Moran walked into the room. The Gang of Eight, all but one of them men, was already seated.

"So was it Jundallah?" one of them asked even as Moran was removing her coat and taking a seat at the head of the briefing table.

"We don't know yet," she answered. "The NSA and CIA briefs are in your—"

"We've seen them," one of the congressional leaders interrupted. "But we want to hear it from you. What's going on here, Madame Secretary?"

"Yes, are we seeing the beginning of an armed conflict between Iran and Saudi Arabia?" demanded another, pounding his fist on the table angrily to emphasize his point. "Is this the Shi'a-Sunni war we've all been afraid of for years?"

"And is the president prepared to stand tough with Iran in the peace talks?" asked another. "He's been lukewarm in his support of Israel in the past, as we all know. Will he shield Israel when the Arab world inevitably blames it for one or more of these attacks?"

Moran took a deep breath. At times like this she longed for the day she could retire from public life and just play board games with her grandchildren. *Very soon,* she thought. *Soon I will be free of these egotistical maniacs.*

"We are looking at each and every possibility and course of action closely," she said calmly. "We have recently redeployed our naval assets to the Mediterranean, the Red Sea, and the northern waters of the Persian Gulf in the event that any of these conflicts escalate."

"Fine," said one of the leaders, "but what will the president *do* if one of these conflicts gets out of hand?"

"And what will he do now to deal with the collapse of the global oil economy?" asked another. "The price of crude is going through the roof. Every business in America—not to mention homeowners and drivers— is going to scream bloody murder at us to do something about it."

"We can't control crude oil pricing or the price of a gallon of gas, as you all know," Moran said soothingly. "Let us be realistic, at least in this room. What you all say to your constituents is another matter. But in here, we need to see the picture clearly, without bias."

"Well, that picture is awfully bleak," offered a fifth leader, who'd been quiet. "So do you have any sort of plan in mind?"

"Actually," Moran said, "I do have some good news. And for at least half of you in this room from the other party, you will likely welcome it. The former vice president from a previous administration who sits on the board of Aladdin Oil has informed us that the new refinery in the Negev is going live even as we speak. They will be refining oil from the Shfela Basin near Jerusalem any moment. The technology is proven, the refinery is built, the Ashkelon-Eilat pipeline is now a two-way pipeline, and the Ceyhan terminal in southern Turkey is ready to start taking shipments from the Caspian Sea oil companies as well. We're at a point where we don't need to rely on the Arab states."

"Thank goodness for that!" one of the leaders said loudly. "At least someone is doing something. Raney always said this thing would work, both here and out west with our own deep oil shale reserves. So we have a shot at dealing with this, even if the Arab states blow sky-high."

"See?" Moran said with a broad smile. "I told you that at least half of you would find this welcome news. Now, some of us still see massive environmental unknowns in this oil shale technology. It's proven, but we're somewhat uncertain on the risks."

"Oh, come on!" one of the leaders said, his face red. "Let me guess. The EPA is going to slap a newfangled regulation on the refining process out west, just because they don't understand the heating process. And right when we need the ability to pull this oil out ourselves. We *need* this technology, and this oil."

"You know," Moran said evenly, "if you all had just committed to clean energy technology sources like solar, wind, and geothermal a few years ago while we still had time, we wouldn't be in this position right now where we have to allow unproven oil-extracting technology out the door."

Thankfully, before the conversation degenerated into the age-old war between the two parties over energy security in the United States—a fight that had been stalemated for more than a decade over whether Congress would invest in clean energy sources or continue to protect the carbon-intensive, fossil-fuel energy sources like oil, coal, and gas—another leader raised her hand.

"So what is this we're hearing about the Twelfth Imam?" she asked. "Is it true, these reports? Did Ali bin Rahman really meet with Reverend Shahidi in Tehran, and is that possibility real?"

"As real as we can imagine," Moran responded, glad for the diversion. "We have no way of knowing the truth behind the news that bin Rahman delivered. But we know that Iran's president certainly believes in the imminent return of the Twelfth Imam. So if such a person shows up, who's to say how he is received? If someone calling himself the Caliph of God appears at the Jamkaran Mosque on the outskirts of Tehran, or in Mecca, who's to say how he will be received?"

"So it's a serious possibility?" the leader pressed.

"As serious as anything else we're dealing with right now," Moran answered. "Time will tell if bin Rahman has a person in his back pocket, and whether the world will buy that this person is the Mahdi, or the Twelfth Imam. We'll deal with that if, or when, it presents itself."

"Don't you think the president should be preparing for that sort of event right now?" the leader asked. "I can't imagine a more destabilizing event in the Arab world than the claim that some pan-Islamic religious authority has shown up in Mecca to lead a new series of revolts. The events of the Arab Spring might be considered child's play if the Arab world gets stirred up by this sort of a figure."

"As I said, we'll deal with it," Moran said firmly. "But I would argue that we need to take these things one at a time. At the present, we're focused on stabilizing our national energy security. Then we'll turn to the regional conflicts erupting in Iraq, Iran, and Saudi Arabia. After that, we'll see if we have to deal with this Twelfth Imam character."

"Fine," the leader of the party that opposed the president said rather loudly. "But I will tell you this. We here in this room, all eight of us, talked among ourselves before you arrived. We plan to call an emergency joint session of Congress to deal with all of this mess if the president does not address it to our satisfaction."

"We have this in hand," Moran said firmly. "The president is the commander in chief, not Congress. We will act, in all of the various regional conflicts."

"Yes, but we declare war—not the president," the leader said. "And we also control the purse strings."

"You don't need to remind me," Moran said. "I'm well aware of the War Powers Act and the fact that Congress approves our budget."

"Good," the leader said. "So please, convey our concerns to President Camara. We're serious about this joint session of Congress. We need to see firm action on his part."

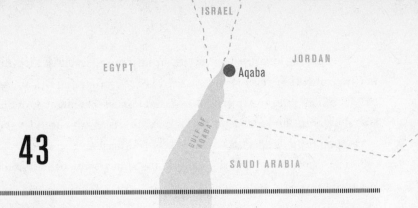

ISRAEL

EGYPT

JORDAN

Aqaba

GULF OF AQABA

SAUDI ARABIA

43

Aqaba, Jordan

General Fahd's inaugural broadcast was awkward, to say the least. He had no idea who might have been listening or how it would be received. He created the audio file, then posted it to a new mVillage account that would feed the many student-led accounts of gossip and political intrigue that careened around freely across the network.

His mVillage account, like the students, was private and anonymous. The Saudi royal family had no access to the mVillage network accounts, though they might have some ability to keep track of the actual mobile numbers.

But he didn't care. It would be known soon enough that he was becoming the voice of an impromptu call for Day of Anger protests in Dammam, Qatif, Medina, Mecca, and even Riyadh in Saudi Arabia. Fahd did not care if they knew where the audio files had originated. Natal wanted the Saudi leadership to know that he was their voice, for his own reasons.

Fahd had promised Natal that he would become the voice of the disaffected in the kingdom. And he was a man of his word.

The words had been carefully scripted. Someone working for Natal in the White Army's intelligence network had pulled files and pictures from mVillage accounts. They'd created a backstory for him, the concept of a new movement tied to the old kingdom of Hejaz, and even a new flag for the movement that was drawn from the old pan-Islamic Arab Revolt flag.

They'd even managed to dig up information recently filed on mVillage about the imminent return of the last, remaining heir to the old Ottoman Empire—a retired librarian named Mehmet Osman, who'd lived in exile in London nearly all of his days—who would make a special appearance in Mecca on the Day of Anger.

Fahd had no idea where any of this information came from, whether it was credible or not, and whether the Saudis would take it seriously. But he also knew enough about the paranoia that often swept through the ranks of the Saudi royal family that it wouldn't take much to tip them over the edge and trigger an overreaction on their part.

The mere fact that a retired Saudi general, in exile but available, who'd once commanded the White Army, would broadcast a call to arms and uprising would almost certainly cause panic in Riyadh. This was precisely why Natal had selected Fahd for the task.

Perception would quickly become reality. No "Free the Kingdom Army" remotely existed as Fahd created his audio broadcast and launched it out onto the chaotic waters of the mVillage network. But Fadh's urgent message about the need to unite the disaffected and oppressed minorities in Saudi Arabia would send the Riyadh leadership into a frenzy.

Fahd wondered, almost in passing, whether they'd send someone after him. But he was old and no longer cared about that. And even if that happened, Natal would likely be the one tasked with such a covert mission on his life.

So General Fahd finished his audio broadcast calling on the "Free the Kingdom Army" to mobilize around the coming Day of Anger and sent it out to the mVillage network.

The audio had been replayed within the hour for both the king and crown prince of the House of Saud in Riyadh. And shortly thereafter, Natal had been called into the king's office with new orders. He obeyed some of them and ignored others.

44

The Ministry of National Infrastructures
Jerusalem, Israel

Abe Zeffren was baffled. Nothing was making a great deal of sense.

When he'd first become Israel's deputy oil commissioner, his mother had been proud. She'd told all of his friends and extended family about the appointment. Never mind that no one discovered oil in Israel, or that the country was wholly dependent on imports for its energy needs and likely would be so for as long as anyone could imagine.

Abe was serious about his job. He'd done everything in his power to encourage legitimate energy exploration companies, make connections that could lead to novel energy sources, and serve as a cheerleader for companies that wanted to drill one dry hole after another in and around northern Israel.

But he was also a realist. He'd long ago come to terms with the fact that, while Arab nations were flush with oil wealth, palaces, and lifestyles of opulence even as they told their own people about how they would one day defeat Israel on one battlefield or another, Israel had no oil wealth and had to carve a place for itself in a land mostly barren of any rich natural resources.

It always seemed more than a little ironic to Abe that Israel was so powerful in the midst of such wealth in the region. He'd often wondered how the world might be different if the tables had been turned.

Abe kept close track of the world's oil and gas economies. He felt like it was part of his job, even if the country itself had no ability to play in such vast export markets. He read the reports online, day after day. He tracked developments on that global media network, mVillage.

And the world was buzzing, spinning, churning, and whirling right now. Word was leaking out in myriad directions about a terrorist attack on the vaunted Saudi Aramco oil complex. News of the attack had sent crude oil prices soaring.

Then there had been word of an attack at the huge West Qurna oil reserve fields in southern Iraq. Abe knew enough to realize that this was an enormous setback for several large oil companies that had hoped the US military war in Iraq had secured a new source of oil there. That effort was now delayed, perhaps for years.

And just this morning there was word of a third body blow to the world's oil economy, a shocking nuclear suitcase attack against the largest oil fields recently discovered in Iran, the vast Azadegan oil field that the Chinese, Russians, and Japanese had just begun to develop.

Like West Qurna, the world's oil powers had hoped that Azadegan would bring new crude oil markets into play. But those efforts would be set back for years as Iran dealt with the nuclear radiation fallout in the region.

Three actions and three significant Arab oil regions were crippled, potentially for years. Abe had never seen, or imagined, anything like this. It was as if some unseen force had simply decided to act against three Arab nation-states all at once. Abe knew that wasn't really possible. But it still seemed odd that Saudi Arabia, Iraq, and Iran would suddenly find themselves struggling to supply the world's oil.

But as disturbing as these actions were to the world's oil economy, they weren't what had Abe confused. No, what was baffling was the steady flow of e-mails and messages raining down on his office in the past twenty-four hours. He was hearing from everyone, from the prime minister's office and aides at the White House in America to Russian Prime Minister Andrei Rowan's office and the Chinese prime minister's office in Beijing.

All were asking the same sets of questions, none of which Abe had any ready answers to supply. Was the Shfela Basin secure? Had the oil reserves been calculated there to any degree? Was there adequate infrastructure that would allow oil mined from there to head south or west? Was the Haifa oil terminal secure? Was there infrastructure at Eilat? Was the pipeline now running both ways between Haifa and Eilat? Who had filed paperwork at the ministry?

Abe had grown accustomed to tracking developments to the world's oil export markets, analyzing them and sending them along for members of the Knesset and the prime minister's office to read about—or ignore, which seemed much more likely.

The sudden explosion of interest in information about Israel's oil and gas infrastructure, its capacity, or its ability to secure passage of oil inside the country's borders had happened swiftly, with no advance warning. Someone, somewhere, had seemingly placed a very large gambling bet on the table. And that table was Israel.

The Russians were especially insistent. Abe had no less than a dozen requests for information from various parts of government agencies in and around Moscow. In fact, there were now so many requests from that part of the world that he'd asked for help from one of the other departments in the same office complex. For whatever reason, someone in Russia was awfully interested in Israel's capacity and infrastructure surrounding its natural resources.

Abe wasn't lazy. But the surge in interest was beyond anything he'd ever seen, even though he'd glimpsed, with his own eyes, the work on the oil pipeline, the beginning of the refining plant in the Negev, and the research underway at the Shfela Basin.

But he couldn't bring himself to believe that Israel, after so many years of being the poor cousin at the party, would find itself the center of attention from wealthy individuals and companies that hoped to explore and build something around natural resources there.

So as he always did when he had too many questions—and far too few answers—Abe decided he'd start his own relentless campaign to get access to information. He'd decide later what to do with that information once it had been assembled.

Abe turned on his computer and sifted through each of the e-mails that had piled up in his inbox over the past twenty-four hours or so. For each e-mail, he fired back more questions in the opposite direction. Russia wanted to know about INOC.

Fine, Abe thought. *I want to know about Russia, and why it has suddenly decided to pay attention to a country that it has never truly had in its sights.*

The American White House wanted to know about the terminal at Eilat, and whether it was secure.

No problem, Abe thought. *I'd like to know what the White House knows about a company called Aladdin Oil and Gas, a subsidiary of another American company that includes uber-wealthy individuals like Wolf Corps' K. Robert Moorhead and a former vice president of the United States.*

Turkish officials wanted to know the status of the oil terminals at Haifa, and whether they were equipped to handle an influx of oil or gas shipments.

Wonderful, Abe thought. *I'd like to know why Turkey, after months of tough talk, has suddenly decided to play its NATO card and seek information about how it might again work with Israeli authorities outside military channels.*

The Chinese wanted to know the status of US peacekeeping and infrastructure improvements in and around Beersheba and its road improvements throughout the Negev desert.

Well, then, Abe thought, *I'd like to know why the Chinese government, after arming our enemies with cruise missiles, planes, and other assorted military exports, is suddenly taking an interest in our affairs? Where in the world did that interest come from? Would oil make its way through Israel and then to China?*

The world's largest private oil companies wanted to know about technology permits needed for one thing or another.

Great, Abe thought, *but what I'd really like to know is why anyone in their right mind would suddenly find anything in Israel worth investing in when they'd paid no attention to the country's natural resources for a generation.*

Abe didn't move for hours. He simply fired off one e-mail after another. For every question posed from one corner of the world or another, Abe fired back three more questions.

He kept his speculation in check as he wrote. He made very few declarative statements in the e-mails. Mostly, he asked questions, one after another. Some sounded downright ridiculous on the surface. But, Abe knew, the most outlandish questions occasionally produced the most unexpected answers.

Abe became so absorbed in his one-man crusade to make sense out of a world that had seemingly descended on his doorstep overnight that he lost all track of time. By the time he'd pressed SEND on his last e-mail to some remote corner of the world that had written to inquire about Israel's oil and gas infrastructure, the sun had already set. His office had grown dark.

So Abe switched on the crummy desk lamp that he rarely used and waited for answers. He read mVillage network reports from around the world. He created new electronic file folders on his computer's desktop while he waited for the world to come to him.

And when the answers began to stream into his computer from around the globe, Abe sat back at his desk and absorbed them. People were willing to speculate about all sorts of interesting things. Sometimes, asking the questions was enough.

As the night advanced, Abe started a new round of memos. But this time, they weren't merely responses to e-mail queries from around the globe. Abe was armed with a few facts of his own, as well as a handful of educated guesses.

The last memo he created was to the executive assistant to Israel's prime minister, Judah Navon. Abe had learned long ago that the route to power advanced through the administrative offices. For this reason, and the fact he was a nice person, Abe had befriended the prime minister's executive assistant in the past two years. She always received Abe's regular memos and promised that the prime minister would receive them. Whether he read them or not was another question.

But Abe put in a special request with this particular memo, asking the assistant to make sure that Navon read the confidential assessment attached. It was important, Abe had written. When he finally turned off his computer, Abe was satisfied. He'd done his job and provided his best assessment of a unique, unfolding situation.

What others did with that information was well beyond his pay grade—despite what his mother might believe and tell her friends.

45

The Gulf of Aden

"Seriously? Those are my orders?"

Captain Bingham rarely questioned his orders. And when he did, it certainly wasn't over the airwaves. Granted, this was a secure communications line, and they could speak freely.

Vice Admiral Truxton knew his orders seemed crazy, so he repeated them. "Yes, Captain Bingham, your orders are to take the *McCain* past Djibouti and into the Red Sea. Make your way up the coastline in Yemen and then Saudi Arabia. Send your planes out when you can."

"Into Saudi Arabia?"

"Yes, into the Saudi mainland."

"And what, exactly, am I looking for?"

"Any evidence of cavalry movement northward, toward Mecca."

"Okay, but I want to make certain I heard that correctly. I'm looking for *cavalry* movements?"

Truxton smiled to himself. Bingham was a very good sailor. He could understand why he was questioning his orders. But he also knew that Bingham would carry them out without question and deliver results.

"Yes, Captain, you're looking for cavalry movements," Truxton said dryly.

Bingham paused. "You *do* realize, sir, that cavalry, well...it sort of died out after the First World War."

"Yes, Captain, I'm well aware of that fact," Truxton said. "I studied at the Naval Academy, too. But if you remember, there was some limited cavalry use during the Second World War."

"And they have tanks now," Bingham added.

Truxton heard the laughter edging Bingham's voice. "I understand. Can you just get moving, please?" Truxton was already trying to move different boats around the region. The vice admiral was simultaneously deploying ships to the northern waters of the Persian Gulf due to the two actions in southern Iraq and Iran.

Now the joint chiefs had given him a highly unusual order. He was to move a handful of ships up the Suez Canal and into the Mediterranean.

The joint chiefs told him there wasn't time to move ships around Africa into the Mediterranean. They needed a presence near Cypress immediately. He'd asked about Cypress. The answer back had been cryptic. The orders would be forthcoming, they'd told him, and involved both Haifa and Turkey.

"Yes, sir, right away," Bingham answered. "But can I ask you something? Does this have anything to do with the strange cargo we discovered in the possession of the Harardhere pirates a few days ago?"

Truxton sighed. "Honestly, I couldn't tell you yet. I'm waiting on orders myself. But my guess is that it does. They seem connected."

"White flags and double-edged swords?"

"Yes, as crazy as this sounds, they're connected to the actions we've seen in both Yemen and the Saudi Aramco complex."

"Really?"

"Yes, really," Truxton said. "We're starting to get all kinds of strange reports about movements."

"Like?"

"Like their goal is to reach Mecca."

"And when they get there?"

"Who knows?" Truxton stated. "We've had folks doing some research. There are legends about an appearance of the Mahdi—or the Twelfth Imam, depending on the source—who arrives at Mecca just as cavalry storms the place and hands the empire over to him."

"So let me guess," Bingham said. "They're carrying white flags and these Zulfiqars?"

"Yes, something like that."

"And the Saudis would stand for that?"

"Hardly. But we've seen stranger things recently. Who'd have thought that students with cell phones could cause so much trouble in capitals around the world recently?"

"I guess," Bingham replied. "But still…"

"I know, but the thing we must pin down is whether there is a cavalry effort massing and about to move up the coastline in Saudi territory. You are our best hope of tracking that. You can send unmanned drones in with eyes. So I need you there, as soon as you move."

"Will do. But you also realize that horses, at best, can only cover twenty or thirty miles a day. It's at least 250 miles from the Yemen-Saudi border. If someone was sending a cavalry up the coastline, we'd have days and days to find it. There's no way they'd escape our coverage."

"I know," Truxton said. "I told that to the joint chiefs. But they told me they didn't care, and that we needed to get eyes in there as soon as possible. But you're right. My guess is that, if something is about to happen, it's going to come off a cargo ship that unloads along the coast of Saudi Arabia."

"So you want to look for that?"

"Yes, please," Truxton said. "That Harardhere pirate nest you tripped across recently was our best clue. They've probably secured a ship, and they're going to deliver live cargo along the coastline—within a day from Mecca." Truxton glanced at the maps on his office wall. "I'd look south of Jeddah. That's the closest, straight line to Mecca from the Red Sea."

"And if I find a ship that's carrying horses and soldiers?"

"Then they're most likely our guys," Truxton said.

"Should I engage?"

"If they're pirates, yes. And if they're still on board."

"And if they're flagged forces—like Yemeni?"

"Then check with me."

"What if they've already made it to land and they're on their way toward Mecca?"

Truxton grunted. "Then it becomes a Saudi problem. We can help, but they'll have to deal with it somehow, in their own fashion. We can't send US troops into the kingdom—not without explicit instructions from the royal family."

As soon as Captain Bingham signed off, Truxton turned to his next task order. The *McCain* would reach Jeddah before the day was out, which meant they'd have information soon.

Truxton had no idea why the Pentagon needed ships in the Mediterranean so quickly. There hadn't been action in that part of the world since the last confrontation between Israel and the relief ships that kept trying to land at Gaza. But that had been months earlier, and the region had been quiet since then.

But he also knew that, once his new orders came through, he'd be able to sort through the picture. Most likely, it had to do with oil. The combination of events in Saudi Arabia, Iraq, and Iran over the past several days had created one of the most unstable moments in the global economy that Truxton could recall.

Everyone was on edge. The classified cables were flying everywhere, all of them speculating about wars and rumors of wars about to break out.

Iran had immediately accused Jundallah of securing a nuclear suitcase from the United States. The peace talks between the two countries were about to fly apart as a result.

The US had denied any role in the attack on the Azadegan oil fields in southern Iran. In fact, Truxton knew, the US was as much in the dark as anyone. They had no idea who'd launched the attack and where they'd procured the nuclear suitcase.

Anti-proliferation experts had warned of the possibility of a suitcase attack for years. Loose nukes had been a threat since the collapse of the Soviet Union. Efforts to tighten the black market had been mostly successful—but not completely.

Until someone took credit for the attack in southern Iran—and no one had yet, beyond unconfirmed reports from rogue individuals loosely attached to Jundallah—everyone would be left guessing. The IRGC had already delivered some damning evidence to the United Nations Security Council tying the explosion to the notorious, violent Sunni opposition group that had attacked the IRGC on occasion in Iran.

But the evidence was circumstantial, and Iran wasn't forthcoming with the origin of the actual nuclear components. Reports from the Mossad and the CIA had already traced at least some of the parts to the North Koreans, which implicated the regime in Tehran.

But Truxton knew from experience they might never know who was responsible. Unless someone came forward out of pride or stupidity to claim credit, it could take years to trace the events backward in time.

Meanwhile, in Iraq, US military forces had moved in swiftly to secure the West Qurna fields, but the damage there had already been done. Iraq's coalition government, still in turmoil, insisted that they lead the investigation and that the US military stand clear.

That was a nonstarter, Truxton knew, but securing West Qurna now was a little like locking the barn door after the cows had fled. Those two attacks, combined with the surprise effort at Saudi Arabia's Aramco complex, had pushed the world's oil economy into a freefall. OPEC was meeting around the clock, but they had no real hope of stabilizing prices at the present.

Saudi Arabia—the country the West relied on to stabilize crude oil prices through OPEC on the world market—was simply not capable of doing so at the moment. Ghawar wasn't producing as it once had, and Saudi reserves weren't sufficient to make up for the crippling of the Aramco complex in the short-term.

There were rumors that at least one or more major, private American oil firms was about to enter the global market and ratchet up production from oil shale in the western United States and, surprisingly, Israel.

There were also reports that Turkey and Israel were talking again and that an oil pipeline connecting Eastern Europe through Israel to Asia was about to go live.

Truxton knew his orders to move ships into the Mediterranean likely had something to do with both of those reports. It was all volatile, though—and highly combustible.

And Israel, in the middle of a collapse of the world oil economy? Even if they had nothing whatsoever to do with any of the actions in Saudi Arabia, Iraq, and Iran, some would still blame and target them. Whatever hopes of peace existed in the region hung by a thread.

But Vice Admiral Truxton was an optimist. If there was some good the American navy could do in the Mediterranean, they would do it.

Truxton was also picking up on other information, though, and had decided to hedge his bets. There were reports of a new military opposition uprising in Saudi Arabia. A retired general in Jordan had broadcast something about a Day of Anger and something he called the "Free the Kingdom Army" that would lead it.

Truxton didn't trust the truth of these nascent uprisings and movements. But something about this new effort that was certain to rile the Saudis didn't feel right to Truxton. So he decided to place more bets on the table and moved a significant presence just off the coast of Bahrain near Qatif and Dammam on the eastern seaboard of Iran.

But he also decided to move a significant American naval presence into the Red Sea, near the coastline of Saudi Arabia. There was no real military need to add to the efforts of the USS *John McCain* in the region. But Truxton could feel there was more at play, and he didn't want to be outflanked or unprepared if something bigger should break.

So he ordered a significant part of the Seventh Fleet into the Red Sea. He also decided to see the conflict personally, as he had during the Persian Gulf conflict with Iran. He would explain his move later to the joint chiefs.

SAUDI ARABIA

ERITREA   RED SEA   YEMEN

SUDAN

Al Hudaydah

46   ETHIOPIA   GULF OF ADEN

DJIBOUTI

Al Hudaydah, Yemen

Sa'id Nouradeen didn't believe in legends. He left that to the masses and to his children.

But if it served the greater good for certain elements to believe that he was al Yamani, the one who would usher in the era of the Twelfth Imam, then so be it. Nouradeen believed only in the cause of war and the power of force.

He'd pushed the Israelis out of southern Lebanon. And with Iran in ascendance, Nouradeen believed the time had finally arrived when the Arab world would rise as one and seize control of the region from the hated powers of the West.

There was only one significant power that stood in the way of progress forward toward a pan-Islamic victory in the region—Saudi Arabia's royal family. But with Iran and the US engaged in peace talks, forces in the region could safely move against the Saudis.

As far as Nouradeen was concerned, it was long overdue. He'd never understood why the leadership in Tehran had waited so patiently for a time to move against the kingdom. But they were moving now. And Nouradeen was pleased to play a part in it.

"Move!" he barked to one of his lieutenants. "We need to get those horses aboard by nightfall."

The cargo ship had been docked at a private terminal at al Hudaydah for nearly a month. It was one of three such ships loaded with the equipment they'd need for their ride to Mecca. One of the three had been taken by pirates and then seized by the Americans. But two had remained, and one was now being loaded by Nouradeen's men.

"Will we leave tonight, sir?" one of the men asked Nouradeen.

"We will if you swine get the horses loaded," he answered.

"And then?"

"And then you shut up and go where I tell you," Nouradeen growled. "I'll give you your orders when we arrive."

"But we will be in Mecca?"

"In two days' time," Nouradeen pledged. "But only if you get those horses loaded."

Nouradeen was pleased. His efforts to combine the two factions had succeeded just as he'd hoped. There was minor grumbling, but Sunni and Shi'a fighters were living, working, training, and willing to fight side by side.

It would surprise the West to see the cooperation. *Well, good*, he thought. *It's about time we surprised them with something.*

The ship was loaded within the hour. Nouradeen made sure the decks were clear, the cargo safely loaded in the hold. And then, with little fanfare, the ship set sail northward along the Yemen coastline. They would make Jeddah before dawn.

SAUDI ARABIA
IRAN

Dammam
Dahran

QATAR

BULF OF OMAN

Riyadh

UNITED ARAB
EMIRATES

OMAN

47

Riyadh, Saudi Arabia

The knock at the hotel door was insistent. Nash looked over at the clock on the nightstand. It was still early. Morning prayers hadn't even been called yet.

He grabbed a jacket, pulled his pants on over the briefs he always slept in, then answered the door. He was greeted by two Saudi soldiers in full combat gear. One wore his helmet. The other wore a simple cloth cap. Both were dressed in drab olive. Both carried guns.

"Mr. Nashua Lee?" one asked.

"Yes, I'm Nash. Can I help you?"

"You are to come with us." The first soldier took a step forward into Nash's hotel room.

"Come with you? Where?" Nash asked.

The second soldier stepped into the hotel room and reached for Nash. "We have a car outside."

"Hey! Wait just a minute," Nash said, trying to keep the fear he felt from his voice. "I'm an American citizen. I need to know where you're taking me."

"We know who you are, Mr. Lee," said the first soldier. "That's why we're here."

"Under whose orders?" Nash glanced over his shoulder. But there was no escaping these two. His room was twenty stories above ground. And even if he could get by these two, where would he go?

"That's not your concern," the second solider said.

"I think it is." Nash's voice rose. "I need to know where you're taking me, and who sent you. Why am I being taken, against my will, by Saudi military forces?"

"We are not military," said the second soldier. "We are with the Saudi National Guard."

"The National Guard?" Nash asked, confused. "You protect the royal family?"

"Among other things," said the first soldier. "But please, we need to go. I have my orders to secure you and take you to the palace."

Nash knew little about the inner workings of the kingdom but enough to realize that if two soldiers from the White Army were here to take him, it was under the direct orders of the royal family. The Saudi Arabian National Guard—the White Army—was small in number and served only the royal family.

They were the elite internal security forces that served as a separate military force inside the kingdom. They protected the royal family and were also charged with protecting the holy places of both Medina and Mecca. They were essentially the king's private army.

"The palace?"

"Yes, we will be going to the king's palace. Now, please, I must insist." The solider took another step into the room.

Nash took a deep breath. *Okay, this isn't so bad*, he thought. *These are the king's men. They aren't military. I'm not being arrested. But what?*

"Can I grab a couple of things?"

"Yes, but do so with haste," said the first solider. "I must have you at the king's palace within the hour."

"Okay, fine." Nash located both his mobile phone and his iPad, stuffed them into his backpack, and slipped on some shoes.

"Are we ready?" asked the second soldier.

"We are," Nash said.

The first soldier wheeled and left the room.

"After you," said the second soldier.

Nash followed the first soldier. He considered the possibility of bolting once he was in the hallway but then thought better of it. *No, I'll see this out*, he thought. *They know who I am. And I can always reach out to someone if I need to. I haven't done anything wrong.*

They left the hotel lobby quickly. It was still dark outside. Only one car, a black SUV, was parked in the circle out front. They opened a rear door and beckoned to Nash to enter. He slid in and was joined by the two soldiers on either side of him.

"So who am I going to see?" Nash asked.

"We'll be there shortly," one of the solders answered.

"So you won't tell me."

"Very soon, Mr. Lee. Please. Be patient. It won't be long."

Nash fell silent. The streets of Riyadh were empty at this time of morning. They rode in silence along King Fahd toward the palace.

Despite the circumstances, Nash couldn't help himself. Once they'd entered the grounds of the king's palace, which spread out over nearly a square mile, Nash stared at the myriad stone walkways, waterways, and pink buildings flooded with light. It was a stunning sight.

Nash was whisked inside once they'd arrived. The soldiers led him down one corridor, through another, and then, finally, to a rather ornate, somber conference room. There were no windows in the room, just a long table ringed by a number of comfortable leather chairs.

The soldiers left him there and closed the door behind them. Nash heard a *click*. He wondered whether they'd locked him in. Not that it made any difference at this point. It wasn't as if he was going to run from the place and try to escape.

He was somewhere within the bowels of the king's palace. He had no hope of finding his way clear. He'd need to find out their game and talk his way through it.

Nash pulled out his mobile while he waited. Not surprisingly, he had no service available. He scanned for an available wireless network. There was nothing there as well. *So there's no hope of contacting anyone from here*, he thought.

He was strangely calm. He didn't precisely *feel* like a prisoner—even though he was here, in this room, largely against his wishes. There was a sense of exhilaration, as if he were about to learn something momentous.

At times like these, Nash had long ago learned to rely on that still, small voice he'd listened for intently for much of his young, adult life. *Life is a gift*, Nash believed, *and you either live it with that in mind, or you live in fear and constant worry*. Nash had always chosen to live a life of implicit meaning. And if that meant he took days such as this in stride, then so be it.

The door to the conference room opened after a nearly ten-minute wait. Three elderly men dressed head to toe in flowing white robes entered. A member of the White Army tried to join them in the room, but the eldest of the men motioned for him to remain outside. One of the others closed the door.

Nash studied the three elderly men. While he'd never met them, he knew them from the many pictures he'd seen in the press. This was the infamous triumvirate that had ruled the kingdom for years—King Faisal, Crown Prince Saud, and his brother, Prince Natal, who commanded the White Army and the intelligence services. Nash was taken aback. He stood to greet the visitors.

"King Faisal," Nash said. "I am honored to meet you. But I am also somewhat surprised at the manner at which I was asked to come here to this meeting."

Faisal held up a hand that shook slightly with some sort of palsy. The man was in his mid-eighties, and his age was showing. "Yes, I regret the inconvenience," the king said. "But there simply wasn't time for niceties. We could not afford the luxury. We required your services urgently, and this seemed the best way to reach you."

"By sending White Army soldiers to sequester me from my hotel room?" Nash asked. His voice, though, was calm and steady. He knew now that he was not in physical danger. What else might take place was difficult to see, but it would require only his wits.

Natal started to speak, but the king gestured for him to remain silent. "Again, my apologies, but I felt it was best," Faisal said.

"But surely, you could have called my office and requested a meeting," Nash said. "I would gladly have arranged to meet with you."

"Yes, and it might have taken days."

"I would have answered your call immediately, King Faisal."

"I appreciate that, but we couldn't take that chance."

"Why?"

"Because," the king said, "we only have a matter of hours to make decisions, and we need to command every resource at our disposal."

"And I am a resource?" Nash asked.

"To be honest, yes, you are," Natal said forcefully, unable to remain silent any longer.

Nash glanced at the minister of the interior—a man well known as a hard-liner within the royal family. Nash instinctively decided to be on his best behavior in his responses to Natal.

"How so?" Nash asked.

"Because your mVillage network has information that we need quite urgently," Natal said. "And—"

"And we wish to impress upon you the great need right now," the king interjected. "We have firm information that war is about to reach inside the kingdom, and we must respond quickly and aggressively."

"Fine, but what does that have to do with me—and the mVillage network?" Nash asked.

"There is an opposition army forming—something participants within your mVillage have called the 'Free the Kingdom Army'—and it is being led by a former general in charge of the White Army who is living in exile in Jordan," the king said.

Nash shrugged. "All right, but I still don't see how I can help. People use mVillage to float all sorts of things. That's nothing new. So I ask again, why have you brought me here?"

The king glanced at Natal and then at the crown prince. Saud nodded, and Faisal continued. "We would like to provide you with a list.

And from that list, we would ask that you provide us with a record of information that was shared or disseminated from those on that list."

"A list?" asked Nash. "What sort of a list?"

The king looked at Natal, who handed a manila folder to him. Faisal slid the folder across the table toward Nash. "You will find a list of mobile telephone numbers inside. This is the list that we must look through quickly. We require specific sets of information, all of which we are quite confident that your mVillage network can provide us."

Nash tried not to turn white as he opened the folder. At any other time, Nash would have stopped the conversation and asked to phone his general counsel's office. Other world leaders had asked his company to provide confidential, private information. But they'd always done so in a formal process, with lawyers involved.

But that didn't seem to be an option here. Nash knew, without asking, that he would need to make a decision here, in this conference room, without his lawyers. And he already knew the answer he would give. He simply could not, under any circumstance, provide the information these rulers were demanding of him. It was not possible—even if it meant he would be imprisoned.

It was a slippery slope when a global information network like mVillage gave up personal information to authorities. China had consistently threatened his company over the years. Nash, and his company, had never given in to the Chinese demands for either curbs on information dissemination or to requests for private information from the network.

"King Faisal," Nash said quietly as he scanned the list of mobile telephone numbers, "you know that I cannot grant your request. I simply cannot reveal personal information from the network. And I cannot provide you this record that you speak of. I can't."

"Please," the king said quickly. "I understand your position. It is one we've heard many times, from others who have access to great stores of information. But I would ask you to consider this and the position we now find ourselves in. We are, at this very moment, under threat of attack from at least three different directions."

"That we know of," Natal offered.

"Yes, that we know of," the king said. "There was the attack at Aramco…"

"Which was well documented by the press," Nash interjected.

"Yes, it was," the king said. "But we still do not know who was directly responsible. We know the groups that carried it out. But we do not know the *root*, the source. That is what we must find. From there, we may be able to discern the true nature of the threat at our doorstep."

"And you think mVillage can help you with that?" Nash asked.

"We are quite certain of that," the king said. "We have had the list of mobile numbers on your list under limited surveillance for some time. But there is only so much we can learn from that surveillance. The true value is contained in the information within your system. By comparing certain words and trends—"

"Again, with all due respect, King Faisal, I am not able to do that," Nash said firmly. "I cannot reveal private information from the network. Not for you and not for any other government leader."

"Then let me rephrase the request," the king continued somberly. "We know of the groups and the nature of the attack at Aramco. What we are trying to ascertain, from the records and data within your network, are the original source of the very first calls to action that went out to certain numbers on that list. From there, we will be able to ascertain root causes.

"But just as importantly, we are trying to determine how coordinated this attack is with movements in two other parts of our country. There are forces at move against one of our holy sites, and we have heard rumors of a coming war on yet another front.

"We must swiftly determine if these are all isolated events—or whether they all have the one, same root cause. We believe evidence of that root cause is contained within the information, data, and records from these mVillage mobile numbers on the list you have before you.

"So what I am asking is this: If we provide you with a road map of items that we would ask you to search, would you be willing to consider the request? And should you find links or connections, would you be willing to provide us with that information? You may keep the personal records safe. We are merely asking for some corroboration of trends, connections, and root causes."

"So you wouldn't ask me to turn over any personal data? We'd do the meta-search ourselves? You're not asking us to turn over the data—only confirm links or connections we might find?"

The king smiled. "Precisely. It is a simple request. Nothing more than that."

Nash shook his head. "It is most definitely *not* a simple request. But I will consider it."

"Wonderful." The king extended a hand. "If you do choose to discuss this further with us, Natal has assured me that he will meet with you alone, and that any information you convey to him will be held in the strictest confidence."

"And if I am unable to provide you with the information you need at the end of our own search, then what? Will I remain a prisoner here?"

"You are our guest here at the king's palace," Faisal said. "We hope that you spend your time wisely and make judicious decisions."

48

Ali Zhubin had never been a patient man. He hadn't gotten to his station in life as the head of Iran's Revolutionary Guards Corps by waiting. But he was being told to wait and be patient by his commander in chief—and it was killing him.

Zhubin understood the grand aims of the Supreme Leader. He and the Reverend Shahidi had talked many times about the bigger play. He got it. He was a loyal soldier to the cause—to the death, if necessary.

Part of being a good soldier—and Zhubin was a very good soldier—was a certain willingness to wait for moments or opportunities during combat.

But the mind-numbing diplomacy of the peace process between the United States and Iran these past several months had long ago driven Zhubin over the edge. The talks had taken place at a bureaucratic level, with little movement. He no longer even asked about the status of the peace talks. As far as Zhubin was concerned, they would eventually break down.

Zhubin trusted the Americans even less than the Israelis. At least the Israelis' military forces were straightforward in their aims. They saw a threat and moved decisively to neutralize it. They didn't wait.

Iran had once secretly tried to position medium-range missiles at the Golan Heights. Every single site had been razed to the ground as the construction was underway. Israel hadn't mentioned it to the world community. The sites were merely turned into rubble. Zhubin admired that sort of action.

But the Americans—that was an entirely different matter. The Iraq conflict was as good an example as any. The war had been about oil. America needed it, and Iraq had it. The US government leaders had signed agreements with every major American oil company within a year of the conclusion of the war there.

So the Iraq war had assured the Americans of another significant source of oil from the Middle East. But the American public had never been told the true aims of that war, and Zhubin was certain they would never fully realize that their leadership was more than willing to wage war over control of the Earth's natural resources.

And now, Zhubin knew, the Americans raced to exploit the chaos and turmoil that had erupted overnight in three of the largest oil-rich Arab states the world had ever known. Russia wasn't far behind, and China was waking up to both the threats and opportunities as well.

All roads seemed to be converging on Israel, which had managed to remain silent throughout the Arab Spring and as principalities and powers fought for control in Saudi Arabia and other parts of the world.

Zhubin knew the secret oil pipeline Iran had once built for Israel, in different times, was poised to reopen shortly. Significant amounts of oil would be flowing in both directions, through Israel to Europe and the Far East. And both the Russians and the Americans were investing heavily in Israel's significant oil shale reserves.

Both of these would place Israel at the epicenter of the world's desperate need for fossil fuels that drove the world economy. It was all very curious indeed.

But Zhubin had other things much more pressing before him— and he needed to act. The nuclear attack against the Azadegan oil fields had been far more crippling than the rest of the world knew. Iran had been counting on the effort to develop new oil reserves. The American economic sanctions had devastated Iran's economy over the years, and they were just beginning to emerge from that long shadow. Azadegan had been central to those plans—and they were now in ruins.

The evidence that had been assembled so far had been laid at the doorstep of the Jundallah, which had been a thorn in Zhubin's side for years. Jundallah had exploded bombs at mosques, killing members of the IRGC.

Materials and chemicals from the bomb site had been traced back to the Jundallah forces. There was no question of that. What was left of the truck that had carried the portable nuclear device had been disassembled and studied extensively. Traces of maps and equipment pointed directly to the Jundallah forces.

The radical Sunni terrorist group was responsible, the IRGC's intelligence services had decided. The Reverend Shahidi and the clerics were convinced and were preparing reprisals against the Jundallah.

But how had the Jundallah acquired nuclear weapons technology from the North Koreans? The IRGC could only conclude that, with the North Koreans supplying technology to Iran over the years, some had been siphoned off.

But Zhubin was not convinced—and with good reason. Al Qaeda had close ties with the Jundallah. The two had worked together on more than one occasion.

After striking his unholy alliance with the Reverend Shahidi and the Shi'a clerics, al Qaeda's leader, Ali bin Rahman, had remained behind in Tehran to wait for developments. So Zhubin had sought him out immediately after the nuclear attack at Azadegan. They'd met for coffee one morning at a private café in downtown Tehran.

"Is it true?" Zhubin had asked bin Rahman.

"What?"

"The attack at Azadegan? Every road leads back to the Jundallah. But I am not convinced. It's all tied up in a neat, little package."

The al Qaeda leader had smiled. "And nothing is ever that simple, is it?"

"Not in my experience. So is it true? Do you believe the Jundallah are responsible for that attack?"

Zhubin didn't trust bin Rahman. He didn't like the notion of a merger, of sorts, between al Qaeda and the Shi'a clerics who ruled Iran.

Zhubin believed in a pan-Islamic world, led by Iran. He realized that alliances were necessary evils during times of war and conflict. And bin Rahman was a necessary evil, a convenient ally at the moment. But he still didn't trust bin Rahman, or what he offered as a new ally. Yet, even with that, Zhubin knew instinctively that bin Rahman was right. *Nothing* is ever that simple.

"What I believe is irrelevant," bin Rahman had said. "What matters— the only thing that is truly important here—is motive. What reason would Jundallah have for bringing utter ruin upon itself by exploding such a device at Azadegan?"

Zhubin had shrugged. "They are a terrorist organization. It's what they do."

"Yes, and al Qaeda is a terrorist organization," bin Rahman had said quietly. "It is what we do as well. And I can assure you, I would never have sanctioned such an attack. It makes no sense. The risk is much greater than the reward. You will utterly destroy Jundallah now, am I right?"

"Yes, we will."

"The Jundallah leadership knows that. I know them. I've worked with them. And I can tell you that they would not take such a course of action."

"Have they told you that?"

"They don't need to," bin Rahman had said. "I know."

"But who, then?"

"Ask yourself this. Who benefits from Azadegan? You'll find your answer there."

"The Israelis," Zhubin had offered. "They are moving into a position of prominence in the world oil economy, and this is a crippling blow against a sworn enemy."

Ali bin Rahman had laughed. "Must all roads *always* lead back to Israel and the Jews? They are a useful foil. But in this particular case, they want to cripple your nuclear ambitions and will take any measure to do so. But attacking Azadegan? No, that's a peripheral interest for them."

"The Americans, then."

"In the middle of the peace process? They have everything to lose and nothing to gain by orchestrating such an attack."

"But they've had economic sanctions against us for years. This is just an extension of those sanctions. And they have nuclear technology."

"Both true—but irrelevant here. The Azadegan attack was not a sanction. It was a direct attack, or retaliation, against Iran—for a very specific aim and reason."

"Which is?"

"To remove Iran from the global oil economy. It delays your re-entry for years, does it not?"

"Yes, it does," Zhubin had mused.

"So who would wish to see that? America? Russia? China? Or someone else? Who is your sworn enemy when it involves oil? Who would that be? And who, at this particular moment in the history of the world, feels most threatened on its own soil, with its economic livelihood at sake? Who benefits if other oil superpowers are likewise crippled, as they are?"

Zhubin had leaned back at this point in the conversation. This particular scenario had never occurred to him. "But they would never initiate such an action. The risks are too great for them. And don't forget, they have no nuclear ambition whatsoever. A generation has passed, and there has been no indication they've ever tried to acquire or build any nuclear weapons."

"Are you so certain of that?" bin Rahman had asked. "The Saudi kingdom is a place of many layers and many mysteries. It is one thing to *say* you do not have something. What you actually do is something else entirely."

"But why? The Saudi royal family has avoided conflict with Iran for years. They've bought peace, with you, for a considerable amount of time."

"Until now," bin Rahman had said. "All of that changed when we brought the war to the kingdom. The attack at the Aramco complex changed everything—and the Saudis know that."

"And if they've concluded that Iran was complicit in that attack, then they would consider some sort of retaliation," Zhubin had mused. "They could not take military action, not while the Americans are engaged in a peace process."

"But they could initiate economic retaliation. I dare say the attack at Azadegan is about as direct an attack on Iran's economic lifeblood as anything I could conceive. And I would ask again, if Iran is not an oil power again for years, then who does that benefit?"

"The Saudis," Zhubin said. "They derive their power from oil."

"And you threatened that at Aramco."

"Which was an attack I would not have sanctioned, had I known about it." Zhubin had scowled.

"Nevertheless, it happened," bin Rahman had said calmly. "It is now done, and the Saudis are going to react predictably."

"So you believe the Saudis are behind Azadegan?"

"It would make the most sense, don't you think?"

"Perhaps. But if there is any proof of that, then you know what that means, don't you? We will have no choice at that point."

"You will wage war in the kingdom," bin Rahman had answered soberly. "And the Western powers may simply sit back and enjoy the theater."

MEDITERRANEAN SEA

IRAN

IRAQ

ISRAEL SAUDI ARABIA

Dammam
Dahran

GULF OF OMAN

QATAR

JORDAN

EGYPT

● Riyadh   SAUDI ARABIA

UNITED ARAB
EMIRATES

OMAN

49

Somewhere in northern Saudi Arabia

They'd left in the dark of night. They'd been riding in trucks through the Arabian desert for the better part of two days, pulling trailers full of horses behind them. But they were nearing their destination and would soon abandon the trucks and mount the horses for a day's ride to Mecca.

"Tell me again—why are we bringing horses?" one of the men had asked before they set off into the desert. "Why aren't we just remaining in the trucks as we get to Mecca?"

"Because the leader demands it from us," said one of the commanders who answered directly to Iran's president.

"And which leader is that?" asked one of the others, a mercenary who'd been through four previous conflicts in different parts of the world.

"Does it matter?" asked a third. "We're being paid handsomely, and it's a just cause."

"Yeah, but swords? That's what we ride into Mecca with?" asked a fourth.

"And what are we supposed to do once we get to Mecca?" asked the first mercenary. "Fight the Saudis off with these Zulfiqars? Seriously?"

"Enough," said the commander. "We'll know more when we get there. We'll have what we need. I trust the leader. It will make sense, once we've reached our destination."

Now, as they rode at night so prying eyes would not know of their covert mission, doubts crept into their minds. It certainly seemed like a suicide mission. Take Mecca with nothing more than horses, black flags, and double-edged swords?

It gave them no comfort to hear that a second wave of cavalry would be approaching Mecca from the south, through southern Arabia. "Twice the number of soldiers armed with nothing but swords doesn't make matters better," they told each other.

Yet these were loyal, hardened, combat-tested soldiers. They'd been hand-picked by Ahmadian from around the globe for this mission. They would do as they were told and would fight with the tools at hand.

And if things did not go well initially during the fight, they were under no special constraints. They could fade away into the desert. All had already been paid, and they were not conscripted by any single government entity.

What they could not have known was that forces well beyond their understanding swirled around them in many different directions as they drove through the deserts of northern Arabia.

Forces of change were beginning to make their voices heard and their presence known in Arabia and other parts of the world connected to the kingdom.

This was not a simple conflict. Myriad powers were at play and games within games at play. The "black flag" cavalry that would ride into Mecca from the north was simply a chess piece on a grand board.

But the men who drove toward Mecca cared nothing about those things. They just knew they'd been hired for a singular, if psychotic, mission by a religious zealot who also happened to be the elected president of an oil-rich Arab nation.

What might ultimately happen if, by some miracle, they were successful was not something they contemplated. That was someone else's plan.

MEDITERRANEAN SEA

ISRAEL

West Bank

Jerusalem

JORDAN

Gaza Strip

Bersheeba

EGYPT

50

Beersheba, Israel

Dr. Thompson rarely got a chance to get out of the refugee camps when she was on the road. So when she had breaks of an hour or so—a real luxury—she took advantage of them.

It had been an especially long morning already at one of the make-shift Beersheba refugee camps already overflowing with new families from Jordan and elsewhere while the peace talks were underway.

She needed the break. Some of the families told her they had no access whatsoever to any healthcare. She was the first doctor many of them had seen in months, if not years. The list of maladies was long and troubling. Elizabeth did her best to triage and move on, but it wasn't easy.

It amazed her that governments did not realize that, when they made promises, ordinary people believed them and acted on those promises. So when powers like the United States and Israel said they would create a new Palestinian state carved out of the wilderness, people actually started to wander across and into that wilderness haven.

This was hardly surprising. Once, in the early years of a nascent American government confined to just the states of the Eastern seaboard of the continental United States, a government had offered plots of land to any settlers willing to cross the wilderness lands in covered wagons.

A flood of people responded and settled nearly every corner of the US territories. Promises made—and occasionally kept—were a powerful thing.

Today, she'd decided to walk into the areas of construction underway in the new settlements rising like magic near Beersheba.

She'd heard about a new coffee shop that served Arabic coffee flavored with mocha. That had been all she'd been able to think about on her walk to the shop.

The aroma was nearly overwhelming as she ordered her mocha coffee. Then she began to look for a seat within the small shop.

The place was completely full. There wasn't a single open table to be found. Elizabeth grabbed her coffee and was beginning to despair when a quiet voice called to her.

"Please," said an older gentleman seated at a two-person table off to the side of the shop. "You are welcome to sit here with me."

"Are you sure?" Elizabeth asked.

"Certainly," said the older man. "You look like you could use the break, and that cup of coffee in your hands is calling out to you."

"Is it that obvious?" Elizabeth pulled the chair back from the small table and sat down. She was grateful for the offer and the company.

"You're holding on to that cup like it contains the water of life." The man laughed. "So yes, it's that obvious."

Elizabeth took a long, careful sip of the mocha coffee. It was everything she'd heard about and more. She could feel her troubles easing, if only for a moment. She eyed the stranger who'd given her a seat at his table. There was something about him that gave her comfort. He had the look of a genuinely nice man.

"Wow, that's a good cup of coffee," Elizabeth said.

The man scanned the crowded shop. "Yes, and it looks like the word is getting around. This is the third time I've been here recently, and it gets busier every time."

"My first time," Elizabeth said. "But I've heard so many good things."

"So what brings you here?"

Elizabeth reached inside the folds of her jacket and pulled out her badge. She unclipped the badge from the chain and handed it across the table so the man could read the ID. "I'm here with World Without

Borders, working with the new refugee camps."

The man nodded. "World Without Borders does great work." He handed the badge back to her. "But you're not just *with* them, Dr. Thompson. You run the organization. You started it. I've heard of you. You're famous."

Elizabeth blushed. She didn't think of herself that way. In fact, she rarely read newspapers or watched television. When camera crews showed up at a refugee camp or at a hospital and interviewed her, she was always gracious. She answered their questions directly, though always modestly. She had no idea what any of them did with their interviews or where the stories were seen.

"Oh, not really…"

"Dr. Thompson, that's not true. I just read about you in *Ha'aretz*. They speculated that you might be a candidate for the Nobel Peace Prize because of your work in the refugee camps. The story was on the front page. It was about the hospital being built in Beersheba for the new Palestinian refugees streaming into the country. There was a picture—of you—on the front page."

"I didn't see that story," Elizabeth said. "I rarely pay attention to those sorts of things. I just do my work. Reporters show up occasionally. There's nothing I can do about that."

"And the BBC ran a big story about the Beersheba camps as well. There was a long section about you and the work of World Without Borders there. Like I said…"

"Really, I never pay attention to those things." She laughed. "I couldn't even tell you when the BBC interviewed me, or why. It's not something I care about all that much. The work is what matters, and there is lots and lots of work to be done in the camps."

The man laughed. "I'm with you, Dr. Thompson. The work is the thing. Pay attention to that, and other things fall in to line. So what does your organization think of the planned settlements at Beersheba? Is there hope? Can it survive?"

"Yes, there is most definitely hope," Elizabeth said, glad to be given the opportunity to move away from media attention about her and the work that her organization did. "It's chaotic right now. There is a *lot* of confusion. Families don't know where to turn for basic information, so they camp outside the US military headquarters and wait for scraps of information."

"I've heard that," the man said. "But the American soldiers are generally gracious. They try to answer questions patiently and give out information that they have."

"They do," Elizabeth agreed. "And I've seen this thing before, in places where conflict and chaos are turning the land upside down. Soldiers get a bad rap. But they are almost always patient, kind, and giving toward ordinary people and families."

"I couldn't agree more. As ironic as this is, soldiers can be extraordinary ambassadors and great peacekeepers."

"The problem, though, is that there's no real, central authority in Beersheba right now." Elizabeth sighed. "The American soldiers are doing their best, but this isn't their country. They don't speak for the Israeli government. And they certainly can't do much for the Palestinian refugees who are arriving here in droves. These people are without a country."

"A good point. It's difficult when a person has no homeland to serve as a beacon. They have nowhere to turn to for authority, meaning, guidance..."

"Or even basic information," Elizabeth said. "I spend a great deal of my time each day just answering simple questions from people. Where can I get aspirin? Where can I go to have my baby, and what should I do to get ready for that day? If I fall into an open fire and burn myself, where can I go to get bandages? These are simple things. But it can be extraordinarily frustrating when it's hard to get easy answers to questions like this."

"And of course, people also make do with incomplete information," the man added. "As a result, information is passed along by word of mouth because there's no other way to receive it."

"Absolutely. For instance, the leaders of every single Palestinian refugee camp that my organization serves are telling me that they're convinced the Americans have an ulterior motive for building in Beersheba. They don't believe, for a moment, that there will be an independent homeland, or that they'll truly be granted a capital."

"So what do they believe?"

"They believe that both the Americans and Israelis have another purpose in making Beersheba important. They point to the massive oil refinery that's been built east of the city as proof."

"Proof of what?" asked the man.

"Proof that the construction in and around Beersheba is mostly about making the city a nexus for refining and transporting oil and gas to world markets. Israelis build and settle, they will tell you. And then they occupy. And they wouldn't build a massive, world-class oil-refining center in the desert and then simply walk away from that. The leaders of the Palestinian refugee camps believe that they're just unwitting pawns in some bigger game that they aren't able to play in. They believe it's mostly about oil—and incredible wealth."

Abe Zeffren leaned forward in his chair ever so slightly. "That's an astute observation, Dr. Thompson. Truly. There may be something to that thought. It makes you wonder what, exactly, is behind much of this activity we see with our own eyes. I've seen interesting developments myself recently in my travels."

"Oh? Like what?"

"I work for the Ministry of Infrastructures, in Jerusalem," Abe said. "I've been out here a half-dozen times to check on developments. And that oil-refining complex you mentioned is perhaps the finest, most expensive in the world, with state-of-the-art technology."

"So I've heard."

"And it's being paired, even as we sit here, with a revolutionary new technology that's allegedly capable of heating shale and rock below the surface, allowing vast stores of trapped oil to rise to the surface, where it can be siphoned and sent down here to this refinery near Beersheba."

"You said allegedly?"

"I haven't seen it for myself," Abe said. "I've only had it described to me. The technology belongs to one of the largest private companies in the world."

"But you said you work for Israel's government?"

"I'm just a bureaucrat." Abe smiled. "This company isn't required to tell me about their technology or their ultimate aims here in Israel and elsewhere in the region. There is only so much I can know or ask about."

She frowned slightly. "I see. That seems unfortunate. I would think it might be in everyone's best interests to have their government know, and communicate, things of this sort."

"I couldn't agree more," Abe said. "But I'm not in charge. I just do my job, ask questions when I can, and provide a service to those who actually make some of those decisions."

"What's that phrase everyone in government always uses?"

"'Above my pay grade'? That one?"

"That's the one." She laughed.

"It's an apt phrase and describes my working life perfectly," Abe said. "But I have to say that your speculation about what the refugee camp leaders think has given me new inspiration today and a thread or two that I intend to follow."

Elizabeth smiled broadly. She couldn't help herself. She liked this man. He seemed so…nice.

"Well, good for you," she said. "I'm glad we connected, and that something I said helped you with your own work. I also wanted to thank you for generously offering me a seat at your table in this crowded shop. It's not often that you get a chance to benefit from the kindness of strangers."

"It is a curious world, Dr. Thompson, full of random encounters and disconnected circumstances," he answered. "We are all strangers only because we choose to be so."

IRAN

SAUDI ARABIA   Dammam
                    Dahran   GULF OF OMAN

                                  QATAR

● Riyadh

UNITED ARAB
EMIRATES   OMAN

51

The King's Palace
Riyadh, Saudi Arabia

In the end, Nash decided he could at least ask his best data mining engineers to take the list of mobile numbers given him by the Saudi monarch and see what they produced. What he would ultimately do with that information once they'd done their work was an altogether different question entirely.

Nash knew, in his heart, that the Saudi monarch was fishing. They had no idea, really, what threats lurked beyond the confines of the palace. The Arab Spring revolts had shaken every dictator or ruler to their very cores.

The revolts were pure chaos. They had no leaders. They were never planned and took sudden, unexpected, random courses of action.

Yet they'd toppled leaders in any number of countries. Saudi Arabia—and Iran, to a lesser degree—had appeared to be immune from such revolts. Until now.

Natal had granted Nash access to his team in New York in a second conference room. He was certain his calls and Internet access were being monitored, so he was circumspect in both his call to his staff as well as the mVillage follow-up e-mails he received as his world-class data engineers went through the list.

Nash was proud of his team. They'd built a novel, first-of-its-kind method of combing through massive stores of data across multiple sites and systems. When given a set task, the system could produce needle-in-a-haystack answers. The engineering team, all of them geeks of the highest order, had affectionately named their system after Frodo, the bearer of the One Ring of the Dark Lord from Tolkien's masterpiece. There was no special reason, really, for the name. They all just loved Frodo and were huge fans of *The Lord of the Rings*.

Through word of mouth alone, their data-mining service had been quietly adopted by several of the intelligence-gathering agencies in Washington. Nash and his team didn't talk about this publicly, largely because they didn't have to. The mVillage network was privately owned. They answered only to the venture funds that had started the enterprise.

So, given a defined data set like the list of mobile telephone numbers and tasked with finding threads and connections, the data-mining team and system would produce certain results. And they did, within the hour.

His lead data-mining engineer called Nash on his mobile. "We've found what you're looking for," he said when they'd connected.

"Careful," Nash said. "Remember that this call is probably monitored. Imagine what the transcript looks like in a cable, the kind that we comb through for threads." He could almost see his lead engineer smiling on the other end.

"Understood. So how should I give you the information?"

"Give me the simple, top-line summary now, over the phone. But be careful."

"Okay, it's this. Mostly, there's nothing there."

"What do you mean—nothing?" Nash asked. "They've been monitoring these mobile numbers for quite some time."

"They're worthless," the engineer said. "That's what I'm telling you. That's our highest-level, top-level algorithm. It's all random, meandering threads with no obvious cross-links. There's no conspiracy, no leadership, no coordinated effort to oppose the Saudi rulers. The numbers don't follow any discernible patterns. We just don't see it."

"How can that be?"

"I'll tell you how," the engineer said. "Nearly all of the numbers they gave you are either of students or family members so far removed from any seat of power or government authority that there's no way they could have any influence. It's all just noise. That's what our system shows."

"So there's *really* nothing there?"

"Well, there is one thing, but it's more of an interesting, potentially significant artifact. There isn't enough there to really give anyone something to go on."

"Try me."

"The one common thread that we *could* find was the Saudi National Guard," the engineer said.

"The White Army?"

"Yes, we found a permanent, consistent thread in the data that clearly connected the Saudi's White Army with al Qaeda, Iran, and even North Korea—"

"Hold that thought," Nash said quickly, cutting him off. "I'd like to go over that with you, but not over the phone."

"Should I send you an e-mail?"

"No, not that way," Nash said. "Do you remember the SIM card application we've been working on?"

"The man-in-the-middle application, the one that overrides some of the SIM card functions from one mobile device to another?"

"Yeah, that one," Nash said. "I have the encryption software loaded on my mobile. So can you send me your thoughts over that direct SMS system?"

The engineer paused. "Outside the data network system?"

"Yes, with no archive capability," Nash said.

"So it will be local once you've received it?" the engineer said.

"Which means I can delete it once I've received it."

"I understand. You know I'll send it to you in bite-sized chunks, right?"

"Yeah, I know. But I don't see any other option."

"Got it," his lead engineer said. "You'll have it shortly."

Nash looked at the short bursts of information several minutes later. He'd just hit the DELETE button on the damning information about the highly unusual connections the data-mining team had connected to the Saudi White Army when Natal burst through the door to the second conference room. Nash was doing his best to process the information. Given what he'd just read, he'd need to be extraordinarily careful in the next few minutes.

Natal closed the door behind him and faced Nash. "Man-in-the-middle?" he asked without preamble.

"It's just something our team has been working on," Nash said, choosing to ignore the fact that Natal and his team had heard every word of his private conversation with his lead engineer. "It's nothing fancy. Sort of like software that runs on an individual mobile device."

"So you received information from our list of mobile numbers?" Natal said.

"Yeah, and you know that they came up with nothing," Nash said, choosing not to play games with the Saudi minister of the interior. Natal already knew what his engineer had shared with him—except the data bursts that had been sent, encrypted, to his mobile device and then deleted.

"But they most certainly did not come up with *nothing*," Natal said evenly. "We both know that. Your team found connections to the White Army that protects the royal family and the holy sites in Mecca and Medina."

Nash didn't blink or look away. "So it would seem," he said simply.

Natal nodded. "I will presume that you are not about to share that information with me. So I am going to make an educated guess or two. First, you found connections to General Fahd, the former head of the White Army, who is now in Aqaba. Second, you found connections between White Army leaders at various levels and some of those mobile devices on the list—perhaps to government leaders in some of the towns that are planning to take part in this so-called Day of Anger. Am I close?"

"As you said, those are educated guesses," Nash responded.

"Very well. And I can also hazard that your team found some connection to the royal family, to those who are within the palace compound. Perhaps even to me," Natal said, his eyes boring into Nash's. "Do I have that about right?"

"You *do* command the White Army," Nash answered. "I would imagine that all roads, in one fashion or another, lead back to you in the kingdom. Intelligence has a way of doing that."

Natal clasped his hands before him. "Yes, that's accurate, to a point. There's a lot that ultimately lands on my desk. But that's far different than saying that something *begins* there."

"I wouldn't know about that."

"No, I guess you would not," the minister said. "So I am going to report to the others what your team found and what you have been willing to share with me."

"But I haven't really shared much, Prince Natal," Nash said.

"Oh, you'd be surprised at what you've managed to reveal to me. And for that, the kingdom will be in your debt." Natal got up to leave.

"Am I free to go?" Nash asked.

"I will let you know shortly," Natal answered. "It depends on how the information I deliver to the king is received."

He left as quickly as he'd entered. Nash knew he only had seconds before his access to the outside world would be cut off. He typed a command into his mobile furiously. *Give White Army/Natal info to NSA right away*, he wrote to his lead engineer, using his encrypted, direct SMS software. He hit SEND and watched as it successfully made it out.

The cell signal on his mobile device faded an instant later. Nash was alone again in the bowels of the king's palace.

MARYLAND

Baltimore

WEST
VIRGINIA

Washington, D.C.

VIRGINIA

52

The Situation Room
The White House
Washington, DC

"This can't be true, General Alton." President Camara stared at the NSA brief in his hand.

"I'm afraid it's very real, Mr. President," said the vice chairman of the joint chiefs of staff who was stationed at the White House.

"Yes, we verified that it came from Nash Lee," said Susan Wright.

There were only the three of them in the Situation Room. Dr. Wright had gotten the urgent brief from NSA and had immediately sought General Alton's counsel. They'd both decided that the president, alone, should see this brief first. They'd bring others into the loop once the president had decided on a course of action.

The president looked up from the brief. "So they're really keeping Nash inside the king's palace, against his wishes?"

"It would appear so," Alton said.

"So get the Saudi ambassador over here immediately," Camara said. "This is unacceptable. There will be repercussions."

"Prince Omar is already on his way," Dr. Wright said. "He will be here shortly."

"And does he know why we've summoned him?" Camara asked.

"He does," Wright answered. "He says Nash is a guest of the king, not a prisoner."

Camara reached for the phone. "I'm calling Faisal. This is—"

"Mr. President," Alton said. "Before you do, can we discuss the second part of that brief—the reason Nash asked his company to call NSA and deliver the message they did?"

President Camara sighed. "Fine. It seems a little...outrageous."

Alton and Wright exchanged glances.

"If I may, Mr. President," Wright said. "I'd like to give you a little background. It may help explain why we believe Nash's report is credible and actionable."

"All right," Camara said, his voice strained. "I'm listening. But be quick about it. I intend to call Faisal. I'm not waiting for his ambassador to get here. I expect to hear from Nash myself by the time I hang up with Faisal."

"I'll get to the point, Mr. President," Wright said. "But first, are you familiar with Frodo?"

"The hobbit from *The Lord of the Rings*?"

Wright smiled. "Well, yes, there's *that* Frodo. But I mean the Frodo system, developed by the data-mining and software engineers Nash hired from MIT, Stanford, and Cal Tech. They built a custom software system for NSA last year."

"Vaguely," Camara said. "I've seen it a few times in the morning briefing reports. It always seemed like a silly name for such a powerful system."

"It's a scientist and engineer thing. They're geeks," Wright said. "But here's the point. Frodo is, by far, the most sophisticated intelligence-gathering system ever devised. It's a generation ahead of its time. It's a little like the Manhattan Project that developed the atomic bomb. In this case, they taught a network of computers how to look through more data than any group of human beings could ever deal with. It's how we've been able to make connections to al Qaeda, Iran, North Korea, you name it."

"I guess I don't want to ask how they do it," Camara said.

"It would take awhile to explain," Wright answered. "But what Frodo can do with a defined set of information, when asked to compare it to big data sets, is nothing short of a miracle."

President Camara wasn't a scientist, but he'd heard enough of these sorts of briefings to jump to the end of the page. "All right, I understand the context for the briefing now. So when the Saudis gave Nash that set of mobile telephone numbers—the ones that the Saudi intelligence agency had been tracking to look for an Arab Revolt thing—and he fed that into Frodo, it kicked out patterns and knowledge it would not otherwise have been able to come up with on its own?"

"Precisely," Wright said, glad her boss was so smart. It made her job that much easier. "It found a couple of needles in the haystack."

"So these Day of Anger protests that are set to occur in..." Camara glanced down at the brief.

"In two days," Alton interjected. "They're going to occur in every city in Saudi Arabia that has any sort of significant Shi'a population— Dammam, Qatif, Medina, Mecca, even Riyadh, we believe."

Camara nodded. "And this Day of Anger is truly spontaneous. That's what Frodo found? They traced it back to three students with mobile numbers on the list the Saudis gave Nash? But they weren't coordinated, or even planned? The students just made things up, sent the information out through mVillage network, and others latched on to it?"

"Exactly," Dr. Wright said. "There's no grand conspiracy—at least among those students. The Day of Anger is truly a random thing, created by some bored students who decided to throw verbal graffiti at the wall on the network."

"That pan-Islamic flag, the Arab Revolt flag?"

"Made up by one of those students," Wright said. "But it's spread like wildfire."

"The notion about bringing back the kingdom of Hejaz? And that Israel is behind it, that they're inciting a war between the Shiites of Iran and the Sunnis of Saudi Arabia?"

"Pure fiction. Made up. Israel has nothing whatsoever to do with any of this."

"But the world won't believe that," Camara said quietly.

"Of course not. Iran is likely to play that card, even though it's patently false. And from the brief, we know that someone within the royal family will as well."

"And this librarian, what's his name?"

"Mehmet Osman," Alton answered. "He's in his eighties now. He's a real heir to the last caliph from the Ottoman Empire."

Camara shook his head. "So do we have someone on the way to find him in London, make sure he's staying put?"

"We've contacted the embassy in London. They're sending someone," Alton reported.

"Good." Camara exhaled in frustration. "That's all we need, is for someone to take advantage of the Day of Anger in these Saudi cities to start something bigger."

"But Mr. President, that's precisely what's happened," Wright said. "That's one of the two needles in that big data haystack that Frodo found. That's one of the reasons Nash had his lead engineer send us the information. It would appear that someone has already taken full advantage of the opportunity presented by the Day of Anger to advance his own cause."

"The White Army?" asked the president.

"Yes, the internal security forces commanded by Prince Natal," Wright said. "Frodo found patterns that nothing else could have found. It is quite obvious that the White Army—or at least some part of it— is deliberately fanning the flames of civil unrest in each of these cities. They are, in fact, turning the Day of Anger into a direct, potentially violent conflict against the royal family.

"They also found a connection between Natal and this retired White Army general, Fahd, who's been broadcasting that he will lead a new Free the Kingdom Army in exile. Not definitive, but an awfully good lead. It would appear that Natal is fomenting unrest in the kingdom, for whatever purpose."

Camara closed his eyes. "But we have no hard proof that Prince Natal is behind this, do we? All we have is this pattern created by a system called Frodo? That's hardly actionable."

"No, it's not actionable," Alton said. "And it's not something you can raise with Faisal, either. But we must prepare for this war that will almost certainly erupt across the Arabian Peninsula in only two days' time. Especially because of the second needle in the haystack that Frodo found."

"The nuclear weapons shipment from North Korea, through Iran?" Camara asked.

"Yes," Alton said. "We knew the North Koreans had only partially given us everything they had. But Frodo found patterns that connect the White Army to Iran's president and then back to North Korea. We have to assume that some sort of a portable nuclear weapon is now inside Saudi territory."

"And you trust this connection?" Camara asked.

"I do...we both do," Wright said. "Frodo has never been wrong. It finds patterns that others can't possibly find."

"And when that thing goes off..."

"It will seem like the gates of hell have opened wide," Alton said grimly. "Natal has a history of blaming Israel whenever possible, and that seed has already been planted across the mVillage network. Iran certainly isn't going to take credit or declare outright war against Saudi Arabia. They always operate through proxies."

"Though I'd say that this will be as close to a declaration of war by Iran as you can possibly get," Wright said. "We may be witnessing the start of a Shi'a-Sunni war—the one we've all been anticipating for some time."

"So we'd better put our troops in Israel, near Beersheba, on alert," Camara reasoned. "What about our ships in the Persian Gulf, the Red Sea, the Mediterranean?"

"All ready, and expecting the worst," Alton reported. "We're ready for a storm, whatever it might be."

The president nodded, satisfied he had enough information to go on. "And we can't warn Faisal about any of this?"

"No, we can't," Wright said. "None of this is dispositive—it's just a set of connections drawn by a very powerful data-mining network. There's no smoking gun."

"But we can take precautions," Alton added. "And we have."

"Well, there is *one* thing I can do," the president said, reaching for the phone. "I can make sure they let Nash walk out of the king's palace unharmed. And as soon as that's done, I plan on calling Nash's father to make sure that Ethan pins the North Koreans' ears back for creating this mess in the first place."

53

Pyongyang, North Korea

"Is everything all right, Ambassador?"

"It's fine, Emma. Everything is fine."

But clearly, everything was *not* fine. Emma Broddle had gotten to know Ambassador Lee well in the past few days. Ethan Lee had joined the stalled peace talks in Pyongyang quite recently. And Emma had learned quickly that he was someone who'd seen and done it all. Almost nothing seemed to faze him. He handled the North Korean generals without blinking.

But the phone call he'd just received had definitely shaken him. He had nearly turned white, before quickly recovering.

They were sitting outside the negotiating room of the interminable peace talks that had been underway in Pyongyang since the day that President Camara had met with the brash, young leader of North Korea on the airport tarmac months earlier.

Ambassador Lee had injected gravitas and a new sense of urgency in the stalled talks, which was likely what the White House had hoped for. But Emma had never seen the ambassador in such a state. The call had affected him deeply.

"You're certain, sir?" Emma asked. "The call…"

Ethan looked over at the young woman and smiled wanly. "It's my son Nash."

"Is he all right?"

"Yes, that was the president. He told me that the Saudi royal family has Nash inside the king's palace as some sort of a prisoner."

"But he'll be all right, won't he?" asked Emma. "I mean, it's Saudi Arabia. They're one of our allies?"

"Yes, but a very dangerous conflict is about to break out in the kingdom," Ethan said. "And I don't know what part Nash has in it—or why he's being held at the king's palace."

"Did the president say what might have caused the problem?"

"He didn't, other than the fact that they were trying to coerce Nash to turn over private information. The Chinese have tried that with his company before. But this is unpardonable. It isn't something you do to *any* American citizen in Arabia."

"Your son will be all right, Ambassador. He will. You'll see."

"I certainly hope so." Ethan stood. "But the president gave me other information, the type I was looking for. And I'm not waiting any longer. We're going to go jump-start these peace talks. It's time we concluded a few things."

"Like making sure that those two prisoners Nash was concerned about, You Moon and Kim Grace, are finally freed?"

"Among other things," the ambassador said, his eyes flashing angrily. "But first, I intend to find out exactly where the North Koreans shipped nuclear materials to Iran—and why they did so without telling us about it."

West Bank

Jerusalem ●

ISRAEL

JORDAN

MEDITERRANEAN SEA

Gaza Strip

EGYPT

54

Shfela Basin
Jerusalem, Israel

The sounds of excavation were pleasing to Nicolai Petrov. He'd wondered if this day would ever arrive. Now that it had, the day seemed anticlimactic.

Russia's future as a world superpower was hanging in the balance. The United States and Israel were about to take a quantum leap into a bold, new energy future. In two short years, the Americans had managed to create leapfrog technology capable of safely extracting oil from vast shale reserves in a way that seemingly did no harm to the environment.

Petrov, for his part, didn't care at all about the environmental implications of the new technology. Neither he nor his boss, Andrei Rowan, was concerned about whether the extraction process harmed the groundwater supplies. He just wanted the oil and was willing to do whatever it took to either steal the new technology or form a partnership with someone who could deliver it to him.

Which explained why the sounds emanating from the brand-new excavation site at the northwestern corner of Shfela Basin were so pleasing. Petrov glanced off to one side at the shiny sign that had recently been planted on the site, identifying the excavation site as a joint venture between INOC and Kosvo Oil.

"Is everything satisfactory?" the crew foreman asked him.

Petrov lifted his hard hat and beamed at the crew. "It is a glorious day—for Russia and for Israel."

Petrov had argued, successfully, that they should use the bankrupt, nationalized Russian oil firm for the joint venture in Israel. No one would be the wiser, he'd argued. Rowan, in turn, had made the case to those who cared in Moscow, and the deal had been struck.

Russia now co-owned a significant oil company operating in central Israel. It had cost them a considerable sum of money, but Rowan believed it was worth it. They had no choice but to go into business with Israel—especially now that three of the largest Arab nations were tied up in knots over their own crude oil capabilities.

Petrov knew it bothered Rowan immensely that his back was against the wall and that he'd been forced to deal with Israel. Rowan was still smarting over the fact that the Israeli Defense Forces had been military advisors to the leadership of Georgia in their border war with Russia years earlier.

But Petrov's boss was a pragmatist and willing to do whatever it took to return Russia to its former greatness. And if giving a great deal of money to Israel so it could co-own a significant, new oil extraction and excavation system near Jerusalem was required, then so be it.

The earthmovers had cleared the path in the past week, making way for the trucks and equipment that could get at the oil shale below. Petrov wasn't entirely sure how INOC planned to refine the oil once it was pulled up, but frankly, he didn't care about that.

The Shfela Basin reserves would yield some 250 billion barrels of oil when all was said and done, with much of that going to Russia since it had concluded its agreement with Judah Navon and INOC's board of directors.

The Russian money was more than enough to assure that Israel could develop both the oil shale reserves as well as the extensive natural gas reserves they'd discovered in the Mediterranean. Israel would soon be energy-independent for the first time in its short history. And Russia was responsible for much of that new capability.

Stalin must surely be turning over in his grave, Petrov thought. *But we do what we must, and there is no other way than to be here, in Israel. The times demand it.*

Rowan, however, had been unsuccessful in convincing the Israeli prime minister to block the Americans' efforts in the Negev. No matter. Russia had what it needed here in the basin. The Americans could have the Negev desert and its massive oil-refining facility near Beersheba.

Someday, perhaps, Russia and America would come to blows over their competing interests in the Shfela Basin. But not on this day. Petrov was just happy to see the beginning of the new Russian-Israeli partnership.

55

Jamkaran Mosque
Tehran, Iran

The floodlit domes and minarets of the grand mosque began to glow with translucent greens and turquoise as night fell. It always inspired President Ahmadian. He reveled in the throng of nearly 200,000 pilgrims who gathered here every Tuesday night.

But this particular Tuesday was no ordinary night at the Jamkaran Mosque. The cars and minibuses that clogged the four-lane highway leading to it had no way of knowing, but they were about to witness history. They made way for the president's car as it approached the mosque.

The pilgrims came to Jamkaran every Tuesday by the tens of thousands. They poured into the concourse in front of the mosque for two hours of prayer—to pray for the return of the Mahdi, the Hidden Imam, the Twelfth successor to the Prophet Muhammad.

Tonight, Ahmadian knew, would be different. For their prayers would be answered.

When the president's car finally arrived, the driver parked behind the mosque in a special place reserved just for him.

Ahmadian was glad they'd agreed to allow the man to make his first appearance here, at Jamkaran. Granted, the imam would make but a brief appearance, and his name would not be uttered. The pilgrims would not even know that the Mahdi was in their midst.

Nevertheless, the mere fact of the hidden imam's appearance here at Jamkaran would fulfill prophecy, and that was all that mattered.

Ahmadian could barely contain himself as he made his way to the inner quarters inside the mosque. Ali bin Rahman had promised to bring the imam to the mosque himself, without escort. There was a risk in this, but the risk would be greater, should word leak that, in fact, the Twelfth Imam was at Jamkaran. The 200,000 pilgrims there for the Tuesday night prayers might overrun the mosque.

Ahmadian asked his aide to remain outside the small room as he came to the last chamber. He paused before entering, said a brief prayer for strength and guidance, and then entered.

There were two men inside. Ahmadian recognized bin Rahman immediately from earlier meetings with the Reverend Shahidi. The other man turned and faced Ahmadian.

"Mr. President," the man said. "I am honored that you have traveled here to meet with me. I have waited a very long time for this day to arrive."

"No, the honor is mine, Imam," the president said humbly.

The man was taller than both bin Rahman and Ahmadian. His hair was black and his face rugged. But his demeanor was kindly, and he immediately extended a hand in Ahmadian's direction. He took a step forward and gazed deeply into Ahmadian's eyes. Iran's president, no stranger to intense encounters with powerful people, did his best not to look away.

"I have been told that you have been so kind as to tell the world of my arrival," the man said. "I am grateful for that. It would be difficult, if not impossible, without efforts such as yours."

Ahmadian glanced at bin Rahman, who was beaming. There would be time later to ask more detailed questions. But today, Ahmadian had only one urgent question he wanted to ask—and it wasn't about the man's lineage or his claims to the succession of the Prophet.

Ahmadian knew the history well. The legends said that Muhammad al Mahdi was the son of the Eleventh Imam. But there was dispute about his mother. Shi'a scholars had identified no less than four different names—Rayhana, Narjis, Ssyqal, or Sawsan—along with various stories about her status as a princess or slave.

That alone, Ahmadian knew, opened the door to possibilities about the Mahdi's true lineage. Scholars across the Arab world would immediately begin to comb through whatever existed in the ancient texts to trace those four names once his appearance became known. The search for connections would be intense, for both the Sunni and Shi'a faithful.

Very little was recorded about the hidden imam's early life. The most legendary story among the masses was that the young imam preached at his father's funeral when he was just five years old, then immediately went into occultation.

But Ahmadian did not want to ask about these things. Instead he asked, doing his best to meet the imam's level gaze, "Imam, may I ask you humbly what country you call home? Is it Iran? Is it another nation? For the world will desperately want to know the answer to that question."

The imam smiled and nodded. "It is a very good question. And yes, you are correct. It is one the world will ask. So I will answer you in this fashion. I am from here, there, and everywhere. No nation may claim me. Yet I serve each and every one of the principalities and powers. I am their prophet."

Ahmadian did his best to hide his disappointment. He had hoped, perhaps unfairly, that the imam would confirm Iran as his home and nationality. But the answer would suffice, for now.

"Thank you. I had hoped you might confirm Iran as your home. But you are here, today, as you appear in public for the first time. That is enough for me. My life has been devoted to you, Imam," Ahmadian said. "Everything I have ever done has led to this day, to this time."

"Good," the man said. "So let us make our appearance together. I would enjoy hearing your words and seeing the pilgrims who gather here every week to pray for my return."

"Gladly." Ahmadian led the way up the stairs, to the portico that overlooked the concourse. He had a brief speech prepared. The imam would be standing by his side, for all to see. But Ahmadian would not introduce him.

No, that moment was reserved for another time—and the proper place. An instant later, the twelfth successor to the Prophet Muhammad stepped out onto the balcony with Iran's president and gazed out at the tens of thousands of pilgrims who were there to pray for his return. The hidden imam smiled and waved to his loyal servants.

EGYPT

Sarum

Mecca

SUDAN

RED SEA

SAUDI ARABIA

YEMEN

56

Sarum, Saudi Arabia

The USS *McCain* trolled as close to the shoreline of the mainland of the Arabian Peninsula as it dared.

As Captain Bingham approached the tiny coastal port of Sarum, the hairs on the back of his neck began to twitch. He could feel it. Their target was here or nearby. His hunter's instincts were rarely wrong.

Sarum was a tiny, nearly uninhabited port south of Jeddah on the western coast of Saudi Arabia. Tourists rarely visited Sarum. There was nothing to see there.

But, Bingham knew, it was a perfect place to land a cargo ship in the dead of night if you wanted to sneak into the Saudi mainland without being detected.

As the *McCain* moved slowly through the shallow waters, Bingham kept his eyes peeled. The dawn was still at least two hours off, but it was a cloudless night. They could make out shapes, at least.

"We've got something, Captain," one of his men called out from the side of the operations center. "Sonar picked it up. We don't have a visual yet."

"What?" Bingham strode across the deck floor and peered at the scope.

The officer pointed at an outline on the scope. "There. It's too big for a port this size. It has to be our ship. It's all the way at the Sarum shoreline."

McCain acted immediately. "Okay, kill our engines. We'll go in with the inflatables. Maybe we can get them while they're unloading."

The inflatable boats were off and headed toward the shore within a matter of minutes. The sailors were all on edge. They had no idea what to expect. Bingham had warned them that the mission was...unusual.

"We're looking for horses, on board a cargo ship?" one of the sailors had asked him during the briefing. "Are we back in World War I?"

"Just keep your wits about you," Bingham had answered. "We're not entirely sure what's occurring here."

"But we're looking for horses?"

"Yes, and Sa'id Nouradeen from Hezbollah, dozens of al Qaeda fighters, maybe Houthi fighters, and who knows what else," Bingham said. "So I mean it. Take this seriously. We don't know what we're walking into."

As the inflatable boats approached the shoreline, the sailors throttled the motors down until the sounds coming from them could hardly be heard above the night's natural background noises. They drifted toward the shore in near silence.

The sailors checked their weapons and sidearms. They all might have joked in the briefing room about looking for horses, but they also knew that Nouradeen, al Qaeda, and the Houthis were real, actual fighters. Whatever they were up to, they'd turn and fight if the American sailors surprised them. The Americans had to be ready for anything.

As they approached the cargo ship, they could all tell it had been forcibly steered well up onto the beach. The ship was listing badly to one side, which meant that it had been run well onto the shore. Whoever had captained the cargo ship wanted to make sure they got to shore and had no intention of returning to sea with the ship. This was a one-way mission.

The first of the inflatables drifted to the side of the cargo ship. The others drifted alongside. One by one, the sailors secured their lines. Bingham gave the signal, and the sailors scaled the side of the cargo ship quickly and boarded. They all hit the deck at roughly the same time.

But the ship was empty and dark. Whoever had been here had

left the cargo hold quickly. The doors had literally been smashed off in their haste to get from the ship to shore.

The hold reeked of animal sweat. The sailors examined the floor quickly. It was covered in horse manure, and the manure was fresh. They'd just missed them.

"They were here all right, with horses," one of the sailors radioed to Bingham.

"But they're gone?" he radioed back on the two-way.

"Gone."

"Anything else on board?"

The sailors combed the cargo ship swiftly and found tire tracks that had rolled right through and over the horse manure. By the look of the tread marks, they'd brought trucks with them as well.

Off to one side, they also found empty crates that had been ripped open. They found two Zulfiqars with broken handles on the ground beside one of the two crates.

And finally, they also found another set of crates at the other side of the cargo ship. This one had contained white flags. A couple had been left behind in their obvious haste to get the cargo off the ship and onto the mainland.

"We found tire marks as well, Captain," the sailor radioed.

"So they loaded the horses, and they're likely driving inland," Bingham said.

"Do we follow them?" the sailor asked. But it was a question with an obvious answer. They were sailors, not infantry. They weren't equipped to go chasing after trucks pulling horses in the dead of night.

"No, we can't," Bingham said. "But at least someone will know what they're looking for now. We'll let the Saudis' White Army forces know. They can decide what to do with the information."

CASPIAN SEA

IRAN

IRAQ

● Tehran

57

Tehran, Iran

This time, Ali bin Rahman chose to be as direct as possible with Reverend Shahidi. The great day that he, and others, had planned for over the past two years was almost upon them. He didn't want to let the opportunity slip past them. Too much was at stake.

The forces were in play. There was only one more puzzle piece to put in place, and bin Rahman felt it was time to reveal that part of the chessboard to Shahidi.

The al Qaeda deputy knew that Shahidi had no intention, at all, of reaching a lasting peace with the Americans or the Israelis. What bin Rahman didn't understand was why Shahidi even bothered to use diplomacy at all. It made no sense to him.

In contrast, bin Rahman was actually a religious man. He was no cleric, but he did genuinely believe that his cause was both just and holy. He believed in a united, pan-Islamic caliphate. He would work toward that unification until his death, if need be.

And he saw, in a way that he hadn't seen before, how Iran was at the epicenter of that effort. In the space of two short years, Iran had managed to take on the Jews in Israel, the Christian infidels in America, and now the corrupted Saudis, who ruled the kingdom with an iron fist, oppressing a Shi'a minority that looked to Iran for guidance.

What bin Rahman had never anticipated—what he could not have predicted—was that they would benefit from someone inside the

House of Saud who saw a common cause in dissent in the kingdom. With Prince Natal's covert help, bin Rahman and General Zhubin believed they could create such turmoil in Saudi Arabia that Iran could very quickly become the region's preeminent superpower and take on Israel directly. The Day of Anger had appeared, magically, at the right moment.

But there was one more puzzle piece they needed—one that would throw the suspicion squarely on the Israelis and their newfound surge toward a status as the crossing point for the world's oil. And bin Rahman wanted to make sure that Shahidi, at least, knew who was responsible.

He also wanted to deliver a final message to Iran's Supreme Leader. Once the Day of Anger had begun in the Saudi cities and his men had delivered a final blow to draw Israel firmly into the equation, bin Rahman had made the decision to leave the safe confines of Iran. He'd already made plans to join the Palestinian cause and fight for control of Beersheba.

It was a gamble and one that would likely end up badly. But bin Rahman knew his time was running out in Iran, and there was little else he could do. Going to stake a claim in the new Palestinian home-land, he felt, was his only play.

At a minimum, it would put Israel to the test. If the Israelis hunted and killed bin Rahman in what was rapidly becoming known as a true, free Palestinian state, then he would be a martyr. But if he survived, he had a chance to lead the country.

Once, Yasser Arafat had managed to make the transition from ter-rorist to world leader. He'd never managed to lead an actual Palestinian homeland—mostly because he could never curb his lust for violent opposition to the Israelis—but he had at least survived to stake a claim.

Bin Rahman hoped to do the same, with much more at stake. The Palestinians were streaming in to southern Israel. American military forces were keeping the peace and making sure that the Israelis did not overrun the tens of thousands of refugees trickling across their borders. The time of decision on the final status of the new Palestinian nation was at hand.

The al Qaeda leader also had one other card to play—one that very few had anticipated. It would become apparent soon, though, and bin Rahman wanted to be at hand when the world took notice.

When the Twelfth Imam did make his reappearance, it would become nearly impossible for world leaders to deal with the phenomenon. And it would be doubly hard once they realized the hidden imam had no nationality to speak of. No country could, or would, be able to claim him. It would seem as if the Mahdi had materialized out of thin air.

Which was the opening bin Rahman would wait for. On that day, he would claim the Twelfth Imam as the central religious authority for the new Palestinian homeland.

If bin Rahman moved swiftly enough, the Mahdi could become the first prophet since Muhammad to lay claim to at least a piece of Jerusalem and the Temple Mount. Some claim to that part of Jerusalem was still very much in the thick of the peace talks over the Palestinian homeland, despite the efforts to make Beersheba the capital of the new state.

And once that happened, all bets were off. The world would have an extraordinarily difficult time dealing with the Mahdi. They were used to principalities and powers belonging to nation-states. When one or two came along without a nation as a home, the game changed.

But first, bin Rahman had a message to deliver to Shahidi and then Ahmadian after that. While the Israelis made plans to reopen the Gulf of Aqaba for oil shipping traffic to the Far East, they were about to see those plans disrupted.

58

"Are you absolutely certain, Vice Admiral?" the captain asked.

"I am," Truxton said. "Cypress can take care of itself. That's a babysitting service. I don't have any interest in keeping track of oil and commerce in the Mediterranean. The action is here, in either the Red Sea or the Gulf of Aqaba. Every single piece of intelligence we have is screaming at us."

"But they're opening the terminus at both Ceyhan and Haifa even as we speak," the captain asked. "You really don't want to be there to make sure no one disrupts it?"

"And what could we *possibly* do there in the Mediterranean?" Truxton asked, annoyed. "That's about oil and gas. They're going to start shipping it north and south to Europe and the Far East. They'll twist a few knobs and turn on the spigots. No one would dare pursue anything militarily in that part of the world. It's the *Mediterranean Sea*, for crying out loud. People vacation on cruise ships there. It's not like this part of the world, where pirates kidnap entire ships at will."

The vice admiral, as he had during the recent Persian Gulf conflict with Iran, had left his desk post and was on a carrier heading toward uncertain conflict. Truxton liked to be near the fighting. It gave him a much better view of the threats. It was an intuitive thing, not easily explained.

And right now, he was on a small convoy of ships headed north up the Gulf of Aqaba, past Sheikh al Sharma, toward the southernmost ports of both Israel and Jordan.

Truxton was making a difficult decision. They had intelligence of threats in so many places that it was difficult to assess what was either imminent or even most important. But the one report that had struck him above all others was word that al Qaeda factions had appeared in Aqaba in the past two days.

The joint chiefs assumed they were there to shadow the retired White Army general, Fahd, who'd been broadcasting to stir up opposition forces in advance of the coming Day of Anger in Saudi cities. Truxton wasn't so sure. There was no need for any sort of al Qaeda escort or shadow in Aqaba. No, they were there for another reason.

Truxton's plan was to travel quickly to the substantially upgraded port at Eilat and then link up with American forces on the ground in southern Israel. The American military was already on heightened alert in southern Israel, protecting the oil pipeline that terminated in Eilat.

The Pentagon's leadership had made it very clear they did *not* want a repeat of what had happened in southern Iraq, when forces had managed to do severe damage to the West Qurna oil fields. The American forces in the region had orders to protect the oil pipeline and terminus at Eilat, regardless.

All of it seemed surreal to Truxton. He had a difficult time wrapping his mind around the fact that Israel was on the cusp of becoming an oil superpower. But things changed—sometimes when you least expected it.

His one nagging thought was the empty cargo ship that Captain Bingham's sailors had found near Jeddah. He'd notified the Saudis' White Army leadership, who'd said they would inform Prince Natal. They'd gladly accepted the information but had said little about it or what it might mean.

But Truxton knew the American forces could only do so much there regardless. It was probably just as well that Bingham's men had not come across the forces making their way inland. The Saudi

National Guard would need to deal with the Day of Anger protests, and whatever was about to transpire in concert with them the following morning.

The sun was beginning to set as they approached the end of the Red Sea. Truxton marveled at how much everything had changed. Aqaba, on Jordan's side, hadn't changed much. But Eilat, a scant two miles to the east on Israel's side, had changed considerably in the past year or so. Massive new structures were in place as far as the eye could see.

Very large oil cargo ships could now be accommodated at Eilat. Israeli naval vessels regularly patrolled the Red Sea. The days that pirates could capture ships at will in the Red Sea were long gone, thanks to the diligent efforts of the Israeli navy forces.

In fact, one of the Israeli ships was heading southward out to sea. Truxton waved at the captain from the deck, then turned his sights back toward shore as they began to pull in to Eilat.

The port of Aqaba was just beginning to disappear from view when an enormous explosion erupted from that direction. The blast was so loud that Truxton could feel the effects on board. There was a second, third, and then a fourth explosion immediately following the first blast.

The reports came in to the operations center quickly. They'd been so close to Aqaba that some of the sailors on the upper decks had been able to see at least one of the explosions. For whatever reason, someone had chosen to destroy much of the tiny, sleepy port of Aqaba just as the American convoy was arriving.

Even from here, they could see that part of Aqaba was in ruins.

59

Aqaba, Jordan

The soldiers made no effort to conceal their identities as they worked their way through the streets of Aqaba. In fact, they came across civilians at least three times and, in all three instances, paused as if to make sure the civilians got a good look at their recognizable uniforms. There would be no question, in the aftermath, that the soldiers were IDF, and that they'd made the sprint across the Israeli border less than two miles away.

Once the investigation had ensued, the soldiers also knew the people would find several abandoned trucks on the outskirts of town that had recently been driven out of the southernmost reaches of Israel. It would be further proof of those responsible for the day's actions in Aqaba.

The soldiers knew what they were doing. They'd drilled and trained for several weeks in a virtual setting that simulated the town of Aqaba.

Still, it was child's play. They met no resistance. Their target was unprotected, unarmed, and generally defenseless.

Once they'd reached their final destination, the handful of soldiers chose a place in the shadows and waited for their signal. While it wasn't crucial, they did want to time it closely.

The first explosion from the Aqaba port was so loud that a few of the soldiers covered their ears. A couple of them smiled broadly as the second, third, and fourth charges went off. They all knew that parts of Aqaba's port would be burning. It was time.

The soldiers made their way up the steps to the top of one of the most expensive villas in Aqaba. They hesitated briefly outside their final destination, checked their location, and then stormed through the door.

General Fahd had just finished his final audio broadcast before the Day of Anger protests that would sweep across a number of Saudi cities in the morning. He was pleased with the broadcast, his sixth. He'd gotten better with each one of the broadcasts. He'd actually begun to think of himself as an exiled leader of the mythical Free the Kingdom Army.

He looked up, startled, as the commando soldiers burst through the front door of his villa. The door nearly split into two pieces. A shard of wood hurtled across the room, slamming against a table and spilling the cup of flavored coffee he'd kept by his side as he'd finished his broadcast.

It never occurred to Fahd to defend himself. He didn't even have a sidearm in the villa. There was no need. He was retired, and this was a vacation home.

Fahd's last thought as the hail of bullets tore through him was a question: Why had the Israelis come for him, and not the Saudis?

60

The memo sat on Judah Navon's desk for nearly three days. Navon would glance over in its direction at odd times during the day. He wondered about the author who would craft such a memo. Who was Abe Zeffren, anyway?

Israel's prime minister was a careful, thoughtful steward of Israel's heritage, its place in history, and its path forward.

The country had faced one challenge to its survival after another over the years—the Six-Day War, the constant threats from neighbors near and far, and the threat of nuclear annihilation from Iran's Shi'a theocracy.

Israel's citizens lived daily with the reminder that life was short, and that you'd better be passionate about your reason for walking the planet and your place on it.

Nearly every person Navon encountered during his daily political life in Israel demanded that he defend and protect its right to exist in the face of constant threats to wipe it off the face of the earth.

But after a generation of struggles, Israel was about to turn a corner for the first time in its history. Many of the same enemies that had fought against Israel early in its history had gone through regime changes in recent years. Still others were caught up in the Arab Spring revolts and had turned their attention inward.

Israel was no longer at the top of their list of concerns.

Meanwhile, bitter enemies like Iran were actively pursuing peace with them. A solution to the intractable Palestinian homeland problem was seemingly just over the horizon. And Israel's woeful, constant search for energy appeared to be poised for a miraculous reversal of fortunes.

Which is precisely why Abe Zeffren's memo troubled Navon so, and why Zeffren was waiting patiently in the outer office.

Navon had glanced casually at the deputy oil commissioner's occasional memos over the years. None had ever been out of the ordinary—just reports on the comings and goings of various efforts to keep Israel from becoming too dependent on any one source of energy.

But this memo from the deputy oil commissioner was different. At its conclusion, Zeffren had asked to meet with him privately to discuss it.

Do not sign an agreement with Russia to finance oil exploration, Abe had written at the end. *If you do, it will mean the end of Israel. We will lose control of our own destiny.*

But Zeffren had condemned the American efforts just as harshly:

> *The refinery in the Negev, coupled with their earth-moving and peacekeeping efforts at Beersheba, is the proverbial nose under the camel's tent. We should never have allowed them to embed themselves so deeply in the affairs of our national economy. For now, I fear, they will never leave.*

All that was left, the deputy oil commissioner had written, was for China to show up at Israel's door and demand a seat at the table. At that point, all three of the world's most dangerous superpowers would be working and operating deeply inside Israel's borders.

Once that had occurred, he'd written, Israel no longer controlled its destiny. Any one of those three economic and military superpowers could decide to wage war against each other over one dispute or another in the Middle East—and Israel would likely be squarely in the crosshairs of the dispute.

Navon had to wonder at Zeffren's prescience on the China guess. China had, in fact, just approached Israel to supply nearly half of its oil and gas. Some would come from Eastern Europe, with the balance made from oil obtained at Shfela in partnership with both the Americans and the Russians. His foreign minister presently was negotiating with the Chinese on the terms.

Navon buzzed his assistant. "Can you send the deputy oil commissioner in? I can see him now. But I only have a few minutes."

"I believe that's all he requires," the assistant said.

Abe had seen the prime minister in public on occasion. He'd never met him, but Abe had always hoped for a chance to at least speak to him. He wasn't nervous. Mostly, he wanted to say his piece and leave.

"Prime Minister, thank you for agreeing to see me," Abe said as he came through the door and took one of the two chairs in front of the desk.

"My pleasure," Navon said. "I enjoyed your memo. It was..."

"Provocative?"

"Yes, that's as good a word as any," Navon said. "And do you believe it, what you wrote?"

Abe nodded. "I do, with every ounce of conviction that I can convey. I asked to see you because I wanted to make a simple request. Israel has never relied on anyone else—not the Americans, not the Soviets once upon a time, not the Chinese—for its destiny. Please don't tie our country to those countries through these arrangements."

"You *do* realize that this is highly unorthodox for a bureaucrat to make such a plea? Your job is to provide background, not necessarily to offer advice," Navon said evenly.

"I understand. But I've been in my job for a considerable amount of time. We've always managed to make do with the meager natural resources at our disposal. Now, in a very short period of time, the world's superpowers show up with offers of riches and gold? Why would we agree to tie our future to theirs?"

"Because it offers us energy independence, for one," Navon said. "And because it gives us resources we might not otherwise have at our disposal. It gives us options."

"Prime Minister, I beg to differ, but it does *not* give us options," Abe said forcefully. "It binds us to them. And like an oxen team that pulls unevenly, we're likely to veer off course when one pulls harder than the other."

"So you're comparing us to oxen?"

"If the analogy works, yes. I cannot emphasize this strongly enough. We don't need America, Russia, or China involved in our own economic affairs."

"And how would you develop the Shfela oil reserves or the natural gas finds off the coast of Haifa?" Navon asked.

"We'll find a way," Abe said. "We always have."

"And if I tell you that the die has already been cast—that we must find a way to work with America, Russia, and China in our land and our national economy, what would you say to that?"

"I would say that Israel had better prepare for a coming storm," Abe said. "With great power come great expectations and inevitable conflict. Those three have a considerable amount of power. Now they will be wielding it within our borders and entangling Israel in their affairs."

London

NORTH SEA

ENGLAND

BEL

ENGLISH CHANNEL

FRANCE

61

London, England

The American embassy officials thought the cable was a joke. Drive over to some old flat to make sure an elderly, retired librarian named Mehmet Osman was still there? And what were they supposed to do about it if he wasn't?

The ambassador bucked the request to the public affairs attaché, who, in turn, sent an intern. The public affairs attaché had better things to do with his time than burn it up chasing after some old coot in London that someone, somewhere, wanted to track down.

It took the intern the better part of an hour to get to the flat. It was in a fairly seedy part of London. He had to take the Tube and then a bus to get there.

When he finally arrived, the door to the flat was locked. He knocked on the door, but there was no answer. He peered in the window, but it was dark inside, and he couldn't see anything.

He was about to head back to the embassy but thought better of it. He started knocking on neighbors' doors.

The first couple didn't know much about the man. But the third neighbor knew Mehmet Osman. He said the man hadn't been seen for the better part of a week. A fourth neighbor knew Osman quite well and often walked to the market with him to pass the time. He, too, had not seen Osman in nearly a week.

But the fifth neighbor proved to be, by far, the most helpful.

He'd been at home one morning and had just happened to see two men knock on Osman's door. When he'd opened the door, the two men had entered quickly, closing the door behind them. This neighbor had never seen these two young men before.

It all looked a bit suspicious, so this particular neighbor had kept an eye on the door to Osman's flat. After nearly a half hour, the two men reemerged. Osman was with them.

The neighbor had called out to Osman, asking him if everything was fine. Yes, Osman had called back. He was good, and everything was fine.

But he had not looked fine, the neighbor said. He was leaving under his own power, but he'd appeared confused. This neighbor had not seen Osman since that day. He'd never returned to the flat. And no one knew where he might have gone.

The intern thanked the neighbor, who asked him why the American embassy would be asking after Osman. The intern didn't know why, he told the neighbor. He'd just been sent here to see whether the elderly, retired librarian was still in his flat.

Neither the intern nor the neighbor knew, of course, that Mehmet Osman was the last descendant of the line of caliphs who had ruled the Ottoman Empire. Osman had never mentioned this to his neighbors. The intern didn't know who Osman was or why anyone would care. But he would file his report when he got back to the embassy. Not that anyone would care, he figured.

EGYPT

Sarum
Mecca

SUDAN

RED SEA

SAUDI ARABIA

YEMEN

62

Al Qirh, Saudi Arabia

It would be a glorious day. It had been a cloudless night, so the sun's light was already beginning to illuminate the eastern horizon.

Nouradeen had considered that, perhaps, they might be challenged at some point on their way to Mecca—either by the Americans at sea or, more likely, by members of the Saudi National Guard once they'd made it inland.

Nouradeen's plan had been simple. They'd brought a considerable amount of weapons with them on board the ship and, now, in the trucks. If challenged, they'd engage in a firefight to the death. But once they were near Mecca, they would ditch the trucks and the weapons. They would ride to Mecca with nothing more than white flags and Zulfiqars.

Al Qirh was a very small town within a day's ride of Mecca. No one would be up in Al Qirh at this time of day. There were no cafés or retail establishments to speak of there and very little in the way of buildings. Nouradeen had chosen a small knoll to the north of the small town. It was a perfect location.

"We'll stop here," Nouradeen ordered. "Pull the trucks well into the trees in the knoll. Tell the men to unload the trailers and line up the trucks to each other."

"Yes, Yamani," his driver said.

All of the men, al Qaeda and Houthi alike, had begun to call him

Yamani from their days at the camp in Yemen. Nouradeen had neither encouraged it nor responded to it. But he also did not tell them not to use the title.

Once the horses had been unloaded, some of the men began to prepare the horses for the long ride to Mecca. Nouradeen directed the others to salt the trucks and trailers with explosives. No one questioned the action or the order. They'd been told this was a one-way mission. They would not be returning to this spot.

"Are we ready?" Nouradeen asked.

The men who'd prepared the horses chose their own mounts. Those who'd prepared the trucks set them ablaze. There was a series of muffled explosions. The trucks and trailers were on fire an instant later. Black smoke billowed briefly skyward.

Now that they were here, and they had not been challenged, Nouradeen knew with certainty that Bahadur had been right. They clearly had a guardian angel of one sort or another inside the White Army. No one had been sent to find them or challenge them.

Bahadur had been confident that they would, in fact, make it to Mecca without intervention. Nouradeen had a difficult time understanding how that was possible. The Saudis were known for crushing dissent with an iron fist. They were more than willing to gas students who even gathered for mild protests at universities.

Granted, they had their hands full with the student protests at cities all across the kingdom that day. Still, it seemed curious.

But he'd also learned to trust Bahadur and General Zhubin over the years. They always seemed one step ahead of their enemies. Predictions became reality. And it was true here yet again. They were not challenged. There was no White Army ready to stop their ride into Mecca.

Bahadur had also promised that there would be other surprises along the way in their journey, and they were not to worry about the final outcome of the battle for Mecca.

"Your job is to get to Mecca," Bahadur had told him in their final call. "We will take care of the rest. Many events will transpire on this

Day of Anger. You must play your part and allow history to unfold as it will."

Nouradeen looked over the mob of Houthi and al Qaeda fighters who'd banded together and were now loyal to him—the Yamani who would ride to Mecca in advance of the coming of the Mahdi, the Twelfth Imam and successor to the Prophet Muhammad.

Nouradeen smiled. It was crazy, psychotic, wildly irrational, and ridiculous beyond reason. He loved it. This was his sort of day.

"We ride," he said and charged north toward Mecca.

SAUDI ARABIA

Dammam
Dahran

BAHRAIN

QATAR

GULF OF OMAN

IRAN

Riyadh

UNITED ARAB
EMIRATES

OMAN

63

The King's Palace
Riyadh, Saudi Arabia

Prince Abdul was stunned when they gave him the news. It hardly seemed possible. But there were many things beyond his grasp today. This was merely one of many. The world seemed to have lost its bearings.

"The White Army took Nashua Lee to the king's palace—against his will? A prominent American citizen, whose father is close to the US president?" Abdul asked.

"Yes, sir, that's correct," said his closest aide, who'd arrived at his private quarters to give him the stunning news. "He is still there, in one of the king's private conference rooms."

Abdul was already dressed for the day. In fact, he'd been up two hours before dawn reading the reports of unrest from all over the Middle East.

There had been a horrific explosion in Aqaba, Jordan, that had decimated the port. The reports were sketchy, but the Israelis were being blamed. They were moving into a position to export oil to China and every other country in the Far East from the northern end of the Red Sea. The oil arrived there from a previously secret oil pipeline that ran the length of the Negev. It connected the Haifa port on the Mediterranean, and then to Europe.

The Israelis wanted control over the northern end of the Red Sea, and they intended to expand their territory. Aqaba was a casualty in that effort, the initial reports said. Jordan wasn't in much of a position to object or get in the way, the reports said, and the Israelis were just expanding territory and settlements, as they always did.

Abdul knew the reports were utter fabrications. There was no way the Israelis, in their wildest imagination, would ever go after a sleepy port like Aqaba. Yes, the Israelis fiercely defended themselves and aggressively pursued settlements and expansions.

They were willing to take the fight outside their borders to Gaza, the Golan Heights, or southern Lebanon when necessary. But Aqaba? That was insane, and Abdul knew it. Any rational person knew it. But the world was not a rational place just now, and there were many who would believe the Israelis were advancing the Zionist cause.

Whoever wanted to cover their tracks for the attack had taken a time-honored route. Israel was an easy, convenient villain. The Jews had been blamed for the world's ills on many occasions. What was one more fanciful story?

What was more shocking to Abdul, though, was the brutal slaying of a retired Saudi National Guard general at his villa in Aqaba. The Israelis, of course, were being blamed for this as well. The initial reports identified members of the IDF who'd been seen advancing on the villa before the slaying.

The speculation was that the Israelis had wanted to remove a radical leader only two miles from their borders before he took power in exile in the midst of citizen uprisings that threatened to destabilize the Saudi kingdom and spark a broader pan-Arab revolt across many nations.

The reports recounted how Fahd had been the voice of the uprising that had led to the Day of Anger protests about to take place across the kingdom. He had become the de facto leader of an army in exile, and the rallying personage for the disaffected who threatened to overturn the monarchy in Saudi Arabia, just as uprisings had removed dictators in Libya, Egypt, and other Arab nations.

The Israelis had no need of a radical leader a stone's throw from their borders, especially one who had begun to give voice to the radicalized anti-Israel sentiment always below the surface in parts of the kingdom and who seemingly could reach out to other disaffected groups in the Arab world. So the IDF, or the Mossad, had neutralized him before he could assume power, the reports had said.

Abdul knew this was absurd as well. There was no way it was true. Yes, the Israelis were known for their ability to reach inside a country such as Iran to assassinate scientists bent on helping their nation acquire nuclear weapons or to track down Hezbollah and Hamas leaders who dared expose themselves at inopportune times.

But this particular assassination made no sense. Israel had no interest in the affairs of the Saudi state. It was far too dangerous for them to entangle themselves in whatever might emerge from a power struggle within the Saudi royal family. This, too, was a convenient lie, well told.

Still, the news saddened Abdul. Fahd had been a good man. Abdul had enjoyed his company when he'd commanded the White Army.

He'd been perplexed, though, as to why Fahd had suddenly taken a radical turn. Abdul had listened to several of his broadcasts, whipping up supporters of the Day of Anger that would take place this day in several Saudi cities.

Fahd was no radical. Yes, he'd married a woman who'd come from a lower-class Shi'a family. He'd kept that fact hidden from others for most of his tenure in the White Army. But that was a personal choice, not a radical one.

Becoming a leader in exile for what, by all accounts, appeared to be a mythical uprising made up out of boasts and child's play did not seem logical to Abdul. He never would have ascribed irrationality and risk taking to Fahd. Loyalty to the White Army and the royal family, yes—but not this sort of lunacy.

Abdul had wondered who, or what, might be driving Fahd. Had someone gotten to him, threatened his family? Or had he just decided to take advantage of a spontaneous movement in the kingdom and see if he couldn't ride its coattails into the history books?

Others had certainly done that in various parts of the world. Whenever there was revolution or sudden change in a nation, there were always winners and losers. And for those who guessed right and were on the right side of history, they were nearly always rewarded with leadership in the ensuing chaos. To the victor went the spoils. Perhaps Fahd had decided to roll the dice.

Abdul doubted that, however. It seemed an unlikely scenario, given what he knew about Fahd and his loyalty to the royal family over the years. More likely was that Fahd had been someone's useful fool, and now he had become a mere footnote in someone's effort to disguise other actions and paint a target on the Israelis' back.

Abdul had been studying Israel closely. The recent attacks in southern Arabia, at the West Qurna oil fields, and at Iran's vast Azadegan oil fields had forever changed the global economic landscape. The world's oil economy was reeling. Saudi Arabia's royal succession—and the protest in the coming Day of Anger—was only a small part of the chaos that had descended in various parts of the world.

Through it all, Israel had emerged nearly unscathed. It was poised to take a seat at the world's economic table. Whether Israel wanted the attention or not, all eyes were turning toward the tiny sliver of land at the eastern end of the Mediterranean.

As someone about to become the Saudi foreign minister, Abdul had made certain that he was fully briefed on a regular basis by the intelligence chiefs. For this reason, Abdul knew that Israel had formed alliances with the Americans, the Russians, and the Chinese that placed them at the very center of the world's vast natural resource economy.

It was a curious position for the Israelis to find themselves in. They'd been dependent on the good graces of others for years. While it had only come to light in recent years, the Iranians had once secretly built an oil pipeline through the Negev so that Israel could import its energy—all while Iran was an avowed enemy of the state.

And now, with everything changing rapidly, Israel found itself about to sit at the head of the table.

But that still didn't explain the actions in Aqaba. Abdul was certain the Israelis were not responsible for the explosions or assassination. But he also knew that history would swallow up the real perpetrators. Israel would remain a convenient, albeit unproven, scapegoat.

Abdul stood up quickly from the desk in his study. *Enough*, he thought. *There are some things beyond my grasp or understanding. But this thing today, with Nash, is something well within my control.*

"Take me to the quarters where they are holding Nash Lee," he told his aide.

His aide didn't move. "I will, but you need to hear the rest of my news first."

"All right," Abdul said. "I will hear your news."

The aide stood straight. "Saud has moved aside. He has already abdicated and given the title to another. It will be announced shortly, in advance of these Day of Anger protests."

Abdul was truly taken aback. The plan had been in the works for days, even weeks. But someone, perhaps the king, had apparently moved up the schedule in an effort to blunt the uprisings about to sweep through the kingdom.

"Saud is no longer the crown prince?"

"As of last night," the aide said. "I have it on the authority of the White Army. They are now protecting a new crown prince."

"Natal?" he asked.

"Yes, Natal," said the aide, a veteran of palace intrigue. It was one of the reasons Abdul liked him so much. "But the statement will read, quite clearly, that this is an interim step, to make way for a new generation of leaders."

Abdul nodded. "So it has begun. This means that Muhammad is the new minister of the interior, and head of the White Army?"

"Yes. The governor of Mecca has been notified, as of last night. And you are soon to become the foreign minister," his aide said, beaming.

"So where are the king and Natal at this moment?" Abdul said.

"I've been told that Natal is on his way to Mecca," the aide said. "He leaves this morning. The king is still in his quarters, conferring with Saud."

"Natal is going to Mecca? Why?"

"To meet with the governor of Mecca, to discuss the transition, I believe," the aide said. "But you know Natal. He never discusses those things, even with his closest aides. It's always an educated guess with him."

Abdul gathered his outer garments. "Well, you're right. This changes everything, save for one thing. Nash Lee needs to be allowed to leave, immediately. I intend to take care of that right now. And perhaps I'll join Natal in Mecca."

"But the new crown prince has given orders to the White Army that the American is not to be approached," the aide said.

"I don't care," Abdul said. "It's not Natal's call. Let the king himself stop me, if he dares."

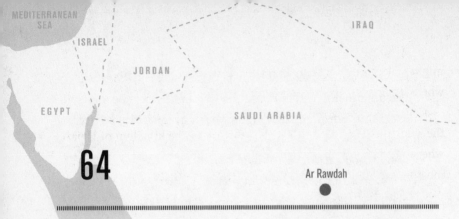

MEDITERRANEAN
SEA

ISRAEL

JORDAN

EGYPT

IRAQ

SAUDI ARABIA

64

Ar Rawdah

Ar Rawdah, Saudi Arabia

"This is insane, sir," the soldier said. "You *do* realize that, don't you?"

"I know," said the bone-weary commander, a close confidant of the internal security forces who surrounded Iran's president. "But we've all been well paid. Mecca is only a day's ride now, and we might be on the right side of history. Who knows? Maybe they'll have a chapter in the history books just about you."

"But seriously, we're riding into the Battle of Mecca—on horseback?" The soldier laughed. "Maybe I'd buy all of this a hundred years ago. Not now."

They'd arrived at the small town of Ar Rawdah, fewer than twenty miles north of Mecca the night before, after three days in the sand of northern Arabia. The men were sick of travel. But they were also a bit mystified as to why they'd never been stopped by the Saudis. It was as if they were ghosts, traveling through the desert.

They ditched and then torched their trucks. The commander radioed his counterpart leading the "white flag" troops from the south. Sa'id Nouradeen told the northern commander they were ready as well and would join up with them at the Kaaba in Mecca. Nouradeen wondered a little about the fact that the "black flag" troops were led by one of Ahmadian's men. It was a risk, but one that Ahmadian and his advisors had been apparently willing to take.

This was the last leg. None of them knew what the end of the day might look like—either here in Mecca, or in other parts of the kingdom where student-led Day of Anger uprisings were planned.

"So who, exactly, are we going after again when we get to Mecca?" the soldier asked. "It's not like the old days of the kingdom of Hejaz, when the sharif or the caliph could be found in Mecca. I mean, it's mostly just a bunch of pilgrims and such now."

"Yes, but it's symbolic," the commander said.

"Okay, then, who's the symbol?"

"The governor of Mecca," the commander answered. "I told you that."

"I know, but I just wanted to hear it again—to make sure. He's a Saudi prince," the soldier said. "So why him?"

"Our patrons have their reasons," the commander said.

"So if he's a Saudi prince, then we can assume the White Army will be there to protect him. How do we get past the guard with just these swords?" The solder held the Zulfiqar aloft, waved it ominously, then burst out laughing. "Seriously. How are we supposed to win a battle against the guard with these things?"

"They've said that others will join us, and that there will be surprises," the commander said. "We just need to make it to Mecca."

The soldiers left on horseback at dawn. They'd be in Mecca well before day's end and would join up with the southern troops at that time.

Those from the north would be carrying black flags and Zulfiqars. Those coming from the south would be carrying white flags and double-edged swords as well.

And what neither group—the "black flag" mercenaries led by a commander from Iran's internal security forces and the "white flag" group of Shi'a and Sunni warriors led by Yamani—knew or much cared about was that they would be fulfilling ancient prophecy as they stormed Mecca.

EGYPT

Hejaz Mountains

Sarum

Mecca

SUDAN

RED SEA

SAUDI ARABIA

YEMEN

65

Hejaz Mountains
Saudi Arabia

Mehmet Osman was thoroughly confused. As he stood on a front porch deck overlooking the holy city of Mecca, he'd already forgotten why he was here.

He'd been suffering from dementia for several years. It had crept up on him even before he'd considered retiring from the public library he'd worked at in downtown London for more than twenty years. There were days when he'd forget what he'd been doing earlier that day.

Osman had long ago resigned himself to the fact that he was the last of the heirs to the long-dead Ottoman Empire caliphate. He'd never married, and he had no children.

But he did not regret that. He'd never had any desire, really, to live in Turkey. And he'd certainly never had any thought of entering politics or becoming involved in affairs of state.

No, Osman had always been content with his small, uneventful life. Every so often, for a bit of fun at a cocktail party or a small gathering, he would reveal that he was an Osman and an heir in the succession of caliphs who'd ruled the Ottoman Empire. He'd get a laugh, a lifted brow, several questions about the job requirements for a caliph, and then the conversation would move on.

In fact, Osman had never truly studied the Ottoman Empire

or what caliphs did. He'd heard stories from his parents and grandparents growing up, of course. But they'd all seemed so distant and remote. It had never occurred to him that he'd need to pay any attention to the stories of his childhood.

Until today. That's why he was confused. Osman wondered why someone had bothered to fly him halfway across the world, to a place in the Hejaz mountains overlooking the holy city of Mecca. He could see Mecca from where he stood. The sun was beginning to rise in the east, so the outlines of the holy city were becoming visible.

The two men who'd come to see Osman at his flat in London had produced identification papers indicating that they were members of the Saudi National Guard. The princes of Saudi Arabia wanted to honor him at a ceremony, they said, and they were willing to pay handsomely if he would agree to accompany them to the kingdom.

The two men had then given him a considerable sum as a gesture of good faith. Osman had nothing better to do, so he'd decided on a whim to travel to Saudi Arabia with them. He'd already decided he would buy two new suits with the money they'd given him.

The men had not explained Osman's role in the ceremony, and he hadn't asked. The sum of money and their identification papers had been convincing. They'd left in a small jet, from a private hangar at Heathrow. There had been no waiting, no checking bags, and no need for security. It had been just the three of them, and two pilots, on the private aircraft.

Osman had stared out the windows for most of the trip. It had been a very long time since he'd come back to this part of the world. He'd lived in London for so long that he'd forgotten how breathtakingly gorgeous the Arabian Peninsula was.

They'd landed the night before and had taken private vehicles up into the Hejaz mountains. When he'd asked about the activities that would occur in the morning, the two men had merely smiled and told him that all would become clear soon enough.

Osman asked about a banner and flag propped up in the corner of the safe home they'd brought him to. It was a unique flag, with a red triangle and green, black, and white stripes. He did not know that it was the last flag of the old kingdom of Hejaz, that it had been used as their symbol for the Arab Revolt early in the twentieth century, or that it had later emerged as the modern Palestinian flag.

As a librarian, Osman should have known that the colors of the Hejaz flag had come to be known as the unofficial pan-Arab colors—should a day ever arrive when there was a reemergence of a pan-Islamic caliphate that crossed country borders and looked like the old Ottoman Empire.

Had he ever inquired about his own heritage and his connection to past events, he would have learned about the disappearance of the kingdom of Hejaz in 1925, when an Emir drove the Hashemites out of Mecca, creating the modern kingdom of Saudi Arabia. The House of Saud had ended any hopes of a pan-Islamic caliphate when it made Arabia a monarchy.

Now, as Osman looked out from Hejaz at Mecca, he noticed men fanning out in all directions across the eastern slope of the Hejaz mountainside. Carrying torches, they set trees on fire as they made their way through the forest. It was a sight to behold.

Osman turned to the two men who'd brought him here. "What is that?" he asked them.

"It is of no concern," said one of the two men.

"But…"

"They are clearing brush," said the second man. "They're firefighters, and they're simply clearing out dead wood in an old growth forest. They're making way for new growth."

Osman nodded. It didn't make sense, but the men were right. It was of no concern. The two men then beckoned to him, urging him to return inside, out of the early morning air. They all needed to rest up for the day ahead, they told him.

Good, Osman thought. *Then I will have time for a nap.*

Several of the larger trees exploded as the raging fire spread throughout the forest that overlooked Mecca. Within hours, the fire would move from the mountains of Hejaz toward Mecca. This, too, would fulfill prophecy about events that must immediately precede the return of the Mahdi.

SAUDI ARABIA

Dammam
Dahran

IRAN

GULF OF OMAN

QATAR

Riyadh

UNITED ARAB
EMIRATES

OMA

66

Riyadh, Saudi Arabia

It had clearly been a long, difficult night for the young American. Nash's clothes were rumpled. His hair was unkempt. The bottom half of his face was dark from two-day-old stubble. He'd been forced to sleep in the conference room. His jacket was folded on top of the backpack that he'd tried to use as a pillow on the hard floor.

"I am so very sorry, Nash. I truly am," Abdul apologized. "There is no justification for this."

Nash stared back at the Saudi prince through haggard, bloodshot eyes. "These things happen. But a bed would have been nice," he said with a lopsided grin. "This floor is awfully hard."

Abdul extended a hand. "You are a good soul, my friend. You have a marvelous spirit of adventure and goodwill about you. That anyone could smile under such circumstances…"

"Hey, it's fine. Really. I've slept in some pretty awful places before. I once had to spend the night in a phone booth in London for an entire evening while it poured down rain. And I spent the night behind the furnace in a boiler room at an apartment complex in Paris." Nash glanced down at the hard floor and then the backpack he'd been forced to use as his pillow. "So this is a piece of cake. I got a few hours of sleep."

"I have come to tell you that you are free to leave," Abdul said. "You have my sincerest apologies. You should never have been detained. It is not the way we do things here."

"Thanks. I appreciate it. But I'm curious. Who did you speak to about this before you came here? King Faisal? Prince Natal? The crown prince?"

Abdul studied Nash. This young American knew more than he was letting on. He was not asking out of idle curiosity. Abdul wondered what exactly had transpired in this room over the previous twelve hours.

"I met with the king," Abdul said. "In fact, I just came from his quarters."

Faisal had been polite but circumspect. He'd confirmed to Abdul that Natal was now the crown prince, that it would be announced within the hour in advance of the Day of Anger protests, and that the move was part of an effort leading to a new change in the country's leadership.

Abdul knew that it would not mollify those who'd begun to identify with the protests in the kingdom. Replacing one elderly crown prince with another member of the House of Saud from the same generation was cosmetic, at best. But he kept his own counsel and simply informed Faisal that he intended to meet with Nash and allow him to leave the king's palace. Faisal had not objected.

"And the king has said I may leave now?" Nash asked.

"He did. I am here to make certain of that. I will escort you personally from the grounds."

"And Natal? What did he have to say?"

Abdul hesitated but only for a moment. There was no reason not to tell Nash about the transfer of power. He would learn of it from the news reports shortly anyway. "Natal is the new crown prince. He is on his way to Mecca even as we speak, to meet with the governor of Mecca about the transition."

The news did not seem to surprise Nash. "This happened last night?"

"Yes. It will be announced shortly."

"I see," Nash said. "And it's done? Natal is the crown prince, next in line to become king?"

"Yes, it is done. But the intention is to make it quite clear that the governor of Mecca, Prince Muhammad, is to become the next king. Natal is crown prince for only a time, through the transition."

Nash stood. He made a quick, intuitive decision, based on this news. It was a risk—but one he felt confident in taking. He trusted this man.

Natal had already orchestrated one attack against a rival for the crown, on American soil. And it appeared he might be poised to do so again, this time in a place where many battles for control of Arab lands had taken place throughout history.

"Prince Abdul," he said, "you and I need to talk—but not here, and not in the king's palace."

"Where, then?"

"On our way to Mecca. And it is important we get there quickly."

"Why?"

"I will explain on the way," he concluded mysteriously. "So are you with me? May we leave?"

Abdul made his own quick decision. There was something about this young American that he liked. He nodded, turned to the door, and beckoned to the guard to allow them to leave. Abdul led Nash through the various corridors that wound through the king's palace and to the outer courtyard.

Neither spoke as they walked. Abdul made one call to his aide, who arranged for a helicopter to meet them in the courtyard. They were on their way to Mecca in a matter of minutes. And once they were away from the king's palace and airborne, Nash began to talk.

By the time they'd arrived in Mecca, Nash had given the same information to Prince Abdul that his staff had delivered to NSA and then the White House the night before.

It would be a long, uncertain day in the kingdom.

67

Tehran, Iran

Ali bin Rahman waited patiently outside the Reverend Shahidi's private study. He'd grown accustomed to waiting for such meetings with Iran's Supreme Leader. It didn't bother him. He was perfectly content to bide his time.

Everything was in place. His men were in place, and events were proceeding just as he'd hoped. *All is well*, he thought. *It is the time of change.*

It was hard for bin Rahman to believe, but years of hatred toward the apostates who ruled the Saudi kingdom were about to be rewarded with a true Day of Anger. The student uprising was a pretext for a much greater outpouring of wrath that would shake the world to its very foundations. Drawing the Kaaba into their plans had been a risk—especially considering that any attack on the shrine would have untold consequences. But it was a risk he'd been willing to take in order to create the necessary chaos.

The door to the study opened. "Please." Shahidi beckoned to the al Qaeda leader. "Let us talk now. I have some time."

It was just the two of them, as it often was. "The day has arrived," bin Rahman said without preamble as he took his customary spot at the small table in Shahidi's study.

"So I've been told," Shahidi said. As always, he was more than content to allow proxies to do his bidding. In this instance, the proxy, al

Qaeda, might surprise the world. But Shahidi was more than willing to enlist uncommon allies as soldiers to the greater cause. "Are your men in place?"

"They are, both in Riyadh and Mecca," bin Rahman said. "They've trained for months. It is the right time, the right place."

"And they have what they need?"

"Yes, thanks to your men at the IRGC. I have already delivered my profound thanks to General Zhubin, as well as Hussein Bahadur. We have precisely what we need for both. The portable devices have been delivered to both locations."

"And what of our illustrious President Ahmadian?" Shahidi asked. "Were you able to give him what he requires? Is he satisfied?"

Bin Rahman laughed. "Yes, he's beside himself, like a little school-girl. He has met his hidden imam. They have appeared to 200,000 pilgrims at the Jamkaran Mosque, fulfilling prophecy—though not a soul there knew who they were seeing for the first time."

"Ah yes, Ahmadian's prophecies," Shahidi said darkly. "He is so concerned with fulfilling those. So he is content? And his new friend is now in place as well?"

"He is. I was told he arrived in Mecca in the past two days. He is ready for his part," bin Rahman said.

Shahidi sighed. "I will say this for our president. He certainly has a feel for what the people like. This new find of his—of yours, actually—will certainly make things interesting. But I must confess that I'm still puzzled by one thing. Where, exactly, is this man from, this hidden imam? What is his true nationality? What nation does he claim as his own?"

"In truth, Reverend Shahidi, it is a mystery," bin Rahman said. "In all of our discussions with him, I must confess that I do not have a satisfactory answer..."

"To either question?" Shahidi asked, somewhat surprised.

"To either question," bin Rahman answered. "He claims no nation as his own, and his true identity, his parentage, his history—it is all still unknown. My men can find no record of his childhood, his birth, any semblance of a life on earth. It is, seemingly, as if he has emerged from occultation, or was born anew just recently."

"That must please Ahmadian," Shahidi said. "It would confirm what he wishes to believe already. But you and I, we will need to discover the truth for ourselves. I, for one, am not content with the absence of an answer to these questions. It matters little to me if we find that this man was an orphan from the streets somewhere, but we still need to know this."

"Absolutely," bin Rahman said. "But all in time. He is quite useful to us, for now. He will move the rest of the world in our direction. And for that I am grateful—regardless of who he is and where he came from."

EGYPT

Sarum
Mecca

SUDAN

RED SEA

SAUDI ARABIA

YEMEN

68

Mecca, Saudi Arabia

It was such a perfect day. Pilgrims who were taking part in Umrah, or the little pilgrimage, would begin to arrive later that day to walk around the Kaaba seven times in a reverse clockwise direction. Even now, in the empty square at the start of the day, the revered black, cuboid-shaped building—the most sacred site in Islam—was magnificent.

But today was even more auspicious for a select few, and the time was nearly upon them. The Kaaba was opened only twice a year, for a ceremony known simply as the "day of cleaning." The first occurred thirty days before the start of the month of Ramadan, and the second took place before the start of Hajj, when millions of pilgrims visited the Kaaba.

One tribe, the Bani Shayba, held the keys to the Kaaba. And on these two days of the year, visitors and foreign diplomats were allowed to participate in the ritual cleaning of the Kaaba. The governor of Mecca would enter the interior of the Kaaba, where he and his honored guests ritually cleaned the structure with brooms.

This day would truly be spectacular. The Saudi National Guard and the Bani Shayba tribesmen had all heard the news—the governor of Mecca had just been named the new minister of the interior and was now in the line of succession to become the next king. The day of cleaning of the Kaaba would be one that they would all remember.

The list of dignitaries visiting the interior of the Kaaba during the cleaning later that day was small. The governor of Mecca had invited only a select few.

The regular members of the White Army were alert, nevertheless. They were extra vigilant, given the recent change in status for Prince Muhammad. They intended to pay close attention to all who approached the Kaaba today.

But there was one person the guard had not checked—and now it would be too late. One of the Bani Shayba tribe had trained for this day in a remote camp in the mountains of Pakistan for months before returning to the kingdom and Mecca.

This man had delivered his carefully constructed package to the interior of the Kaaba just that morning, before the others had arrived. It was stowed safely in a closet off to one side of the interior of the Kaaba. When the governor and his group of dignitaries were allowed inside, this man would be with them, to assure that this device fulfilled its mission. He would die in the blast, of course, but that was to be expected. His reward was in heaven.

The timing had to be perfect, this man knew. But he was ready. As soon as the two groups of horses and men charged the square, he was prepared to act. His months of preparation were at an end.

The new crown prince, Natal, was meeting with the governor of Mecca as they made preparations for the day of cleaning ceremony. Natal had shown up unexpectedly, but the national guard had been told that he would not be joining the ceremony within the Kaaba.

Instead, Natal had told them, he planned to return to Riyadh. He'd seen the inside of the Kaaba before, he'd joked with some in the White Army. He had no interest in sweeping it with a broom again.

69

**The White House
Washington, DC**

President Camara always had a difficult time sleeping, but especially at times such as this. So it was almost a welcome relief to see the soft red light glowing on the phone beside his bed. He glanced over at his wife to make sure he wasn't disturbing her, then answered the call.

"Mr. President, I'm sorry to disturb you," General Alton said. "But you'd asked to be briefed when we had news about Nash Lee."

"Yes, is he all right?" The president was accustomed to receiving bad news. But he fervently hoped that was not the case here.

"He's fine," Alton reported. "In fact, we just heard from Ambassador Lee. Nash called his father from the helicopter shortly after it left the grounds of the king's palace. He was accompanying Prince Abdul."

Camara sat up in bed. "Abdul? What does he have to do with any of this?"

"Well, there's been some other news, which will break over there shortly as the day starts there. They're making Abdul the new foreign minister. Prince Muhammad, the governor of Mecca, is now the minister of interior. And Saud has stepped aside. Natal is the new crown prince."

Camara smiled. So Susan Wright had called it from the beginning. The grandsons were, in fact, taking power in the kingdom. Natal was a wild card, and he wondered how that might play out.

"But Nash is fine? I can cross that off my list of worries?"

"Yes, sir."

"And what of the Day of Anger protests today? Can we help? Do we have folks in place? What about other parts of the world, in case this spills over?"

"We have ships to the east and west of Saudi Arabia, on both coasts—the Red Sea and the Persian Gulf," Alton said. "But you do realize that we can't help the Saudis? This is their fight. We can't do much else except observe."

"I understand. But I'm still glad they're close by. If the Saudis ask for our help, we'll be nearby."

The president closed his eyes, wondering what the world might look like soon. Light was starting to peek over the horizon and work its way into the bedroom. He decided that the night was over. It was time to work on a speech he was considering to a secret joint session of Congress. Whether he gave such a speech would depend on events.

"Thank you, General Alton," the president said. "Call if you have any other news."

IRAN

SAUDI ARABIA

Dammam
Dahran

QATAR

GULF OF OMAN

Riyadh

70

UNITED ARAB
EMIRATES

OMAN

The King's Palace
Riyadh, Saudi Arabia

It was a simple task, really. The device had been placed in the king's bedchambers the previous evening, while Faisal was meeting with Natal and the crown prince.

The man had allowed a small crew to enter the palace grounds. They'd secured it safely in the king's chambers and then left quickly.

The al Qaeda operative had been on the king's cleaning staff for the past two years. He'd scrubbed toilets, washed floors, and gathered up soiled clothes for months, waiting for this day to arrive.

He had no special knowledge of the device. But that wasn't required. It had all been assembled for him. All he was required to do was activate it at the proper moment.

He was more than willing to play his part in changing the future course of events in the world. He knew that his family would be honored for the part he was about to play, and he was glad for that.

The device was powerful enough that no one could possibly survive it. At least, that was what he'd been told. The blast radius for the portable nuclear device—which contained pieces freshly exported from North Korea, recently delivered to Iran, and later carried to the king's palace by carefully selected couriers—was sufficient that it would kill the king, his immediate family, and everyone else on two floors of the king's palace.

It would, in one effort, take out much of the Saudi royal family. Only those who were fortunate enough to be somewhere else—not in the king's palace—would survive the blast.

The man said his final prayers and began to make his afternoon cleaning rounds. The elderly king always took a late afternoon nap. The al Qaeda operative who'd managed to infiltrate the cleaning staff waited nearly fifteen minutes to make sure the king was settled in his chambers.

He knocked on the door. Hearing no answer from within, he entered. The king was sleeping peacefully at the far corner of the room.

The man walked over to the closet and opened it calmly. He'd been instructed not to set a remote timer. Instead, he was told to activate it directly and wait to make certain that it fulfilled its mission.

The portable device was small and innocuous. It looked like a suitcase, a piece of luggage. He spread the suitcase on the ground and opened the two latches.

Everything was in place. He followed the instructions he'd been given. He heard several *clicks*. A machine of some sort came to life.

The man sat down and waited. He wasn't entirely sure when it would go off. But he'd made his peace with God. He was ready.

An instant later, the nuclear suitcase detonated, vaporizing the man sitting calmly next to the suitcase. The king's chamber—as well as the floors above and below it—was turned to rubble upon impact. The king died immediately, in his sleep.

MARYLAND

Baltimore

WEST
VIRGINIA

Washington, D.C.

VIRGINIA

71

The Capitol Building
Washington, DC

"You're sure the press won't be there?" Camara asked. He glanced
out the window of the presidential town car as they made their way
through the southern gate of the White House complex. Even now, so
early in the morning, there were a few tourists who snapped pictures of
the presidential motorcade as it made its way out of the complex.

"Absolutely," Anshel Gould answered. "We've made certain of it.
The galleries—both for the public and the press—will be empty."

"How did you manage it?" the president asked. "Is the press
screaming?"

"DJ is managing it," the president's chief of staff said evenly. "It isn't
pretty. But he's explaining to them that we're providing highly classified information to Congress. That closes it to the press."

"Even though it's to a joint session of Congress—not just to a secret
session of the Senate that they're all accustomed to when we give them
classified information?"

The motorcade was small and would only tie up traffic for several
minutes this early in the morning. Commuter traffic wouldn't kick in
for an hour or so. For all anyone knew, the president was on his way for
a round of golf at Andrews Air Force Base—not to an early morning
speech to a closed, joint session of Congress at the Capitol.

Camara had already been considering a speech to Congress. The news of the assassination of the Saudi king, coming on the heels of the attacks at Aqaba, had made an address an imperative. For all he and anyone else knew, war was about to break out in the Saudi kingdom, southern Israel, or the Persian Gulf.

The uneasy peace with Iran, likely behind the attacks in both places, might end as well and turn into fighting that would include US troops. And while he didn't need to consult with Congress under the War Powers Act when American troops were already engaged, the president felt an urgency to bring another branch of the US government into the picture.

"It doesn't matter," Gould said. "You're presenting information based on highly classified intelligence. We closed it based on that alone. This is nothing more than our usual briefing during a secret session of the Senate. We've just invited the House to take part."

Gould and the president rode alone in the back of the presidential limousine. Susan Wright and General Alton were in the second limousine that trailed the motorcade. DJ was riding with the small press pool that was coming along but would be forced to wait outside the halls of Congress while the president spoke to the members of Congress in a closed session.

"But we both know the information I present won't hold for long," the president said. "Half of the senators and congressmen will leak the information the moment the doors open."

"Most likely," Gould stated. "But we have to let them know about the events. No one can predict where this thing will go—not now that the Saudi kingdom is on the edge of the abyss. If the attacks that are headed to Mecca are somehow successful in removing the governor of Mecca, Prince Muhammad, and a real revolution starts in the kingdom, then we'll have our hands full for some time."

Camara grimaced. "Natal and the conservative forces will close ranks in the kingdom. They'll shut down every attempt at moderation. But he will have unleashed powerful forces—ones that he can't control. I wonder if he realizes he's playing with fire by dallying with Tehran as he has."

"Absolutely," Gould nodded. "Natal is playing a very dangerous game—especially with talk of the return of a caliphate and an imam who shows up from nowhere, it seems, claiming to be a hidden imam and the Mahdi. Who know what chaos Natal has set loose?"

The president turned in the car seat to look directly at his chief of staff. "I wanted to make certain of something. I can't mention Natal's role in the assassination of the king? I can't talk of his complicity with Tehran?"

"No, you can't," Gould said firmly.

"Not even with the information Nash Lee provided us? Don't we have a responsibility to at least let the Saudis know?"

"We can't," Gould said. "The royal family will need to sort this out on their own. We can't help them here, not with troops on the ground, and not with intelligence that we can't back up with hard facts. This is their fight, not ours."

"But if this second nuclear suitcase bomb that NSA has warned us about is there, in Mecca?" the president asked. "What if it goes off? It will create chaos and panic nearly everywhere. What then?"

"Let us hope that the intelligence is wrong," Gould said quietly. "Or that it somehow does not succeed. Either way, it is the Saudis' war—not ours. We can only be prepared for the time that it spills outside the kingdom, in the direction of our troops on the ground elsewhere. That is the message you have to deliver to Congress today."

The motorcade made the turn in to the driveway at the western side of the Capitol. Construction workers were already there, working away at the endless efforts to refurbish the Capitol dome building's aging exterior. The motorcade worked its way in and around the construction and pulled into the underground garage. They made their way toward a private entrance that led up to the chamber where the Senate met.

The underground parking garage was half full, despite the early morning hour. The word had gotten around in time to the members of Congress. It was obvious that a decent number had been able to make it to the Capitol for the closed session.

The president didn't wait for the other cars in the motorcade to park. He left the limousine and made his way up the steps to the Senate chamber. He was anxious to get this session behind him. Gould moved quickly to keep up. He glanced over his shoulder as they entered the stairwell. DJ was holding the press back, while Susan Wright and General Alton hurried to catch up to them.

When the president entered the hall of the Senate through a side entrance, he was greeted by half of the members of the Gang of Eight leaders. He shook hands briefly, then entered the hall. He did not have a prepared speech with him or a teleprompter. He'd decided to make this more informal. He was going to talk to the members of Congress directly.

Dr. Gould, Dr. Wright, and General Alton took seats in the front row. The Senate was overflowing. With so many House members there, every seat was taken, and it was standing-room only in the aisles. The president walked over to the podium, opened his notebook, and glanced up at the galleries to make sure that no press had been able to make their way in. The galleries were empty.

The president waited until the hall had grown quiet. "Thank you for arriving at such an early hour," he said, his voice unnaturally loud in the now-still Senate chamber. "I know this is unusual, but there is a great deal happening in the world at the present time. I felt it best to speak to you here, in person, so that we could have an honest discussion about the events."

Camara gestured at the podium. "As you can all see, I'm not here with a teleprompter. I don't have a prepared speech. I have some notes, and I wanted to share some information. But I'm not here to try to convince you of the need to act, to declare war, or to end our peace with Iran. I simply wanted to make sure that you all are aware of the gravity of several actions, and to be prepared.

"I've been told that similar sessions are occurring nearly simultaneously. For instance, Judah Navon is addressing a closed session of the Knesset, and the prime minister of Russia is meeting with the Duma leadership. I'm sure there are other similar discussions underway.

"First, with the attacks on oil fields in Saudi Arabia, Iran, and Iraq, I know that all of us are concerned about the imminent collapse of the world oil markets. Crude oil speculation has tripled prices on spot markets. If events spin out of control in Saudi Arabia today, then OPEC will essentially lose control of the world's oil economy. We'll be in free fall.

"However, I wanted to assure you that Russia, China, and US leadership have discussed contingency plans in the event that this happens. There are other sources of oil beyond the Middle East. Israel has agreed to handle all of that traffic, from the Caspian Sea and elsewhere. In fact, that oil is flowing even now. We'll be fine.

"I know you've all heard about the attacks at Aqaba as well, and that the Israelis are being blamed. But it is my firm belief that Israel is not responsible for those attacks. It appears that both of those attacks were orchestrated by Iran's proxies.

"Nevertheless, we will be hard-pressed to roll back that perception. It will become conventional wisdom to the world community that Israel was behind those attacks. There is not much we can do about that, unfortunately. The real perpetrators—and their motives—will be lost in time.

"We also know that al Qaeda's new leader, Ali bin Rahman, has made common cause with Tehran. While this is unusual, it should not be surprising. Half of al Qaeda's leadership has hidden inside Iran for years. What is unusual, though, is the news that Ali bin Rahman has come out of hiding and is on his way to the emerging Palestinian homeland in southern Israel.

"There is also surprising news out of London. Depending on events that will shortly play out one way or another in Saudi Arabia, this news may—or may not—become important. The last remaining heir to the caliphate of the Ottoman Empire has been seen in Saudi Arabia. New pan-Arab flags representing the old kingdom of Hejaz have been seen in circulation as well.

"What makes his appearance problematic is that there are military forces advancing on Mecca from both the north and south. They are, surprisingly, on horseback, and they're carrying white and black flags, and double-edged swords.

"These rather unusual military forces are being led by Sa'id Nouradeen, Hezbollah's leader in southern Lebanon. They are calling him al Yamani, the mythical legend who appears before the coming of the Mahdi, of perhaps the Twelfth Imam. From all accounts, this is being orchestrated to usher in chaos and fulfill certain prophetic requirements before the appearance of this Twelfth Imam.

"As for this Twelfth Imam, the president of Iran has begun to tell those around him that this person is quite real and that he has now made his first appearance to tens of thousands of people. He believes this imam is real. So for the time being, we must also take the Iranian president at his word. If he says the Twelfth Imam is real, and that he has returned—and he has made this quite clear to the people—then we are forced to deal with that. We have no choice.

"Now, before any of you ask me about my opinion of this so-called Twelfth Imam, I will say this. He is a real person. We know that. What we cannot ascertain—at least not yet—is where he came from, his background and training, or even what nationality he calls his own. As soon as we can, we will give you that information.

"But for the time being, we will likely be forced to recognize this personage—if only because Iran's leadership recognizes him. And if the likes of al Qaeda's leadership recognize him as some sort of religious authority for a pan-Arab community, it will even further complicate matters."

President Camara paused and glanced at his notes. The Senate chamber remained silent. This was a considerable amount of information to take in.

"Still, all of that pales in comparison to the additional news that I wanted to give you here today," he said, keeping his voice steady. "It is this. Our worst fears were realized a short time ago. Some of you in this chamber, in fact, have been predicting for some time that the nuclear genie would escape—that portable nuclear devices would become readily available to terror networks willing to use them to create chaos.

"This has, in fact, just occurred. Our intelligence networks have confirmed that the king of Saudi Arabia was assassinated within the hour by a nuclear suitcase bomb. Countless members of the royal family and staff were killed in the blast. We don't know yet who was behind the nuclear terrorist attack, but I believe we can all hazard a good guess.

"But as if that wasn't bad enough, we have learned that there is a second nuclear suitcase bomb in circulation. Our intelligence reports are fairly confident on this. And that second suitcase, if the reports are to be believed, may be detonated in Mecca, perhaps at the holiest site in Islam, the Kaaba, as the military forces descend on the city.

"And if that were to happen—if a nuclear terrorist attack should destroy the Kaaba at a time of surging violence in the Saudi kingdom— it will almost certainly trigger chaos, conflict, and violence across the planet. War, in many places, becomes inevitable. All of us can only hope, and pray, that someone or something intervenes before an event like this occurs."

EGYPT

Sarum
● Mecca

SUDAN

RED SEA

SAUDI ARABIA

YEMEN

72

Mecca, Saudi Arabia

Given what he'd heard from Nash on the ride to Mecca, Prince Abdul decided to ignore the niceties of diplomacy and ceremony. There wasn't time.

The day was waning. They'd gotten reports of the Day of Anger protests throughout their flight from Riyadh to Mecca. Most of them had been largely peaceful and uneventful. The protests in Dammam and Qatif, especially, had been mild. Students had shown up, waved their cell phone cameras around for a while, and eventually dispersed.

They'd gotten two disturbing reports as they neared Mecca—both of which they'd need to confront once they'd landed. The first was that a brush fire had engulfed much of the forestland to the west of Mecca and was making its way down the slope. There had also been strange reports of hordes of horses approaching Mecca from both the north and the south. Both would arrive within the hour, the reports said.

While he didn't pay much attention to such things, Abdul knew that the fire and the cavalry charges from the north and south were prophecies that tens of millions had read about in popular novels about the return of the Mahdi. And today they would be witness to such prophecies, no matter how absurd.

But it was possible that none of this mattered. It might all be for show. The game was here, in Mecca, at the Kaaba. He couldn't say precisely what Natal was up to, but if he was here in Mecca, it was for a reason.

Three mobile phones went off. Nash glanced at his. He didn't recognize the number. But Abdul answered his mobile. As he listened, a look of horror crept onto his face.

"There was an explosion at the king's palace," Abdul said once he'd hung up and regained his composure. "A portable nuclear device. It destroyed three floors. King Faisal was killed immediately."

Nash turned white. They'd been there, hours before. He'd only met Faisal—and now the king was dead. Even in the midst of this chaos, Nash couldn't help but wonder—and marvel—at Natal's ability to orchestrate these events.

"I'm sorry," Nash murmured. "I can only imagine your pain. But this means that…"

"Natal is king," Abdul said.

"And the only other true rival to keep him from remaining king is Prince Muhammad—here, in Mecca," Nash concluded.

Abdul leaned forward to get the pilot's attention. "Land the helicopter in the square," he told him. "As soon as possible."

The pilot turned, horrified. "The square of the Kaaba? Are you certain?"

"I am certain," Abdul said. "Land it in one of the corners. The pilgrims will largely have finished by now. There should be room to land safely."

The pilot obeyed. The helicopter was built for long-haul missions, but it could also hover and land in tight spaces. He'd have no problem landing it safely in the Kaaba square.

As they made their approach, Nash was still in shock from the news. He looked out to the west. Much of the eastern slope of the Hejaz mountainside was ablaze. Black smoke billowed skyward.

"Do you see it—that fire coming toward Mecca from the mountainside?" Nash asked.

Abdul nodded. "It fulfills prophecy—just like the cavalry charges."

"Prophecy about what?" Nash asked.

"The return of the Mahdi, or the Twelfth Imam," Abdul said. "If you believe in such things."

Nash said nothing. Too much had happened in the previous twenty-four hours for him to process this news. At this point, he wasn't sure what, or whom, to believe any longer.

The helicopter banked hard and swept out over the square. A few people were still walking around the Kaaba, but most had made their pilgrimage and had left the square. The pilot was able to land the craft safely. Nash and Prince Abdul hurried off toward the nearest door at the outer edge of the square.

"Where is Natal?" Abdul asked a guard, a member of the White Army, as they left the square. "I need to see him immediately."

"He is with the governor, within the Kaaba. They are there for the ceremony, the cleaning. But I believe he is about to leave the compound, before the ceremony is finished," the guard said. "We—we have all heard the news. I believe the new king is about to return to Riyadh. The governor will remain behind and finish the ceremonial day of cleaning."

Abdul and Nash exchanged glances. An unspoken thought occurred to both of them at the same moment. They were running out of time.

"Take us to the Kaaba. Now," the prince ordered. "We need to see the new king before he leaves for Riyadh."

"But sir, the ceremony has already begun. They are inside the Kaaba. I can't..."

Abdul turned and walked back into the square. He strode purposefully toward the square black building. Nash followed him. Guards hurried to catch up.

Nash felt helpless. He had no idea what was happening. But he trusted Abdul's instincts. By the time they'd crossed the square and arrived at the entrance to the Kaaba, Nash was actually winded. Between the largely sleepless night and then the wild ride from Riyadh to Mecca, he was running on fumes.

Natal was just coming down the stairs that led into the Kaaba as they'd arrived. The pilgrims still in the square stared in fascination as two members of the royal family confronted each other in front of Islam's holiest site.

As he arrived at the bottom of the stairs, Natal glanced first at Abdul and then at Nash. He was clearly taken by surprise, both by Abdul's arrival here, at the Kaaba, and by Nash's presence with him. But he recovered quickly.

"What is the meaning of this?" he demanded. "Why are you here?"

"I needed to see you," Abdul said. "So I am here."

Natal was agitated. Both Nash and Abdul could see on the new king's face that he wanted to be anywhere but here at this moment. It was painfully obvious.

"I know you've received word of the horrific incident at the palace," Natal said, visibly angry. "So I must return to Riyadh. Immediately. There is not a moment to lose." Natal started to move away from the prince. There was no doubt he wanted to leave this place. Quickly.

Abdul stepped in front of him, physically preventing Natal from leaving. Nash held his breath. "Natal," Abdul said quietly, so only the three of them could hear his words, "I know what you've done. I *know*. But we will leave that discussion for another day.

"For now, I insist that you remain here, with me. We will take part in the day of cleaning, with the governor of Mecca. For today, we will all be one big, happy family. Wherever you go, for at least the foreseeable future, I wish to make sure that both the governor of Mecca and I remain with you."

Natal, the new king, and Abdul, who would soon become foreign minister, stood facing each other. Nash could see that Natal wished to flee the Kaaba. Every fiber of his being screamed it to the heavens. The fear emanating from Natal was palpable.

"I am your king," Natal said. "I do not answer to you."

"True. And right now, I would invite you in the strongest possible terms to enjoy this glorious day of cleaning inside the Kaaba with the governor and myself."

Abdul, the younger man, took Natal by the arm and steered him back toward the entrance to the Kaaba. Nash trailed behind, still not quite certain what was happening. But he was determined to keep up.

In the end, Natal did not resist. For what could he do? Flee? An elderly king, running in abject fear from the Kaaba as pilgrims watched? Hardly.

Natal went to work immediately. He did not have a moment to lose. There was some risk to him in what he was about to do, but there was no other choice. He was trapped here, inside the shrine, and there were no allies here to help him. He had to act.

Once inside the Kaaba, Natal left Abdul and Nash, ignored the dignitaries sweeping the floor with ceremonial brooms, and approached one of the White Army guards. He, in turn, then found two more additional guards. The three of them approached a hapless member of the cleaning crew.

The man panicked. He tried to sprint for a closet to one side of the interior of the Kaaba. "Stop him!" one of the guards called out. A fourth guard intercepted the man. They collapsed to the ground in a flurry of tangled arms and legs.

One of the approaching guards opened the door of the closet the man had been trying to reach. He recoiled immediately and took two quick steps backward. It was obvious, even to his untrained eye, that it was some sort of an explosive device.

"Everyone needs to leave this place," the guard said loudly. "Right now. There's a bomb here."

It was like yelling *fire* in a crowded movie theater. All of the dignitaries dropped their brooms and rushed toward the exit as one. It wasn't pretty. They all tried to shove and push their way through the door by force in order to escape what they feared was a death trap. Natal, Abdul, and Nash were nearly crushed in the sudden, mad dash for the exit. They were fortunate to escape.

But just as they'd reached the stairs, they were greeted with pandemonium on the other side of the doorway. Dozens, perhaps hundreds, of soldiers mounted on horses streamed into the square, carrying white and black flags, waving menacing swords above their heads and shouting to the heavens. Members of the White Army moved quickly to cut them off before they could reach the Kaaba. Bursts of gunfire echoed throughout the square.

Some of the remaining pilgrims trapped inside the square— at least those who knew the legends about the return of the Mahdi— immediately recognized the prophesied signs. But there wasn't time to process these thoughts. Everything was happening too quickly.

An instant later, a small, five-seat, white helicopter with twin propellers hurtled over the top of the onrushing cavalry. It navigated to the center of the square, slowed, and then came to rest—directly atop the Kaaba.

73

The events in the holy city of Mecca had shocked the world. While there had been no television cameras to capture the cavalry charge, the bomb scare and its peaceful aftermath, or the surreal site of a white helicopter landing on top of Islam's holiest site, cell phone videos immediately circulated widely. Within an hour, nearly every person on the planet had seen some version of the events.

With more than a billion practicing Muslims around the world, speculation about the true meaning of the day's events in Mecca, at the Kaaba, careened wildly in all directions. Some predicted the end of days. Others predicted the return of a pan-Arab caliphate. Still others were convinced that the kingdom of Hejaz had returned, replacing the House of Saud in Arabia.

At the heart of the mystery was the appearance—captured by dozens of cell phone videos and immediately carried around the world on the mVillage network—of what many were calling the Mahdi, the Twelfth Imam, the successor to the Prophet Muhammad.

The videos all showed the same scene. A small, white helicopter landed on top of the Kaaba. Two men emerged from the craft and addressed the soldiers, the pilgrims, and the dignitaries still trapped on the stairs as they tried to exit the interior of the Kaaba.

News anchors and reports across the planet, commenting on the extraordinary mobile videos, were able to identify the members of the royal family witnessing the event—including the new Saudi king, Natal, who'd only been named crown prince hours before King Faisal's assassination in Riyadh.

The commentators were also able to identify Nash Lee, the young CEO of the very same mVillage network that was now broadcasting these very same mobile videos to a global audience that numbered in the billions.

None of the reports mentioned the uneventful conclusion to the day of cleaning at the Kaaba, or the peaceful manner in which dozens of cavalry riders had eventually dispersed at the Kaaba square and drifted away, into the desert. The twin-rotor white helicopter—a smaller version of the new Sikorsky X2 under development that looked remarkably like the mythological Pegasus, or al Buraq—had dominated their stories.

They were eventually able to identify one of the two men who'd emerged from the white helicopter that had landed on the Kaaba. He was, quite amazingly, an elderly, retired librarian from London—but also the last heir to the caliphate of the Ottoman Empire. No one quite knew what to make of that news, or what it might signify.

But the second man who'd emerged from the helicopter to address the square at the Kaaba had, so far, eluded either definition or identification. He was truly a man of mystery. No one knew who he was, where he'd come from, or what his nationality might be.

The mobile videos all concluded with an equally eerie scene. Just one of the two—the man people were calling the Mahdi—re-entered the white helicopter. The elderly librarian, the last heir to the Ottoman caliphate, remained behind as the helicopter lifted off and took flight again.

It was at this point that the international news media had managed to find its way into the emerging story. For the white helicopter that really did look like Pegasus in flight did not remain in Saudi Arabia.

It headed north, toward Jerusalem. No one was certain, but the craft's occupant seemed, by some accounts, to be re-creating the

Prophet Muhammad's night flight from Mecca to the "farthest mosque." Television crews began to scramble in Jerusalem, all of them eager to get close to the Al Aqsa mosque believed to be the place the Prophet Muhammad landed.

It was four hundred miles or so as the crow flies from Mecca to Jerusalem, the commentators said. It would take the craft about three hours to reach Jerusalem and the Temple Mount—if that, in fact, was its final destination.

Both American and Israeli military helicopters picked him up, in flight, as he crossed over into Israeli airspace. But they didn't dare fire on the helicopter. Several private aircraft were tracking the helicopter, with television crews feeding live coverage via satellite to networks around the world.

Presidents and prime ministers alike were riveted by the unfolding drama—along with billions of ordinary people who were glad to follow the developments live. Several of the American news networks reported that President Camara had just spoken to a secret, joint session of Congress to brief them on the developments of the past twenty-four hours. But the White House, as yet, had not confirmed it, or what the president might have said.

The white helicopter continued its flight north. It was clearly headed directly to Jerusalem, the commentators said. One of them had computer artists create an interactive graphic that traced the craft's current trajectory from Mecca, indicating when it would arrive at the Temple Mount.

By the time the white helicopter arrived in Jerusalem, anyone who was awake anywhere in the world was tuned in, live, to see who this brazen mystery man might be—this Mahdi who'd appeared atop the Kaaba in Mecca and was seemingly about to land on the Temple Mount in Jerusalem.

When the white helicopter did finally land—at the southeast corner inside the grounds of the Temple Mount—several television cameras in helicopters hovering nearby were able to record the scene. A man, the same one who had spoken at the Kaaba, emerged.

With the world watching and wondering, the man took off his shoes and walked purposefully across the land, toward a grove of trees that had grown up over an ancient pile of rubble now filled in with dirt. He stopped at a fountain to purify himself.

And then, for a reason that only he would be able to explain to the world at some point, he chose a precise spot a few feet from the fountain that was equidistant from both the golden Dome of the Rock to the north and the Al Aqsa mosque to the south, knelt to the ground, and kissed it.

ABOUT THE AUTHOR

Jeff Nesbit has been a national journalist, the communications director to the vice president at the White House, and the director of public affairs for two prominent science agencies in Washington, the National Science Foundation and the Food and Drug Administration. He's written eighteen novels for adults and teens.

Nesbit authored *PEACE* and *OIL*, the first two books in the Principalities and Powers series, after extensive research into the truth about the conflict between Israel and Iran threatening to destabilize the Middle East. He also managed a successful strategic communications business for nearly fifteen years. His clients and projects included dozens of national nonprofit, trade associations, media companies, Fortune 500 companies, major health foundations, public relations agencies, and advocacy organizations.

Nesbit was also a national journalist with media organizations such as Knight-Ridder Newspapers (now McClatchy), ABC News' Satellite News Channels (acquired by CNN), States News Service (when it was managed by *The New York Times*), nationally syndicated columnist Jack Anderson, and newspapers in Virginia and South Carolina.